2/06/

MOORESTOWN LIBRARY
856-234-0333

3 2030 00200 8075

W9-BTF-084

Mystery
Ful   Fulmer, David
         Rampart Street

RAMPART STREET

ALSO BY DAVID FULMER

Jass

Chasing the Devil's Tail

RAMPART STREET

DAVID FULMER

HARCOURT, INC.

ORLANDO   AUSTIN   NEW YORK   SAN DIEGO   TORONTO   LONDON

Copyright © 2006 by David Fulmer

All rights reserved. No part of this publication may be reproduced or
transmitted in any form or by any means, electronic or mechanical,
including photocopy, recording, or any information storage and retrieval
system, without permission in writing from the publisher.

Requests for permission to make copies of any part of the work should
be mailed to the following address: Permissions Department, Harcourt, Inc.,
6277 Sea Harbor Drive, Orlando, Florida 32887-6777.

www.HarcourtBooks.com

This is a work of fiction. Names, characters, places, organizations,
and events are the products of the author's imagination or are
used fictitiously for verisimilitude.

Library of Congress Cataloging-in-Publication Data
Fulmer, David.
Rampart Street/David Fulmer.—1st ed.
p. cm.
1. St. Cyr, Valentin (Fictitious character)—Fiction. 2. Police—Louisiana—New
Orleans—Fiction. 3. Rich people—Crimes against—Fiction.
4. New Orleans (La.)—Fiction. 5. Creoles—Fiction. I. Title.
PS3606.U56R36 2006
813'.6—dc22 2005015509
ISBN-13: 978-0151-01024-0 ISBN-10: 0-15-101024-2

Text set in Sabon
Designed by Cathy Riggs

Printed in the United States of America
First edition

A C E G I K J H F D B

Rampart Street, Rampart Street
Walkin' down on Rampart Street,
Ain't no tellin who you might meet
Walkin' down on Rampart Street.

—FROM "WALKIN' DOWN ON RAMPART STREET"
  TRADITIONAL, CIRCA 1904

RAMPART STREET

ONE

The moment he turned the corner onto Rampart Street, he knew he was a dead man.

A shadow was moving directly in his path, a phantom in a dark duster, one arm outstretched and pointing a Navy .45. He started to say, *Not me!* But he only got as far as the first word when the other hand came up, the palm out, shushing him.

From down past Second Street, he heard a trumpet blowing, a slow run of dirty brass. *Jass* they called it. He fixed on that odd word for a moment, seeking escape. Then he was back facing the pistol, feeling its ghostly touch over twelve feet of space.

He had lived for years with the fear that someone would come for him. He had paid in sleepless nights. He had seen a shady figure in his dreams, stepping out of a darkness just like this one. It wasn't fair. He wasn't the villain; he was the one who wanted to set things right.

He was blurting "Damn your—" when the pistol shouted and the .45 slug caught him under the chin, snapping his head back and choking off the words in a bloody cough. The shot echoed down Rampart Street as he staggered and toppled over, clutching at his throat, his life bleeding out to seep around the cobblestones.

The shadow faded back into the inky New Orleans night. Across the narrow street, a curtain opened, hung suspended for a moment, and then closed.

One minute passed in silence. It lingered into a second, then a third. The stream of blood ran to the gutter, a feast for the flies at the first light of day.

There was a patter of footsteps, rat quick, from the far side of the street. A crabbed figure bent over the body, rustling through pockets, pulling the heavy piece from the right-hand ring finger. When the wedding band wouldn't budge from the left hand, a blade flashed on its way to dismembering the digit and the ring that wrapped it above the knuckle.

But before the job could be done, a trio of men appeared, the last dregs flushed out onto the street from Johnny O's Saloon, hooting drunkenly as they staggered up to the corner. In the one-two-three order of a vaudeville routine, they came to a stop. Their mouths dropped and six bleary eyes swam over to the body lying in the street and the other form that was bending over it.

One of the drunks, finding his voice, yelled, "Hey, now!"

The crabbed figure jerked back and scurried away just as fast as he'd come. The three fellows slowed to a series of nervous baby steps as they drew up on the body. The first one saw the ugly hole in the victim's throat and said, "Sweet Jesus! Look at that!"

A stunned few seconds passed, and then the fellow who had spoken up went stumbling back to the call box that was mounted on the light post, just down Rampart Street.

TWO

Earlier on, in the last week of January of that same year of 1910, the New Orleans City Council allotted municipal funds to hire a balloonist to float aloft and carry along a photographer to record a series of aerial views of the city. It was a windy late winter, and it was only on their fourth attempt that they could lift to a decent altitude without the risk of being blown halfway to Cuba.

The brave photographer came back down with two full cases of exposed glass negatives. When the negatives were developed, printed into positive images, and put on display, local residents and visitors from outside New Orleans Parish alike marveled to see panoramas of the Crescent City stretching out in mile-wide swaths, as a bird might view them.

Among the photographs was one that detailed those blocks that extended northwest from the French Quarter. For twelve years this section of the city had gone by the sobriquet "Storyville." For all of those twelve years and, in fact, for most of the eighty prior, it had come to be known as one of the most infamous red-light districts in the world. At its busy height, thousands of carnal acts were purchased and performed within one sweep of the clock. This went on day after day and week upon month, as efficiently as the assembly lines that Henry Ford was adapting to produce the vehicles that were mobilizing America. This astonishing activity, along with the more pedestrian diversions provided by the restaurants, saloons, and music halls, made Storyville—or "the District," as it was more commonly known—quite the destination.

So the photograph that included those twenty blocks, displayed with the others in the rotunda of City Hall, got more attention than any other. Gentlemen lingered there, snickering and employing broad winks as they pointed out the landmarks: the grandest sporting houses of Basin Street, the fine dining rooms, the classy cabarets, and the best-known drinking establishments. Those with sharp eyes could also pick out the rows of tiny pale squares on the back end of the District, the outlines of the cribs that the lowest class of scarlet women rented for ten cents a day. Two large plots of white, one at the northwest and another at the southeast corner—St. Louis Cemetery No. 1 and No. 2—provided foursquare reminders of a certain grim fate that awaited one and all.

Figuring most prominently in this photograph was the building on the corner of Basin and Iberville streets that took up a fair portion of the block. It had a broad, swooping roof that was dappled with gables and fairly bristled with chimney stacks from the fireplaces that were only now being replaced by coal-burning furnaces.

This was Anderson's Café and Annex, the keystone of the District and its magnetic core. Those who were most familiar with the location could peer at the photograph and point out the window of the King of Storyville's office, on the second floor and with a view all the way along Basin Street.

It was there, on a quiet Wednesday evening in the late spring, that Tom Anderson, the king himself, was settling back to wait out the eternity being defined by the babbling tongue of his guest, Alderman Alphonse Badel.

Anderson, seated at his heavy oak desk, gazed blankly at the alderman, taking in the flabbering jowls, heavy, wet lips, thick spike of a nose, black hair slicked oily, and small, pale green eyes, all perched upon a body that was barely stuffed into the Queen Anne chair. Anderson shifted in his own chair, a regal affair of dark oak and oxblood leather, tapping thick fingers on the top of his desk as he waited.

He had no idea why the alderman was going on and on, since he had gathered all the information he needed within the first minute of the visit: a certain resident from Badel's Esplanade Ridge ward had been discovered lying dead in a gutter, far out on Rampart Street. It was a sad and sordid affair, true; and yet Anderson still did not understand what it had to do with him.

Of course, he could have bullied the monologue to a halt at any point. As impressive as his guest's bulk, he was the larger man by any measure, tall, broad, and growing ever heavier around the middle, as if his girth was the gauge of his wealth and influence. A wide forehead, round cheeks, and noble ball of a chin proclaimed the pride of power. His silverish hair was parted down the middle in the fashion of the day, and he kept a thick but tidy handlebar mustache, steel gray and lightly waxed. His brow was like cut stone over blue eyes that could shine kindly or glitter fiercely, depending on the moment's mood. When he wore his metal-framed spectacles, he much resembled the man who had left the White House the year before.

He was even more substantial by reputation. Now in his late fifties, he was the red-light district's proud monarch, lording over the madams in their grand mansions, the sporting girls in fine upstairs rooms and dime-a-trick cribs, the rounders and gamblers and sports, the criminals petty and heeled, the saloon keepers who served them, and all the other characters in Storyville's shifting cast. His election to the state senate eight years earlier was his nod to the general concept of democracy; though, of course, he had neither the need nor the desire to practice it with particular vigor. He was now in his second term in the senate and well into his second decade in Storyville, and it had never occurred to anyone to challenge his prominence in either domain.

He held the respect of a fair share of the city's upstairs and downstairs populations. He was a friend to men of wealth and influence, and Teddy Roosevelt himself had slapped his broad back jovially and called him "Tom." At the same time, he knew most of the harlots, pimps, rounders, drunkards, hopheads, and musicians in his territory by their first names. As an old man, he would come to his Savior and renounce this sinful history; but for now, he took much pleasure in and grew rich from ruling Storyville.

With all this power and prestige came certain burdens. He was responsible for the welfare and safety of the women who staffed the mansions and cribs as well as their patrons. Matters of crime and punishment that were beyond the purview of the penal system fell to his judgment. He engaged in delicate political dances as stylized as waltzes. Swirling about were the endless and strange details of running a piece of territory that was dedicated to the commerce of sin.

It was a chore keeping the lid on a cauldron where passions ran loose and could be brought to a boil in the blink of an eye. Jealousies led to bloody violence. Whiskey, opium, and cocaine to fuel the mayhem were there for the asking. Serious amounts of money traded hands, tempting the foolish. It was always worse in the summer, when the New Orleans heat clung to bodies like a net. A hard hand on the wheel was required, lest it all fall into bedlam, a disaster for everyone, since the pyramid of wealth depended on the security of paying customers. Tom Anderson kept the streets generally peaceful and the cash rolling in without pause, and so grew more powerful and wealthier with every tick of the clock.

Though he was by no means without his failings. Along with his considerable gifts came appetites that now and then led him into trouble. He had launched a torrent of delirious gossip when, right under the nose of his mistress, Hilma Burt, he began a dalliance with Josie Arlington, once a sporting girl of legendary skills and now the youngest and prettiest of the Basin Street madams. The whole bawdy affair had been like some ongoing production at the Opera House, and Storyville was enthralled.

It didn't last long. Managing the District while these women tried to tear him in two was too much. When his esteemed colleagues in the state senate began snickering behind his back and he realized what a ridiculous figure he was cutting, he came to his senses and negotiated a truce between the squabbling madams. Chastened, he fixed his attentions on Storyville. His desires were checked, or at least hidden from prying eyes, much to the disappointment of those who had delighted in all the comedy. Once again, he was their sober leader, with responsibilities weighing on his broad shoulders.

Along with his greater burdens came petty irritations, among them a requirement to suffer fools, which was why he now sat fidgeting at his desk on a warm spring night, listening to the likes of Alphonse Badel prattling on and on as if neither one of them had anything better to do.

He put up with it for a while longer, then let out a small sigh and glanced at the door. The alderman, sensing his host's impatience, slowed his jabbering and then stopped completely.

Anderson leaned forward and turned his thick hands palms up. "I don't know how I can help you," he said. "I don't have anything to do with what goes on out there."

Badel gave him a shrewd look and said, "Don't be so modest, Tom."

Anderson ignored the compliment. "Have the police investigated?" he asked.

Badel turned snappish. "Not that you'd know it! They acted like it was just another Rampart Street murder. It was only when they got him downtown and found out who he was that anyone gave a damn about it. By then it was too late. They had a look, but they didn't find anything."

"Maybe because there was nothing to find."

Badel blinked. "What, now?"

"How do you know it wasn't just some spat that went badly?"

The alderman shook his head. "The coppers asked the same thing. There wasn't no trouble of that sort."

"As far as you know," Anderson murmured.

Badel's jowls flushed and jiggled. "I'm acquainted with the family," he exclaimed. "They're good, God-fearing Christian Americans. The fellow didn't gamble, didn't drink, didn't run with loose women. His hands are clean. It doesn't make sense. A gentleman like that, shot down, and on Rampart Street, of all places. It's some odd business and someone needs to look into it."

Now Tom Anderson raised a thoughtful brow, as if pondering the request, all the while trying to figure exactly what Badel was up to. It could be as simple as placating a family that had suffered the tragic loss and sought answers to ease their grief. Or it could be something else entirely. It was important, that was for sure, or the alderman wouldn't have come knocking on the devil's back door.

His guest was known as one of those righteous types who drew attention by roundly cursing Storyville as a sinful blight and demanding that it be shut down. Anderson recalled that in a recent screed, Badel had proclaimed to some temperance group or other that not only should the District be closed, but razed to the ground, with every stick burned, every brick buried, and the entire scarlet populace run out of town on rails. It would have been laughable, except there were more than a few important citizens of the city of New Orleans and the state of Louisiana who took such foolishness seriously.

"What about this fellow St. Cyr?" Badel broke into his thoughts, pronouncing the name with a rough French curl of his lip: *Sawn-sear.*

Anderson cocked one eyebrow, truly surprised at the turn in the conversation. "What about him?"

"Well, he fixed that Black Rose business a few years ago, didn't he? And that trouble about those jass players?" The King of Storyville nodded vaguely. He himself considered both terrible episodes as history, fixed and finished; the Creole detective St. Cyr, on the other hand, would say there was much left behind. If he spoke about them at all.

"Perhaps we could ask him to look into this," Badel said.

Now Anderson studied the alderman even more carefully. So that was it. He had come to request the services of St. Cyr specifically. The King of Storyville was more than a little astonished, as St. Cyr had been doing his best to stay out of sight and out of mind since he had suddenly reappeared in New Orleans earlier that year.

In any case, Anderson wasn't inclined to lend the detective out like some common laborer. Still, it puzzled him that Badel was going to so much trouble over an incident that would most likely end up swept under a rug. He thought about it a little more and realized that the alderman was presenting him an opportunity to kill two birds with the one stone. He would do a favor that would have to be repaid; more important, he'd find out if there was anything left of Valentin St. Cyr's skills.

"Well, we can ask him," the King of Storyville said, keeping his tone offhand. "It so happens he's downstairs right now."

Anderson had always taken a certain private delight in presenting Valentin St. Cyr to a stranger. It was always the same: the unsuspecting victim would look and then look again, brow furrowing in puzzlement. Though St. Cyr appeared at first glance to be a Creole of the French-Spanish variety, there was something not quite right about the picture. His flesh had an olive tint, his nose was bent a bit, and his black hair curled about like an Arab's. His gray eyes had a Mediterranean cast while his lips were almost as full as a Negro's. So if he turned one way in a certain light, he was clearly dago. Another half turn of his head and there was no doubt he was colored. And then he'd turn the other way and appear to be just one of those white men with odd features, not uncommon with New Orleans' racial mélange. In any case, it was enough to keep people guessing. He was just below medium height and built wiry, and he moved in a poised way that was just short of tense, as if there was violence stirring just under his skin. He was quiet, still as a stone for the most part, with a certain insolence resting in his cool expression and lazy posture.

It was that exact posture that St. Cyr assumed as he stepped into the doorway. Anderson put on his best innocent gaze, all the while watching Badel's face out of the side of one eye and allowing himself a small smile. He glanced at the detective and tilted his head in the direction of his guest. "This is Alderman Badel," he announced.

Valentin looked at the Frenchman who was wedged into the Queen Anne chair and murmured something that sounded like "sir," though Badel couldn't be sure. He knew of the detective only by reputation and frankly had been expecting someone less…*puzzling.*

"He has a problem and he'd like our help," Anderson explained. "Having to do with a murder that happened on Rampart Street on Sunday night."

When St. Cyr didn't respond directly, Badel took it for modesty before superiors and spoke up. "The victim of this terrible crime was one of my constituents. He was shot down in the middle of the street."

"*Rampart* Street," Anderson repeated. Valentin gave a blank nod. "Out beyond Third." Still there was no response from the

Creole detective. "I told the alderman we might extend him the courtesy of looking into it," he finished.

"That would be police business," St. Cyr said.

"They investigated and came up with nothing," Badel said. "We need another opinion on the matter."

Though the detective's gaze was fixed on the alderman, it was blank, as if he was actually listening to the noise from the Café below. Badel frowned, annoyed at the indifference.

Tom Anderson was watching Valentin and trying to fathom what was going on behind that stony visage. This former New Orleans police officer and sharp-minded private detective had to be bored doing nothing but working the floor of the Café four or five nights a week. Why wouldn't he be curious about a well-to-do white man shot down so far back-of-town? It was an odd matter, just as the alderman described it, the sort of puzzle that St. Cyr would jump to untangle. Or at least would have, before the troubles that had driven him away.

No matter; he was back, and it was high time that Tom Anderson found out what he was worth, if anything at all. "So perhaps you can help our guest," he prodded him.

Valentin nodded again slightly and returned his attention to the alderman. After a quiet moment, he asked, "What was the man's name?"

Badel leaned back and his chair creaked. "Mr. John Benedict," he said.

Anderson had dismissed St. Cyr, and he and the alderman waited until the footsteps had moved along the short hallway and receded down the stairs.

Badel said, "He didn't seem all that interested."

"He's quiet," Anderson said. "Discreet. It's what you want in a situation like this."

"Well, you know best, Tom." The alderman huffed brusquely, then with some difficulty pushed himself out of the chair. "Now, if you'll excuse me, I have an appointment." Having done his duty, he was eager to be on his way.

"Of course." Anderson stood up. He happened to know that Badel was on his way to visit a certain octoroon girl three doors down at Josie Arlington's. It did not strike him as the least bit odd that the alderman would pose as his sworn enemy by day, railing up and down the Crescent City about the terrible malady that festered in uptown, and then, since he was already in that den of iniquity anyway, help himself to those same delightful pleasures of the flesh by night. The man was not a priest, after all; he was a politician, and a New Orleans politician at that.

Anderson escorted him through the door, along the short corridor, and down the steep staircase. Once he had ushered him safely out the side door, he went back through the kitchen, nodding good-evenings to the sweating cooks and rushing waiters, and peered out through the round window in the door and into the big room.

It was thrumming like a happy machine. Anderson's Café and Annex was an elegantly appointed palace of its proprietor's personal crafting, the best address south and west of New York City for the diversion of gentlemen. The proprietor's deft hand was in evidence at every turn, from the cut glass in the doors, to the ornate crystal chandeliers, to the floor of Italian marble crisscrossed with dark carpeting, to the bloodred brocade above the wainscoting that ran along the walls. The bar with a constellation of colorful bottles and a long mirror held up one wall. The floor was filled with tables for drinking, fine dining, gambling, and political conniving. There was a small salon in the back for the ladies, their eyes shielded from the men and their diversions by drawn curtains.

On this night the tables were crowded and the games at full throttle. The Storyville sharps had descended on the Café, intent on plucking clean some fellow with more cash than skills. St. Cyr had sworn, and Tom Anderson had come to agree, that a

fair number of the marks showed up with their fat bankrolls for
the express purpose of being cleaned out. It would be something
to talk about for years to come over glasses of good whiskey
back home in Dallas or St. Louis.

The King of Storyville took another look around the big
room, saw that all was well as could be. St. Cyr had taken up a
post on the landing near the front door and his gaze moved over
the crowd in a distracted way, as if he wasn't really seeing any of
it. Anderson shook his head and muttered under his breath, wondering again if he had made a mistake. The man looked more like
one of the derelicts who sometimes wandered in off the street, the
same sort of miscreants St. Cyr was hired to keep off the premises.

Anderson went back upstairs and spent the next hour engaged in business by way of the brass-and-walnut telephone set
on his desk. He received two visitors, both with disagreements
that were too far wide of the courts. He took the problems under
advisement, promised solutions, and accepted payment in the
form of some future service. It was a normal night.

After the last guest departed, he made ready to slip out for
his visit with the girl at Gipsy Shafer's mansion. He knew both
Hilma Burt and Josie Arlington had their spies watching him.
Still, he had his ways: Miss Shafer had a private entrance that
led to a private stairwell that led to a private room.

He didn't leave right away. Instead, he loosened his necktie,
unbuttoned his vest, poured a glass of fine brandy from the decanter on the corner table, and carried it to the front window.
Though his bones ached with weariness, the mere sight of the
boulevard all aglitter with newly installed electric lights cheered
him. Standing there, brandy in hand, he let his mind wander
back over his day, going from hour to hour and putting all in
order in his head. This review was something that he did most
nights, the attention to detail one mark of his genius.

He wound his way through the morning and afternoon to
arrive at the evening visit from Alderman Badel and stop there.

It was a curious matter that had been laid before him. Of course, there was more to it than Badel had let on; the man had skittish eyes, and *schemer* was written all over his face. The crime had happened far out on Rampart Street, another world entirely, mean, loud, and bloody. The women and the whiskey along that avenue were dirt cheap, the rounders as low-down as they came, the type to kill a man over a wrong look.

They all drank Raleigh Rye by the gallon, smoked pills of hop, whiffed cocaine, and stuck needles of morphine sulfate in their craggy veins. Most of the men and half the women carried hideaway pistols, straight razors, or spring knives, which they employed with ill-tempered abandon. And the bands in the saloons and dance halls still played jass in the fast-and-furious style that crazy King Bolden had started.

By morning light the bodies of niggers, mulattoes, various other kinds of colored, and poor white trash were collected off the street, all good-for-nothings who deserved their sorry fates. This time, though, it had been a well-to-do American from the high-priced neighborhood on Esplanade Ridge.

Watching the swirl of the crowds on the banquettes below, Anderson pondered Badel's fussy insistence that someone look into the crime, even though it was the sort of shameful mess that most families would want buried along with the victim's remains. Not just someone; Badel was willing to risk the wrath of the police by bringing in Valentin St. Cyr, a fellow that coppers generally despised, instead of a Pinkerton or some other private copper.

It was odd, indeed, that Badel had picked St. Cyr, of all people, and he wondered how much the alderman knew about him. The Creole detective had only recently come back to the city. Where he had gone and what he had done for the fifteen months he was away was anyone's guess. He hadn't said. All Anderson knew was that he showed up at the Café door one chilly Tuesday afternoon after the turn of the New Year to ask humbly, like a stranger, if there might be any suitable employment for him.

The King of Storyville had been sitting at his usual downstairs table. He masked his surprise, regarding St. Cyr with frank appraisal. The Creole looked the worse for wear. His clothes were hanging loose and dirty. He had lost weight, and there was a certain hungry edge about him, like a stray dog that had been scrapping for food. The King of Storyville thought about it for a moment, then told him that he could work the floor of the Café as needed. The detective had responded to the offer with such an odd, absent look that Anderson had wondered if there was something wrong with him.

When he asked where he would be staying, St. Cyr muttered something about a room on Clio Street. The King of Storyville knew in an instant that there was no such room, and that the poor fellow would be sleeping that night in a flophouse, in the park, or in some doorway. So he offered an advance on the first week's pay, five Liberty dollars. St. Cyr had stared at the coins for a long time before picking them up. Then he thanked Anderson quietly and took his leave. A few days later, he announced that he had taken a room over Frank Mangetta's Saloon and Grocery on Marais Street.

The Creole detective who carried a history that had taken on aspects of legend had come back, and yet there was no fanfare at all, only whispers in the saloons and the parlors of the sporting houses. Of course, fifteen months was a long time to be gone, and memories in this part of the world tended to be short.

Except for working late nights at Anderson's Café, he stayed out of sight. If he was visiting any sporting girls, no one talked about it. Everyone assumed he was just finding his way and left him alone. That couldn't last, though; indeed, there were already rumors floating about that Tom Anderson was already losing patience with him.

In fact, after just a few days, the King of Storyville had discovered that he was dealing with a different Valentin St. Cyr altogether. Though the detective had never been able to afford the best clothes, he had at least taken some care with what he did own. Not anymore; he appeared at the Café in the same dingy suit every night. He had been known to keep a sharp eye and a firm hand on the nightly crowds, respecting those customers who behaved and dispatching those who didn't. In fact, the blunt way he'd dealt with the miscreants had been a source of some entertainment for the patrons. Now he barely paid attention, and there were complaints that some of the local pickpockets had been having a field day right under his nose.

Anderson sighed and brought his thoughts back to the business of the murder on Rampart Street. A case this simple would either get the Creole detective back on his horse or prove that he truly had lost his once-extraordinary skills. If that was so, he would no longer be of any use to the King of Storyville.

There was no trouble that night. Valentin left at 4 A.M., after the stragglers with nowhere else to go had shuffled out the door and into the last shadows of the New Orleans night.

He wandered down Basin Street, turned the corner at Iberville, and walked three blocks to Marais Street. At this hour even Mangetta's Saloon, the noisiest music hall in Storyville, was as silent as a bier. As he stepped into the alley that ran alongside the building, he looked in through the wide front window to see two drunks sprawled unconscious over tables while a bartender swept the sawdust across the floor in a weary rhythm.

He climbed the creaking metal stairs and let himself into his room, a cramped and dingy affair, as uncluttered as a cell, with a sagging iron-framed bed, a closet, a chest of drawers, and a night table. The walls were bare except for a 1909 calendar and a crucifix that had been hung there by the former tenant. Valentin had left both where they were. Two suits hung on the back of the door. The tools of his former trade—an Iver Johnson pistol, a stiletto in an ankle sheath, and a whalebone sap—were tucked far in a corner of the top drawer.

No one else but the cleaning girl entered the room. His landlord, respecting his privacy, was still waiting for an invitation. Anyone else who might have visited him was gone: Bolden, long lost in Jackson; Jelly Roll Morton in St. Louis and Chicago, playing music for the high rollers; the few others scattered far and wide. Justine, the dove who had shared his rooms on Magazine Street for the better part of two years, hadn't come calling, though she had to know that he was back in town. He'd taken pains to avoid her, and he guessed that she was doing the same. Though he now had the money for a sporting woman, it didn't occur to him to visit one.

On the nights that he wasn't working, he walked the streets of the city from one end to the other, often with his head bent as if searching for something that he had lost. It was an old habit. If the weather was poor or he was just worn out, he would stay in and listen to the music and shouts and laughter from the saloon downstairs. The jass—muted by the building's heavy beams, plaster ceilings, and hardwood floors—sounded like a faraway echo of the crazy gumbo that the Kid Bolden Band had created back in 1901. He still heard echoes of the way Bolden had played, and liked to listen even when it kept him awake. He didn't have anything better to do. There was a stack of books under his bed for when it got too quiet.

He wasn't quite ready to sleep this morning, so he opened the window and sat on the sill to take the breeze. As he sat there above the dark and silent streets, his thoughts meandered to the exchange that took place in Anderson's office earlier in the evening.

He had almost turned around and walked out when he realized what Badel and Anderson wanted. The alderman's gaze had been conniving and his voice shady as he talked about the hapless white man murdered in the dark end of town.

It was a puzzle why they had summoned him at all. There were Pinkertons and other private police all over the city; a few even had skills. And yet Alderman Badel had come to Anderson, and Anderson had turned to him. He didn't know what the two men were expecting, and it didn't really matter. Valentin hadn't come back to New Orleans to plunge into detective work again. He thought that was understood.

Anyway, he already knew what had happened. This Benedict fellow had gone to Rampart Street for the wrong pleasures, wandered off in the wrong direction, and crossed paths with the wrong person. The man's family should have wanted it swept from sight. So why insist on an investigation and why call him? Maybe, Valentin reflected with a grim smile, because they weren't looking for a real detective after all. That part, at least, made some sense.

He pondered for a while longer, until his head began to droop. He couldn't think anymore. He came back inside and closed the window as the first light of day, dark crimson, edged along the northeast horizon. The city would be coming to life soon. He stretched out on the bed and closed his eyes to the creeping dawn.

THREE

Justine Mancarre walked her gentleman caller down the stairs and out the door onto the gallery. His company motorcar, a forest green Maxwell with thin gold piping painted along its panels and fenders, idled at the curb, sitting high on bright yellow wheels. It was still early enough that she could step onto the gallery in her nightdress without being a spectacle. The breeze from the east lifted the hem as she watched Mr. George descend the gallery steps and cross the banquette to heave himself into the backseat of the automobile. The driver fixed his goggles over his eyes, engaged the gearshift, and turned his head to check the traffic. Mr. George gave a jaunty wave from the backseat as the automobile jerked forward and chattered away over the cobblestones. She knew he would now race home to the American side of town, change into clean clothes, and hurry off to his good job as president of the shipping business down by the river.

Her smile, already thin, evaporated. She took a moment to survey the banquette. Basin Street was tranquil, sleeping off the prior night's revels. It was a quiet and lonely time of day. She turned around and trudged back inside and up the stairs.

She was halfway to the landing when one of the maids came into the foyer and called up to her. Miss Antonia was requesting a moment of her time. Justine wasn't in the mood and thought about offering an excuse, perhaps claiming a headache. It wasn't worth it. The madam would just pester her all morning. She told the maid she'd be back down in a few minutes and continued up the steps.

Valentin woke to someone in the store below gabbling excitedly in Sicilian dialect. The voice came down a bit and the singsong lilt brought a memory of his father, who would lapse from his mangled English into Sicilian dialect when he was feeling especially gentle or agitated. His mother knew some words and, with the help of her backwoods Creole French, could talk back to him. He remembered lying in his bed, listening as his younger sister and brother slept. It was like the quiet moments in an opera, sweetly muted. It had been a long time ago, and yet he could still conjure all that at the sound of a single vowel.

He turned his head to see that the sun was up well over the rooftops. More voices rose, calls back and forth on subjects of mortadella and prosciutto. The grocery was open for business. He lay there for a while longer, listening to the voices and the rough music of the streets and alleys, getting busy with traffic.

He got up and headed to the bathroom at the far end of the silent hallway. There was only one other boarder on the floor, a serious and mysterious fellow who spoke a few gruff words in Italian when he spoke at all. Whatever his true name, Frank Mangetta referred to him only as "Signore Angelo." He had a peasant body, too, solid muscle. His skin was dark olive, his blue-black hair was oiled and combed, and his mustache waxed.

Where he had come from and what he was doing there were never explained. Angelo was always up and gone by first light and didn't come back until dusk or after, then went into his room, closed the door, and didn't come out again. Where he took his meals and life's other pleasures was a mystery as well. Though Valentin was curious, he didn't intrude. Whatever the Sicilian was hiding—or hiding from—was none of his business. The few times their paths had crossed, they had exchanged a brief greeting in Italian and Valentin had peered into black eyes that were like pools of private woe. It appeared that Angelo carried some cursed history on his broad back. Respecting his privacy, Mangetta did not share any information, either.

Since he and Angelo came and went at opposite hours, Valentin mostly had the upper floor to himself. He could enjoy a bath and a shave at leisure. Frank had installed a new toilet with a flushing mechanism so there was no longer any need to visit the back-alley privy in the damp chill of winter or the blistering, fly-swarming heat of high summer.

After his bath Valentin went back to his room and put on a pair of gray linen trousers and a white cotton shirt, both worn to the threads. He tied his shoes, pulled up his suspenders, draped a jacket over one shoulder, and went downstairs by way of the inside stairwell that led down to the storeroom.

Mangetta's was divided into two high-ceilinged rooms, the saloon on one side and an Italian grocery on the other. From the early hours of the day until late afternoon, the grocery, a compact and tidy establishment, catered to the District's floating population and the Sicilians who lived or worked nearby, as the proprietor kept the shelves stocked with foodstuffs, wines, and newspapers from the old country.

The saloon, twice the size of the store, opened at the stroke of twelve for cold lunches and an afternoon of casual drinking. No dinner was served, though cold plates were available. When the streetlights gleamed, the grocery doors were locked and the saloon became one of New Orleans' rowdier music halls. A four- or five-piece band would hold down the low riser in the corner, blasting jass for a crowd of drunken revelers, Creole, Italian, and American. There were plenty of sporting girls and rounders, though Mangetta kept neither rooms for the doves to ply the trade nor a gambling parlor for the men to lose their earnings that way. A violinist of modest skills, he had years back taken the role of padrone to the back-of-town music community. His saloon had been the beachhead when jass first crossed over Canal from the filthy bucket-of-blood music halls on Rampart Street. Now a dozen Storyville addresses featured jass bands regularly. Indeed, the onetime outlaw music was slowly edging in toward respectable.

The saloon was quiet in the morning and served as a private refuge for the proprietor and one of his tenants.

Valentin stepped though the storeroom and into the grocery to find Frank stocking shelves while his clerks took care of the line of customers, southern Italians and maids from the nearby bordellos. Though many stores lately had begun to allow patrons to select their own goods from the shelves, Frank wouldn't hear of it; he liked doing things the old way.

Valentin received a brief nod of greeting from the proprietor as he passed into the saloon, picking up the copy of the morning *Picayune* that was lying on the butcher block next to the archway. He took down two chairs and got himself situated just as Mangetta appeared with coffee in hand. The Sicilian placed the steaming cup at his elbow and disappeared to the kitchen behind the bar. The two men didn't exchange a word. Valentin took a sip of his coffee, noting that the storekeeper had thought to add a drop of *anisetta*. He opened his newspaper.

The stories on the front page described jagged bits of chaos. In Philadelphia, a streetcar strike had blossomed into a general work stoppage. Strikebreakers were on the way and riots were predicted. There was flooding in Ohio, with dozens dead and thousands uprooted from their homes, all because a dam had been built with inferior materials and had come down under the onslaught of spring rains and melting snow.

Valentin smiled over an article about a group of Chicago saloon owners creating a ten-million-dollar fund to battle the temperance movement, which was determined to close all the drinking establishments in the city. He tried to imagine someone going after the New Orleans saloons. Finally, there was a sad story about an argument between two friends over a coveted space at one of New Orleans' markets turning into a fight that left one of them dead on the floor.

There was no doubt about it, these were unruly days almost everywhere, and all up and down the economic ladder.

It was quiet here, though, and within a few minutes, aromas were wafting off the big cast-iron stove in back. Frank emerged from the kitchen, carrying a plate heaped with sausage and eggs. At the first whiff of sage and black pepper, Valentin's stomach started to churn. There was superb food all around the city; indeed, New Orleans was world famous for its cuisine. And yet no downtown restaurant could serve a peasant Italian dish to match Frank Mangetta's. Valentin sometimes wondered if the real reason he had come back to the city was that he missed the cooking.

Frank, born Franco Mangetta outside Siracusa, was as round as one of his waxed provolones and had a florid face adorned with a broad swoop of a waxed mustache and topped by a broader swoop of oiled black hair. He had known Valentin's father in the old country, and had remained a friend the detective could count on. When he was small, Valentin called him "Zi' Franco"—Uncle Frank—and he had memories of sweets dropped secretly into his hand during Saturday-afternoon visits to the store.

Later Mangetta had witnessed the terrible tragedies the family endured. Valentin went away after that happened, and when he came back, the Sicilian had taken a paternal interest. He had been dubious about the young man's foray into police work and guessed correctly that he was more interested in finding out about those responsible for his father's death and about the fate of his mother than in law enforcement. His career was mercifully short, and when it was over, he went to work for Tom Anderson. That had been almost ten years ago.

After two difficult cases in three years, Valentin had disappeared from the city and the Sicilian wondered if he'd ever see him again. At one point there was a penny postcard from Kansas City, but that was all. When Valentin finally did come back, Frank was glad to offer him a place to lay his head and some good Italian meals, *come una famiglia,* as he put it. It made him feel better to have the young man whom he considered a godson under his roof.

They had a morning ritual. Once Frank brought breakfast to the table, he would fetch himself a cup of coffee and then sit down for a chat. The proprietor would have preferred to carry it out in his native tongue, however Valentin had lost far too much to converse with any ease—just as almost all of the French that his Creole mother spoke had deserted him years ago.

The detective now put his paper aside and let out a sigh of pleasure as he turned his attention to his meal. Mangetta tended to some business in the store, then reappeared, coffee cup in hand.

The two of them talked about this and that, and eventually Valentin got around to his latest bit of news. "I'm going to be doing a little job for Mr. Anderson," he said.

"Yeah? What kind of a job?"

Valentin took a sip of his coffee. "An investigation." He told him about Alderman Badel, Mr. John Benedict, and Rampart Street.

Mangetta listened, wrinkling his thick nose in finicky disgust. "Why you want to work for them people?" he said. "There ain't enough trouble around here?"

Valentin understood; *them people* referred to the Americans. "I'm just doing a favor for Anderson," he said, explaining that it was a simple matter, a rich man paying for his depravity with his life. He would be finished with it in no time.

He felt himself stuttering over the explanation. Frank eyed him, frowning. Before he could say what was on his mind, though, one of the clerks called out from the grocery about a case of cannellini filled with dented cans. He got to his feet with a grunt of annoyance.

"*Mang'*," he said. "Eat. You're still skin and bones."

Miss Antonia's phone tinkled merrily just as Justine reached the door of her office. The madam picked up the handset with one hand and held up a bejeweled finger of the other, a signal for her to wait. Justine leaned in the doorway, lending half an ear as Miss Antonia crooned honey-dripping words of flattery, which meant the person on the other end of the line was a man of means, one of those whom they depended upon to eat, to pay their rent, to buy their fine clothes. It was their business; still, Justine was always stung by these little reminders of her return to the sporting life.

At the same time, she knew a thousand women would that very morning trade places with her. She kept a room in one of the best houses on the main line of one of the most infamous red-light districts in the world. Her looks and able wits meant she entertained only wealthy downtown gentlemen and the occasional uptown sport flush with winnings. She was not hiking her bloomers for a dozen strangers a night. She did not go through cartons of stockings from spending so much time on her knees, like the women in the French houses. She did not have to take beatings to satisfy some madman's desires. She didn't have to perform lewd acts of every description for the entertainment of crowds of cigar-smoking gentlemen, as they did in French Emma Johnson's Circus. She did not pay visits to the doctor for the treatment of a disease, and she'd never had to summon Dago

Annie to clean away the first traces of a trick baby. In short, she did not walk the kind of rough road that would turn her into an old woman by thirty. Indeed, if she kept her good looks and taut body, she might well end up as a mistress or even the wife of some well-to-do gentleman—though her last try had ended poorly. Being kept was not to her taste.

So her life had settled into an adequate routine that lasted until the morning Miss Antonia put her head in a spin by whispering that Valentin St. Cyr was back in town. The next days brought reports that he'd been sighted here and there, and that he was looking as ragged as a tramp. When he didn't appear on her doorstep, she had to quell an urge to go see him.

Some days later she learned that he was back in the employ of Tom Anderson and was staying in a room over Mangetta's. He was working within spitting distance of Miss Antonia's and living not too much farther away, and yet he never came to see her. Somehow she wasn't surprised. She couldn't blame him, not after she had ended up back in the same place where—

"Justine!" Miss Antonia was watching her with a vexed expression.

She blinked. "I'm sorry, what?"

"Mr. George."

"What about him?"

"I was saying that he's quite pleased with you," the madam commented. "You'll want to keep it that way. He's the head of Gulf Shipping." She acted as if Justine hadn't already heard this information a dozen times. "It's one of the largest companies on the river."

Justine stared at her blankly, and Miss Antonia let out a little hiss of irritation. She waved a hand to one of the café chairs. "Please, have a seat," she said.

Justine pulled the chair away from the wall and sat down with some reluctance. It was time for her daily grilling, the one where Miss Antonia went searching for signs that she was about to bolt out the door on the trail of a certain Creole detective.

At the same moment Justine was settling into the chair, Valentin was crossing to the south side of Basin Street, heading toward Canal. He did not look over as he passed Antonia Gonzales's mansion. A few minutes later, he was hopping on an Esplanade Line car. Another quarter hour and he stepped off at the corner of Rendon and started south.

The neighborhood Valentin entered, intersected by Esplanade, was one of the city's most pristine American enclaves. The houses were large, mostly classic French in design, many of stucco or whitewashed brick, with mansard roofs and balconies of ornate wrought iron. The windows were tall for light and ventilation. Each one sat on a large plot of land with gardens in front and large yards behind the houses, some of which backed up to the line of yew trees that defined the borders of the Jockey Club. There was not quite so much attention to family tradition here as in some older sections of town. Those who had the funds could take their place, and those who couldn't were not welcome. In fact, it was uniquely democratic in that way, though, of course, no one of color need apply.

As lovely and secure as the streets appeared, and no matter how sweet their beds of roses and camellias, Valentin knew too well what kinds of corruption dwelt behind some of the facades. He'd seen it firsthand; and it was one such scandal that had brought him there this morning.

He arrived at the Benedict address on St. Philip, feeling something like a beggar as he stepped under the balcony to knock on the heavy oak and cut-glass door adorned with a wreath of somber black roses. It gave him a long moment's pause.

The door was opened by a young mulatto girl. Though she was dressed down in black, she regarded him with bright, curious eyes and a smile that was almost impish. His first thought was that she looked familiar, and he was trying to place her when an elderly and elegantly attired Frenchman came to the foyer to greet him.

"Mr. St. Cyr?" he said, offering a thin hand. "Maurice Delouche. The Benedict family attorney." His posture was bent and his features narrow, an aging fox. His eyes were a light blue just a shade away from transparent. He glanced at the detective's worn ensemble and sighed in disappointment. Valentin guessed that the fellow had expected a Pinkerton in a three-piece suit.

The attorney bent his head to whisper. "The late Mr. Benedict's wife and daughter have requested the services of an investigator to look into his unfortunate death." He sniffed disapproval. "You should know that it was over my objection. I don't see what's to be gained. But they insist." He regarded the detective for another troubled moment, then gestured with one of his frail hands. "They're waiting in the sitting room."

With the colored maid following behind, he ushered Valentin along a corridor. The detective took a quick look into a living room and dining room and saw an assembly of white people standing around in suits and dark dresses, holding cups and glasses and little trays of food and talking in low voices. If the mourners saw him at all, they ignored him.

Delouche led him into a small parlor, where four armchairs were arranged around a coffee table and the two women were waiting.

The attorney murmured the introductions. "Mr. St. Cyr, allow me to present Mrs. Grace Benedict, the widow, and Miss Anne Marie Benedict, his daughter." He looked from one woman to the other. "Mr. Valentin St. Cyr is a private investigator referred to us by Alderman Badel." Neither the name Tom Anderson nor the word Storyville was mentioned.

Finishing his little speech, Delouche invited Valentin to take one of the vacant chairs while he took the other one.

Mrs. Benedict cleared her throat and asked in a low voice if their guest would like some refreshment. The maid who had greeted him at the front door was waiting. When Valentin shook his head, the widow flicked a hand and the girl faded away.

The detective took the moment to study the widow and the deceased's daughter. Both women had regal profiles, patrician noses, full lips, striking blue-green eyes. They were dressed alike as well, with their black skirts draping to the floor and black shirtwaists buttoned at the neck. The widow's visage, though haughty, was somehow blurred, as if out of focus. At a second glimpse, Valentin noticed that her face was hollow beneath the powder, as if she was made of fine china, and dark shadows curved under her eyes. He had seen it before and knew what it meant. By contrast, the daughter's posture was stiff and her gaze intense, like she was on alert. There was something not quite right about the poses they presented; on the other hand, he knew grief did strange things to people.

It didn't matter. He had no particular sympathy for their grief, and a flush of annoyance brought a sour taste to his mouth. These people and their privilege. With fortunes built on the sweating backs of generations of poor folk, they passed their lives untouched by the dirty world outside and its dangers. They broke rules and never paid a price. He knew for a fact that among their number were those who had gotten away with murder. Now one of theirs had died, they were desperate for help, and he had been called.

With a solemn sigh, Delouche said, "Well, then. Shall we begin?"

The daughter, who had been regarding their visitor with her steady eyes, said, "Thank you for coming, Mr. St. Cyr." She spoke the name with a Parisian lilt, barely moving her mouth as she softened each letter.

"Yes, ma'am," Valentin said, keeping his voice flat.

Mrs. Benedict raised eyes that were as glassy as a doll's and

said, "We want to find out what happened to my husband." She
had tried for a note of command, but her voice warbled. "I hope
you can help us."

Valentin took his hands off the arms of the chair and made
a steeple before his chest. "My understanding is that your husband was alone in a dangerous part of the city," he stated directly. "He ran up on some criminal and it cost him his life."

Mrs. Benedict's gaze skipped to the attorney and then back
to him, her lip beginning to quiver. "But he wasn't...he had no
reason to be in that...that *place*."

"And yet he was," Valentin said briskly. "He could have been
killed elsewhere and his body moved there, but I doubt it."

Both women winced and the attorney let out an angry hiss
of breath. A pronounced silence followed. Mrs. Benedict held his
eyes, then looked away. The daughter continued to gaze at him
fixedly, and now seemed to be biting her lip.

Valentin gave their stares right back to them. "It would help
to know what he was after on Rampart Street in the dead of
night."

It came out cool and insinuating, the same tone of voice he
used when he grilled suspects. The small spots of color on the
widow's cheeks faded to a dead white, even as the daughter's
eyes flashed hotly. It was if they were noticing him in their midst
for the first time. He shifted his blank gaze to some point in
space.

Mrs. Benedict held herself together for another moment,
then began to sob quietly, dabbing her eyes with a silk handkerchief. Anne Marie put a protective arm around her mother's
shoulders and glared at Valentin, her face taut and lips tight with
anger. He refused to engage her, so she turned to Delouche,
sending a message.

The attorney, who had been trying to get his attention all
along, leaned over to deliver a sharp whisper. Valentin stood up,
gave a cursory bow to his hosts, and followed the attorney out

of the room. They stepped into the pantry, a narrow space that adjoined a large, sunny kitchen. The door swung closed behind them. Valentin settled against one of the sideboards and studied the arrangement of fine china in the cupboards as Delouche drew his thin body up, clenching his hands at his sides.

"What do you think you're doing?" the attorney hissed. "You don't speak to ladies like that!"

Valentin eyed him. "Like what?"

"John Benedict was buried yesterday. They're grieving. You aren't on Basin Street, sir. You can't—"

"This is a waste of time."

Delouche cocked his head, stunned at the detective's insolence. He said, "I beg your pardon?"

"This is a waste of time," Valentin repeated. The attorney opened his mouth to protest. Valentin barged on. "They can tell any story they want, but you know he went out there for a woman. Or maybe it was a man. Or something else. And he was murdered." He shrugged. "That's all there is to this."

By now Delouche's cheeks were crimson and his lips fairly trembled with anger. "Are you finished?"

"I am." Then, as if reading the attorney's thoughts, Valentin said, "You can hire yourself another detective, if you like. You'll likely get someone who will drag it along and milk the widow out there for as long as she'll put up with it. And then he'll come to the same conclusion I did. So I just saved her a good bit of time and money."

The lawyer grimaced with distaste. "Thank you for that advice," he said acidly. "You may show yourself out."

After Miss Antonia dismissed her, Justine went upstairs, eager to draw her bath and wash away the previous night's amours.

Since it was still early, there was plenty of hot water and a thick cloud of steam filled the bathroom. She slipped out of her nightdress and hung it on the back of the door. As she drew the long pins to let her hair down, she studied herself in the mirror on the wall. Her African and Cherokee blood had given her features an exotic cast that sometimes drew stares on the street. Her skin was au-lait brown, her eyes oval and slanted over high cheekbones. Her nose had a gentle Indian curve and when she smiled her mouth was a full bow.

She had kept a good body, too. Her hips and bust were full curves on a short and slender frame that carried little fat. It was such a fine figure that she could have rested on it alone and earned herself a good living. But unlike most of the Storyville doves, she wasn't a shallow woman. She had gone to school; she knew how to read and she could write with some skill. She had finished every book Valentin had kept in their rooms, and she regularly bought penny novels from the sellers on the street. Valentin had even discussed his cases with her, and had asked for her opinions. He was the only man who had ever treated her that way.

The bathtub was full. She tested it before slipping into steaming water that was all fragrant with the scent of camellias. She sank down and put her head back until all but her face was submerged, and house and the world outside fell into a watery silence. She closed her eyes, felt her muscles flow away from her bones. It was always at times like this that her musings drifted to Valentin. After her little chat with Miss Antonia, those thoughts made a beeline.

She had gone away from him after the Black Rose murders, and then they were thrown together in a terrible dance during the jass killings. A few days after that case ended, he got on a train and left New Orleans. Justine's sadness at his departure was tinged with relief that all her anguish over him was finished. She went back to the sporting life. It was her profession, for good or ill; and for the first time in a long time, she felt a little peace.

Over the months that followed, she would sometimes sit at her window on quiet nights, looking out into the darkness and wondering where he was. She pictured him walking down the back street of some dirty city or along a narrow, dusty country road, and always alone. As time went by and he didn't return, he seemed to dim in her mind, grow smaller, more distant.

Then, five weeks ago, he reappeared. He made no effort to find her, and part of her didn't want to see him, either, so she stayed away. It appeared they were settling into an unspoken agreement to avoid each other, even as they walked the same banquettes every day.

For a few seconds she dropped into the deeper silence beneath the water, then pushed her face out again. She knew it couldn't go on like that forever. Sooner or later they would meet, by choice or accident. She tried to imagine the look on his face and what words might come out of his mouth when it finally did happen and came up with nothing, as if he really was a stranger.

When Valentin got back to Marais Street, the kid who went by the moniker Beansoup came rushing out the front door of Mangetta's Grocery to intercept him.

"Mr. Valentin!" Beansoup yelled, louder than was necessary. "Hey, Mr. Valentin!"

The detective saw that the kid, now a professional street Arab of some skills, had replaced his usual ragged shirt and trousers with a suit he'd found somewhere, a bad-fitting ensemble of light brown checks. It was too long and too wide, and his white limbs poked out like stalks. A derby of darker brown was perched atop his ball of a head. Beansoup's face was pale in the winter and splotchy pink in summer. His eyes were lazy blue, and there was a first hint of fuzz on his upper lip. Now fifteen, he worked hard to assume the posture of a rounder without much success; he didn't have the required poised, sullen reserve. He looked like a cartoon drawing or like a child dressed up in his father's old clothes, except that Beansoup wouldn't know his father if he tripped over him. He was a ward of the city, and his home, when he chose to claim one, was St. Mary's Orphanage.

When he caught up with the detective around the side of the building, he had an Italian roll stuffed with sausage in one dirty hand and a Chero-Cola in the other, both no doubt provided by that kind soul Frank Mangetta. He swallowed the contents of his mouth, took a swig of his cola, and spoke up in his cracking voice.

"I got a message from Mr. Tom," he piped.

Valentin grunted with frustration. Almost everyone of means in New Orleans now owned a telephone set these days, and the lawyer Delouche had wasted no time in using his. "What's he want?"

"He wants you at the Café. Right away." Beansoup went to stuffing his mouth. "What the hell'd you do?" he said, spraying crumbs. "He's hot as a goddamn pistol."

Valentin found the King of Storyville at his usual table near the end of the bar, talking to Billy Struve, a District gadabout and Anderson's most able spy. He treated the detective to a short glance, said, "Wait in my office," then returned to the whispered discussion.

Valentin went through the kitchen and into the hallway, then climbed the stairs. Once in the second-floor office, he leaned against the wall and looked over Anderson's desk. Only a single brass lamp, a green felt blotter that was replaced weekly, and an ornate telephone in a walnut box adorned the polished surface. Stacks of papers were laid out on a long library table that was pushed against the opposite wall, so Anderson would take only what he needed to his desk or, more commonly, to his preferred table at the end of the bar downstairs. He loved to work in the midst of the bustle of getting the Café repaired from the previous night and ready for the next. He did all his workaday tasks and entertained those who came to him on more mundane matters downstairs.

He used his office when the Café was open and when there was serious business to conduct. He greeted the most important visitors and handled his most private communications there. Rumor had it that the desk was also pressed into service during visits from certain young ladies. If it was so, Valentin mused, it would have been when Anderson was a younger man. And a lighter one; sturdy as it was, the desk might not take the weight of two persons if one of them was Tom Anderson.

As if to underscore that thought, leaden steps at that moment came thumping up the stairwell. Valentin turned around and composed his face into a stolid mask. He knew what was coming.

Anderson stepped through the door and crossed directly to the desk. He kept Valentin standing as he dropped into his leather chair and folded his hands before him in a stiff bridge. The Creole detective had seen his employer strike that pose a few times, and it was always a bad sign. Anderson now regarded the younger man with his coolest stare.

"That damned Badel called me," he said. "He was in a state. Because he got a call from this Delouche, the lawyer. Who said you insulted the widow and daughter and then told him you weren't going to continue the investigation."

"I didn't say I—"

"Be quiet!" The white man jabbed a thick finger. "You stood right there and heard me promise results. Or at least the courtesy of an effort. That's why I sent you."

"All I did was tell them it's better left alone."

Anderson glowered for a moment, then shook his head and folded his hands on his blotter once more. "You listen to me, Valentin. I wanted to give you a chance to get on your feet again. But I can make a call and have someone else on the job in ten minutes. If that's what you want, just say so." He actually made as if he was about to reach for the telephone.

Valentin felt the room closing in and his gaze went to the window. To the east, over the slate rooftops, he could see the crescent of the Mississippi and partway to the Gulf. He wondered what he'd been expecting. The King of Storyville had lost patience with him, and if he gave the wrong answer, he'd be going back to his room to start packing.

Anderson shifted in his chair. Another few ticks of the clock went by. Valentin sighed quietly and said, "I'll do it."

"Without wearing a face? Or telling those people what you think of them?"

"I'll be fine," Valentin said.

"Then you'll have to go see Delouche and make amends. And hope he accepts your apology."

"And what if he doesn't?"

"Then you'll want to think about a situation somewhere else," Tom Anderson said.

The detective understood that he was on shaky ground. Still, he allowed himself a dim smile. Anderson caught it and said, "What?"

"Lieutenant Picot's not going to like this at all."

"When has that ever mattered to you?" Tom Anderson waved the detective out the door with one hand and reached for his ornate telephone with the other.

The offices of Dremont, Castell and Delouche, Attorneys-at-Law, occupied both floors of a staid brick building on St. Charles, a few blocks past Poydras. Valentin stepped up to double doors that were mounted in a brass-plated frame and set with leaded glass in which the name of the firm was etched.

He crossed the lobby to stand before a desk that was large enough to serve dinner for six. Once he announced himself to the gray-haired woman seated there, he was asked to wait in an armchair that he found so plush he could have napped in it. Long minutes passed before a young fellow in a shirt and tie appeared to escort him along the hallway that extended off the lobby. Delouche's office was at the far end, as befitted a senior partner.

The room was lined with books, wall to wall, ceiling to floor. In one of the corners was a low table and two armchairs, upholstered in brocade. Tall windows looked out on St. Charles. The thick carpet of deep, sober blue muffled any and all sound.

The desk at the center of the room was a ponderous affair of old cherrywood that was polished to a dark glow. From behind it, Maurice Delouche coughed and said, "Mr. St. Cyr," in a creaking voice that held a feigned note of surprise. He waved a hand and Valentin took one of the chairs opposite.

The attorney, for all his frailty, still managed to summon from some corner of his being a certain firmness of stature and tone, and he regarded his visitor with a cool and brittle gaze. "How can I help you?" The delivery was completely deadpan. Valentin guessed that in the time it had taken him to get there, Anderson had spoken to Badel, who had in turn called Delouche. The attorney knew exactly why he was there.

"It's about the Benedict case," Valentin said.

Delouche raised an eyebrow. "What about it?"

Valentin understood that he was going to have to pay for his earlier insolence. "I'd like permission to continue the investigation."

The attorney now took an elegant pause, settling back to study him with a certain sly light in his eyes. Valentin bit down on his bile and waited.

Delouche swiveled in his chair a quarter turn so he could gaze out one of his tall windows. "The Benedicts are a good American family, and they've been in that Esplanade Ridge neighborhood for more than thirty years," he intoned. "John was a very successful businessman and a stalwart of the community. The ladies have attended the finest finishing schools and have taken part in society. They are active in the church. They have been very supportive of a number of charities. In other words"—the chair came back around and the flat gaze settled on Valentin once more—"not the type of people to go wandering around on Rampart Street in the dead of night."

"Then what was he doing there?"

The attorney said, dryly, "I'm quite sure he just got lost. But to my mind, it doesn't matter how that happened, or why. My concern is the survivors, Mrs. Benedict and Anne Marie. I don't want the family name dragged in the dirt. Except for the report of the crime, I've managed to keep the whole mess out of the newspapers, but until it's settled, there's a risk of scandal. So we don't really need an investigation, sir. We need a conclusion."

Delouche tugged at his vest, a small gesture of impatience. "What happened was a tragic mistake and that's all it was. Now it needs to be laid to rest. Do I make myself clear?" Valentin hesitated and the attorney cocked his head. "Mr. St. Cyr?"

"I understand."

"Very well," Delouche said. "Then let's get the whole sad matter handled as soon as possible." He picked up a pen. "Now, if you'll please excuse me..." He returned his attention to the document on his desk. He did not look up as Valentin made his exit.

Outside, the afternoon had turned windy and high clouds were coming in from the Gulf. Valentin walked down St. Charles to Lafayette Square and made a circuit of the statue of the great Frenchman, absently running his hand over the wrought-iron spikes as he passed along.

Now he understood. No one wanted an investigation, merely the appearance of one, and he was going to be a willing player in this fiction. *The poor fellow got lost and...* He was expected to deliver a report that would insulate the family. Whatever had actually happened to Benedict would remain forever unknown.

He began another circuit of the square. His task would be

easy enough. If he performed this simple service, he'd be taking a step in the direction of reviving some semblance of his career. Whether he wanted to or not.

And yet he knew old habits died hard and he couldn't shake the thorns that kept pricking at him from the edges. Beginning with the most obvious: What *was* John Benedict doing alone on Rampart Street at that hour? Was he so foolish that he got lost, or was he there for some purpose? Either way, why wasn't anyone watching out for him? The man was wealthy. Where was the protection that people of means employed?

Valentin arrived back to the St. Charles Avenue banquette and stopped short. What was he thinking? It was none of his affair what happened to John Benedict. He had agreed, mostly by his silence, to go through the farce of an investigation, in order to placate a troubled widow and daughter. That was all there was to it and he needed to leave it alone.

Anyway, it was well after the lunch hour and he hadn't eaten since breakfast. He turned northeast, heading for home.

The telephone bell jangled and Anne Marie Benedict lifted her skirts and hurried to the foyer to answer it before it woke her mother. She pushed back her hair, held the polished brass hand piece to her ear, and studied the design in the glass that framed the front door as she listened to Mr. Delouche explain the situation.

Valentin St. Cyr, the private detective who had shown up at their door with a surly face and sharp tongue, had apparently seen the error of his ways and now wished to continue the investigation, if the family would allow it. The attorney reported that the man had been chastened roundly. There would be no more disrespect. He said that while Tom Anderson still insisted that St. Cyr was the man for the job, there were many other competent investigators about.

She counted to five, feigning deliberation, then made her

voice sound grudging as she stated her preference to keep Mr. St. Cyr on. His experience with the rough streets of the city couldn't be discounted. After thanking the attorney, she replaced the telephone in its cradle.

She turned around and went up the stairs to the second floor. As she reached the master bedroom, she peeked through the crack in the door. Her mother was still asleep, thankfully, exhausted by grief and her medications. Their maid Betsy was busy in the kitchen. The house was silent. The visitors had been asked to leave by two o'clock out of respect for the family.

She continued down the hall to her room, closed the door behind her, and immediately went to the chest of drawers and the tray with a bottle of brandy and three glasses that sat on top. She poured one of the glasses half full, took a sip, then another, feeling the heat in her stomach and the tight pressure in her forehead wash away. As she sat down on the edge of her bed, a sudden memory of the Creole detective gliding into the armchair caught and held her.

The moment the lawyer Delouche began talking about St. Cyr, her heart had thumped like a drum and then a peculiar quiver ran down her spine when he told her that the detective wished to investigate her father's murder after all. She had felt a giddy delight and a jagged spike of dread, both amid the melancholy weight of her poor father's death.

A rush of guilt and sorrow assailed her, and she put a hand to her face and sobbed, thinking of her father's horrible death, shot down and dying alone like that and in that place.

After a few moments, she got hold of herself, sat up, and dabbed her eyes. She carried her glass to the window to watch the quiet street.

The first terrible days after the murder had passed and the funeral was over. As her mind cleared, she tried to understand what had happened. She had only the vaguest notion of Rampart Street, had heard only whispers about what went on out there, with the loose women, the vicious men, and the wild music. It was no place for a gentleman like her father. And yet he had gone there. Not knowing what was waiting...

She drank off more of the brandy and noticed there was only a half inch left in her glass. She went for the bottle, telling herself that she had to stop doing this so early in the day. She filled the glass one more time and went back to the window to gaze out at the clouding sky.

The police officers who had come to the house were courteous but blankly dismissive, assuming that she and her mother were hiding what they knew in order to protect the family name. She saw the glances they exchanged. They thanked her for her time, promised to look into it, and went away, no doubt snickering up their sleeves.

When Alderman Badel appeared at the wake, his round face composed in bereavement, she took him and the attorney Delouche aside to express her dismay over the police work. Surely, there was something more to the tragedy than some stupid mistake. She told them she wanted to hire someone to look into it. The attorney disapproved. Better to lay it to rest, he had whispered in that craggy voice of his, along with the body. Much to his displeasure, however, the alderman jumped to volunteer his help. The next day he reported that he'd found a man who had worked those same vile back-of-town streets. A regular Pinkerton would barely know where to begin. Anne Marie guessed right away that Badel was somehow serving his own interests as he minded hers. She didn't care; she understood that sometimes things worked that way. One thing led to the next, and Valentin St. Cyr appeared at their door.

Even through her grief, she couldn't mistake the insolence in his face and posture, as if he had the tragedy and the family that endured it all figured out in advance. Bored, he was there by no choice of his own. He was barely interested, which intrigued her all the more. Indeed, malice came off him like he had a sign on his forehead. He didn't like them, didn't want to be in their home or their employ. Still, she sensed that he was the man for the job, and so she wanted him on it.

Though she had heard the words "rounder" and "sport" bandied about, she never actually met one. Once, when she was fourteen or so, their carriage had been diverted down Basin Street and her father made her put her hands over her eyes so as not to witness the scarlet parade on that famous avenue. She had peeked anyway and caught glimpses of sporting girls and madams and some dangerous-looking men like St. Cyr.

She finished her brandy and put her glass up, then went downstairs to the kitchen, where she found Betsy snapping beans into a pot.

The maid took her instructions with a sly grin spreading across her face. She put up her work and hurried out the door and off to Storyville, a place she seemed to know quite well for someone who claimed to have been a domestic servant since the age of twelve.

Valentin stopped by the Café to tell the King of Storyville that he had gone to see Delouche and would finish the investigation.

"You're doing the right thing," Anderson counseled him. "It will be over in no time, and we can all get back to business."

The detective nodded politely and excused himself, murmuring about coming to work that evening. Though he worked to keep his voice even and his face blank, Anderson could tell he wasn't pleased. Well, he mused, that was just too bad for him.

By the end of the afternoon, Betsy hadn't come back and Anne Marie was beginning to wonder if the maid had decided to spend the time in Storyville earning some extra money. Anne Marie went ahead and made her mother a dinner of light broth, a small salad, and a French roll and put it all on a tray. When she carried it into the bedroom, Mrs. Benedict took one look at the food and made a face.

"I'll have it later," she said.

Anne Marie's gaze roamed to the small wooden box, saw that it was open and that the syringe was in plain view. She closed it with a deft hand. With another urging for her mother to eat, she went down the hall to change clothes, knowing that when she came back, the tray would be untouched and her mother would be asleep again.

It was after six o'clock when Anne Marie heard the key jiggle in the front-door lock. She forced herself to walk slowly to the head of the stairs. Betsy was looking up at her and smiling, wide and white and devious, and she felt a rush of excitement.

She came down the steps in a glide, took the maid's elbow, and steered her through the downstairs rooms and into the kitchen. They sat down at the table. Impatiently, Anne Marie said, "Well?"

Even though there was no one else about, Betsy dropped her voice to a whisper. "Mr. Valentin St. Cyr ain't what you think," she said. She took a dramatic pause, then said, "First thing you need to know..."

She let it hang there until Anne Marie said, "What? What is it?"

The maid grinned like an imp. "The man is *colored*."

It took a good half hour for Betsy to finish. Afterward, she got up from the table and went about preparing an evening meal for the two of them, leaving Miss Anne Marie at the table, her chin resting in her hands, gazing blankly at the vase of flowers.

The detective had quite a tale, and that he was a person of color was only the beginning. She wondered where the maid had gotten so much information in such a short time.

That his true name wasn't St. Cyr, for example. According

to Betsy, he was born Valentino Saracena and was a Creole-of-color on his mother's side and Sicilian on his father's. No matter what the color of his face, blood was blood, and the man she had agreed to engage was part Negro and part dago.

He had grown up in the polyglot neighborhood around First and Liberty streets, to the west of the city and above South Rampart Street. His life was unremarkable until the troubles of the 1890s, when mobs of white Americans turned on the Sicilian community with raw violence. His father was one of the victims, murdered by a gang.

Anne Marie interrupted to ask Betsy to repeat that part for her. Then she told her to continue.

Valentino was sent away to a nun's school in Chicago. He came back to New Orleans to learn that his mother had one day left their home and simply wandered off like some madwoman, or so the neighbors claimed, and was not seen again.

He had remained in the city, using the moniker St. Cyr. He was a policeman for a while, working the streets of Storyville. When he left the force under a cloud, Mr. Tom Anderson offered him a position. That had been almost ten years ago.

There was more in the shadows of his biography. Murder, madness, and a whole palette of mayhem had swirled around him. A café-au-lait sporting girl out of a Basin Street mansion was woven into the tale. So was Tom Anderson, of course; and a horn player named Bolden, who had made crazy jass music in the saloons and dance halls along the same Rampart Street where her father had died. There were whispers about a black-skinned island girl and about a Georgia guitar player lying dead on the sawdust floor of a beer hall across the river in Algiers.

It was some story, and Betsy had gathered it all up in the course of a single afternoon.

Anne Marie thought about it some more and realized that she needed both her mulatto maid and the Creole detective, no matter what kind of blood ran in their veins. Though if St. Cyr's history ever got around, she'd have to claim that she'd been deceived, like everyone else, and send him away.

Charles Kane stood on the gallery of his house on Third Street, a tumbler of whiskey in one hand and a Cuban cigar in the other. His wife nagged him so much about the smell that he had finally given up smoking in the house and started taking his pleasure outdoors. This had a benefit of giving him an escape from her and their sons for a while. Lately he found them aggravating, listening endlessly to recordings of coon songs on the Harvard phonograph that he'd so foolishly purchased. His wife had told him that *everyone* had one, and so twelve dollars of his money went out the window. Now the parlor echoed nightly with plinking banjo music and minstrel singers yelping about darkies stealing chickens and other such nonsense.

That's about all the niggers were good for, Charles brooded sourly as he blew a fragrant cloud and watched it swirl away in the night breeze. Stealing and lying and lazing about when they weren't making more useless litters; them and the rest of the intruders.

He was mulling these thoughts, his head down and brow beetling, when he became aware of something moving along the edge of his vision. He gave a start, turned slightly, and then stepped closer to the railing. There had been a shift in the shadows between the two houses across the street. Or maybe not; he kept staring, but nothing else moved.

It gave him pause. He had sensed a shady presence that wasn't the product of the liquor he drank in healthy amounts, and it had started the day after John Benedict had been found dead on Rampart Street.

He stood watching the space across the street, but picturing Benedict in that part of the city in the darkest part of the night.

The fool! What he must have thought when he turned the corner to see a figure emerge from the darkness. He had to have known what was coming and that he didn't stand a chance.

It was the last senseless act in a drama that never should have happened. They had all done things in the past that should have been left there. Who hadn't? Benedict wouldn't leave it be, though, and look what had happened. Now Charles knew that if he had ever opened his mouth, it would be him lying dead in some place like Rampart Street.

With that thought chilling him, he tossed the half-smoked Cuban off the porch and into the gutter, and went back inside, just in time to catch the last verse of a song about darkies sewing buttons on their overcoats.

A few moments after the door closed, footsteps padded close to the porch. There was a light thump as a weight landed on the welcome mat. The footsteps padded off again, into the dark of the night.

FOUR

Valentin was up so early Friday morning that as he went shuffling down the hall to the bathroom, he caught sight of Signore Angelo's hulking figure descending the back stairs.

After his bath and shave, he went back to his room and put on his one good suit, the gray-checked cassimere that he had left with Mangetta when he went away, along with the few other things he wanted to keep, not knowing if he would ever be back to claim any of it. The suit had been an odd vanity in that way; certainly, he had no idea if he would wear such an ensemble again, except maybe in his coffin. It was an expensive purchase, over twenty dollars, a good two weeks' pay. Though it had been fitted expertly by Myers, the tailor on Ursulines, it now hung on him loosely. He had also left one plain bosom with Frank and had donned it as well. The collar was missing, so on his way to catch the Esplanade Line car, he stepped into a haberdasher's and bought one of white linen for a nickel. He decided not to bother with a tie. He wasn't going to his wedding. For all he knew, Miss Benedict was going to slam the door in his face.

While he waited for the streetcar, he stepped into a five-and-dime and spent another six cents on a small notebook and a pencil.

———

When he stepped onto the Benedicts' gallery and knocked on the door, it flew open as if on a spring. The mulatto maid waved him inside, her eyes bright. He had a good memory for faces, and he knew for sure that he'd seen her before in Storyville, though he couldn't place when or where.

"This way, please," she said. "Miss Anne Marie is expecting you."

She led him back to the sitting room, stealing sly glances all the way. He found Miss Benedict seated in one of the high-backed chairs, her spine straight and shoulders back. Still in mourning, she was wearing a dark gray shirtwaist with a Dutch neck and pleats down the front that defined the line of her bust. Her hands were folded in the lap of her black walking skirt. Though she tried to look prim and proper, this modesty had rendered her all the more alluring.

She turned her head when the maid ushered their visitor into the room. "Mr. St. Cyr," she said, speaking the name with the same near-perfect French lilt.

As Valentin stepped closer, she lifted her right hand from her lap and held it out. For an uncertain moment, he wondered if she expected him to kiss it, which he absolutely would not do. He didn't care if it ended the interview, the job, and his life as a citizen of New Orleans right then and there. He had already sunk low enough.

Before it came to that, she turned the hand so he could take it in his own. Something flashed in her aquamarine eyes that told him she had just played a trick on him. She released his hand and gestured to the opposite chair.

"We have tea, if you'd like some," she said.

He shook his head. She let her gaze linger on him for a moment, then glanced at the maid, sending a signal. The mulatto girl went away from the door, though no more than a few steps.

Anne Marie returned her attention to her guest. "Mr. Delouche tells me that you want to continue the investigation."

Valentin tugged at his stiff new collar. "I was impolite during my last visit," he said. "I apologize for that."

Anne Marie regarded him steadily, and he could see something stirring in her gaze. She let him think about it for a few moments, then said, "I'll guess there are more than a few private detectives in New Orleans."

"There are, yes." Valentin, surprised by the utterance, now wondered if she'd allowed him into her home just so she could fire him.

"Are any of them better than you?" she asked.

He watched her with more interest. "No one I can name," he said.

"So, then," she said. "Are you going to investigate what happened to my father or just put on a show?" He had not seen any of this coming. Before he could summon an answer, she said, "Because that's what Mr. Delouche told you to do, isn't it? Come up with a story that will allow us to bury this?"

The detective managed to cover his surprise at her frankness. "He thinks it's better for all concerned if it's settled as soon as possible," he said.

"I'm sure he does," she retorted. "But he's not the one paying you. I am. So I want to know what *you* think."

She was being forthright and he returned the favor. "There are some things that don't fit at all. Some questions that need to be answered."

She nodded, and her shoulders came down from their stiff angles. "Then I want a proper investigation. Nothing less and nothing more. If you find that this was some random crime, so be it. If it was something else"—again she faltered for a moment—"then I want to know that, too. Do we have an understanding?"

It was the second time in two days that the question had been posed. This one canceled the other.

"Yes, ma'am," he said.

He met her gaze, saw an odd light that was there and gone in an instant. "What's the fee for your services?" she inquired.

"Five dollars a day," he told her. It was at least twice his normal rate, but he saw no reason to be cheap. Not in this part of town. And not when he was stirring a hornet's nest.

Anne Marie shrugged absently. "Betsy will see that you're paid." She pondered for a moment, then drew herself up. "Well, then..."

As Valentin got to his feet, she offered her hand again. He turned to find the maid standing in the doorway, wearing her curious smile.

Walking along St. Philip Street, he mused on what had transpired in those few quick minutes in the sitting room of the fine house, and wondered what had happened to the fellow who had sworn off the life of a private detective. If he did what Miss Benedict asked and started digging, there would be hell to pay from several quarters, beginning with the New Orleans Police Department. What bothered him more was the shrewd look in her eyes, as if she already knew things about him. He could thank the maid Betsy for that. A small voice in the back of his mind told him to turn around, go back, and quit before it went any further. He didn't, though, and as he arrived on Esplanade, he managed a smile as he imagined the look on the dry, pink face of the attorney Delouche when he learned of what Miss Anne Marie Benedict had started.

Anne Marie waited until she heard Betsy murmur a saucy good-bye to the Creole detective and close the door to sag back into the chair. She sat for a moment to catch her breath, then got up and went to the window. Pulling the curtain aside a few inches, she watched St. Cyr walk away. With his head up and watchful and his careful stride, he looked like he was stalking something.

She watched his figure grow smaller. She knew that there was still time to send Betsy running after him to explain that she'd had a change of heart and she wouldn't require his services after all. Instead, she let her gaze rest on his back until he turned the far corner.

She sensed the maid stepping to the doorway. Without turning around, she said, "Look in on Mother, please, Betsy. And then fetch the brandy, if you would."

Eleven o'clock found Valentin climbing the stone steps to the doorway of Parish Prison, the cube of grim gray stone that took up the better part of the block between Conti and St. Louis streets. He laid a hand on the brass door handle and hesitated for a moment. The place held some bad memories that took a moment to push aside before he went in.

A cavernous lobby with a marble floor occupied the street level, with six courtrooms. One floor up were offices for a police precinct and for the criminal administration. In the basement was a cold, damp, and lightless jail with white and colored sections splitting the lower level in two. Though he had never had the misfortune to be locked away in one of the dank underground cells, the very sight and smell of the place was quite enough.

Police Lieutenant J. Picot looked up from his paperwork and stared, startled to see St. Cyr walk in the door and speak to the desk sergeant. Picot had neither seen nor heard anything from the Creole detective since he'd arrived back in New Orleans. As the weeks went by, he began to relax, thinking that the gossip about a weak copy of the former St. Cyr was true. But now here he was, back at his door, so he was about to find out for himself.

The desk sergeant appeared in the doorway of his office. "Fellow out there says he wants to talk to you," he stated.

Picot looked past the sergeant and at the visitor at the front desk. "Yeah? Talk to me about what?"

"That homicide out on Rampart Street."

"Is that so?" The lieutenant drummed his thick fingers on his desk blotter in an absent rhythm. Then he pushed his chair back and stood up.

Valentin had to wait while Picot made his gradual way across the room, stopping at most of the desks and several file cabinets. He understood it was the copper's lumpish way of reminding him where he was. Whatever business had brought St. Cyr to his door would have to wait until Lieutenant J. Picot was good and ready. The crude little maneuver was a feature of the uneasy truce between the two men.

They had already spent years crossing swords. Picot regarded the detective St. Cyr as a meddler and walking embarrassment for the New Orleans Police Department. For his part, Valentin thought Picot a bumbler at best, a cruel bully and sneak in his worst moments. Neither man cared for the other, though they had stopped shooting daggers from their eyes each time their paths crossed—which had been just often enough to keep their feud alive.

Theirs was an odder standoff with much at stake, because both men had African blood and yet managed to pass for white. The difference was that Valentin did not engage in convolutions to hide his black and Sicilian bloodlines, while Picot, if cornered, would deny the colored side of his family to his grave. Beyond that, though, they were bound together by darker secrets that neither one dared divulge.

Though they hadn't met in a year and a half, they didn't bother with a greeting. "What's this?" Picot inquired in a clipped voice, his face already pinched in sour petulance.

"I'm looking into the murder of John Benedict," Valentin said.

Picot took an idle moment to eye St. Cyr up and down. There was something different about him, like he wasn't all there. "Says who?" he asked.

"The family, by way of an alderman named Badel and their attorney, Mr. Delouche. And with Mr. Anderson's permission."

Picot let out a grunt of annoyance. He wouldn't dare defy such an array of authority, and they both knew it. "It's not our case," he said. "That's nigger town. Sixth Precinct."

"The victim was from Esplanade Ridge."

"That's right, he was!" The copper threw out his hands. "Does this look like that part of town to you?"

"I thought this office was handling all the homicides within the city limits," Valentin said quietly.

Picot grimaced; the detective had been reading the newspapers.

"The family wants someone besides the police to look into it, that's all," Valentin said, keeping his voice just shy of sheepish.

It worked. The lieutenant's muddy green eyes narrowed and his short spike of a nose twitched as if he was sniffing blood. This was not the St. Cyr he had known before. The Creole's former cold pride was nowhere in sight. He looked almost embarrassed to be there at the bidding of rich Americans. Picot glanced over his shoulder. The desk sergeant and two patrolmen were lounging nearby, too close for comfort. He came around the counter and headed out the door, crooking a finger for St. Cyr to follow him. Once out in the cavernous hallway, he produced a cigarillo. He hesitated for a moment, then took out another one and offered it to the Creole detective.

St. Cyr studied it, then put it into his pocket. "For later," he said.

The lieutenant dug for a pack of lucifers, snapped a flame, and puffed a small cloud. "All right, then," he said. "We figure this fellow likely went over there looking for something in one of those houses." His mouth dipped in disdain. "These rich ones could have the finest octoroon in New Orleans, and they go off after some filthy back-of-town street whore. Anyway, this Benedict gets what he came for, probably in one of them cribs, finishes his business, and walks out on the street. He gets turned around and heads off the wrong way. One of them crazy niggers over there comes along and figures he's got himself an easy mark. Benedict tries to fight"—he shrugged—"and that's the end of him."

"That makes sense," Valentin said. "Though from what I hear, he was a straight-arrow sort."

"Yeah, that's what they always say." Picot snickered. "Well, this straight arrow ended up dead on Rampart Street. Shot in the throat with a .45 pistol."

"What about the investigation?"

"Good as it could be for those parts," the lieutenant said, shifting on his feet and frowning. "We sent a couple detectives. They took a picture of Benedict and showed it around. They had to slap a few faces, as usual. Even so, no one remembered seeing him about." He tapped the ash from his cigarillo. "You ever hear what kind of sound a .45 makes? Like a goddamn artillery round. But nobody heard a thing. These three fellows come out of a saloon and see some street rat bending over the body. It could have been him did the killing, or he could have come along after and decided to help himself to the victim's goods." He turned around, stiffened slightly, and eased his mouth into a cloying smile as two gentlemen in suits approached and then passed down the marbled corridor. The smile disappeared. "Are we finished here?" he said brusquely.

"I'll need to visit the scene," Valentin said.

"It's Rampart Street," Picot said with a shrug. "Who's stopping you?"

"And I want to talk to the patrolman who caught the call."

Now the copper gave him a sharp look. "What the hell for? He didn't see nothing."

"I've been hired to do a job, Lieutenant."

Picot considered. He didn't like it. Grudgingly, he said, "Be out there at three o'clock. I'll send the officer. His name's McKinney."

"I want to talk to those fellows who came up on the body, too."

Picot shook his head and muttered something under his breath. "They got their names at the desk," he said.

"What about the autopsy report?"

"What about it?"

"I need to have a look at it."

"It's the family's decision to release it," the lieutenant said curtly. "What else?"

"I don't know," Valentin said. "Is there anything you're not telling me?"

Picot smiled now, a cool twist of his lips. "Why, there's always something I'm not telling you, St. Cyr."

He tossed the butt of the cigarillo into the spittoon that was against the opposite wall, turned around, and strolled back to his office.

Tom Anderson collected his papers and was on his way out of his office to go downstairs and start his workday when his telephone rang. He picked up and was greeted by the greasy voice of Alderman Badel, taking a moment to thank him for getting St. Cyr on the Benedict case. The alderman's effusion switched to a tone of mourning about the poor man's passing, then turned brisk over his hopes for a quick ending to the investigation.

Anderson agreed with everything and got off as quickly as he could, dropping the hand piece in the cradle. There was something about Badel that made him feel like he had just stepped in something on the street.

The alderman might think that all was well; Anderson wasn't so sure. He couldn't see St. Cyr dancing like a trained monkey to the whims of some rich Americans from Esplanade Ridge, not now, or ever. As he started down the narrow staircase, he wondered frankly when he was going to learn his lesson.

The onetime Pinkerton named Nelson answered the telephone in the foyer of the plantation house on the river at Nine Mile Point. He listened for a moment, then put a hand over the mouthpiece of the handset and stuck his head around the doorway into the sitting room, where William Little, executive assistant to Mr. Henry Harris, was at the antique desk, poring over a ledger.

"It's that Badel fellow," Nelson said. Little glanced up and responded with a curt wave of his hand.

"He's not here now," Nelson said. He listened for a moment, then said, "I'll tell him," and dropped the hand piece in the cradle. "He says he spoke to Anderson, and everything's been taken care of."

Little barely nodded as he continued working.

Jackson Square was a small carnival that ran every day in the midst of the busy city. Along the winding walks, a dozen food carts offered a variety of fare, from fruits to sweets. Valentin stepped up to one, and ordered two boudin sandwiches. While he waited for the food, he looked over the square. The color, noise, and motion were a relief from the close air inside the Parish Prison building.

Booksellers set up tables, the kind he used to browse all the time. Now he couldn't recall when he'd last bought a nickel volume. He used to stash novels all over his rooms on Magazine

Street, as if hiding a shameful vice, then pore over the printed pages like a hungry man devouring a rich soup. Not anymore. Not in a long time.

A one-man band was performing on the street side, the old Negro plucking a banjo, thumping drums with his feet, blowing a variety of horns and whistles, and singing "Mammy's Little Coon," a popular minstrel show tune. In another corner an Italian, dressed in a dusty and worn tuxedo, was playing opera arias on a violin, his eyes closed over a grand black mustache that was waxed to curlicues on the ends. As always, there was the usual small squad of rascals, pickpockets, and other miscreants, darting like rodents. The two uniformed coppers strolling the perimeter of the square ignored them.

He paid for the sandwiches and was turning to leave when he saw Beansoup come in through the Decatur Street gate on the heels of a rough-looking Negro carrying an odd instrument, a banjo with six strings instead of four or five. Valentin stopped to watch with interest as the pair took up a place along the walk. He had all but forgotten about Beansoup taking up the harmonica after his street pal Louis had gone off to ride Bernstein's junk wagon and play the drum in the Colored Waif's Band. Now, it seemed, the kid had found himself a partner, and Valentin recognized him.

The Negro, Charley Johnson, strummed the strings of his curious instrument one time for attention, then began to play, plucking with the fingers of his right hand and sliding the back of a straight razor up the neck to make a raw and sweeping whine. After a few bars, Beansoup started blowing notes on a harmonica, his face pale with panic and his eyes flicking between Charley and the guitar as he struggled to keep pace.

Johnson began singing in a voice that was sand rough, the banjo vamping in the background and Beansoup's harmonica filling in some of the holes.

Well, it's twinkle, twinkle, twinkle, little star
Well, along come Brady in his 'lectric car
Got a mean look all in his eye
Gonna shoot somebody just to see him die
He been on the job too long

The song was "Duncan and Brady," a retelling of a bloody altercation between a saloon keeper named Jim Duncan and High Sheriff Louis Brady in 1890 East St. Louis. Valentin had heard the song on the road, more than once, and was now delighted to hear it again.

Duncan, Duncan, Duncan was tending the bar
When along come Brady with his shiny star
Brady said, "Duncan, you're under arrest"
And Duncan shot a hole right in Brady's chest
He been on the job too long

Charley did not smile at all. He stared at the people who stopped to listen as if accusing them of the crime described in the song. Beansoup hung back, working his cheeks like a huffing steam engine. Charley sang:

Well, old King Brady was a big fat man
Well, the doctor reached out, grabbed hold of his hand
Felt for his pulse, then the doctor, he said:
"I believe to my soul King Brady's dead"
He been on that job too long

Beansoup added some notes and full chords, growing a little more assured with every measure. Valentin shook his head in wonder that it didn't insult his ears.

When the womens all heard King Brady was dead,
Well, they go back home, get all re-ragged in red

Come a-slippin' and a-shufflin' and a-slidin' down the
*   street*
In their old Mother Hubbards and their stockin' feet
He been on that job too long

Beansoup finally saw the detective and his face flushed as
Charley sang on.

Well, a hard-tailed carriage was standin' around
For to take King Brady to his burying ground
Hard-tailed carriage, double-seated hack
Took him to the graveyard but they didn't bring him back
He been on that job too long

It was an odd contrast. Valentin could have taken a few steps
back and he'd hear an old man playing a coon song about grinning, foolish, watermelon-eating darkies, then turn around and
find a mean-looking fellow singing a dark tale of bloody murder
committed by a Negro with nothing to lose.

Valentin shook his head, bemused. Just as soon as one low-
down brand of Negro music had been tamed, along came another. While jass was crossing over from Rampart Street, the
gutbucket blues got dressed up and came into town from the
farm fields and country crossroads and especially from the plan-
tations of the Mississippi Delta, landing in the heart of New Orleans, right before Valentin's eyes.

Charley now slapped his razor up the strings in a metallic
wail as Beansoup blew hard to stay with him, and for one instant he didn't look so much like a boy. He looked like a man
with some age on him as he shared an ancient ritual of song.

Well, it's twinkle, twinkle, twinkle, little star
Well, along come Brady in his 'lectric car
Got a mean look all in his eye

Gonna shoot somebody just to see him die
He been on the job too long
Been on the job too long...

They ended in a cascade of crying notes. With a round of applause, coins clinked into the cup at Charley's feet. Beansoup's face got all pink with pride. He looked like a kid again.

When they started the next song, Valentin walked over to drop a Liberty quarter in their cup and give Beansoup a quick wink. Charley Johnson fixed his eyes on him in a prison stare. The man was an absolute ray of sunshine. The detective hoped Beansoup would be on his toes with this character.

All the way back to Marais Street, the sound of the music and the sight of his young friend playing it stayed with him. He had known Beansoup as little more than a child, and now he was closing in on grown-up and working the streets as a gutbucket blues man, no less.

Valentin got to the *Daily Picayune* office, a three-story brick building on the corner of Camp and Poydras, at one in the afternoon. He went around to the alley in back of the building and pushed the button next to the door that was down a short flight of brick steps. Inside, a buzzer croaked. He waited. He waited some more.

Presently, he heard the sounds of movement and growls from beyond the wall. The door creaked open and the face of Joe Kimball appeared, red and glaring. Then it broke into a bleary grin.

"God*damn*!" he cried happily. "Son of a bitch! I heard you were back!" He grabbed Valentin's shoulder in a meaty paw and dragged him inside. "Where the fucking hell have you been?"

Even in the bizarre menagerie of New Orleans characters, Kimball was a standout. Some people thought he was crazy.

Others dismissed him as a common sot. He was loud and abrasive and hated his bosses as much as they despised him. They couldn't do without him, though, and so there he stayed, dwelling like a mole in a maze of shelves and stacks and file cabinets that made up the *Daily Picayune*'s morgue. The day his liver gave out, as it surely would, the morgue would fall into hopeless chaos. As long as he remained upright, however, he was more than useful. He was a walking library of information about the city and its residents.

Like some rare nocturnal creature, he was rarely spotted outside his habitat in the dark and shadowy bowels of the *Picayune* building. He had a house somewhere along the river that no one had ever seen. Most nights he slept on a cot or just dropped his head on his desk.

Luckily for Valentin and a lot of other people, Kimball was such a diligent drunkard that he had ceased to function as a reporter. Otherwise, they would all lose an irreplaceable font of information, especially about business and political leaders and their respective scandals, of which there was never any lack.

Valentin had last seen him a few days before he'd left town. In fact, if it wasn't for Kimball and the files that were stored in his basement cave, he might not have broken that last case at all.

Now, tracking him through the first and second low-ceiling rooms that were crowded with boxes and files, the detective noted that in the eighteen months since he'd last been there, nothing had changed. It was the same mad clutter, the same trash heap of an office in back, the same desk lost under stacks of the paper, the same Joe Kimball in all his inebriated glory.

Lurching into his office and the chair behind his desk, Kimball grunted and said, "What time is it?"

"It's right about one," Valentin said.

"*One?* Already?" The yell echoed along the low rafters. "Jesus Christ Almighty! I need a *drink!*"

Valentin knew that whatever time he announced would have gotten the same response. Kimball went digging into his desk and produced a short bottle of his favored Raleigh Rye and two dirty glasses. He poured one finger in one and four in the other, handed the short glass to Valentin, and took its taller partner for himself. Valentin watched him down half of the whiskey in one long swallow, then lower the glass and let out a sigh of satisfaction. He licked a few drops from his mustache, and there were more golden drops that he missed gleaming in his beard. He smiled, his teeth as yellow as the orbs of his eyes.

"You ain't drinkin'?"

Valentin took an obligatory sip. The liquor was raw in his throat and he coughed. Kimball chortled.

"Little early in the day for me, Joe," Valentin said, wiping his eyes. He put the glass down on the desk, then placed the sack he was carrying next to it. The newspaperman stared at the sack, wrinkling his broad red nose as if he was smelling something foul.

"What's that?" he asked suspiciously.

"I brought lunch."

"Lunch. That's why you came by? To bring me lunch?" He took another sip of his whiskey and his eyes got sly. "Or is there something else on your mind?"

"I've got a case," Valentin told him.

"A case. Is that so? Are you getting back in the game?"

Valentin gave him a small smile. "I'm just doing this one thing. Did you hear about the murder on Rampart Street last Sunday night?"

Kimball frowned. "John Benedict. From, uh...Esplanade Ridge?"

"That's right."

The newspaperman gave him a critical look. "That's not your territory."

"I'm just doing a favor for Anderson. Who's doing a favor for someone else."

Kimball drank the rest of the whiskey in the glass and put it down. "The man gets killed on Rampart Street," he mused. "You'd think the family would want it left alone."

"You'd think so. They don't, though. So here I am."

"And I suppose you need the word on poor Mr. Benedict."

The detective nodded. "I'll wrap this up as quick as I can."

Kimball poured four more fingers of whiskey in his glass. "Oh? And what if there's something more to it?"

"Then I'll tell you first, Joe. Just like always."

Kimball nodded, mollified. Information was his coin, and the more sordid, the more gilded. He picked up his glass, rolled it between his thick fingers, took a sip, closed his eyes, and began.

"John Benedict was from one of those families that managed to hold on to their money after the war. They did very well. There were judgeships, state senators, one congressman. And they did especially well in business. Benedict was in shipping. He was in with Henry Harris."

Valentin, who had been listening with one ear, sat up. "What now?"

"Benedict did business with Henry Harris," Kimball said. "Supplied him with something or other. That's where he made all his money."

The detective mulled the information. Everyone in the city knew the Harris name from that gentleman's business empire. Indeed, it was common to hear a rounder brag about being "as flush as Henry Harris." Valentin recalled that one of the scores of ditties Jelly Roll Morton had made up included the line "strolling the gay streets of Paris, as heeled as Henry Harris."

There was more: in addition to business, Harris had dabbled in politics, energized by his well-trumpeted vitriol for anyone who wasn't white or native-born. His disdain for those he considered inferiors—the colored, southern Europeans, Turks, Arabs, and Orientals—was a matter of public record. Over the years he had rallied supporters to him merely by waving that particular red flag. It had served him well, and he had been widely regarded as a defender of white America and Christianity, a profile that was stark against the backdrop of New Orleans, that festering pool of mixed-blood malignance.

The lawyer Delouche hadn't said a word about Benedict's connection with Harris. Neither had Anderson, Badel, or Picot. Though they all surely knew. It seemed an odd oversight, akin to skipping over the fact that the victim had done business with the Rockefellers. Did they think he wouldn't find out?

"Valentin?" The detective blinked. Kimball was watching him over the rim of his whiskey glass. "You hear me?"

"Sorry," Valentin said. "What was it again?"

"I said that Benedict made enough to stop working a few years ago. He was on some boards, and that gave him a good income right there. He and his wife were still active in the Opera House and all that shit. So if he turned up at all lately, it would be on those goddamn society pages. And I can't help you with that."

Can't meant *won't*. Kimball was vehement in his refusal to read or catalog that section of the paper.

"Who do I talk to?" Valentin asked.

Kimball yawned and raised a thumb to the ceiling. "Upstairs. Third floor. Robert Dodge." He treated Valentin to a sudden piercing look. "Why are you doing this?" he asked.

"Because I said I would, Joe," Valentin murmured. "I mean, what the hell else am I going to do?"

Kimball didn't have an answer for that. After a moment he said, "You want me to call Dodge for you? You can go up there now."

"I can't," Valentin said. "I'm meeting a copper in an hour. I'll come back."

"You do that. He's an interesting fellow." He grinned lazily and began unscrewing the cap from his bottle. "Hey, you want another one before you go?"

It was past two o'clock when Valentin stepped onto the South Rampart Line car that rumbled away from the District and into the colored and Italian neighborhoods of back-of-town New Orleans.

As the car rattled over Erato Street, he looked to his right. Two blocks up was black Storyville, the four-block square of houses and cribs offering diversions to Negro gentlemen. A few blocks farther, on the left side, he could catch a glimpse of the alleys and the back walls of the saloons and dance halls along Rampart Street.

Five minutes later the car crossed First Street, and he was now within a short walk from the very house where he had grown up, from St. Francis de Sales School for Colored, from the empty lots where he had played as a child.

He wouldn't be visiting any of those places, not today or anytime soon. When the car stopped at the corner of Fourth Street, he stepped down and made his way directly a block west.

When the patrolman noticed him, he ceased his pacing, took off his round-topped helmet, and put it under his arm, coming halfway to attention. The unconscious gesture of respect gave Valentin pause. He wasn't used to that sort of treatment from a copper.

The young officer introduced himself as Patrolman McKinney. He was a burly fellow, pale Irish, with a broad elfin face. His hair, reddish blond, badly cut, was parted in the middle and slicked down.

"What did Lieutenant Picot tell you?" Valentin asked him.

"He told me you wanted to know about the murder that happened here." Translated, this meant McKinney was expected to spy and report to the lieutenant.

Valentin said, "I know he wasn't happy about this."

The patrolman laughed nervously. "No, sir, he wasn't."

"Don't worry. I'm not going to make this difficult for you."

McKinney let out a small breath of relief.

"I understand that you were the first on the scene that morning," Valentin said.

The patrolman nodded. "Yes, sir. Call come in from the box down the street. Someone says there's a body in the street. I was on patrol so..." He nodded to a spot on the cobblestones a few feet away. "When I got here, he was over there."

"What was the first thing you noticed about him?"

McKinney blinked. "Sir?"

"When you came upon the body. What was the first thing you noticed?"

The patrolman's brow stitched in concentration. "I thought he was dressed way too fine for this part of town," he said. "From what I could see, I mean. There was blood on him and in the street here, too. He was on his back and his head was tilted back." He put a finger to a spot right under his chin. "He had a hole right there." He made a space with his thumb and forefinger about the size of a Liberty quarter. "Like that."

"How close did you look?"

"I got right down on him," McKinney said. "I knew it wasn't likely, but just in case, I wanted to see if he was still alive."

Valentin gave a quick nod of approval. "Did you notice powder on him?" he continued. "Or how about any red from a burn?"

McKinney smiled. "I had a look. I didn't see none of that."

"Had he been robbed?" Valentin said.

"Well, he didn't have no purse on him," the copper said. "His clothes was messed up like somebody had gone through his pockets right quick. One of those men that come up on the scene said that fellow that was bent down over the body had a knife out and was just about to take off his finger for a ring. He must have tried to get his watch and then dropped it, because we found the pieces in the street."

Valentin said, "Did you see it?"

"What, the watch? Yes, sir, I'm the one collected it. The pieces, I mean."

"Was there blood on any of it?"

"There was blood on all of it."

The detective considered for a moment, then stepped into the street. "The body was lying which way?" he asked.

McKinney gestured with both hands. "Sort of this way," he said. "He was on his back, like I said. His head was back here and his feet was out this way."

Valentin pointed to the west, toward Fifth Street. "So the shot came from this direction?"

"That's right," McKinney said. "Since there wasn't no powder and no burns, he must have been standing back a good bit."

"Eight, maybe ten paces," Valentin murmured.

He walked around the scene in widening circles while the patrolman waited. It didn't make sense. The nearest streetcar line was two streets south. The closest of the music halls was another block back toward town, and the first of the sporting houses was another block beyond that. There was a row of cribs rented by the cheapest whores on the other side of the street. There was no good reason for a man like Benedict to be wandering around alone at that hour. If he had gotten lost, it was more likely that he'd go toward the lights and the noise, rather than to the shadowy end of the avenue. It was common knowledge that the characters that slithered around that neighborhood would cut a man's throat for a dollar and change. Mr. Benedict had either made a terrible mistake or he had come there for something that was worth the risk.

Whatever had brought him there, Valentin knew that when Benedict and his assailant met in the street, the other person had drawn down from a distance and shot a hole in the victim's throat. That didn't seem at all like a robbery; more like an assassination.

With the policeman watching earnestly, he made wider circles, dodging the light hack and automobile traffic until he had covered the street from one banquette to the other. He found nothing of interest lying about the cobblestones. He spent some time surveying the buildings on both sides, noting again the line of decrepit shotgun doubles, a row of cribs, and one structure that looked like an abandoned stable.

Picot was correct in his observation that a shot from the .45 would have echoed like a cannon at that quiet hour. Of course, such an uproar wouldn't bring anyone running, not in this part of town. These citizens would hit the floor and stay low until they were sure it wasn't the start of a gun battle. It didn't happen often, but when it did, balls of lead flew everywhere. If it was a lone killing, no one would want to see who had delivered a fatal shot. Eyewitnesses in these parts could find both coppers and killers breathing down their necks.

He walked back to where he had started to tell Officer McKinney that he was finished and thanked him for his time.

The copper said, "All right, sir." He lifted a hand, walked away a few steps, then stopped and came back. "Can I ask you a question, Mr. St. Cyr?" he said.

"What's that?" Valentin was frowning absently at the stain of dried blood that marked the place on the cobblestones where the victim had fallen.

"I was wondering...is it true what I heard about you? That you was on the force and they put you off because you threatened to kill your sergeant?"

It was a bold question; and yet McKinney didn't seem to mean any harm. He was just curious.

Valentin said, "I didn't say I was going to kill him."

"But you drew your weapon on him."

"That's right." Valentin looked at him. The young fellow was probably no more than a year or two on the force. About his own age at the time that the incident had occurred. He almost smiled at the memory of the crazy episode, now ten or twelve years in the past.

"The sergeant was drunk," he explained. "He was beating on a whore in an alley because she wouldn't give him French. He punched her in the face, and when she went down, he started kicking her. He was in a rage and I thought he meant to beat her to death. He wouldn't stop, so I pulled my revolver and put it in his ear. He did stop then."

"What happened to the girl?" McKinney asked in a hushed voice.

"She died from her injuries."

"What about the sergeant?"

"He was put at a desk for a few months. Then he was back on duty."

"And you were thrown off the force?"

"No, but I wasn't welcome after that, so I left," Valentin said quietly. He glanced over at McKinney, who continued to watch him with wide eyes. "Something else?"

"You was on those Black Rose murders. And when those jass players was being killed year before last."

"What about them?"

"Some officers talk about you down at the precinct. That's all."

Valentin could imagine what they said and had no interest in hearing any details.

"I'm finished here," he said, and started away. "You can tell Lieutenant Picot that I found nothing of value." He felt the patrolman's gaze follow him as he moved along the banquette.

He turned down Fourth Street, doubled back after a dozen paces, slipped to the corner of the building, and peeked around. As he expected, McKinney had remained at the scene and was studying the same section of cobblestones that he himself had examined just a few minutes ago. He was an ambitious sort and not a bad young fellow. He probably still believed that most policemen were on the job to serve the public good. He'd learn soon enough.

Valentin leaned against the corner bricks of a closed saloon and went digging for the cigarillo Picot had given him and a lucifer. He struck a flame against a brick and smoked as he waited for the patrolman to go away.

He gazed along the street. To his right, heading south, the street was cobbled for only two more blocks before it turned to gravel and dirt. Both sides of the street were patched with untidy shotgun doubles and a few run-down storefronts. The banquettes were no more than wooden slats, and there were no streetlights at all. It would be a frightful place at night. He turned in the other direction and saw a photograph that he carried in his head come alive.

Rampart Street. Even the name affected him. He now picked out the familiar facades: Longshoreman's Hall, Pelliot's Cabaret, Jack's Corner Saloon, the Crescent Club. These addresses were interspersed with a selection of narrow stores that served as gambling parlors during the daylight hours. Sam Abel's barbershop held down a corner. The narrow walkways between buildings provided cover for all manner of sin once the sun went down. Standing there, the cigarillo burning away between his fingers, Valentin read the street, past and future.

From the time he was old enough to understand, it had held a wicked allure, humming all rowdy and raucous six nights a week. Buddy Bolden's heyday, 1905 and 1906, had been the shining moment for the avenue, and yet Valentin could see how it was dying with the echoes his friend had left behind. From their ragged shingles, it appeared that Pelliot's and the Crescent were out of business. Another few years and all the clubs probably would be closed. Jass was no longer derelict music that needed a home. They were dancing to its bouncing strains all around the District and beyond. He'd heard jass sounds in St.

Louis and Kansas City; and hadn't Jelly Roll Morton and Professor Tony Jackson both gone up north to preach the jass gospel? It was spreading like an infection.

Likewise, the good players had packed up their horns for the greener and safer pastures on the other side of Canal Street. Only the most incorrigible among them, those who were too wild for the proper gentlemen and their high-toned sporting girls, had remained behind. They were a dying breed, heading for hell any way they could get there. Even gutbucket players like Charley Johnson who stood on the corners moaning and growling their dark cants had taken their acts to the better parts of town.

Once Rampart Street was gone, there'd be nothing to replace it. And if a few more men like John Benedict ended up dead there, its demise would come sooner rather than later.

Valentin saw McKinney finally strolling away. He waited until the copper went out of sight at the corner of Second Street to step out.

He spent the better part of an hour moving up one side of the street and down the other, knocking on doors. Most were homes of working people who were out for the day, and he got no response. Bleary-eyed whores appeared at two of the addresses. One slammed the door in his face when she realized he was not there to do business. The other listened and then shook her head. She couldn't remember if she had been there or not on Sunday night. She sure didn't recall any shots fired in the middle of the night. She had the face of a dead-end drunk, the type who would sleep through an earthquake. She roused herself enough to offer him any pleasure he preferred for a Liberty half. He declined politely.

Just past the last house was a building that contained a half-dozen cribs in a row. The first one was vacant. The next door down also slammed in his face, accompanied by a hearty curse. The third also brought no response. When he banged on the next one in line, he heard a shuffle of movement inside.

"Who's out there?" a woman's voice croaked.

"A friend," Valentin said. It was an all-purpose greeting in these parts.

The door opened a crack on a woman's homely face, medium brown with a yellowish tinge. The eyes were an odd color, too: muddy green. Her nappy hair was pulled back in stiff blades. She was short and thin and wearing a worn shift of dirty gray cotton.

She looked Valentin up and down, her open mouth showing the gaps of missing teeth. Her expression was dull, like she might be slow in the head.

"My name is St. Cyr," he said. "I want to ask you a few questions."

The woman blinked. He had used his best official voice, and she had come to attention, assuming he was a policeman. "You wan' come inside?" she asked, and stepped back a little.

Valentin got a whiff of the odor of the room behind her and shook his head. "What's your name?"

"Caroline," she said, pausing to size him up some more. "West."

"Were you here last Sunday?"

Caroline West's brow furrowed. She coughed once, a dry, rattling sound, and shuffled her dirty feet. "Believe I was, yes, sir. I'm here most every night."

"Did you by chance hear a gunshot out on the street?"

Her mouth closed and opened, and she drew in a breath as if she was about to speak. Before she did, though, it seemed something crossed her mind. "Don't think so, no, sir," she said.

He turned and pointed. "Happened right out there," he said. "A man shot down. You would have heard."

"I didn't, though," she replied too quickly.

"How about any of your customers that night? It would have been late."

"I don't remember, no," she whispered. "I'm sick. Doctor say—"

"If you were here, you would have heard," he repeated.

"I got to take my medicine," she said, and began to close the door.

He put a flat hand out and settled the sole of his walking shoe on the threshold. "I'll come back until you tell me what you saw and heard," he told her. "You won't be able to do business for the trouble." He was slipping back into his old voice and posture, the detective who would not brook any resistance.

Caroline West's face got all fretful and she fidgeted. "I'm sick, I tell you. I didn't see nothin'. Didn't hear nothin'."

"You heard the shot."

She held out for a good five seconds, then nodded. "It was the middle of the night," she said in a low voice. "Musta been four o'clock."

"Did you have company?"

"Yes, sir..."

"Who was it?"

"Ain't never seen him before. I ain't been over here but two weeks. I was on Robertson Street and they run—"

"What about the man?"

She coughed. "Skinny little red-haired nigger. Red in the face, too. Like one of them Cherokee niggers." She saw that Valentin was waiting for more. "I just finished wit' him, and he was buttonin' his britches and that's when we heard it." She dipped her head an inch or so. "He ducked down like somebody was shootin' at him. Then we didn't hear nothin' else, and he went to the window and opened the curtain."

"And?"

"And he said, 'Damn, lookit there,' or somethin' like that. I didn't know what he was talkin' about. Then he said, 'They's someone layin' in the street.'"

Valentin began to picture what happened next. "Did he go out?"

The whore's eyes shifted. "I tole him stay in and leave it be. But he hooked up his britches and ran on out there."

"Did you see what he did?"

"I didn't. I didn't want to."

Valentin believed her. "Did he come back?" She hesitated, then nodded. "With valuables?"

Now Caroline said, "I don't want to get in no trouble."

"You won't. Just tell me what happened."

"I heard some mens yellin' somethin' out there. I peeked out then, and this nigger was gone away. A little while after that the police come by. Then I heard somebody knockin' on the back door. It was him. He'd been hidin' down where they had the stables, but then the coppers were about and he had to leave out of there."

"So you let him in. Did he have any loot?"

"He had a bunch of Liberty dollars in a little purse." She looked at St. Cyr and looked away. "He gimme three of 'em. Tole me not to say nothin' about it." She twisted her fingers together. "I thought I mighta saw some kind of a ring. But I can't be sure 'bout that."

"And you're sure you don't know this fellow?"

"No, sir. Ain't never seen him befo'. He didn't say his name."

"You wouldn't be protecting him?"

"I wouldn't do that. He wa'n't nothin' to me but a twenty-five-cent trick."

Valentin stepped back. "If you happen to see him around, or if he comes back to visit, you could let me know. Send a kid by Anderson's Café or Mangetta's on Marais Street. Or there's a patrolman named McKinney. This is his beat. You can tell him."

It took her a moment to assemble her thoughts. She frowned. "You ain't a copper?" she said.

"No, I'm private security. I work for Mr. Anderson." Her eyes widened, the reaction he expected. He went into his pocket and placed a Liberty half in her palm. "I appreciate your cooperation."

She stared at the coin for a moment, then came up with a ghastly grin. "You want to come inside? I'll treat you all right. I'm a good goddamn—"

"Just send a message if you have anything for me. All right?"

She nodded rapidly. "Yes, sir, I see him, I'll let you know. You know I will."

McKinney stood in the doorway, his blue helmet tucked under his arm. Picot waved him inside, and he walked over to join the lieutenant at the window that looked down on Royal Street.

"You met up with St. Cyr?" Picot said.

"Yes, sir."

"So?"

McKinney shifted his weight. "He asked me about what I saw that night and I told him. He walked around the scene for a little while. He didn't find nothing, though. Not that I could tell. We were only there maybe ten, fifteen minutes."

Picot's eyes narrowed. "Then what?"

"Then he left."

"How long did you remain on the scene?"

McKinney swallowed as the lieutenant's drift began to sink in. "I didn't know I was supposed to stay after—"

"How long, Officer?"

"Couple minutes. Maybe five. I came in and did my report. Then I went back on patrol."

Picot said, "St. Cyr is not a policeman. He was, but he's not anymore."

"Yes, sir, I know. But you sent—"

"I know. I sent you out there. You did your duty and now you're done with it. The people of New Orleans don't pay us to assist private parties. Especially that one. You understand?"

"Yes, sir."

"Good." Picot jerked his head, and the patrolman walked

out of the office and into the hallway. If he had looked back, he would have seen the lieutenant stepping into his office doorway and crooking a finger to gather his officers around him.

Valentin worked the Café that night. Before he went out on the floor, Anderson appeared and took him aside to ask for a report. The detective kept his voice low as he related Anne Marie Benedict's request that he conduct a proper investigation. The King of Storyville frowned, but didn't comment. Valentin then told him about going to see Picot and the lieutenant's reaction. He shared what he had gathered from Joe Kimball. When he got to the part about Benedict's position in Henry Harris's shipping empire, Anderson's brow stitched further.

"What else?" he asked in a terse voice.

The detective described his visit to the crime scene and the hour or so he had spent going from door to door. He described Caroline West and the red-haired Negro customer who had run out onto the street and come back after filching goods off the dying or dead John Benedict. He drew this last part out, knowing how much Anderson enjoyed talk of the street, and the more wicked, the better.

"It wasn't the Negro who killed him," Valentin said. "Whoever it was shot him down, then just walked away and left him there to die."

The King of Storyville said, "So if it wasn't a robbery..." His silver eyebrows arched. "You think it was a trap? Somebody lured him out there to—"

"I don't know that," Valentin cut in quickly. "Maybe it was just a dispute that got settled with a pistol."

The white man caught the retreat and eyed him narrowly. "On Rampart Street?" Valentin shrugged and he let it go. He considered for a few moments, then said, "Benedict was in cahoots with Henry Harris?"

"They did business. Benedict's company supplied Harris's shipbuilders." He noticed that Anderson looked troubled by the news and said, "Why?"

"I was just wondering," said Anderson, who never "just wondered" about anything. "So what about this nigger that robbed the body? Did you find him?"

"I'll track him down. He won't have much to say, though."

"Do it anyway," Anderson said. "Give the daughter what she wants and finish this so the poor man can rest in peace."

Anderson now seemed vaguely irritated, and Valentin considered reminding him that it was his idea to get involved in it in the first place. He decided that wouldn't be received well at all and went back to work.

Picot's officers had it all wrapped up by nine o'clock that night. First they canvassed the neighborhood until they found Caroline West, then shut her down and braced her until she told them about the red-haired Negro. They fanned out up and down the saloons along Rampart Street, asking after anyone who fit the description. They soon narrowed it down to two suspects. The first one, who went by the moniker Little Chink because of the Asian cast of his features, proved to be elsewhere. That left a half-breed Cherokee who called himself Ten Penny due to the copper tinge of his skin. His true name was Thomas Lee, and he was known as one of those ne'er-do-wells who lived off petty thefts and would sell a friend for a Liberty dollar, if he'd had a friend to sell. Some time back he had earned pocket money by snitching to the police, until it was discovered that at least half the information he was selling was false. Now he made his way by begging, stealing, and scavenging. He was so ragged, dirty, and foul smelling that he was no longer permitted in even the lowest dives on Rampart Street.

The coppers found Ten Penny in an alley off Willow Street

where he had built a lean-to of discarded packing crates. He was cooking hot whiskey over an open fire when they kicked the boards of the shack apart and dragged him out by his kinky hair. Within the hour he had been carried downtown to Parish Prison and duly charged with the murder of John Louis Benedict.

FIVE

It was late morning and Valentin was just settling down with his coffee when Frank came in from the store, a cup in one hand and a copy of Saturday's *Daily Picayune* in the other.

"What was the name of that fellow got murdered on Rampart Street?" he said.

Valentin lowered his own cup. "John Benedict. Why?"

Mangetta dropped the newspaper onto the table. "It says here they caught the fellow that killed him."

When Valentin got to the end of the piece, he put the paper aside and said, "I need to use the telephone."

A phone call interrupted Lieutenant Picot's lunch, but what he heard destroyed his appetite, anyway.

He made it from his house on Bell Street to Parish Prison in twenty furious minutes and raced down the two flights of steps to the basement, moving as fast as his thick legs would propel him without him breaking his neck. He came blustering along the hallway that led to the colored section. At the anteroom where the jailer had his desk, he found St. Cyr slouched against the wall in an insolent posture that set his blood to stewing.

"What's this?" he demanded of the jailer.

"He's got permission."

"Permission from who?"

The jailer held out a sheet of paper. Picot snatched it away and read down, his mouth settling into a hard line. His muddy eyes flicked at St. Cyr. "Jesus Christ!" he muttered. "What are you doing here?"

Valentin said, "I'm working this case, Lieutenant. And you made an arrest."

"That's right, we did!" Picot barked. "It's what we do when we find guilty parties. And this one's guilty as hell."

"Has he confessed?"

"He will soon enough."

"Did you find the weapon?"

"It's likely at the bottom of the damn river. I don't have to explain this to you." Picot gave Valentin a resentful look. "You just can't keep your nose out of our business, can you? You want to know if he did it? He did. We're going to put this one away. You'll be out of a job, but we're doing the family a *favor* here, goddamnit! This one's over and done."

Valentin kept his expression flat, ignoring Picot's bluster. He knew what was going on. When he was a copper, he had heard the same routine a hundred times. Once a suspect had been picked, there was an answer for everything. Ten Penny was their man, and his guilt or innocence was not germane. He might well hang for a crime that he probably didn't commit.

"I'd like to talk to him, anyway," the detective said.

Picot fumed, glared. "I guess I can't say no, can I? You got a note here from O'Connor." He waved the page in the air, making a snapping sound. "How the hell did you manage that?"

"It was Mr. Anderson's doing."

Picot rolled his olive-brown eyes. "Well, he's the boss, isn't he? Even the damned chief of police dances to his tune." He shoved the letter in the direction of the jailer, a splotch-faced old bull. "Make sure you go in there with him," Picot said, then lowered his voice to mutter something else that Valentin couldn't hear. He didn't look at the Creole detective as he stalked off.

Valentin soon discovered what the lieutenant had told the jailer, because he found himself waiting around for no reason for the better part of an hour. From down the corridor, he heard the occasional rude shout or low groan, and he smelled urine, shit, sour sweat, and the general rot of the damp and filthy place. It reminded him of the coarse air around the cages at the zoo. The only difference was that the animals received better care.

At 1:30 the jailer stood up, hefted his ring of keys, jerked his head, and said, "Come along, then."

Valentin followed him down the corridor. From each of the first six cells, eyes glared out at him. The seventh cell was empty. The eighth held six prisoners, and among them was a short, thin, copper-skinned Negro who sat in the corner with his knees folded before him and his bony arms dangling.

The jailer put the key in the lock and threw the door open with a crack that echoed down the corridor. The half-dozen hopeful faces looked up. The jailer barked, "Lee!" and the fellow who was on the floor got to his feet as the faces of his cell mates went dull again.

The jailer pushed Ten Penny with a rough hand, herding him outside and then into the empty cell next door. He glanced at Valentin. "Go on," he said, and when the detective went in, parked himself in the doorframe and crossed his arms.

Valentin waved the prisoner to one end of the lone steel bunk while he took the other end. He spent a moment studying Ten Penny. Close-up the Negro had a small, feral face, with a hooked nose and close-set eyes. His crooked mouth was missing half its teeth, and the ones that were left were brown with rot. Even though he had gone through the prison's shower and delousing, there was a rank smell coming off him, as if the stench of the streets had settled too deeply into his pores for such curatives to reach. His black eyes flicked like skittering marbles from the

Creole detective to the jailer. He put on a street rat's cloying smirk, already trying to figure if his visitor could get him out of the mess.

The detective spoke in a low voice. "My name's St. Cyr. I want to talk to you about what happened Sunday night. Or Monday morning. With that fellow on the street. The one they say you murdered."

"I didn't!" Ten Penny's voice was high and grating. "I didn't kill nobody!"

"Then tell me what happened over there."

The Negro glanced at the jailer, who let out a grunt, then looked away.

"Go ahead," Valentin said.

"I had me a little money and I was lookin' to get some, and I was in there with that crib whore," Ten Penny whispered, and then came up with a grotesque grin. "You know what I'm talkin' about? Anyways, we was just done and I heard this damn shot go off. I runned over and look out the window. I saw that fellow a-lying out there."

"Did you see anyone else?"

"Maybe so." Ten Penny's eyes shifted. "They was still smoke off a pistol in the air. And then I mighta saw somebody in one of them long coats. Walkin' away. Backwards kinda."

"Toward Fourth Street?"

"Thas right. To Fourth Street."

"Did you see this person's face?"

"Naw . . . it was too dark for that."

"All right, then what?"

"I waited for a minute. Then I went to see if I could help."

Valentin snickered at Ten Penny's earnest expression. "He was dead when you got out there?"

"He was finished."

"So you went ahead and robbed him."

Ten Penny's eyes did a nervous hop toward the jailer. "Well, somebody was gonna get it."

"You took his purse. What else?"

"That was all."

"No, it wasn't," Valentin said tersely. "You grabbed his watch, but it fell and broke apart. You were about to take his finger to get his wedding band. So I'm asking again. What else?"

Ten Penny shook his head one way and then the other, attempting to appear innocent.

"Was there a ring on his right hand?"

"Naw, nothin' like that."

"What happened to it?"

"I don't know what you—"

"What happened to the fucking ring?" Valentin snarled suddenly.

Ten Penny gave a start. "All right, all right!" He cleared his throat. "I got one, all right. But I want somethin' for it."

"You'll get something for it," Valentin said. "I might be able to save your life. Or I could just go out there and toss the alley and see if I can find it myself. And then let these coppers have at you. You'll be lucky if you last a day."

"No, I'll tell you," Ten Penny said quickly. He described a loose brick next to a doorframe.

Valentin got to his feet. With his back to the jailer, he said, "You better hope it's still there."

"Say, you gonna get me out of this?" Ten Penny called to him. "They like to put a rope round my neck."

Valentin looked through the bars. "I'll do what I can."

"Do what you can? What if that ain't enough?"

"Then they'll notify your next of kin."

He could still hear Ten Penny squawking as he went up the steps to leave the building.

Valentin had stopped gambling the night in Algiers that a game went wrong and he ended up putting a hole in the chest of one Eddie McTier, a backwoods Georgia guitar player and rounder who was an even worse shot than he was a cheater. McTier, caught double-dealing, had snapped his Stevens Tip-Up .22 in Valentin's face. The problem was that the Tip-Up only had one bullet in the chamber, and a second after it whizzed past his ear, his Iver Johnson had dropped McTier onto the sawdust floor and five feet three inches closer to hell.

Though he had sworn off games of chance that night, it was always a good bet that Picot would put a man on him. Since Valentin was too quick to pick up a tail, it seemed that the lieutenant just wanted to let him know that he was being watched. The man would be pulled off if he was needed elsewhere.

This afternoon Picot had sent a character from the shifting cast of part-time Pinkertons and private coppers that roamed downtown and uptown New Orleans. Indeed, pick any saloon and every other fellow at the bar would be carrying some kind of badge. This one was tall and rail thin, on the consumptive side, with a long nose and drooping mustache, dressed in a gray serge suit and black derby hat. He held a handkerchief in one hand that he coughed into repeatedly. That alone was like a bell on a cat.

Valentin thought about losing him just to show Picot that he could still do it, then decided to hold that card. He walked down to Canal Street and waited patiently, letting the next car pass, so that Picot's string bean could keep up.

He and his traveling companion switched to the South Rampart Line and rode for twenty blocks. Valentin hopped down at the corner of First Street and took his time strolling north. He picked up his pace a little bit as they crossed into the darker streets, taking a long way around, intentionally avoiding the blocks nearest the First and Liberty intersection.

As he came up on Willow Street, he made a sharp jag and cut down the alley. He was pleased to find that he was still deft at such maneuvers and could always slip away from anyone if need be. He left the string bean gawking and pacing in a panic. His prey had blown away like smoke.

In a minute Valentin had found what was left of Ten Penny's hovel and located the loose brick alongside the doorjamb in the back of the building, just as the Negro had described it. He snatched the ring, replaced the brick, and made his way back to the street. When he came up behind Picot's man, he slowed his steps and ambled around him as if it was Sunday afternoon in Jackson Square.

He heard the string bean let out a loud breath of relief. He kept his pace modest, trailing his new companion and leaving those rough streets behind.

Anne Marie Benedict had just finished her bath and was drying herself when Betsy pushed the door open without knocking. Anne Marie gave a start and pulled the towel around her. The girl was too fresh, and she was about to scold her for the hundredth time about keeping her place when she noticed that Betsy's coffee-brown face was all giddy with excitement.

"It's that *detective*," the maid whispered. "Mr. St. Cyr. He's down on the gallery."

Anne Marie felt a flutter in her chest. "What's he want?"

"He says he needs to see you right away." She giggled. "Go on and go down like that. I dare you."

Anne Marie clenched her jaw to stifle a laugh and kept a stern face as she sent Betsy to tend to their visitor. She hurried down the hall to her bedroom, where she picked a beige high-collared shirtwaist and a dark blue skirt. She had decided in that moment that it was time to change from mourning black and gray. Still, she pinned her hair rather severely. She was in too much of a rush to notice that the flush in her cheeks was giving her away.

She assumed that the Creole detective had come by to report the arrest of the suspect named Lee. There had already been telephone calls from the police, from the lawyer Delouche, from Alderman Badel, everyone expressing relief that the terrible episode could finally be laid to rest.

She realized that if this was indeed the case, the detective she had hired—the *colored* detective—would have no more business there and would fade back into the fetid slough of Storyville, and most likely she'd never see him again. With that thought in mind, she turned away from the mirror.

When she came downstairs, she found him seated on one end of the divan. Betsy was hovering in the doorway, casting glances his way and trying not to grin. She straightened and pulled her eyes off him when Miss Anne Marie approached.

He stood up, not with a nervous jerk like most men; instead, he rose as smoothly as a serpent uncoiling. Anne Marie caught her breath as she settled carefully into the opposite chair.

"Mr. St. Cyr," she said, clearing the catch from her throat. "Please, sit down." He resumed his seat as deftly as he had left it. "Did Betsy..." She stopped, began again. "Have you been offered refreshment?"

"He didn't want nothing," Betsy piped up. Anne Marie frowned at the maid's tart tongue. She thought to chase her away, but she would only find some other place to lurk and eavesdrop. She returned her attention to the detective. "Are you here about the arrest of this Negro suspect?" she inquired.

Valentin wasn't surprised that she already knew about it. "I am," he said.

"Is he guilty?"

"I doubt it."

Anne Marie stared, glanced at Betsy, looked at him again.

"I questioned him," Valentin told her. "And I went to Rampart Street yesterday afternoon. I visited the scene of the crime, and I spoke to a woman who was with him when the shooting occurred."

"Was the woman a prostitute?" Anne Marie asked.

"Yes, ma'am. A crib woman."

Betsy said, "That means she—"

"I know what it means." She gave the maid a sharp glance, then returned her attention to St. Cyr. "And Mr. Lee was her customer?"

"That's right."

She eyed him closely. "You said you questioned him?"

"Yes, ma'am. This afternoon, in Parish Prison."

"What did he say happened?"

"He said that he and the woman heard a shot fired, and then he looked out the window and saw the body on the street. When nothing else happened, he ran out there. He said your father was already dead. He went through his pockets. That's all he did. So he said."

"And do you believe him and the woman?"

"They both told the same story," Valentin told her. "They could have put their heads together to make up an alibi, but I don't think they have the wits for it."

"Then why did the police arrest him?"

"To clear the case," he said, as if it was obvious.

"How can they do that, if he's not guilty?"

"Oh, they'll produce evidence and make sure he confesses," Valentin explained matter-of-factly. "It happens all the time. They'll get what they need on him, one way or another."

"Then what?"

"He'll be tried and convicted and hung in the yard," he said simply, adding, "and it will be over."

Her brow furrowed. "But that means an innocent man will lose his life."

Valentin smiled then, a lazy tilting of his mouth that brightened his gray eyes and softened his face. Anne Marie blinked in confusion and the thump in her chest came so hard she was sure he could hear it. She didn't dare turn her head to look at Betsy, who had let out a soft purr of her own.

"Mr. Lee isn't *innocent*, if that's your concern," Valentin went on, keeping the smile in place. "He's most likely gotten away with crimes just as bad." He thought about mentioning Ten Penny caught in the act of slicing off her father's finger, then thought better of it. "Anyway, this is only what I believe is true," he told her. "The police think they have their man."

Her eyes came back at him full of light, and now it was his turn to be a bit dazzled.

"If Mr. Lee didn't murder my father, I want to know who did." Her voice trembled and her face took on a blush of emotion. "I don't care what the police say. I want you to continue the investigation."

Valentin said, "All right, then."

"So do you—"

There came a sudden pounding from the floor above. Anne Marie's eyes flashed at Betsy and the maid scurried away.

"Is there something wrong?" Valentin inquired.

"No, not at all," Anne Marie said. "Are we finished now?"

Valentin said, "You should know that if I continue, I'll have to dig around your father's affairs. I mean business and personal."

She hesitated for a moment and he sensed her wavering. Then she said, "If that's what's required."

"And the first thing I need is for you to allow the release of the autopsy report to me."

She shifted, looking discomfited. "How do I do that?"

"Mr. Delouche will take care of it, on your instructions."

"I'll call him, then." Her voice was fading. "Anything else?"

"Not right now," he said.

She let out a breath of relief. Footsteps were padding back down the staircase. "Betsy will see you out," she said.

Sauntering along with Picot's man following like a tired hound, he rehashed the visit. Though he had to admire her mettle, he wondered if she understood that keeping him on the case could end up ruining her family name. Probably so; she was no dunce. So she knew, and was still willing to face a grim conclusion. She had her reasons, of course. He couldn't figure out what they were. But he would, sooner or later.

A streetcar was coming down the tracks, and he hopped on and found himself a seat by the window. Turning his head slightly, he saw his tail hurry to grab the rail and pull himself aboard, causing a clumsy commotion with the other passengers. The fellow might just as well have shouted out loud that he was following the Creole in the gray suit.

Valentin chuckled over this, then let out a sigh, thinking how little regard Picot must have for him to send such a sad sack. At the same time, he wouldn't put it past the lieutenant to have picked out the worst of his crew, just to make that point.

Anne Marie wandered into her father's study and she sat down at his desk, a large walnut affair with two reading lamps of polished brass. The afternoon sun hid beyond the curtains, casting a faint light across the Turkish rug. It was cozy there, a favorite place. When she was a little girl, she used to play under the desk, all safe and secure, until her father came in to work and chased her off. Later, she would curl up with a book in the leather chair that sat in the corner. On the rare occasion, they would share a rainy evening in sweet silence, she reading and he laboring over his papers. He never seemed to stop working.

After a few more moments in reverie, she opened the drawer, rummaged under a sheaf of papers, and took out a single sheet, which she held in her hands without reading.

In that very room, four weeks before, she had opened the drawer looking for her old diploma from Madame D'Orly's Academy for Ladies and came across the envelope that contained the letter. Curious, she took it out and saw that it was addressed to her father from Henry Harris himself, and that it was almost twenty years old. After she read it, she sat unmoving for a long minute. Then she put it back where she had found it.

The next morning she rode the streetcar to the city library, where she asked to see copies of the local newspapers from the early 1890s. Three days later she took the letter out again, carried it to the kitchen, where her father was drinking a cup of coffee, and laid it before him.

She remembered how he had stared at it, silent and unmoving, his face going pale, as if he was aging before her eyes. At one point he had started to speak, then couldn't get any words out.

"Is it true?" she had asked. "Did you do this?"

He gave her a sick look, his face draining of blood, as if something he had long feared, some nightmare, had come to life at last. It took another tortured half minute for him to give a slow nod.

She swallowed, holding back the sob that had risen into her throat.

"It was so long ago," he said in a whisper. "There's nothing I can do."

"You can't just leave it like this," she said tightly, her face flushing. "You can't."

He said nothing to that as he continued to gaze somberly at the letter with eyes that held a terrible grief.

"You've got to do something," she told him. To which he said not a word.

Less than two weeks later, he was dead.

She put the letter back in the drawer and closed it. The study seemed dark and close now, as if his ghost was lingering, and she decided she needed to get out of the house. She went to the foyer and called up the staircase that she was going for a walk, then put on a hat, wrapped a thin shawl over her shoulders, and stepped onto the gallery.

It was a dry afternoon and just a bit windy. She knew a lot of her neighbors still didn't consider it quite proper that a girl of her station wander the banquettes alone, but she didn't care. She was in the aftermath of a death in the family, and she needed to walk and to breathe something other than dying flowers.

As she started down the banquette, it occurred to her that those same neighbors likely thought there was something wrong with her, anyway. She was unmarried at twenty-two. Her brother was so derelict that he had appeared at the funeral for one agonized hour, then disappeared again, back to Mobile or Baton Rouge or Memphis, wherever his negligent shoes took him. Now she had a rough-looking detective going in and out her front door.

She had started something when she took the letter to her father that day. The arrest of the Negro named Lee offered a chance to lay it to rest again. All she had to do was let things be. As Mr. St. Cyr had said with that feral smile of his, Lee had to be guilty of something. It was a simple solution and might spare her and her mother from a nightmare. Instead, she had retained the services of a man who was most definitely the wrong kind of Creole for her part of town and put him to the task of digging all the way to the bottom.

She passed two matrons on the banquette. They were from the neighborhood and familiar, and yet she was so lost in thought that she didn't hear their murmured greetings as they went by. They looked over their shoulders, whispering and shaking their heads.

Though she had worked to keep the upper hand, she admitted that St. Cyr was having an effect on her. She didn't understand it, and it bothered her. She was not a silly schoolgirl who was prone to losing her wits. Indeed, with a weak mother and a father who wasn't there much of the time, she was left to her own devices.

Anyway, she wasn't like the other girls, who seemed to dream only of marriage and children. She read all the newspapers, knew about women clamoring for suffrage, and thought it a good thing. She took her own steps in that direction. She smoked tobacco when she felt like it, even in public, drank brandy—too much, of late—and only rarely wore a corset, much to her mother's dismay.

Even worse, she had for months taken to reading Betsy's copies of the *Mascot*. At first, she had filched them from the trash bin in back and carried them to her room, feeling shamed and wicked. Then she just started studying them openly. Her mother was too dazed and her father too absent to notice. From those pulp pages and the questions she asked the mulatto maid, she got an education in the sordid commerce of the north side of Basin Street and beyond.

So far, reading was as far as it went. She had not been "ruined" in the parlance of the day. She had only been touched in private places on a few occasions, and the boys were such oafs that she called a halt to it out of sheer annoyance. At the same time, she knew she couldn't wait much longer. She wasn't about to become an old maid. She was already often the only unmarried young woman at parties.

She reached the corner of St. Ann Street and stopped to consider that she could get on the next streetcar on Orleans Avenue and be on that same infamous Basin Street in twenty-odd minutes. She'd told herself she'd do it someday. With a private smile at the thought, she walked on.

Though she was considered something of an odd duck, proper, finely bred, and handsome young gentlemen had come around, potential suitors. And yet for some reason, her carnal musings, frequent of late, always brought men like St. Cyr and women like Betsy to mind. They were like another species to her, alien and bewitching. She knew St. Cyr was what they called a rounder, and she had no doubt that Betsy, though only eighteen, *had* been ruined, and not recently, either. Anne Marie imagined the trading winks, gestures, and words behind her back in the language of their scarlet world.

Though they might well think her a pampered child, she was still in charge. Betsy worked for her, not the other way around. As for St. Cyr, she wanted him to investigate her father's death on her behalf, and that was all.

She now found herself on the edge of City Park and decided to sit awhile and watch the birds before going home and taking up her troubles again.

The telephone lines that led to the ornate set on Tom Anderson's desk were sizzling. First it was Alderman Badel, followed by Delouche the attorney, then Chief of Police John O'Connor.

Badel said, "He's not playing along..."

"...with the understanding that we had." Delouche sniffed. "That he would..."

"...leave this to my officers to handle," the chief finished.

Anderson was at pains to hide that he was just as surprised as they were. Not three days ago, St. Cyr had to be dragged into the investigation like a stubborn mule. Now he had jumped into it with both feet. He was on Rampart Street, he was in the colored jail at Parish Prison, he was at the Benedict home, he was wandering around alleys north of Rampart Street, and who knew where and what else?

After Anderson hung up from the last call, he seethed for a moment, then sent for Beansoup, who seemed to possess a special nose for locating the Creole detective. The kid appeared at the Café and within an hour was back with St. Cyr in tow, having intercepted him on his way to his room on Marais Street.

Anderson thought to embarrass the detective by letting Beansoup stand by while he got dressed down. Instead, he flipped the kid a whole Liberty dollar with a wink and a muttered thank-you. Beansoup, stunned with pleasure by this blessing from on high, tottered back out onto the banquette, clutching the silver coin tight in his fist.

The King of Storyville glared at the detective. "What the hell is going on?" he demanded. "You've got half the city raising a ruckus. Did your signals get crossed? I thought you were going to finish this and put it away."

"Miss Benedict wants to know what happened to her father."

"So tell her. The man got lost and was murdered. They have a suspect under arrest."

"She won't buy that."

Anderson lifted his chin as if catching a scent. "Why not?"

Valentin leaned his arm on the bar. "She asked me if I thought Ten Penny was guilty. I told her no."

"You did *what*?" The King of Storyville's bark echoed in the empty room and janitors froze in place.

"I told her Ten Penny isn't guilty," the detective said.

Anderson looked around, as if seeking someone who made sense. "What do you think you're doing?"

"This could be as simple as everyone says it is," Valentin said. "Or there might be something more to it."

Anderson rolled his eyes, his face turning a darker shade of pink. "Do you know how many times I've heard you say that? And every time it means trouble."

"And there would have been more if I hadn't done anything," Valentin said curtly.

Anderson thought about it, then waved a hand in the air. "Yes, I know. I know."

"I'll quit it, if that's what you want," Valentin said.

"Oh, will you?" The King of Storyville produced a mirthless grin. "Somehow, I don't think you will. Let me tell you something. That girl is in for a shock when she finds out her father was out there fucking some nigger crib girl. Or doing who knows what else. There won't be any way to keep it quiet. It will be all over town. She has to know that."

"She does."

Anderson muttered something that Valentin did not catch. "Sir?" he said.

"I said, I never should have let you out of Storyville." He leaned back, drumming his fingers, considering. Valentin could almost read his thoughts, another sign that he was slipping back into old habits. Anderson was figuring a way to play his hand. As if on cue, he straightened and said, "Is Miss Benedict paying you a decent amount?"

Valentin nodded, sensing what was coming.

"Then I don't need you here right now," Anderson said bluntly. "We both know you're not doing the job, anyway. I have criminals stealing from our customers right under your nose. Every card cheat in the city is coming around, because the word's out that you're not putting the arm on anyone. I can't have that." He mulled for another quick moment. "So you work tonight and then you'll be finished."

"Are you firing me?" Valentin tried to remember if this was the third or fourth time.

Anderson's blue eyes flicked. "I'll keep you on half pay. You just won't come to work for a while."

Valentin understood the King of Storyville's game instantly. There was nothing the chief of police or Delouche or Badel could say if St. Cyr was no longer in his employ. They couldn't ask him to run him out of town—at least not yet. Of course, Anderson would expect something for the money he would be paying under the table: any information he might use to his own benefit. Valentin had to admire the footwork. It was a sleek move for such a lumbering man, but he'd had a lifetime of practice. And what he said was true: he didn't care and had been doing a terrible job. He considered for another moment, then shrugged his agreement.

"I'll fix it for Beansoup or someone else to deliver the money to you," Anderson said, and then waved him out with a word of warning. "One more thing. To my mind, there's something not right about this young lady. Why does she want to have a scab like this pulled back? I'd watch her, if I was you. And I mean carefully."

The caution wasn't really necessary. Valentin already knew that there was more to Anne Marie Benedict and the sad little drama of her father's death.

She went by Betsy James, though it was nowhere close to what was on her birth certificate. Sometimes she had to think to recall the name her mama had given her eighteen years before in Chula, Mississippi. She barely remembered the woman who had died when she was a child, leaving her and her sisters to raise themselves.

How she had landed in the home of the family on Esplanade Ridge was some story, one she preferred to keep to herself. Why she stayed there was not such a mystery. It was a good place to hide from her past. Mrs. Benedict and Anne Marie had come to count on her so much that she was as close to a member of the family as she could manage without bleaching herself white. She was more capable of running the house than either woman and certainly knew more about the world than the two of them put together.

She took advantage of the wealth around her, helping herself to little things that would not be missed. She found out where the money was hidden and filched a dollar or two now and then, though she was clever enough to make sure that no one noticed. Or maybe they knew and didn't care. In the wake of Mr. Benedict's death, they seemed to be barely holding themselves together. The mother could only do it with the help of her prescription, and Anne Marie had a growing hankering for her brandy. She seemed sad and defeated, and didn't seem to care much about anything else.

Until Mr. Valentin St. Cyr came along, and Betsy quite suddenly found herself traveling familiar ground around Storyville to gather information.

She was stunned to learn that St. Cyr was a Creole, all right, but on the dark side of that line. He was by any definition a colored man and yet managed to pass, at least enough to move around in proper society. It was a trick that he seemed to have perfected. He had spent most of his years in the District working for Tom Anderson, handling security for some of the houses down the line, and those were not jobs for niggers, dagos, or anyone in between.

Still, she was not completely surprised that Anne Marie did not send the detective away after learning this. Indeed, she seemed all the more entranced by him and his story. Betsy wondered frankly if the white woman understood that she was playing with a very dangerous fire. Not that she could blame her; St. Cyr had a way about him. She had noticed it, too, the first time she'd laid eyes on him.

Betsy had scrounged the information quickly and cleverly, which was how she made her way through life. She thought of herself as a cunning bayou critter, a mink or a martin, small, sleek, very sly, and not to be crossed. She had asked around and found a sharp who worked the scarlet streets and seemed to know everything there was to know about the Creole detective. She flirted, letting him think he might get what was tucked in her satin drawers. After a day or two, she had the poor fellow panting like a dog and was thinking she should give him his reward for doing such a good job.

Not yet, though. She needed more from him. She knew too well that once men got what they wanted from a woman, it made them lazy. She needed this one hungry.

On this evening she rode the loop line car and got off on the corner of Villere and St. Louis. She was wearing a simple day dress of soft blue cotton, a typical maid's garment. She would go unnoticed, another colored servant out on errands. As she went about her secret mission, she recalled tales she'd heard about the infamous Marie Laveau, who had begun her long career spying on French and American families and ended up a wealthy woman and the greatest voodoo queen in Louisiana history. She, like Miss Betsy James, had started out humbly.

Betsy kept her head bent to the banquette, as if modest in her servitude. It was really to hide her face. She made her way one block west to Conti, then turned south another block to Marais and went around the corner and into Eclipse Alley.

He was waiting for her, as they had arranged, slouching against a storefront. When he saw her, he smiled and winked. She smiled back prettily and took his arm. He led her to a saloon where they served colored customers. She would have a brandy and he would nurse a glass of beer. She reminded herself to call him "Emile," instead of the moniker that he despised, for it wasn't a rounder's name: Beansoup.

Anyone passing on the Algiers side of the Mississippi River Bridge might have heard a splash in the water, as if a heavy carp had broken the surface, but the sound was lost in the wash of a freighter heading out for the Gulf, bound for Port of Spain.

SIX

A little past three o'clock, just as the night was winding down, the girl came into the dining room to announce that Justine's gentleman Mr. George was out in the foyer.

George Reynolds was a well-to-do man, and any dove would be satisfied to be in his favor. Though it was true that, for all his money, he showed little refinement, wearing flowery colognes that assaulted her nose every time she got close to him. He didn't take care of his appearance. His wardrobe was fine and yet his clothes often had an unwashed smell—which meant his wife wasn't doing her duty at home.

On the other hand, he wasn't all that demanding of her. He seemed mostly another lonely fellow who desired the affections of a pretty young woman. His business success seemed to have brought him little joy. It was something she had seen in other men of means and never understood. He liked to complain about his lazy, empty-headed spouse and spoiled children. His other favorite subject involved the conniving businessmen who crossed his path. He was a success, but when he got to her room, he was a weak and flaccid man altogether. For his pleasure, she bent over the bed and lifted her skirts or kneeled before him as he sat in a chair. Either way, it was over in no time. There was rarely any spooning or other such silliness. When he stayed through the night, sleeping in a torrent of snores, he made it worth her while. She didn't know what Mr. George was telling his wife and didn't care. He paid her a princely twenty-seven dollars a week for the personal service. She gave a third of it to Miss Antonia for her room and meals. It was a good living, two or three times what any other young working woman in New Orleans might earn.

With all that, she and Mr. George still had an unspoken arrangement; if he didn't appear by ten, she was free to do whatever she wanted. After all, this was a Basin Street mansion, not some back-alley whorehouse, and she wasn't some common trollop, either. She was surprised and a little annoyed that he had come so late, but there he was.

She was about to have the girl tell him that she wasn't feeling well. Then she saw Miss Antonia giving her a look from across the room. She was expected to set an example for the other girls. You did not turn away a well-heeled gentleman like George Reynolds because your sorry bones were too lazy, even this late. So she got up from her chair and followed the girl to the front of the house.

As soon as she laid eyes on him, she could see that there was something wrong. He was even paler than usual and clearly agitated, his eyes blinking rapidly as he fidgeted with his hat. She took his arm and steered him up the stairs.

As befitted the prettiest dove, Justine kept the largest and best-appointed room, after the madam's. On the front corner, it had a high ceiling and arched windows with a broad view of the lights of Basin Street. There was enough space for a large bed, a wardrobe, an armchair, a love seat, and a dressing table. There were knickknacks, decorated pillows, and throws. She could afford it. She was earning it.

She led Mr. George in, got him settled on the love seat, and fetched him a short glass of whiskey. He quaffed it in a single gulp and held out the glass for more. With a second drink in hand, he settled back, let out a loud breath, and drew out his handkerchief to mop his brow.

"What's upsetting you so?"

He took another sip of his drink and his hand still trembled.

"The strangest thing," he said, and then, in a hushed voice, proceeded to tell her the story.

Dauphine Street was fairly quiet for a Saturday night, the breeze coming up from the south like a warm breath. It was late, well past two, and the banquettes were already all but deserted as George Reynolds and Charles Kane, both of them woozy from the cocktails they'd enjoyed in the Napoleon House, negotiated the narrow avenue, weaving this way and that.

Kane muttered that his motorcar, a new Oldsmobile, was waiting one block over on St. Peter Street. He offered his friend a ride home in the fine cabriolet, which he drove himself, rather than leave the chore to some "goddamn nigger monkey," as he loudly put it. George declined, explaining that he had plans to visit a young lady in a house on Basin Street. This was true. He was also weary of Kane, who couldn't take a sip of liquor without launching into a crimson-faced diatribe about how the coons, dagos, kikes, chinks, and all the rest of them were ruining decent American society. It was positively appalling when he went on one of these rants, mindless (or perhaps mind*ful*) of the colored, Italian, and Chinese serving folk who watched and listened with who-knew-what murderous thoughts festering behind their blank gazes. He was white, though, and moneyed, a man of some importance, so not a word was spoken, even by those like George, who secretly despised his notions.

The only time Charles quieted down was when he spoke about John Benedict. George caught the name coming back around like an echo, and it stopped him cold. Kane went to muttering under his breath, a string of curses, and George could have sworn that somewhere in there he heard what sounded like "got what he goddamn well had coming," though he couldn't be sure. Charles seemed mostly to be talking to himself.

They paid their bill and went out onto the street and through the Quarter with him still uttering the occasional drunken snarl that was coupled with Benedict's name.

When George said, "What about him?" something raw flashed in Kane's eyes and he fell silent, turning inward for a few moments.

"That's what he gets!" he said. A second later he looked like he was going to be sick. "There was a rat on my gallery," he half moaned.

"What?" George said. "What are you talking about?"

"I found a sack with a dead rat in it on my doorstep! You know what that means?"

He stalked off and a few seconds later he was back to railing at the world around him with his usual hateful volume. George didn't even want to think about what was simmering behind this strange behavior.

And yet George had never challenged him, never told him that he was an imbecile and should shut his vicious mouth. It wasn't his way, and it would only make things worse. If Kane had any idea that he was on his way to visit a woman of color, he'd be shocked, disgusted, enraged. God knows what he'd say—or do. So he was only too glad when Charles veered off down St. Peter to reunite with his fine automobile.

As he watched him walk away, he went digging into his pockets for a plug of tobacco, wondering why he still bothered with him. He didn't like him much at all. They weren't friends, not really. Charles Kane didn't have friends. Reynolds had worked for the man at one time and that was all. That was *all*.

He bit off half a plug. Charles was a short block down, crossing over Burgundy, when George was startled to see a sudden shadow fall and, a second later, a shape that looked like a huge bird swoop from one of the doorways. There was a rough shout, and in one instant Kane and the dark shape were gone as if they had both been erased from the night. It was such a jolting sight that George couldn't quite believe his eyes and peered hard, trying to define shadow from solid form. He waited, expecting at any second to see Kane lurch into sight once more. The street remained still. A woman's laugh trebled from around a distant corner. Something was wrong.

George edged along in Kane's footsteps and began calling his name as he came up on the corner of Burgundy. He noticed a walkway between two of the storefronts on the other side of the intersection, a three-foot space that led into an alleyway behind. George stepped closer and peered along the dim gap, shading his eyes. The darkness along this narrow cavern was a brownish tint that made it impossible to see anything. It was as if a shroud had been dropped over his eyes. He called again: "Charles! Charles Kane!" and heard his voice carry down the narrow cavern.

He backed away, feeling a throb of fear, as if the wet darkness might reach out and suck him in, too. His thoughts were skittering to and fro. It had to be that Charles had simply stepped into the walkway to relieve his bladder. Then where had he gone? Helplessly, he looked up and down the street. There was not another person in sight.

When another tense minute went by and Kane still didn't appear, George hurried around the corner and down a block to North Rampart Street, where he found a police corporal and a patrolman, strolling the banquette in their round-topped helmets, their nightsticks atwirl. He rushed up and began to explain what had happened, but the whole thing sounded so bizarre on his tongue that he could only stumble along in starts and stops. The two policemen studied him with incredulous frowns. There he was, a white man of means, and the two blue-suited minions were regarding him as they would some common drunkard or a babbling idiot.

What? How did this happen? It looked like a bird? The more George described what he'd seen, the more he sounded like a lunatic. He kept trying to explain and finally, grudgingly, the two coppers accompanied him back to the scene.

The junior officer lit his portable gas lamp and, holding it high, stepped into the walkway. His footsteps clicked off into silence. Nothing happened for a few moments and then they heard him again. He came out with a shrug, reporting that there was nothing to see but an empty courtyard where trash was collected. And the usual squadron of rats, of course.

The policemen now took turns staring at George, trying to determine if he was drunk or insane. Then the corporal yawned and mumbled something about making a report. They left him there and went back to their rounds. A moment later, feeling the shadows creeping about, he hurried out of the Quarter and crossed over Basin Street to Miss Antonia's door.

Justine listened to the story. It fascinated her, not that she cared at all about Mr. George's friend, but because she was enthralled by the macabre way it progressed, and the ending was like an Edgar Allan Poe tale. She wondered if he was making it up. He looked truly upset, though, and she told him not to worry, that it was probably one of those things, shadows of the night, and that his friend was likely sleeping at home that very moment. George nodded, though his eyes continued to make nervous tics.

She remembered her duties then and reached to unbutton his vest. "Can I calm you now?"

He sighed, a huffing sound. "Yes, dear, that would be pleasant."

In a half minute, she had him all undone and had settled to her knees between his spread thighs. He sighed and leaned his head back. When he closed his eyes, though, he envisioned the corner, the dark-winged swooping shape, the empty place where his acquaintance had been standing just a second before. It required Justine's most expert ministrations to chase the visions away.

The body that had been swept through the wake of the Trinidad-bound freighter finally washed to shore a mile down the river, beyond Algiers.

The police were called and arrived promptly at the scene. They found the sodden corpse dressed well, in a tailored three-piece suit. He bore no identification; however, someone at the parish morgue thought he recognized the face, even though it was blotched, bruised, and scarred by tiny claws and teeth. There had been a photograph in the newspaper, the witness recalled. So the man might well be someone of note. A telephone call went over to New Orleans, where a police clerk wrote down the particulars and promised to pass it on. It was Sunday, though, and there was no one to pass it to, so the clerk put it on the nail for attention first thing Monday morning.

No more than a half hour later, a patrolman walking a beat on St. Peter Street saw that the fine Oldsmobile cabriolet that had been parked unattended since the night before had not been moved. He thought nothing of it and went on about his rounds.

It was late afternoon when Valentin stepped onto a quiet Marais Street, having slept a good part of the day away. The street was almost empty of traffic, the usual for a Sunday. He stood on the corner of the alley, trying to decide where to go for an early dinner.

Right away, he noticed a Buick touring car painted a red so deep it was almost burgundy, with white-spoked wheels, parked down the block and across the intersection of Bienville Street. Two men were sitting in the front seat, both wearing jackets and derbies that were pulled down low over their faces. Even from that distance, Valentin sensed them watching him. He turned and began strolling down the banquette in the direction of Iberville Street, wishing for a moment that he hadn't left his pistol in his dresser drawer.

He wasn't surprised to hear the engine of the Buick cough to life. The putter of the four cylinders rose and fell, and the car pulled up to the curbing ten paces ahead of him. The man who was riding shotgun swung down onto the banquette, not quite blocking his path, though close enough so that there was no mistaking his intent.

He was tall, broad across the shoulders, and sported a pronounced mustache on a face that bore prominent scars. The nose had been broken at least once, and the eyes above it were flat, cold, and unfriendly.

He held up a gloved hand and said, "St. Cyr," pronouncing it *Saint,* the American way. Valentin made as if he was going around, then stopped at the last second. The detective caught a flash of white teeth and glanced at the driver, who had noticed and enjoyed the ploy. His face was relaxed and curious, as if he was an idle observer to this comedy. His eyes were clear green and his hair was long, pushed behind his ears and reaching his collar in back.

Valentin returned his attention to the man before him and waited.

"My name's Nelson," the tall man said. "I've got a message for you, friend." He rolled his shoulders a bit, like a prizefighter getting ready for action. "The message is that you're spending too much time on Esplanade Ridge."

Valentin looked between the two men. "Who says so?" he asked politely.

"You don't fucking worry about who says so," the tall man muttered. "Let's say I work for a man who works for a man who doesn't want to be bothered."

"What does that mean?"

Nelson's face went pink. He wasn't in the mood for back talk. "Listen, goddamnit, you—"

"Our employer thinks you might be taking advantage of a young lady who's grieving," the driver cut in, sounding like the height of reason. "He'd like it to stop."

"That's right," Nelson said. "Stop. And that means now."

"Or what?" Valentin inquired.

Nelson gaped at him, then looked at his companion. "He wants to know *or what.*"

The driver gave Valentin a cool smile. "He knows," he said. Then, "Let's go."

"You've been warned," Nelson said as he grabbed the hand bar. "You stay where you fucking belong!" He pulled himself up into the seat. The driver engaged the clutch and they drove off. Once they turned the corner at Iberville, the puttering of the engine faded and the Sunday-afternoon peace returned.

SEVEN

Frank Mangetta came out of the kitchen, pulled up a chair, broke off the heel of the Italian loaf that was on the side plate, and cut a chunk of provolone to go with it. He picked up a section of the *Daily Picayune,* and he and Valentin ate and read in silence.

Presently, the detective put down his paper as a way of breaking the silence and without preamble recounted what had happened Saturday and Sunday, starting from the moment Frank showed him the article about the arrest of Ten Penny and ending with the visit from the two fellows in the Buick.

After he finished, the saloon keeper frowned and said, "See what I told you? So who sent them?"

"I think it was Henry Harris."

Frank's cup clattered and some of the coffee spilled out. He gaped at Valentin. "Henry Harris! *Gesù!*" he cried in Italian. "What the hell have you got yourself into?"

"I don't know. That's what I'm wondering. Why did he bother to send those two?"

The saloon keeper sat back, his mouth tight, regarding Valentin critically. "No, the question is why the hell are you doing this?"

"I told you. Because the daughter's paying me."

"Oh? Because she's paying you." Frank gave him a sardonic look. "Is that all?"

"What else?"

"She a peach?"

Valentin smiled slightly. "If you like your women cagey, she'd probably be all right."

"What's that mean?"

"It means she's a sharp one, that's all." He let it go at that.

Frank shook his head in distraction, then drained his cup, got up from his chair, and ambled off to the grocery, leaving Valentin alone with his thoughts.

A half hour later, the Creole detective stepped outside to find Beansoup eyeing the young maids out of the mansions who were passing by on their morning errands, and making comments that would have gotten his face slapped if he did not present such a comical figure. The girls, most of whom knew him and his antics, just laughed and went about their business. He took advantage of the quiet moments to blow some blue notes on his harmonica.

When he spied Valentin, he put the harmonica in his shirt pocket, strolled over, sniffed once, hitched his trousers, and rubbed his hands together. "What you got for me?" he asked, his voice curiously deep.

Valentin gave him his instructions and sent him on his harmonica-tootling way.

The detective climbed the three flights to the *Daily Picayune* newsroom and asked to see Robert Dodge. The reporter appeared after a few moments, a short, thick man in his forties, dressed in a white shirt that was going yellow and the trousers and vest of a three-piece suit. He had mouse-gray hair over a broad face that was fringed by an erratic beard. The eyes behind his tiny wire-rimmed glasses were the bloodshot red of a veteran drinking man. Even as they shook hands, Valentin caught a whiff of something on Dodge's breath and wondered frankly if anyone in the building was sober.

He said, "My name's Valentin St. Cyr, Mr. Dodge. I'd like a few minutes of your time. Joe Kimball told me to come see you."

"Kimball?" Dodge's gaze was wary.

"That's right."

Grudgingly, the reporter ushered him through the swinging gate and then through one of the doors behind the front desk.

The air in the room they entered was thick with smoke from dozens of cigars and cigarettes, and fairly vibrating with sound. Typing machines clattered under the gray cloud as copyboys streaked around the desks like fleet mice while the men at the desks barked commands. Indeed, amid that din, anyone who wanted to speak at all had to yell. It was like a battlefield in there.

The detective trailed Dodge to the back corner of the room, where the noise and the smoke were diminished. The reporter gestured to the chair opposite his desk and sank into the one behind it, a swivel affair with torn leather covering.

Valentin, regarding his host, thought Dodge had about him a look of ruined gentility that he had seen before. Usually, it was scions of families that had lost everything in the war and went about drinking themselves into oblivion as they mourned the Confederacy along with their lost wealth and glory. Dodge had somehow managed to hang on to enough of this former opulence to make an appearance in that company. Though who knew how? Even now, seated in his creaking chair, he displayed a collapsing posture that, along with those watery red eyes, marked a lifelong drinker. There would be a bottle in the desk, and Valentin knew that before the hands on the clock advanced much further, Dodge would go in search of it.

The reporter now regarded him with a wet gaze, as if something had just dawned on him. "I know you," he announced abruptly. "You caught the one who committed those Black Rose murders in the District in '07."

Valentin's mouth barely tilted. "I believe someone here at the paper made up that name."

"And the business with those jass players." It sounded like an accusation.

"That, too," Valentin said, shifting his chair.

Dodge regarded him vaguely, his brow in an absent furrow, as if his thoughts had gone elsewhere. The detective wondered for an idle moment if this scribbler might be the one who used the byline "Bas Bleu" for the *Picayune* columns he wrote excoriating the high and mighty uptown and down-, an anonymous thorn in the side of the city's hoi polloi. As far as Valentin knew, the man's (or woman's) identity was still a secret. As for Robert Dodge, he looked too flaccid to excoriate anyone.

The detective went directly to the subject at hand. "I'm interested in information that you might be able to provide."

Dodge stared fixedly at his guest. "About John Benedict?"

Valentin kept his face impassive, wondering how the besotted Dodge knew this. "That's right," he said.

"And you want information?"

"Yes."

"For which I would get what?" the reporter asked archly.

"A return of the favor someday."

Dodge considered for a moment, then sat up in his chair and drew open the drawer to his right. "You care for a drink?" Now his tone was almost jovial.

"I wouldn't say no," Valentin said. Any other response would likely end the interview right there.

Dodge went about pouring whiskey into two glasses. It was all done one-handed and out of sight in the drawer. He handed Valentin a glass, raised his own in a small toast, then downed its contents in one quick swallow. The glass went back into the drawer. It had taken all of five seconds. Valentin sipped more gently, cupping the glass between his palms. It was only ten o'clock.

"So," Dodge said, leaning back with a quiet smack of his lips.

"Whatever you can tell me about Mr. Benedict would be helpful."

Dodge considered, nodding. "Yes, I suppose it would," he said with sudden irritation. "I suppose it would be very helpful to you if I told you who shot him to death on Rampart Street. That would be pleasant. Except that I don't *know*."

Valentin, perplexed by the bizarre rant, said, "I didn't think you did."

Dodge now nodded his head with blank melancholy. He seemed to be a man who fell into moods at the drop of a hat. Valentin wondered if he was going to be able to keep him on the subject.

"The Benedicts are an old-line American family," he began. "The grandfather was in shipping after the war. John, Senior, married into acreage in St. Martin Parish. He had three sons and a daughter. John Louis, the one who was killed, was the eldest. I don't quite recall the others' names. They all went into shipping, except for the daughter, of course. She lives in the Garden District. She married one of the..." He blinked, hesitating. "...the, uh...uh..."

"Carters," a voice piped up.

Valentin turned to see a young man of perhaps twenty standing by the next desk over, a sheaf of papers in his hand.

"Did someone ask you for that?" Dodge snapped at him.

The young man's face flushed. "Excuse me," he said. He dropped some papers on the desk and hurried off. The reporter watched him go, his brow furrowing with petulance. He paused to open the drawer to pour another quick drink.

"Some people get rich from hard work," he said suddenly, brow furrowing. "Just as many get rich from no work at all. Either way, they learn how to use their money. They don't get harmed by messy business. Embarrassments of a criminal sort never reach a courtroom. Things get fixed. Charges are dismissed. Wounded parties receive a monetary award. And life goes on."

Valentin got the impression that Dodge had strayed off and was waxing philosophical on American New Orleans' particular brand of corruption. He himself preferred Storyville, where the sins were in full view of anyone who bothered to cast an eye about.

"I understand he was an associate of Henry Harris," he said.

Dodge hesitated, then nodded. "I think that's right."

Valentin thought of something and threw it out. "And then he retired at a fairly early age."

Dodge's eyes shifted. "Well, good for him, I suppose." It was an odd thing to say; Dodge seemed to be nursing a vague disdain for the very people he was paid to write about. Maybe he knew them too well.

Valentin said, "Joe said he's been mentioned in the society pages."

Dodge shrugged. "He and his wife were active in the Opera House and some other social events, but that's all. The usual."

"I'd like to—"

"Rampart Street," Dodge interrupted dolefully. "What a place for a man like him to die." Abruptly, he leaned forward, all furtive, his eyes shifting. "Have you asked yourself what the hell was he doing there?"

"I have wondered about that," Valentin said, careful to keep his voice matter-of-fact.

Dodge winked and came up with a devious smile. He was just about to add something, when his eyes shifted and locked on something or someone over Valentin's shoulder. His Adam's apple bobbed, his cheeks paled, and he gave a slight nod. The detective had to make an effort not to turn his head to see who had engaged Dodge's attention at that moment.

Dodge let his gaze slide back to him and straightened in his creaking leather chair. "I won't be a party to this dreadful business!" His voice went up a notch. "If that's what you came for, you wasted your time."

Valentin almost snickered at the haughty pronouncement, delivered as only a drunkard could manage, and for the benefit of anyone listening nearby. He placed his glass with its remaining half inch of whiskey on the desk where anyone who happened to glance their way would see it. It was a deliberate rudeness. Dodge glared, snatched the glass between two fingers, depositing it out of sight in his desk drawer. His eyes batted in annoyance as he pulled a soiled handkerchief from his pocket and began swiping at the whiskey that had sloshed over the rim.

"I'm not here to do your work for you," he said, now all crabby. "You're the damned Pinkerton." He was pouting, his lower lip hanging and his eyes dull with rebuke.

Valentin said, "I'm not a Pink—"

"Maybe you'd have more luck elsewhere." Now Dodge was snappish. "Maybe you should go back down to that damned dungeon and see your friend Kimball."

"Maybe I should." Valentin got to his feet.

"Because you're wasting your time here!" It came out much too loud.

"Thank you for the hospitality," the detective said dryly.

Dodge didn't speak and didn't look up. Valentin turned on his heel and made his way across the room, walking a maze path between the desks. He looked around casually, to see if anyone was taking an interest in him, perhaps the person who had passed Robert Dodge the silent message. No one caught his eye, and he walked out of the room, through the door into the lobby, and down the staircase to the street.

———

He had gone only a half block when he heard his name called. The young man who had blurted the information about the Carters hurried to catch up with him.

"Mr. St. Cyr? My name's Reynard Vernel. I'd like a moment of your time." He took a furtive glance over his shoulder, then pointed farther up the street. "There's a place on the next corner, if you can spare me a few minutes."

The place on the next corner was the Red Bird Café, a drinking establishment with a small dining area in the back. The doors had just opened for the day and the proprietor, an old Frenchman, greeted them with broom in hand. He murmured a welcome and waved to the bar and a platter arrayed with cheese, cold meats, and bread, the typical New Orleans free lunch.

Valentin helped himself. Reynard Vernel didn't take any of the food, but asked the detective if he wanted something to drink. Valentin told him he preferred a cup of coffee.

A minute later they were seated at a small round table in the corner of a back room that the sun through the front windows didn't illuminate. Though there was still enough light for the detective to get a fair look at his companion.

He was slightly tan in the face, with dark hair cut badly and a light mustache on his upper lip. In a suit that was either a hand-me-down or purchased secondhand and worn walking shoes, he was just shy of ragged, though his expression was bright with eager good humor.

He pushed Valentin's cup across the table. He had ordered a mug of beer for himself, and was so nervous that when he drank that, the glass rattled against his front teeth.

Valentin sipped his coffee and began nibbling the food on his plate. "What can I do for you?" he inquired.

"I know who you are, Mr. St. Cyr. I've read about your cases in the paper. And I've heard people talk." Vernel swallowed nervously. "And I...I thought I might...I want to *write* about you," he blurted.

The detective cocked an eyebrow. "Do what?"

"Write about you," Vernel said. "Follow you on a case and then write about it."

Valentin smiled as if he thought it was a joke. "Write about what? I don't understand."

"I would follow you and write about how to solve a case," Vernel said. "Like the murder of this Benedict fellow. I think that right there would make a grand story."

Valentin took a bite of ham. "And this would be for the *Picayune?*"

Reynard Vernel gave up a nervous laugh. "Oh, no. They'd never print anything like that. It would be for a magazine. Maybe one in New York. There's got to be an editor who'd be interested. They enjoy things like that. They think that once you get beyond Pittsburgh, it's the Wild West down here."

He saw the baffled look on Valentin's face and plunged on. "I have plans, Mr. St. Cyr," he stated with some impatience. "I want to be a real correspondent. If I stay at the *Picayune,* I'll write obituaries and business stories for the next five years and then I might be allowed to cover a news beat, and after that, if I'm lucky, write articles of interest to anyone but me. I'll be an old man by then. I don't want to wait. I want to get my career going, and I think this is a good way to do it."

Valentin thought about it for a short second. "I don't think so."

Vernel's face fell. "Why not?"

The detective gestured dismissively. "First of all, you'd be in my way. Sometimes what I do can be dangerous. I can't be responsible for you. And, anyway, I don't want anyone writing about me. I don't need to see my name in any magazine." His gray eyes flicked with dry humor. "You should be talking to the Pinkertons. They like that kind of thing."

Vernel opened his mouth to argue. Valentin got there first.

"Look, I'm not one of these penny-novel fellows," he said. "It's not like that. I don't rush from one exciting moment to the next with my pistol blazing. It can be boring, especially in a case like this. There's not that much to it, because the man was likely shot down by some criminal. If it's not the fellow they have in Parish Prison, then it's some other scofflaw. But whatever I do find out, I won't be able to talk about, because of the family. That's the way it works. I'm not a policeman. What I do is not on the record. That's why they call it *private* detective."

Vernel's face was twisting up in chagrin. It was too bad for him. It couldn't be any other way. The whole idea was ridiculous. Valentin finished the last morsel from his plate and sipped his coffee as he mulled the rest of his day and waited for the younger man to take his disappointment and leave.

"What if I can offer you something in return?" Vernel said, breaking into his thoughts.

Valentin put his cup down. "Such as?"

"Information you could use."

Valentin studied the younger man's face. "Like who got Dodge to shut his mouth back there?"

"Sure," Vernel said. "Could be. And could be more. I can find out and tell you what Dodge wouldn't."

Valentin pondered it for another moment. "I'm sorry, no," he said. "I can't have that. I'll just have to figure it out for myself." He got to his feet and Vernel followed suit. "I'm sure you'll find something else to write about. This is New Orleans. There's trouble everywhere you look. There must be a hundred good stories, right under your nose."

Vernel was getting ready to plead his case some more. Then he saw the look on the Creole detective's face. With a huff of frustration, he walked off a few paces, then stopped and came back.

"The fellow who shut him up was an editor named Collins," he said in a low voice. "I heard him ask who Dodge was talking to, and one of the reporters said, 'It's St. Cyr, that fellow who works for Tom Anderson.' And then he went over there and made like this..." Vernel put a stiff finger to his lips. "Dodge shut his mouth, just like that."

"What would he care?"

"He wouldn't want you coming around asking questions," Vernel said with a shrug. "He's related to the publisher of the paper, see? That's how he got the job. He hasn't got much to do except stick his nose in other people's business. He's got no talents at all, except for drinking."

Valentin laughed at the last comment. Vernel smiled ruefully and said, "I guess I'm about the only one around there who doesn't have that problem." He got serious again. "Nobody's going to discuss anything having to do with Henry Harris, Mr. St. Cyr."

"Who said anything about Henry Harris?"

Vernel smiled slyly. "Benedict ran one of his companies. He sat on a board of directors. And along with everything else he owns, Harris is a big stockholder in the newspaper. You should know that you're not going to get anything that touches him from anyone in that place. Except me."

Valentin mulled this for a moment, then said, "Thank you for your help."

Vernel tugged at his tie, a nervous gesture. "You know where I am if you need me," he said, and headed for the door.

George Reynolds picked up the telephone on his desk in his house on Russell Street, gave the operator a number, and asked to be connected.

One of Charles Kane's sons answered. George forced his voice steady. "Is your father at home?" he asked.

"No," the son said, sounding bored. "Haven't seen him, not today."

"Do you have any idea where he might be?"

"Nope," the young lout said. "He didn't say."

"When do you expect him back?"

"Don't know," the boy said breezily. "He does that all the time. Stays off over the weekends. On business."

George wanted to ask what matters of business would keep the man occupied through a New Orleans Saturday night, all of Sunday, and well into Monday. He was tempted to recount the bizarre tableau he had witnessed on the dark French Quarter street and see if the son would care about *that*. Instead, he simply thanked him and left a message to have his father contact him as soon as he arrived home. He wondered if the boy could hear how hollow his voice sounded.

George went to the front window and stared out over the gallery at the street. He was supposed to be at work. He should have left hours ago but found himself benumbed, unable to summon the gumption to move. The memory of what had happened on Burgundy Street wouldn't leave him be, tying him in knots and bringing a chill to his very bones.

Charles Kane would not be going home. George was sure that he had witnessed the abduction that had ended with the man's death.

He felt his stomach heave. He had not a week ago read about John Benedict, also the victim of a senseless murder. He had attended the funeral and paid his respects, hearing the murmurs travel from mouth to ear about how Benedict had died on Rampart Street, that raucous and sin-soaked avenue. No one could guess what he was doing there in the dead of night; or, rather, no one would say out loud. Those words would be whispered outside the house.

George recalled how Charles had stood by, glowering in grim silence, a knowing light in his eyes, and wondered for a crazy moment if he might have done the deed himself. Though he couldn't imagine why.

Charles had known something, though. George could see it

in his face and hear it in his drunken mutterings. He never found out what it was, because a phantom rose from a dark void to sweep Kane from the street with what appeared to be a supernatural force. Though New Orleans was a violent town, what were the chances that two men he knew would meet grim fates in less than a week? It could be coincidence. Benedict might have run into trouble on Rampart Street, and one of the dagos or the niggers that Kane maligned might have finally heard enough. He tried to convince himself of this, but his gut wouldn't let him.

He pondered for a minute more, then picked up the thin paperbound book that listed all the four-digit phone numbers for the city of New Orleans and paged through it again. He lifted the receiver and waited for the operator. When she came on, he asked her to connect him to number 4337, the home of the late John Benedict.

It had turned into a pleasant spring day, the air sweet with warm spring breezes, and Valentin decided to walk to Peters Street. He strolled along Canal Street, the widest artery in the city. The banquette was crowded and the street was swarming with streetcars, bicyclists, horse-drawn hacks, and a variety of automobiles that coughed, puttered, rattled, squeaked, and belched gray clouds. Though a good share were stolid black Model R Fords, Valentin also picked out another dozen roadsters and cabriolets in various gleaming shades: green Wells, blue Packard, yellow Winton, red Marmon, white Sears, and on and on. People complained all the time about the noise, smell, and smoke, and yet every day it seemed there were even more motorcars zooming this way and that, and every new edition seemed to go faster.

At least some did; as he walked along, he noticed a police truck dragging a fine Oldsmobile cabriolet behind it, moving north at a grudging pace toward the garages on Fulton Street.

He turned the corner at Magazine, walked one block to Common Street, and stopped. He spied the balcony of his former residence a half block down. He had occupied the rooms of the second-floor flat over Gaspare's Tobacco Store for seven years, then gave them up when he had left the city.

He turned east again. At Peters Street, he headed south for two blocks, crossing over Poydras. The address he was seeking was squeezed in between two proper storefronts. Three glass globes hanging in a triangle over the door announced a pawnbroker's.

He stepped up and rapped a knuckle on a pane. Some moments passed and slippered feet slid across the floor. An eye peered out through one of the panes, the lock turned, and the door opened just wide enough to let him pass.

"Mr. Valentin!" The proprietor, a Hebrew named Solomon, greeted him with surprise. His skin was like Mediterranean leather, his eyes pale and birdlike, his nose a bow that would have done one of Valentin's Sicilian relatives proud. He was short and thin, balding on top with a fringe of gray hair the rest of the way around his narrow head. Valentin guessed he was now close to fifty, though he looked at least ten years older.

He was an able artisan, the son and grandson of diamond merchants. He also managed a successful pawn brokerage, and in fact it was to Solomon that the local jass players came to buy a horn or get a quick loan on one they already owned. A good-hearted fellow, he was known throughout the music community for his fair shakes. Valentin had always thought him too easy a touch.

Soft touch or not, Solomon was still such an astute merchant that he might have been wealthy, except for the fact that he spent every extra penny in a desperate effort to save his daughter Sophie, a resident of the row of sporting houses called the Jew Colony on Bienville Street between Villere and Robertson.

No matter how many times Solomon dragged her off that street, Sophie went back. He had gone to her rooms and made such an uproar that the madams had seen fit to put him off the

premises. He had cursed his daughter with Old Testament righ-
teousness, even accused her of causing the death of her poor
mother. When all else failed, he resorted to paying men to purchase her and then not take advantage. Some did as he asked;
others just took the money and enjoyed the girl, anyway.

Nothing worked. Sophie—raven-haired, full-bodied, with
striking gypsy features—was also clearly crazy and likely a hopeless case. Sober, she was just a problem. When she drank, she
was as wild as a crib girl, with an impressive record of arrests
for drunk-and-disorderly conduct. She wasn't quite crazy enough
for the bughouse. That she hadn't been locked away for good in
the women's prison was a small miracle. Valentin guessed that
her long-suffering father had long ago prepared his prayers for
the dead.

Valentin had first encountered Sophie at a time when she
could still keep a room in one of the better Jew Colony houses
on the Villere end of the section. He knew Solomon at the time,
though the pawnbroker had been too ashamed to mention his
errant daughter.

Later, when they became more familiar, Valentin had listened
to the tragic tale of a good girl gone bad for mysterious reasons
and had accepted a small sum of money to find and deliver her
back to the safety of her father's home.

Valentin realized right away that it was no use. Sophie
Solomon was out of control. He was in her room not one minute
when she let out a crazy laugh, dropped to her knees, and tried
to unbutton his trousers. He rebuffed her, so she laid back on
the braided rug, hitched up her petticoats, and began gyrating
like a Turkish dancer. When he didn't succumb to these charms,
she went about entertaining herself. He left her there, huffing
and gasping and thrashing her pelvis this way and that, all the
while babbling like a madwoman.

He went back to return Solomon's money and tell him the
bad news, leaving out the graphic parts. It was accepted with a

slow nod of grief. Valentin was not unmoved, however, and took it upon himself to keep an eye on the girl and try to keep her from serious harm.

Solomon expressed his gratitude by proffering the occasional gift of a special stickpin or a pair of cuff links that had come across his counter. Once or twice, when Valentin had a need to pawn something, Solomon was far too generous. Three years had passed since they had first met and done business, and the poor man's back seemed to bend another inch with each orbit of the earth around the sun.

"So," he said as he hobbled behind the counter. "What a surprise this is. It's been some good while since I've seen your face."

"I've been away," Valentin said.

"I heard, I heard." Solomon's brow stitched in sudden worry. "What brings you to my door? Have you seen So—"

"I haven't seen or heard anything about her," Valentin said quickly.

The older man closed his eyes for a moment. "I haven't, either. She could be dead, for all I know."

Valentin didn't have anything to say to that. To break the mood, he took out John Benedict's ring and placed it on the little rubber mat that was atop the glass case. The jeweler took a breath that was at least half sigh to shake off his melancholy and peered down at it through his thick spectacles.

"What's this?" he asked momentarily. He picked it up and held it to the light, its heavy gold band gleaming bright. "Very nice. Very nice." He looked at Valentin. "What? You want to sell it?"

"No, it's not mine. It has to do with an investigation."

The jeweler came up with a rare smile of small, gray-tinged teeth. "An investigation? In Storyville? I heard you were through with all that."

"I was," Valentin said shortly. "And it's not Storyville."

Solomon looked perplexed.

"What about the ring?" Valentin said.

"The ring...Oh, yes, fine piece," Solomon pronounced. "First-rate work, a beautiful stone. About perfect." His judicious eye shifted. "Is this evidence in a crime?"

"It turned up among the possessions of a dead man."

Solomon nodded sagely. "Your dead man was wealthy."

"I'd like to know where it might have come from," Valentin said. "Who made it, anything unusual about it, that sort of thing."

The pawnbroker now regarded Valentin deliberately. "Of course, I want to help you," he said. "As kind as you've been to me. I'll have to ask around a little bit. Show it. Without making a lot of noise, of course." He patted Valentin's wrist. "Don't worry. It's not the first time I've handled queer merchandise."

It was true, of course. Who knew how many ill-gotten items were hanging from the walls. The detective could trust Solomon to keep his lips sealed. "I'd appreciate anything you can find out," he said.

"We'll see what we can do," Solomon told him. "I'll send you a message. You're at...?"

"Mangetta's," Valentin told him.

"Mangetta's... of course. I guess some things don't change."

Valentin took that bit of wisdom out the door with him.

They brought the body into town and deposited it at the city morgue at one o'clock. There was no doctor on duty, and so the corpse, wrapped in linen, was laid out on a cooling board in the vault. Then everyone went to lunch.

When they came back a languid hour later, someone went to check and learned that the police had no reports of a missing person that matched the victim's description. Since the man on the board was obviously no derelict, a kid was sent to the offices of the *Daily Picayune* to collect one of the photographers who made portraits of local gentlemen of influence for the society pages.

While they were waiting, the attendants and coppers on hand eyed the corpse, taking special note of the beautiful pocket watch that was still ticking away despite the soaking in the river and the ring that was on the right hand, a heavy gold affair with a dark blue stone at the center. It was too late, though; sooner or later, the fellow's family would come for him and would want to know what had happened to his fine accessories.

A photographer named Grady showed up an hour later and with some reluctance went inside to view the body. Though he did not personally recall the gentleman, he mentioned a portrait that had appeared in the paper in a story having to do with the christening of a new freight vessel. If that was true, Grady said, then the photograph had likely been taken by the crippled Frenchman, Bellocq, who had made portraits for one or another of the shipbuilders. He offered to go through all the files to try to find a negative if someone was willing to pay.

After a round of discussion, they decided it would be easier just to get the Frenchman to identify the body. A policeman was summoned who knew the narrow back alleys of the Vieux Carré, along one of which Bellocq kept a room and a small studio. The copper was sent off with instructions to roust the photographer and get him downtown by the end of the afternoon.

When Valentin got back to Marais Street, he found Beansoup waiting in the saloon with the news that he had located two of the three characters that were first on the scene of John Benedict's murder, and that they would be waiting at Fewclothes Cabaret at eight o'clock that very evening.

Valentin was astonished. "How did you manage that?" he said.

Beansoup's chest puffed. " 'Cause I know what's what, that's how. Turns out the three of them is regulars back-of-town. Two of them work at the same place, too. In the office of a brick-works out toward Metairie." He gave a broad wink and snapped his fingers. "So I run them down."

"What about the third one?" Valentin asked.

Beansoup deflated a little. "That son of a bitch ran off."

"Ran off where?"

"I ain't got no idea. He works for a butcher at the French Market. I went in and asked for him. The butcher went in back and come out and said he'd run off. I guess he heard me asking about him."

"He's probably got some trouble with the law."

"Don't worry about it," Beansoup said. "I'll keep at it."

"You did a damn good job," Valentin said, and laid a Liberty dollar in the boy's palm. Beansoup came up with a grin that split his face like a jack-o'-lantern's.

It was midafternoon when E. J. Bellocq was roused from a ragged slumber by a pounding on his door. At first, he thought it was part of the crazy dream he was having, one of the many. But when it went on, he opened his eyes and growled a curse, figuring another gang of street urchins had come to torment him. Then he heard the shouted word "Police!"

At that, his heart went to chugging as he grabbed for one of his metal crutches. With a grunt of pain, he lurched to his feet and clanked his way to the door.

The patrolman, a hard-looking sort, was standing there in his round-topped helmet, just lifting his nightstick to rap the jamb some more. He took a step back from the smell of the rooms, a fetid odor of damp rot and chemicals in a closed space. He regarded the little Frenchman with disgust, then in a rough voice told him that he was wanted at the morgue at Parish Prison. Sooner rather than later.

"The morgue?" Bellocq squawked in a voice that was often compared to a duck's. "What for?"

"Just make sure you go," the patrolman growled. "I damned sure don't want to come back here." He wrinkled his nose. "Christ Almighty!" He turned to stalk off down the alleyway.

"Who wants me down there?" Bellocq cried after him. "What is this?" The copper ignored him and kept going.

The little Frenchman closed the door and locked it tight, then leaned on the wall to catch his breath. The police? What did they want with him? And at the morgue! What had he done?

Indeed, what *could* he do, even if he had an urge? The various ailments that had cursed Ernest J. Bellocq's body since he was a child had grown harsher over the past year. He was only in his late thirties, and yet he looked like an old man, and an old man in ill health at that. His entire body seemed to be clenching into a crabbed fist, ever tighter. He was sure he was growing shorter as his freakish, hydrocephalic head gained weight. His yellow hair was thinning, and his bulbous, pale blue eyes were often bright with pain. It took an effort for him to move ten steps. So what could he have done that demanded the attention of the police?

It couldn't be the paregoric he took for his pain or the opium he used to ease his sleep; those potions could be purchased by a schoolboy at almost every apothecary and chink laundry in the city.

He thought of his collection of photographs of Storyville prostitutes, taken over a period of years. But he didn't do that work anymore. He didn't get around as well, couldn't mount the gallery steps to the houses and the stairs to the second-floor rooms, and failed to persuade the girls to pose for him. They wanted money now, and he couldn't pay. When he insisted in his strange fierce voice that people would be gazing upon their visages on the walls of museums a hundred years in the future, the girls just laughed and sent him away.

Not that his prints could bring trouble in any case. They were chaste by the standards of the day. Far worse fare was offered for sale at various shops around the District. And the Circus at French Emma Johnson's featured live displays of the crudest sorts, involving men, women, even animals. So his photographs could hardly be suspect.

After he ruminated some more, he thought of Valentin St. Cyr and immediately felt a knot in his stomach. The Creole detective had something to do with the summons to the precinct. He didn't know how, only that it was true.

Valentin was one of the few people he had ever considered a friend. Their paths tangled in the middle of the Black Rose murders, and when it was over, Valentin had stopped coming around—as if he didn't want to encounter anyone who had anything to do with that nightmare. Later the Frenchman found out that he had packed up and left New Orleans. That was in the fall of 1908, and now he was back and delivering trouble directly to Ernest Bellocq's door.

With a grunt of displeasure, Bellocq made his way to his back room to begin to dress for the long trip downtown.

Valentin took a table at Mangetta's front window. A manila envelope had been waiting for him when he got back, and he now opened it and drew out a one-page duplicate of the autopsy report. Whoever had done the work had been careless by intent or habit, because it was a scribbled mess.

His brow knit as he tried to decipher the pen scratches; after a few minutes, he could pick out enough to make some headway. It was all very simple. The victim John Benedict had received a fatal gunshot wound to the throat. The shot had been neatly placed, just chipping the top of Benedict's sternum and entering the soft part beneath his Adam's apple. The trauma was critical and the victim expired within seconds from blood loss and asphyxiation. It didn't say which came first. Not that it mattered. The slug that was recovered was a .45 caliber, not a marksman's pistol by any means. There was no mention of powder burns on the victim's flesh or clothing, either. Taken together, the facts confirmed Valentin's initial judgment that the shot had come from a short distance away, twelve paces at the outside.

He closed his eyes, revisiting the scene on Rampart Street. He could picture the two figures, Benedict and his assailant, meeting on the cobblestones in the dead of night. Since no one had heard any voices raised in argument, it was probably finished quickly. An arm came up and a finger squeezed a trigger. There was an explosion, and Benedict went toppling over, dead within seconds. The killer slipped away into shadows before the echo had died.

Valentin opened his eyes. What had happened on Rampart Street was no robbery, nor was it some spat that got out of hand. It was a planned murder. If he'd had any doubt before, it was gone now.

He viewed the report for another minute, found nothing more, and laid it aside. He picked up the copy of the *Sun* that had been left on the next table over. On page 5, near the bottom, he read that the arraignment of one Thomas Lee, a Negro, aka Ten Penny, had been held on Saturday afternoon, and that sufficient grounds were found to indict the suspect for the murder of John Benedict. The farce was going forward, even though there was more than enough evidence that Ten Penny didn't commit the crime. Valentin wondered if they had gotten a confession out of him. The article didn't say.

They were going ahead with their case against the suspect, which meant that someone downtown was pushing to have it closed in a hurry. Someone else had to be pushing that someone.

Valentin mused for a moment on what Lieutenant Picot must be thinking now. Even as this bit of fraud went forward and powers above bore down on him, he would be aware of a certain Creole detective circling like an alligator in a Louisiana swamp, moving closer to chewing the case to bits. He'd take the blame if that happened; his superiors would make sure of it. He had jumped to arrest Ten Penny for the killing before he had any real evidence. The Negro had already been sitting in jail without a shred of evidence against him and none in sight. Picot had to be sweating.

Valentin folded the paper and pushed it aside. Too bad for him, too.

He got up from the table and went through the saloon and grocery and upstairs to rest for a little while. Just as he put the key in his lock, something moved on the periphery of his vision. He turned his head slightly, casually, and saw Signore Angelo's door in the process of closing. Angelo's dark gaze rested on him for a moment, like the calm stare of an animal. It was rare that the Sicilian was at home during the day, and Valentin wondered if he might be ill. He almost greeted his neighbor but instinct told him to let it be. Angelo's door closed and the lock clacked.

Papá Bellocq could not clamber into a hack without help and he couldn't handle a bicycle, so he walked wherever he went. Though "walk" didn't truly describe his gait, a wheedling, staggering business that he managed only with the aid of steel crutches that banged like castanets on the boards of the banquettes. He drew looks of pity, pointed fingers, rude catcalls. Other pedestrians just looked away from him. No one offered even the smallest word of greeting. He responded to one and all with an inflamed eye.

In this manner he made his way out of the old town and west on Burgundy Street, a tortuous journey. He was thankful that New Orleans was so flat or it would have been impossible for him to get anywhere. Still, it was after five o'clock before he rounded the building and made his creaking way along the alley to the steps that led down to the morgue. He negotiated the stairs like a windup toy in constant danger of collapsing into a broken heap. Red, sweating, and cursing in his native tongue, he crept along the long hallway to the room where they kept the bodies.

He heard the snickers and whispers in the background while he waited for them to roll the gurney out of the vault. In the past he held himself above these cruelties, refusing to give his tormentors the pleasure of a response. Now he looked from one to the next, catching their eyes and glaring until they turned away.

One of the attendants pulled back the sheet. He knew the face, as he knew every face he had ever photographed. He had a complete album in his head. This one was even easier; he had seen it not six months before.

"Charles Kane," he announced. "Runs one of the companies that outfit ships. Or he did. I took his photograph, more than one time."

"You sure?" one of the coppers asked him.

He just looked at the policeman and said, "Am I done here?" He didn't wait for an answer before walking out, clanking down the hall, sounding like a rusty old machine with bad gears.

Valentin found the two men, as arranged, at Fewclothes Cabaret, a noisy Basin Street music hall at night but a more genteel saloon during the afternoon and early evening. From the bar or one of the window tables, a fellow could watch the curious parade that passed up and down the line and get a world of information from a simple posture: the rounders took a slow pace, eyes flicking hawklike; the erring married men scurrying by on nervous feet, their shoulders hunched. The college boys out for a lark strutted along like young cocks. And then there were the dregs: drunks, hopheads, and the cheapest whores, who as often as not staggered about the banquette, making their miserable ways on unsteady legs.

The two men were standing at the curve of the bar, leaning back with one foot up on the rail. Each man had a mug of beer in front of him. The younger fellow, who went by the name of

Willis, was portly and dark-haired, sporting a slick mustache, and appeared quite pleased to be there. Witnessing the aftermath of a bloody crime on Rampart Street suited him, and he pumped Valentin's hand with vigor. The older, thinner Mr. Royston had a pinched, bearded, and altogether glum face. It was just as clear that he would rather be elsewhere. When Valentin asked after the third of their party, Willis announced that Mr. Bedford would not be joining them, being the "no-good, damned coward that he was."

"I think he's run off," Valentin said.

Willis stared, then looked at his friend, smiling slightly. Royston gave a shrug, as if this came as no surprise.

"I want to thank you gentlemen for your cooperation," Valentin said.

Royston said, "What is it you want?"

"Just for you to tell me what happened that night."

Willis fell to the task with relish. "We come out of Johnny O's, on the corner of Third Street. They had a jass band there; they were tearing it up, all right. This here trombone player— big nigger must have gone three hundred pounds—he was workin' that thing, had every—"

"After you left," Valentin murmured.

Willis blinked. "Oh, yeah. They run us out of there. It was late. The band was done. We were about the last ones."

"What time?"

"It was..." Willis frowned. "I'm not sure...Maybe four A.M.?"

"It was after," Royston muttered.

Valentin and Willis both turned to stare at him. He kept his mournful eyes fixed on the street beyond the window. "I heard the bells on the quarter hour."

"Well, then," Willis continued momentarily. "We went out there on the banquette and got to talking about what we was going to do next. Bedford and me, we wanted to see if we could find us one more door was still open." He tilted his head and smiled dimly. "This citizen wanted to pack in and go home."

Valentin glanced at Royston. The man didn't comment.

"Well, we wasn't thinking about where we was going, and the next thing I know, I heard something sounded like a shot. There wasn't nothing more, and we didn't give it any thought. Course we'd all had a good bit to drink. Then we got on Rampart Street and..." He took a dramatic pause. "...that's when we saw him." He took a swill from his glass. "First we saw someone bending down, looked like a damn crow on a rat. When we got closer, I saw the blade. I yelled and he jumped up and run away. We come up to the one in the street, and the first thing I saw was that hole in his throat. He was looking up at the sky and his eyes was open. Good Lord, it was awful!" He shuddered. "I run right to the call box. Then we waited around till the coppers come."

Valentin nodded. It was mostly what he had already noted from the police reports. "Outside the saloon...did you see anyone?"

"What's that?"

"Was there anyone on the street?"

"No, we didn't see a soul out," Willis said. "It was pretty dark out there and nothin' was moving, not a—"

"I did," Royston cut in, as much, it seemed, to get his companion to shut up as to offer the information. Again, Valentin and Willis had cause to stop and gape at him.

"You saw what?" Willis said.

"I saw someone on the street." Royston still refused to pull his gaze from the window.

Valentin studied him. "Someone you recognized?"

Royston shook his head and his eyes made the briefest flinch. "No one I knew," he said.

"Can you describe him?"

"No, I can't," Royston said, sounding short and sour. "All I know is he was wearing one of those long coats. A duster. That's the only reason I noticed. Don't see them much anymore. Not in the city. Couldn't see his face, though."

"When the hell was this?" Willis crabbed, irked at losing his position at center stage.

"It was while we were standing on the corner," Royston said. "He was across the street."

"Then how come I didn't see it?"

"Because you and Bedford was too busy having a spat about where you were going next. And you were stumbling drunk." He paused. "But Bedford saw him, too."

"Can you tell me if he was short or tall?" Valentin said.

"More like tall," Royston said. "I think."

"What happened to this person?"

"Don't know. He was there for a few seconds and then he was gone." His frown deepened. "Hell, maybe I didn't see anyone at all." He looked at Valentin for the first time since they'd walked in. "Are we finished?" he said. "I've got business."

Valentin looked at Willis. "Can you think of anything else?"

"I, uh...uh..." Willis shook his head, chagrined at having nothing more to tell.

"Thank you both," Valentin said.

Willis issued a cheery good-night. Royston barely nodded, and the two men ambled out into the falling night.

Valentin was about to leave as well, then decided to sit for a while. The saloon was still quiet, so he ordered a small whiskey and carried it to the table near the window, where he could watch the eddies along Basin Street.

The street traffic picked up, and more souls began drifting through the door. In another two hours, there would be a small crowd on hand. Sunday was often regarded as a day of rest and Monday a day to open quietly. Though Fewclothes would be plenty rowdy the rest of the week, this night they would have only a professor at the piano. The sporting girls and their rounders would come by, taking the night off from the action. Who knew who might walk in? The thought gave Valentin a start, and he drank off his whiskey, left a Liberty quarter on the table, and made his way out the door, heading for home.

EIGHT

The whispers first broke out when the maid who had greeted the policemen at the Kanes' door told the maid at the next address, who told the lady of the house, who told her friend across the street. Soon tongues were wagging like flags in a stiff breeze as the word went over picket and wrought-iron fences, up and down the banquettes, and into the stores, so that hours before the story in the afternoon edition of the *Daily Picayune* and the *Sun* hit the street, it was already old news from one end of the Garden District to the other.

At the stroke of ten, a black carriage pulled up to the Kane home on Third Street, and a man in a tall black hat and a shiny black suit stepped down and went inside. Before he left, his driver carried a wreath of black roses that was in back of the carriage and placed it on the front door.

Anne Marie Benedict heard about what had happened in a telephone call from Mr. Delouche. The attorney first asked after her mother's health, then her own, then took a dramatic pause and proceeded to relate in a few somber sentences that over the weekend Charles Kane had fallen into the river and drowned. A dreadful accident, he explained, and took another of his leaden pauses.

It was all she could do to steady herself. It was a good thing they were speaking on the telephone or he surely would have seen the way the blood drained from her face. She felt her stomach churn, and for a few seconds she thought she was going to be sick.

She knew from the silence that Delouche was waiting for her to say something. She couldn't speak, though, and stared at the wall before her, hoping that the attorney would excuse himself and ring off. He wouldn't, of course, so she made herself breathe deeply and hold on.

She had known Mr. Kane. Like her father, he'd been a major figure in New Orleans' shipping industry. She recalled absently that there had once been talk about one of his sons coming round to court her, which she nipped as soon as she met the young lout. He was too much like his father, a blustering, bullying sort. Finally, Kane's name had been on the letter she had pulled from the desk drawer, the same one she had laid before her father.

She blinked in concentration, trying to grab hold of the thoughts that were tumbling around in her brain. While she had always disliked Kane, she hadn't wished him dead. Not him or anyone else. He was, though, and only a week after her father's murder. The deaths had to be connected. Probably the same person had caused both, and it surely wasn't the poor Negro who was sitting in Parish Prison. Whoever committed the crime, she sensed that she was the one who had set it in motion. Though she didn't understand how. And that, she now realized, was why she needed St. Cyr.

She wanted Mr. Delouche to go away so she could think. No such luck; the lawyer, still unwilling to keep his nose out of the family's affairs, where it had been parked for the better part of two decades, stayed on the line. He went about addressing some minor matters relating to the estate that she couldn't follow.

Anne Marie was too distracted and didn't catch a word of it. Then she heard the name "St. Cyr."

"I'm sorry, what did you say?"

"I was asking if Mr. St. Cyr has come up with any useful information." She could tell by his clipped tone that he was still peeved about her going against his advice and hiring the detective. Though he'd had no better luck dissuading her when she called him on Saturday about the autopsy report, he wasn't giving up.

"Please consider setting a limit on his time," the attorney was saying, the pout still in his voice. "Otherwise, he'll bleed you dry."

Oh, yes, and that's your job, Anne Marie was thinking. What she said was, "He'll be on the job for a while. He believes this Lee is a scapegoat."

"The police say otherwise," Delouche retorted.

"I don't think the police know a damn thing and I don't think they care, either," she said, too sharply. Abruptly switching to a smooth tone, she added, "But, of course, you'll be my first call if he comes up with any useful information."

The beat of thick silence told her that he didn't believe she'd do anything of the kind. He murmured a sighing good-bye.

Relieved, Anne Marie laid the hand piece back in the cradle. She wasn't about to give the attorney news about St. Cyr. She hadn't told him or the detective about the call she received the day before from a man named George Reynolds. Now it came back to her.

The phone had rung and when she picked it up, Reynolds identified himself, half stuttering over the introduction. She remembered his name in the funeral guest book, though she didn't recall meeting him.

"I was wondering... has there been any more word about this terrible tragedy?" He sounded like he was gasping for breath.

"What kind of word?"

"Who might have been responsible..."

"We don't know that."

"What do the police have to say?"

She'd had one too many brandies, and without thinking about it, blurted out that the police had made only a halfhearted effort, then arrested a man who wasn't guilty. So she had engaged a private detective to look into it. When Reynolds asked if the detective was a Pinkerton, she told him it was a fellow who knew the back-of-town streets better that any of those operatives out of the Hibernia Bank Building, and that she had confidence that he would do a good job. She heard herself speaking these bleary words and wondered precisely when she had become an expert on the relative worth of New Orleans' private investigators.

Reynolds didn't say why he was so concerned, and before she could ask him, he thanked her and broke the connection.

Thinking about that call, the one from Delouche, and the news about Charles Kane, she conjured an image of a tangled knot of dirty twine, the world of the men who had been her father's associates. And Mr. Henry Harris had his fingers on every strand.

She had known Harris's hovering presence through all the years she was growing up. He was more an institution than a person, the embodiment of an organization that tainted everyone who worked in the industry, from the lowliest colored janitor right up to men like her father, who looked up to him as some kind of deity. Even after her father was dead and done, Harris's hand reached out to touch her.

Harris had a public presence as well. He had never been shy about his views, and he seemed to believe that his wealth was in direct proportion to his wisdom. She had read his screeds in the newspaper, filled with an imperial disdain for those he considered of lower class. He was known to have funded various organizations dedicated to the supremacy of what he considered true Americans.

She had met him once or twice as a young girl and had disliked him instantly, even at that young age sensing the cruelty that enlivened his eyes and put a knife edge on his speech. Now she remembered with a small smile that she always thought Harris looked like the groom on a wedding cake. His riches couldn't buy him physical stature. He would always be a small man.

As the years passed and his wealth grew to fantastic proportions, he stayed in their lives. Her father had been a part of his royal court; willingly, and without shame, or so she thought until she laid the letter before him as he sat at the kitchen table.

She didn't want to think about that now. Turning away, she went into the kitchen to fetch a cup of coffee and carry it upstairs to wake her mother.

As Betsy placed the cup and cream and sugar on the tray, Anne Marie became aware that the maid had said something to her. "Excuse me?"

Betsy gazed at her, frowning. "Are you all right? You look a little sick."

"I'm fine," Anne Marie told her. "What did you just say?"

"I said your mother wouldn't let me change the bed this morning."

"I'll take care of it," Anne Marie said. She carried the tray to the door and stopped there. "Betsy, do you know who Henry Harris is?"

"I've heard the name," she said. "He's some rich man, ain't he? What about him?"

"Nothing," Anne Marie said, and went out of the room.

Mrs. Benedict roused herself enough to sit up in the bed, and the sheets and blankets gave up a musty smell. Anne Marie decided she wasn't going to get into a battle over it this morning.

"How are you feeling?" she asked.

"Who called on the telephone?" Mrs. Benedict inquired. She had gotten an idea in her head that Betsy and Anne Marie were deflecting important calls.

"It was Mr. Delouche," Anne Marie told her.

"Did he wish to speak to me?"

"No, Mother, he wanted to tell me something." She offered the cup and saucer, and her mother took it, though reluctantly. "Do you remember Charles Kane?"

Mrs. Benedict began to shake her head, then stopped. "He was one of them," she said.

"One of whom?"

The older woman's mouth set grimly. "Why do you ask?" she said. "Is he dead?"

Anne Marie was taken aback. "Well...he is, yes."

Mrs. Benedict nodded. "Of course," she murmured. "He sold his soul."

"Who? Kane?"

"No, your father." She gave Anne Marie a sly look. "You know very well what I mean."

Anne Marie sat down on the bed. Her mother was having a rare lucid morning, and she wanted to make the most of it. "He didn't do anything of the kind," she said quietly.

"Where do you think all this came from?" Mrs. Benedict said, suddenly throwing her thin arms out to the walls and the rest of the house beyond. "Your father sold his soul to the devil."

Anne Marie felt sudden tears welling in her eyes. "Stop it. He could have made a success of himself no matter what he did," she said.

"But he didn't, did he?"

"No," Anne Marie said. "He didn't."

Mrs. Benedict sagged back on the pillows. "Oh, well...," she murmured. Then: "Is that nigger detective in the house? Or dago or Greek or whatever he is?"

"Mother…" Anne Marie caught herself. "He's not, no."

"Good, because he doesn't belong here."

"I've hired him to finish the investigation. I told you that."

"Yes, you did." The older woman gazed toward the window, wearily. "And you'll be sorry."

Anne Marie stood up. "Are we ever going to get rid of him, Mother?" she said.

Mrs. Benedict looked at her again, blinking. "Who?"

Now it was Anne Marie's turn for a sly smile. "Drink your coffee," she said. "Betsy will be up with your breakfast."

She went down the hall to her room to change her clothes. She had a feeling Mr. St. Cyr was going to show up, and she wanted to be ready for him. So engaged, for a few quiet moments, she was able to keep Charles Kane, George Reynolds, and especially Henry Harris out of her thoughts.

It had taken awhile for Kane's name to circulate through the police ranks and for the patrolmen to come forward to report encountering a gentleman who claimed to have witnessed something very strange happen to the victim. It took more hours for the detectives to identify and locate the individual in question.

Two police detectives arrived on George Reynolds's gallery at a few minutes past noon, having first visited the subject's place of employment and learning that he had stayed home sick that day. George opened the door, took one look at their faces, and immediately felt a sinking weight in his gut.

The two men were dressed in suit coats and high-collared shirts, and each wore a derby. They looked much like twins, except one had a trimmed beard and the other only a mustache. They regarded him with the same practiced copper stares.

He ushered them into the front parlor and had the maid fetch coffee. Once they were seated and served, they took turns stating the facts. The body of Charles Kane had washed up on the banks of the river two days before. The coroner guessed that he had been in the water twelve to twenty-four hours, which meant he had gone in sometime between late Saturday night and early Sunday morning. The official cause of death was drowning, though the investigation was still open. They said they had a report from two beat coppers noting that on Saturday night, a Mr. Reynolds had claimed that Kane had been abducted right before his eyes. Then they waited.

George steadied himself and recounted the evening to the best of his memory, feeling his face flushing from the first word.

"He was walking away...and when he got to the corner of Burgundy, something happened. I saw a shape, a dark shape, come up on him, and at first I thought it looked like a bird, and then he wasn't there. He had just, uh...disappeared."

"What kind of bird?" the bearded detective said. George wasn't sure if he was making sport of him or not.

"I didn't say it was a bird," he said. "It just looked that way. It was very dark out there."

The two detectives exchanged the same sort of glance the patrolmen had shared that night on the banquette. Only these two followed it with looks of suspicion, as if they were thinking he had created the bizarre tale to cover his own guilt.

He was startled. The idea that he could have murdered Kane and then dumped his body in the river brought a clumsy smile, followed by a strained laugh.

"Did we say something funny?" the detective with the mustache inquired.

George shook his head, sobering. He was dazed by the coppers' act, switching from a yawning boredom to sharp interest, two lizards sleeping on a sunny rock, snapping awake when something edible came into range. They posed more questions, back and forth, like they were tossing a ball. Their queries seemed rather pointless, and once they figured that he likely wasn't guilty of anything, their inquiries became perfunctory, as if they were reading down a list. They requested the telephone number at his office and told him to be available for more questions. He saw them to the door. He had to force his hand steady to turn the bolt.

Early as it was, he wanted nothing so much as to rush to Basin Street and find Justine. He needed a place to hide. He knew she cared little for him, that her affections were offered at a certain price, and if he didn't pay, he wouldn't get past her door. Those were the rules, of course. He wasn't even thinking about that now. He simply yearned for her sweet calm and the refuge of her upstairs room, where no one could find him.

He felt confused and frightened. It hadn't been a dream or a mirage, no matter what those detectives thought. Someone or something had rushed from the shadows of Burgundy Street and swept Charles Kane away, turning him invisible, and sometime later had dropped his body in the brown waters of the Mississippi. He wondered for a blank moment if Charles had been dead before he went in.

He recalled again how they studied him with their cool copper stares, as if he was something they were getting ready to devour. Then their gazes went flat, passing over him and on to other matters.

He caught a movement out of the corner of his eye and turned his head to see his wife standing in the doorway. Before she could start worrying him for information that she would turn into gossip to chew over with the other useless wives, he muttered something about having to get to his office, grabbed his coat and hat, and hurried out the door.

When Valentin walked into the empty saloon, he found Beansoup at a table, digging into a pile of peppered eggs and Italian sausage. The kid gave a start, his face flushed pink, and he looked a little nervous.

The detective said, "Good afternoon," and treated him to a puzzled glance.

Frank Mangetta came out from behind the bar with a coffee for Valentin. "He's got some news for you," the Sicilian said.

Valentin pulled out the chair. The kid emptied his mouth, took a swallow of his own coffee, and said, "You hear about the fellow they pulled out of the river?"

"What fellow?"

Beansoup produced a furtive, eyeball-shifting look that was so comical that Valentin almost laughed out loud. He was serious, though.

"They pulled this fellow name of Kane out of the river on Sunday," he said. "He fell in and drowned."

"Too bad for him."

"That ain't it, though. Word is he was on the docks and did business with Henry Harris, just like the one that got killed on Rampart Street."

Valentin's cup stopped in midair. "How do you know about this?"

"Well, I *listen*," Beansoup said, as if it was a foolish question.

The detective stared at him. Frank raised his eyebrows.

"You hear this?" he asked the saloon keeper, tilting his head toward Beansoup.

"I heard it," Frank said, shaking his head and frowning.

When Justine passed Miss Antonia in the hallway, the madam was wearing a familiar look, the one that broadcast that she had a delicious piece of gossip that she was just aching to share. Usually, it was about one of their regular customers. One time, a high police official had been spotted dancing in the parlor of one of the houses on Conti Street where men dressed as women. Another patron was caught embezzling from the family business in order to support the morphine habit of a thirteen-year-old paramour. The wife of yet another had walked in on her husband and two girls at Grace Lloyd's, and hell would freeze over before he finished paying for that indiscretion.

Justine did her best to avoid this overheated gossipmonger-ing. She didn't need any more reminders of just how tawdry Storyville could be.

This was something else, though. After they passed each other, Miss Antonia said, "Justine, dear? A bird flew in my win-dow, just this morning."

Justine stopped out of courtesy. "Yes, ma'am?"

"There's a rumor going round about Mr. Valentin and a white girl."

Justine did her best to keep her face passive. "Well, he does manage to pass," she said, knowing how weak it sounded.

"A white woman can bewitch a fellow, if he's not careful," the madam said in a singsong voice. "Even that one." She shook her head slightly. "Maybe he's leaving Storyville behind altogether."

Justine knew that Miss Antonia was delivering this piece of news in the hopes that it would turn her away from the Creole detective. The truth was, it did nothing at all. She didn't expect anything from him, anyway. Though the madam was right about white women. They were pale and thin, and many of them looked like they couldn't fuck any good if their lives depended on it, but they did seem to cast spells on men of color. She just never figured Valentin for one to fall for it. Though he wasn't the same person, any more than she was.

An hour later, as Valentin was unlatching the Benedicts' front gate, he happened to glance up to see the widow's figure at one of the second-floor windows. Her silhouette went away as he stepped onto the gallery and up to the door.

This time Betsy led him to the back gallery, which ran the entire width of the house and was enclosed with screening. He had a view of a flower garden that needed tending. Wisteria and morning glories hung over the fence and trellises and around the gazebo. Betsy offered him a chair, and he sat for a few minutes, watching the butterflies float and bees levitate from bloom to bloom in the dappled sunlight.

Anne Marie appeared, wearing a simple walking dress. She had decided to forgo her fancier attire for something more common. Valentin knew enough about women's private appointments to guess that she would be wearing only a thin camisole rather than a full corset underneath. He was enjoying the image that went with these thoughts as he stood to greet her.

She said, "Sit down, please. Betsy's bringing coffee." Apparently, Betsy had not been aware of this and she looked surprised, then piqued, at being ordered away.

Anne Marie settled into the second chair. Instead of facing the garden, she turned in his direction, her hands clasped in her lap. It was something of a bold move for a young lady of class, and he got the distinct impression that it had been calculated.

"What do you have to report?" She came up with a thin smile. "Mr. Delouche has been inquiring."

"Not very much," he admitted. "I saw the autopsy. There were no surprises. I can tell you that what happened was not a robbery."

"How do you know?"

"Whoever shot your father stood back a ways to fire."

"And why is that not a robbery?"

"Because a thief will step up, show his weapon, and demand the goods," he explained. "So he's fairly close in. If the victim resists or tries to fight, he might shoot. That would be close range. No more than three or four feet."

"So how do you—?"

"A pistol fired at close range leaves powder on the clothing and the flesh," he said. "There was no mention of powder in the report. Also, there was some information..." He hesitated. "...about the nature of the wound itself that tells me the shot came from a distance."

Anne Marie's face paled a little. "I see." She twisted her fingers into a nervous knot. "But this person could have decided he wanted Father's possessions and the easiest way was to...to just...draw his pistol...and kill him." She looked up. "Isn't that possible?"

He shrugged. It was possible, though not likely. A Rampart Street thief would know how to pull off a heist. It wasn't something he wished to debate, though.

"What else?" she said.

"Have you heard about Charles Kane?"

"Yes, I heard what happened." She had answered too quickly, meaning she had prepared for the question.

"Your father and he had shipping companies on the river. They both did business with Henry Harris."

"That's right."

"And both died in the space of a week."

"My father was murdered. Mr. Kane drowned in the river."

"That doesn't mean they're not connected."

"How would that be?"

"Perhaps you can tell me."

She gave a start. "Excuse me?"

He backed up, shrugging casually. "Is there any reason you can think of why someone would want both your father and this Kane fellow dead?"

Her brow stitched and her lips pursed, as if the question was preposterous. It was a good act.

"I don't," she said. "I barely knew Mr. Kane."

"When was the last time your father saw him?"

"Years ago, I'm sure."

"Two men ran companies in the same business in the same place, and they both die less than a week apart. I don't think it's a coincidence."

"Well, you're the detective," she said archly.

"I am, yes, ma'am," he said.

The tense silence that followed was interrupted when Betsy stepped in with coffee. He was thinking of a different tack when Anne Marie said, "My father was a decent man. No matter what anyone says." Her tone wasn't defensive at all; more ruminative, as if a door in her memory had opened and she was peering inside. "He used to have quite a name around New Orleans," she went on. "He did very well in business. He was in all the prestigious social clubs. We had everything we needed and more. As you can see." She looked at him directly, though her stare was not clear. "My father was successful. He was *important*. And not because of Henry Harris, either."

She looked like she expected him to dispute this. Then she switched again, picking up a cup and holding it in her hands as if warming them. Valentin looked at her, then stole a glance at Betsy, who had retreated to the kitchen doorway to listen. He took the second cup and returned his attention to Anne Marie. "Is there anything you want to tell me?" he asked.

"About what?" Her voice remained distant.

"About your father. And this Kane fellow."

Her gaze came to rest on him, and again he saw something strange in her eyes. "I don't know anything more," she said deliberately. "But maybe his mistress does."

Valentin stopped to stare at her. "Excuse me?"

She all but laughed in his face. "He kept a quadroon," she said. "You didn't know about that? Oh, yes. I knew all about her. So did Mother. She's very pretty. She was at Father's funeral. She stayed in the back, but she was mourning like she was his wife."

Valentin again glanced at Betsy, then returned his attention to Anne Marie. "Your mother knew?"

"Oh, yes. It had been going on for years. It's not uncommon. As I'm sure you know."

Valentin was thinking of a way to approach the subject that had come immediately to mind when she said, "If you've got an idea that what happened to him was a scorned wife's revenge,

the answer is no. My mother didn't care. Not one bit. She wel-
comed it." She leaned a few inches closer and lowered her voice
confidentially. "She's one of those women who found acts of
love...*distasteful*. As far as I know, her last act of passion with
my father was the one that produced me."

She sat back, a coy smile playing faintly around her mouth.
Valentin felt his face getting hot. He had spent more nights than
he could count frolicking with sporting girls who sometimes
cried out in the crudest language, but something about this
pretty American miss making a vague reference to that same act
embarrassed him. She noticed the color in his cheeks and gave
him a cunning look.

He quickly moved on. "If not your mother, then perhaps this
other woman..."

"Her name is Sylvia Cardin."

"Maybe it had to do with her. Maybe there was someone
else in the picture. Someone else interested in her favors. I've seen
those kinds of disputes before."

"I haven't thought of that," she said. Valentin again detected
the hesitation in her voice. "I suppose it could be." She stirred
her coffee in an absent swirl, her gaze now troubled. He guessed
that she was wrestling with the notion that she had blurted too
much. Though he would have found out anyway.

"Do you know where she lives?" he said.

"In the French Quarter, I believe. You'll have to ask Mr. Delouche. He was the one who took care of her needs and gave her
money."

She seemed to be indulging a certain sniveling delight that
she had sprung something on him, something he should have
known. In any case, he needed to counter her in some manner.

"How is your mother feeling?" he asked.

"Mother? She's"—her smile went away—"doing as well as
can be expected."

"What medication is she using?"

"Excuse me?" Her eyes flashed at Betsy for a brief second.

"Oh, she didn't say anything," Valentin told her. "I know the signs." Anne Marie's face took a cool set. "How serious is her addiction?"

"She doesn't have an *addiction*," Anne Marie said. "She has a prescription from her doctor." Her back stiffened. "What does this have to do with your investigation?"

"Probably nothing."

"Then we don't need to discuss it, do we?"

"No, ma'am."

"Are you finished with your coffee?" she said.

He put the cup down, got to his feet, and thanked her for her time.

Betsy followed him out, her dark eyes all sly. He didn't hear the door closing until he had reached the banquette.

Solomon's customer cradled his horn to his chest like it was a child, threw his free hand up in grateful farewell, and went out the door. Before the pawnbroker could come around to the counter to lock it, it swung open sharply. A shadow blocked the light from the street and Solomon blinked, just barely making out a man's hulking figure.

"Yes, sir, can I help you?"

The customer didn't answer. Solomon made a shuffling retreat behind his counter. Though he was by nature a peaceful man, he kept a loaded .32 pistol handy. The items on his walls and especially those in the glass cases were just too tempting. He'd pulled the weapon a half-dozen times and felt no hesitation about firing it if he had to. He now dropped his hand to grasp the wooden grip of the revolver.

"How can I help you?" he repeated.

"You can help yourself," the tall man said.

"How's that?" Solomon inquired politely.

"Are you doing business with St. Cyr?"

The question caught the pawnbroker by surprise. Then he recovered. "I do business with a lot of people," he said.

The tall man stepped forward, now all but looming over the counter. Solomon took in his features: a broad, scarred face; stiff, wide mustache; blank, pale eyes.

"Listen to me, Jew, I didn't ask you about a lot of people, I asked about St. Cyr."

Solomon lifted his chin to regard his visitor through his spectacles. "Do you have something to pawn? Or do you wish to make a purchase?"

The tall man studied him, almost smiling. "I want to purchase whatever that fucking Creole brought in here."

"Not for sale," Solomon said.

Leaning forward, eyes glinting, the tall man said, "Then I'll just take it."

A second later, he was staring down the barrel of an Aubrey Hammerless.

The pawnbroker said, "As I mentioned, it's not for sale." His birdlike eyes were dead calm.

The tall man took a hesitant step back. He regarded Solomon for a moment, giving a slight shake of his head. Then he turned for the door. Before he made his exit, he paused to say, "I'll give your regards to Sophie." He winked, put a silencing finger to his lips, and went out, banging the door behind him. Only then did the pawnbroker go pale and let out a shuddering breath.

In another half hour, Valentin was on St. Charles Avenue, stepping to the door of Maurice Delouche's law office. It seemed the attorney had taken a page out of Picot's book, because Valentin was made to wait the better part of an hour before he was summoned. He spent the time reading through a copy of *Harper's Weekly* that was on the low table.

Delouche offered him neither a greeting nor a seat. He

merely raised his eyebrows in the most perfunctory way. Two could do that dance. The detective helped himself to one of the chairs and returned the attorney's stare. Delouche tolerated it for as long as he could, then dropped his pen with a snap and said, "Well? Are you going to sit there all day? What do you want?"

"Sylvia Cardin," Valentin said.

The attorney looked surprised, then closed his eyes as if he was enduring a spasm of pain. "Who told you...?" He sighed. "What about her?"

"I want to see her," Valentin said.

"She doesn't know anything," the attorney said. Valentin didn't bother to argue. Delouche sat back, looking old again. "You want me to arrange it?"

"I don't need you to arrange anything. I just need her address."

There was a long pause, and then the attorney gave a little cough and pulled open his desk drawer. He drew out a leather-bound book and opened it with his thin white fingers. He stopped at a certain page, picked up his pen, and wrote something on a slip of cream-colored paper. He put the pen down, closed the book, and stored it back in the drawer. Then he folded the slip of paper and pushed it to the edge of his desk. This was all performed in a moody silence, the only sound the ticking of the Junghaus clock on the wall behind Valentin's head.

The detective picked up the folded sheet and tucked it in his pocket.

Delouche lifted his pen once more and said, "Now, if you'll excuse—"

"How long has Mrs. Benedict been addicted to morphine?"

The pen hung suspended in midair, and Delouche regarded him with a blank gaze, his dry lips in a straight line. He looked like a fish that had been pulled onto a riverbank and stunned with a rock.

"Mr. Delouche?"

The eyes shifted. "What was the question?"

"Mrs. Benedict has an addiction to morphine."

"She has a prescription from her doctor," Delouche protested faintly.

"For what condition?"

"Some female problem, I believe." Valentin could barely hear him.

"So she gets morphine?"

"That's none of my affair." Delouche grimaced. "So I've been told."

For a moment he felt charitable toward the old charlatan. It seemed he had at least one soft spot. He mulled that, then put it away. "What was the ring that Benedict wore on his right hand?" he inquired.

Now the attorney looked startled, as if shocked back to the present. Color rose to his ivory cheeks, and his thin eyebrows dipped fiercely.

"What's that again?"

"Mr. Benedict was wearing a ring on his right hand the night he died. Gold with a large blue stone."

The attorney hesitated, then said, "What if he was?"

"Do you know if it had some special meaning to him?"

A moment went by and Delouche moved his head slowly from one side to the other. "I don't recall any such ring. I only saw the man once every few months."

Valentin waited, but the attorney seemed to have deflated into a glum sack of skin over frail bones. He stood up. "Thank you for your assistance," he said.

He had just reached the door when Delouche called his name. He stopped and waited.

"We have no further business," the attorney said. "Don't come here anymore."

At that, Valentin realized he was getting somewhere.

———

When he got back to his room, he found a note that someone had tacked to his door. Solomon the jeweler wanted to see him at his convenience. After a visit to the bathroom to splash some water on his face, he hitched his suspenders and headed out once more.

Just as he reached Basin Street, a new Maxwell cabriolet whipped by, stitching like a sewing machine, a driver in livery at the wheel and a heavyset citizen bouncing in the backseat. He watched the automobile chatter along the street and then slide to a sharp stop in front of Antonia Gonzales's mansion. The stout fellow lurched down and climbed the steps to the gallery.

Valentin crossed over and turned west for Canal Street.

Justine was summoned and she greeted Mr. George in the foyer. The man was getting to be a pain. Still, she knew Miss Antonia wouldn't stand for her sending him away, so she led him up the stairs to her room. Along the way, she called to one of the maids to bring a tray of coffee.

Once she had him in her room, she took his coat, undid the buttons on his vest, and settled him on the love seat. The maid came and Justine took the tray and poured for him.

"Could I have something else in there?" he asked. "I think I need it."

She took a decanter of whiskey from the corner table and dropped a healthy slug in his cup. She fixed an attentive gaze on his face, all part of the act.

He started muttering about the fellow who had disappeared again. "Do you know that two police detectives were at my door at noon today? They asked all kinds of questions. Made me go through what happened again. I know they thought I was an idiot. Or making the whole thing up."

Justine kept her face bland. She had been thinking exactly the same thing.

"They even gave me the eye, like I was the one who had

snatched him like that!" The thought of it made his face turn pale. He took another swallow of his fortified coffee and went back to his tale.

She pretended to listen as he babbled away. She had already heard the story and thought it was silly for a grown man to be going on so. She was beginning to think maybe he had gotten drunk and the whole thing was a product of his addled mind. Bodies were fished out of those murky waters every day of the week.

She was nodding with feigned sympathy and gazing long-ingly at the book on her bedside table when something he said caught her ear. She snapped out of her daze. "What was that?"

"What?" He stopped. "I said that...that Benedict's daugh-ter hired herself a detective. She's got this—"

"And who is Benedict?"

He gave her an exasperated look, as if he wondered if she'd been listening to him. "John Benedict," he repeated. "The first one who died. It was just a week before Kane did. I said Bene-dict's daughter hired a detective, some sharp from back-of-town, to look into it."

"Did she say his name?" Justine said.

"All I know is that he isn't a Pinkerton. Why?"

She waved a hand. "It's nothing. I know a few of those fel-lows, that's all." She took a deliberate moment, then composed her face into a mask of studied interest. "Can you tell me again from the start what happened?"

He frowned. "Again?"

"I'm just a little slow sometimes," she said demurely. "I really would like to hear it." She moved closer, laying one hand on the back of his neck and the other on his heavy thigh. "It's like a ghost story. And you tell it so well."

He swallowed, and then smiled thinly, putting on a brave front. "All right, my dear."

———

Beansoup walked along St. Louis Street, keeping an eye out for Charley Johnson, though there was no telling where the Negro might be. Anywhere from Canal Street to the edge of town, standing on some street corner and singing for enough money to buy himself a pint of Raleigh Rye or hunched in some doorway if he had one. Beansoup didn't mind. It was only because of his drinking that Charley allowed a young white boy to dog his steps and sometimes play a tune with him.

Beansoup was glad he did, though. He felt like he had finally found something he could hang his hat on. Up until a year ago, he had traveled the streets with Louis, a Negro boy out of the Colored Waif's Home. Then they split up. Louis rode the junk wagon and pounded a drum and blew a horn in the Colored Waif's marching band. Stung by what he saw as the younger boy's betrayal, Beansoup had started following Charley Johnson, who had come to town from the Delta to earn some dollars with his six-string banjo.

Even as a kid, Beansoup had been known to bawl out a raw and bawdy Negro song at a moment's notice. He had purchased a rusted, spit-encrusted harmonica at a pawnshop and tootled along with Charley whenever the singer was too drunk to care, and on his own whenever the fancy took him. After the used harmonica fell apart, he got the sisters at St. Mary's to order him a good one out of the Sears, Roebuck catalog, and he occasionally surprised those within earshot by playing something that was not a form of torture. Other than that, he roamed around Storyville in his seedy clothes, always on the lookout for a bit of action.

Now, as he walked along, blowing a song called "Country Blues" and clapping his free hand against his thigh for rhythm, a young colored girl stepped into his path. He stopped.

"You the one they call Beansoup?" the girl asked.

He nodded and winced; he had to get rid of the silly moniker. It made him sound like a little kid or a grown-up clown.

"I got message from Miss Justine Mancarre over at Miss Antonia Gon—"

"I know who she is," Beansoup said. "What's the message?"

"She want to see you whenever you can come along."

Beansoup digested the news. "Tell her I'll be there in a little bit," he said. He gave the girl a broad wink and dropped a quarter of his own in her palm, just like a regular rounder.

Valentin turned down Poydras Street and then three blocks east on Peters. Solomon had two customers, so he lolled about for a few minutes, examining the fine pieces of jewelry and the horns, guitars, and mandolins that were hanging on the walls. For a brief moment, he conjured a vision of a Sicilian with a broad mustache, some cousin of his father's, standing in their living room, plucking a *mandolinu* and singing a lament in a minor key. The door opened and closed as one of the customers made an exit, and the vision went away.

He stepped to a jewelry case and looked over a collection of diamond stickpins that would have done any uptown sport proud. Somewhere along the line, they had been pawned, always a sign of trouble. He wondered idly if any of them had been taken off a dead man and which—

"Mr. Valentin." The bell over the door tinkled as the second customer left, and Solomon was regarding him over the tops of his spectacles. "You got my message."

Valentin's first glance told him something was wrong. Solomon looked neither his cheerful nor somber self, but agitated, as if unnerved by something. It seemed odd for this gentle man. He was about to ask if there was some problem when the pawnbroker said, "I've got something to show you. Over here, please." Valentin caught the tiny slide in his voice.

He waved the Creole detective to the glass-topped counter and then went rummaging into one of the cabinets behind him. He turned back to place a tiny felt sachet on the counter and plucked out John Benedict's ring. He had to steady his hands before he could hold it up and direct a magnifying glass at it. Valentin gave him another curious glance.

"I showed your piece around," Solomon said. "I wasn't able to find out where it came from. It's not a local piece. Then I took a closer look, and it seems you have a *partikler* item here. I'm going to show you why." He handed over the glass and ring. "If you look into the stone and turn it to the light, you can see, there in the setting, some letters engraved. You see?"

Valentin held the glass over the stone and turned the ring until he saw a tiny impression emerge as if it was under dark water. Some sort of design. He drew the glass farther away to try and enlarge it, but the design only blurred.

"Never mind, you won't be able to read it without a loupe," Solomon said. "They're letters. Three of them, with a line underneath. Here..." He went into his vest pocket and retrieved a stub of a pencil. He found his receipt pad, licked the point of the pencil, and started drawing with a careful hand. When he finished, he turned the pad so Valentin could see.

<u>V V V</u>

"Is that supposed to be three V's?" he said. "Does it mean something?"

Solomon waggled some fingers. "I asked around about that, too. No one knows. It might be a fraternity of some kind."

"A college fraternity?"

"No, not like that. There's no V in the Greek alphabet. It's something else. Right now, I don't know what. The other question is why would you want to hide the letters in the first place. You only see them if you know they're in there. I think it's maybe a code. Something secret. Anyway, it's a first-class piece. Worth, I don't know, maybe four, five hundred dollars. A lot of money for a ring."

He dropped it in the little sack, tied it up, and handed it back to Valentin with a nervous motion.

"Maybe I should leave it here," the detective said.

The pawnbroker's eyes shifted worriedly. "Is that necessary?"

Now Valentin said, "What's wrong, Solomon?"

A few seconds went by, and Solomon sighed and related the visit from the tall man. When he finished, the detective said, "I know who he is."

"What's this about?"

Valentin held up the ring. "This."

"He...he said something about Sophie. About visiting her. How does he know?"

"I don't know," Valentin lied. The truth was a few simple questions would lead to the poor man's daughter.

"I'm afraid for her," Solomon said. "You think you could maybe take a moment and go see...just to make sure she's..." His voice cracked a little and he stopped.

"I'll do it today or tomorrow," Valentin promised.

"I'd be grateful." Solomon coughed. "Tell her...Tell her that her father says the door is still open here."

As Valentin left, the jeweler managed a wan smile and said, "I'll find out about those three V's for you."

Justine was sitting at the big oak table in the kitchen, drinking chicoried coffee and looking at a charcoal sketch that had been slipped into her hand.

It belied a secret. Thanks to her comely figure, she had gained an extra vocation. Once a week, she made her way out of the District and rode a St. Charles Line streetcar to Tulane University, then walked across the campus to a room in the basement of one of the austere buildings, where she stripped off her dress and posed naked before a dozen young men, art students all.

She never looked at the earnest fellows with their scratching pencils. They were only a few years younger than she, and yet seemed like such children to her. She did what the professor asked, collected her money, and went back to her life as a Storyville prostitute. She would have preferred that she was the one seated in a classroom, but that was of course impossible. Women weren't permitted as students in those halls. Still, it was a far step away from Basin Street and important to her because it meant she was something other than just a receptacle for a man's yancy. What she held in her hand was proof.

Though her eye was not practiced, the sketch seemed to her clumsy but heartfelt. It wasn't an accurate rendition, either; her breasts were not quite so heavy nor her hips that wide. Her face was not clear in the drawing, just a few rough scratches that were meant to suggest her features idealized in the young fellow's mind.

She couldn't remember much about him, just that he had bright eyes and red cheeks. None of the other young men had ever bothered to give her a drawing; and of course she'd not had any before. The one photograph she'd had taken years back had been lost. Valentin had never expressed an interest in having pictures of any kind. Which was strange, because he was friends with the cripple Bellocq, who was famous for his photographs of Storyville doves.

She put the drawing aside, and her thoughts shifted. It was no surprise that Mr. George had a connection to the case Valentin was working. Storyville was a small town in a small city and odd threads entwined. It was that simple. So she decided to contact him, to break down the wall that had risen between them.

She had been going through a terrible time just before he left, with a yen for paregoric that she couldn't put down. He had saved her from a dire fate when a deep secret had come to light right in the middle of the bloody case he was working. When it was over, he went away. When he didn't come back, she returned to the life of a sporting girl, to selling her charms and affections to the highest bidder. It was the only profession she had ever known; and a woman of her looks and skills earned well. From what she could surmise, Valentin considered this a final betrayal.

Her heart started to race. He had disappeared without so much as a good-bye and now had the nerve to be rankled because she had gone back to what she had been when he first found her? She was good enough for him then, wasn't she? What had he expected her to do? Become a nun? Go to work in a shop? Clean toilets? Just to protect his wounded feelings? Probably so; a man whose pride was offended would expect exactly that.

Things had been so peaceful. She was lonely, but that was nothing new. The gentlemen she entertained were well-to-do dullards who seemed unable to think of anything but money. She was used to that, too. Why couldn't he just stay away and let things be? Why couldn't he keep traveling through those dark and empty American nights until he found whatever his brooding heart longed for, instead of coming back and upsetting her entire life?

Miss Antonia had passed on the gossip about the white woman, and then Mr. George had mentioned the daughter of the man named Benedict hiring a detective who worked Storyville. Justine had to consider that what she was doing was nothing more than meddling for her own purposes, and that annoyed her all the more.

She found herself sitting upright, her brow furrowed, as if he was at that moment across the table, receiving a round scolding. She was so *angry* at him. So angry that it made her laugh at her own foolishness.

She was so caught up in the moment that she was startled to look up and see someone standing on the gallery, peering in through the glass. She recognized the face and beckoned with her hand.

When he stepped inside, she felt a catch in her throat. She had known Beansoup since the days when she lived with Valentin on Magazine Street. He had been a regular visitor then, often sleeping overnight on the couch in the front room and eating at their table. Though he had a bed with the nuns at St. Mary's and was most at home on the streets. Somewhere along the way he had taken it upon himself to look out for them. When they went apart, he tried playing cupid to bring them back together. It seemed very important to him.

Now he sidled inside and asked how she was doing this fine afternoon, playing it casual, as if he wasn't eager to see her again. His little performance was ruined when the maid who had delivered the message came in the door moments later. He had rushed there so fast that he had beaten her back to the mansion. He blushed, all abashed, and jerked his head. "She says you want to see me?"

Justine gave him a severe look that was full of affection and said, "Why don't you visit anymore?"

Beansoup's face turned a darker shade of pink. They both knew the reason. He had seen her, day by day, in the rooms she shared with Mr. Valentin on Magazine Street. Now she was a resident of a grand Basin Street sporting house. She saw the disappointment in his pale eyes.

He said, "I've got...I'm busy, you know...and I..." He went through the words like he was driving down a bumpy road. "...with this and that...you know..."

She had mercy and told him to take a seat. She got up to fix him lunch of a thick slice of bread, some Swiss cheese, a chicken drumstick, and an apple, along with a cup of coffee from the pot.

As she moved about, his eyes kept flicking below her face. She was wearing a thin shift, and the curves of her body swelled against the fabric with every motion. As silly as it seemed, he had always posed as some kind of pint-sized sport and ladies' man. Now he was old enough to be one in his own funny way. Yet he remained enough of a boy that she couldn't take offense.

She brought the plate to the table and slid it in front of him. As usual, he attacked the food. He was always hungry.

She watched him eat. "So what's this I hear, you're a musician now?"

He blushed some more. "Naw, nothin' like that...I just play along with this here gutbucket singer now and then."

"I heard you're pretty good at it."

"I wish I was," he said, and she was moved by the way he said it. Like he meant it. He ate some more, then took a sip of his coffee and said, "So, um...what was it you wanted?"

She sighed, and he watched her chest heave with some fascination. "It's about Valentin."

He looked up and cocked his head warily. "Oh. What about him?"

"I know you've seen him since he's been back."

Beansoup's pale eyes shifted. "He's around, sure."

"And how is he doing?"

"He's doin' all right, I guess," the kid said. "He was working at the Café. But he stopped that now. He's back at detective work. For some rich lady out Esplanade by the Jockey Club. She's a—" He stopped before he gave too much away.

"I know what he's working on," Justine said. "That's what I need to talk to him about. And I need you to carry a message to him."

The kid's eyes slid one way, then the other. "Well, I guess I can do that."

"Tell him I have information about his case," she said, dropping her voice. "If he doesn't want to see me, I can write it all down. Or we can talk on the telephone."

"All right, I'll tell him."

"Thank you." She gave him her most endearing smile and saw the color rise to his cheeks. "More coffee?" she asked.

Valentin was taking his time walking west on Canal Street. He stopped at the corner of Loyola, waiting to cross, when the Buick pulled up. The driver that had been with Nelson on Marais Street tilted his head toward the passenger seat.

"Someone wants to talk to you," he said over the chugging engine. It wasn't a threat, more a polite request. Valentin recalled how this fellow had seemed humored by the way he had talked to Nelson, and he got into the seat.

They turned the corner and went back east on Canal. When they reached Decatur Street, the driver cut north, past Jackson Square. The wind and road noise made it impossible to talk. It didn't matter; within another few minutes, they came to a stop in front of La Grenouille, one of the city's better French restaurants. Valentin knew for a fact that such establishments were only open for dinner and gave the driver a puzzled glance.

"Go on in," the driver said. "The door's open."

Valentin stepped down. "What's your name?" he asked.

"Louis Stoneman, sir." The voice was polite.

"Have we met?"

"Long time ago. In the District." He nodded toward the door. "Man's waiting for you," he said.

Valentin stepped onto the banquette and to the heavy door. As he pulled it open, Stoneman drove away from the curb.

He found Nelson standing in the archway between the foyer and the dining room. "In here," he said, and turned a thumb toward the dining room. Valentin walked in to find the room empty, the tables all set with white cloths and fine china and glasses in preparation for the evening. Then he noticed a man sitting at a table in the back corner of the room.

"Let's go," Nelson said, and led him across the floor.

The man at the table said, "Thank you, Mr. Nelson," and Nelson dipped his head and mumbled something in response. He backed away.

"Have a seat, Mr. St. Cyr," the man at the table said. "My name's William Little. I'd like a few minutes of your time."

Valentin sat, regarding William Little carefully. He guessed him to be in his fifties. Though he held himself stiff, in a carriage of cold command, there was something distinctly delicate about his features. His thin hair was going gray, parted on the side, and as neat as a pin, and his mustache was near white and trimmed to a tidy brush. The suit he wore was well tailored, a solid brown. If Valentin had to guess, he would peg Little as an accountant or banker. There was a glass filled with water, no ice, before him.

Eyes of a very pale blue studied the detective in return. "I'm a special assistant to Mr. Henry Harris," Little began. He waited for a reaction, got none, though it took a small effort on Valentin's part. Little studied him, frowned, sighed slightly. "You're conducting an investigation into the unfortunate death of John Benedict." Again, Valentin didn't respond. Little's gaze settled. "We'd like to put a stop to it," he said.

"Why is that?" Valentin asked.

Little looked perturbed by the question. His lips pursed for a petulant moment. "You know that Mr. Benedict and Mr. Harris did business over the years. He sat on our board after he retired. That makes it our concern."

Valentin frowned and scratched his ear, as if he didn't get the connection. Little clearly didn't care whether he got it or not.

"I'm sure you're aware that a man, a Negro named Lee, was arrested for Mr. Benedict's murder," he said with an air of impatience.

"I know about that," Valentin said.

"And yet you're still investigating."

"I'm working for Mr. Benedict's daughter. She's not satisfied that Lee's the guilty party."

"Why is that?" Little inquired. "Because you said so?" He didn't wait for an answer. "It seems that what we have here is a distraught daughter who is letting her emotions run away with her."

Valentin said, "She seems reasonable to me."

"There's more to this," he said, his tone shifting to snappish. "Mr. Harris is considering announcing his candidacy for United States senator. This would be a distraction. A man of his stature has enemies. There are newspapers in this town that delight in attacking him. The point is that they'll make more of this than is actually there. I'm sure you understand."

Valentin watched thoughtfully as Little came up with a faint and false smile.

"Mr. Harris is not one to allow cooperation to go unrewarded," he said. "So I'm prepared to make you an offer. You inform Miss Benedict that you're not available to continue your investigation. In return, we'll find a position for you. Security of some type. You'll be paid generously, certainly more than a pimp like Tom Anderson can offer. Though I understand you're not working for him any longer, anyway."

Valentin was not surprised that Little already had this information. It was on the street. What did concern him was that they had been watching him and he hadn't caught on. Picot's bumbling crew was one thing; this was something else, and he had to respect it.

At the same time, he detected disdain at having to do this particular piece of dirty work in Little's expression. His thin nose was all but curling as if he smelled a foul odor.

"Miss Benedict can dismiss me if she wishes," Valentin said. "I'm not going to quit."

"Tell her you changed your mind," Little said curtly. "Or that you looked into it and you now believe this nigger Lee is guilty after all. I'm sure you can think of something." He picked up his water glass. "That's simple enough, isn't it?" After taking a sip, he said, "Please understand that this isn't a negotiation. It's an offer for this one time."

Valentin thought it over for another few seconds, then pushed his chair back and stood up. "I've got to go back to work," he said. "Anyway, Mr. Harris doesn't really want to hire the likes of me, does he?" He smiled. "I just wouldn't *fit*."

Little sat back in his chair, his mouth turning downward as he regarded the detective with the kind of blank fixation usually afforded the victim of an accident. For a moment Valentin considered that he was making a serious mistake. If that was the case, it was too late now. He turned around and walked away from the table.

Nelson, standing by at the door, came on point like a hound, and Valentin wondered if he could get his sap around quickly enough to drop him. Nelson just glared, though, and let him pass.

"You're a goddamned fool," Nelson muttered.

"That I am." Valentin stopped. Without meeting the tall man's stare, he said, "You want to stay off of Peters Street. And out of the Jew Colony."

Nelson looked down at him, smiling. "What, you making a threat?"

"It's a suggestion," the detective said vaguely.

He went out the doors onto the banquette. Stoneman and the Buick were not in sight.

As he walked along, he considered that he had just said no to one of the two or three wealthiest and most powerful men in New Orleans. And yet Little had made no argument and no threats. These people were above that. He crossed the street through the late-afternoon shadows, realizing that, in some way, they would make him pay.

The sun was beginning to fall, turning the evening sky red as Valentin turned the corner, came up on Mangetta's, and saw two figures pacing the banquette. One was Beansoup, and the other one was the newspaperman Reynard Vernel.

They were so intent on eyeing each other that they didn't see him until he was two doors down the banquette. Beansoup broke away first. Vernel was right on his heels. They came to a stumbling stop, both talking at once. Valentin picked "Justine," "drowned," and "Benedict" out of the chatter. He raised a finger and glared, and they both shut up.

"What the hell's going on here?"

"I've got a message from Miss Justine," Beansoup blurted. "She wants—"

"I have something for you on the Benedict case," Vernel said before he could finish.

"I told him he could have told me and I would have passed it on," Beansoup said, glaring at the reporter.

Valentin said, "Justine?"

Beansoup turned back to the detective with a smile and a quick nod. "She said—"

"Wait a minute," Valentin interrupted. "What's this about Benedict?"

"A man was dragged out of the river," Vernel said. "They just identified his body yesterday. His name's Charles Kane. It turns out he worked with John Benedict."

"I know about that. It's all over town."

Beansoup gave a triumphant snicker. Vernel shot him a look, flagging only for a moment. "There's a good deal more to it," he said.

Valentin noticed Beansoup fidgeting so he turned to him and said, "Mr. Vernel's a guest. We should hear what he has to say."

As he hoped, put that way, Beansoup was mollified. "Sure," he said with a sidelong glance at the reporter. "Let's hear it."

"Inside," Valentin said, and opened the saloon door.

They found the room early evening quiet and took the table near the window. Valentin went to the bar and got a glass of whiskey for himself and Vernel and a root beer for Beansoup. He was halfway to the table when he turned around and went back. He told the bartender to dump the soda and add another whiskey in its stead. When he brought the three drinks to the table, he saw Beansoup's eyes light up. It wasn't the first time the kid had tasted hard liquor, of course. It was the first time he had sat at a table in a saloon like Mangetta's with two adults with drinks all around. As Valentin placed the short glass in front of him, his eyes flashed a message for the kid to go easy. Beansoup nodded innocently.

Valentin sat down. "All right, then," he said to Vernel. "Let's hear what you've got."

The reporter ran through it briefly. The body had washed up on Sunday. It had taken awhile to identify the victim. It turned out that they had to go find a crippled photographer named Bellocq to—

"Bellocq?" Valentin said quizzically. "Why him?"

"One of our photographers said that he was the one who took his picture. So the police sent someone, and Bellocq came in and looked at the body and said who he was right away."

Valentin took a sip of his whiskey. He stole a glance at Beansoup's glass, saw it was still full. He returned his attention to Vernel. "This is interesting and I appreciate you taking the trouble to come by. There's not much I can do with it, though."

Vernel caught the dismissal in the detective's tone. "It's some coincidence. The two of them dying so close together."

Valentin didn't want to engage the question with the reporter, so he said, "I'm looking into that."

"Because they were both in the shipping business. Did you know that?"

Valentin said, "I did."

"Did you know that they were both in a partnership with Henry Harris?"

The detective stopped to gaze at the younger man, his brow furrowing. "What partnership?"

"They started a company that ended up taking over a good-sized piece of the shipping business on the docks. And no one really knew about it. It was never mentioned in the newspaper."

"Then how do you know about it?"

"From the business licenses. They have to file one. And it has to be posted in the legal notices."

Valentin said, quietly, "When was this?"

"Twenty years ago—1890 or thereabouts. And now both the partners in that business are dead in the space of a week. I'm no *private detective,* but I'd guess that there might be something to that."

Valentin smiled. "So would I."

The reporter's face flushed with pleasure. "So maybe I'll write down some notes. What do you think?"

Valentin thought about it and said, "Be my guest."

Vernel drew himself up, his face flushing with delight. "Well, then, can I ask if you're done for the night?"

"I'll finish this and then I'm going to go pay a visit to Joe Kimball," the detective said. "I'd invite you along but don't think you want to be seen with me."

"I can't," Vernel said fretfully. "If I got caught..."

"I understand. You can catch up with me tomorrow."

Vernel drank off the rest of his whiskey and pushed his chair back from the table.

"Thank you again," Valentin said, and stood to shake his hand. Then he shook Beansoup's hand, though grudgingly.

Beansoup watched the reporter go out the door and turn west toward Bienville Street. He had a worried look on his face, as if he wanted to run outside and make sure Vernel kept going.

Valentin sat mulling the information the reporter had delivered. Then he turned to the kid, who was fidgeting about, and said, "Now, what's this about Justine?"

"She asked me to give you a message." He cleared his throat

and then went ahead and repeated the information. Valentin didn't comment at all. "So what do you want me to do?"

"Don't do anything," Valentin said.

"Ain't polite to just leave it hanging."

"I'll think about it." He ignored the kid's grimace and nodded to his whiskey glass. "Are you going to drink that?"

"I never liked it much," Beansoup said in a low voice.

Valentin glanced over his shoulder. No one was paying attention to them. Deftly, he switched Beansoup's glass with his empty one. The kid smiled quietly, then hunched his shoulders and got all serious again.

"You goin' to go see Miss Justine?" he asked once more.

Valentin was about to snap at him, then he noticed the look on his face, a mutt who gets kicked and still remains loyal.

"I will," he said. "Probably tomorrow."

Beansoup sighed with satisfaction.

"Now you need to be on your way," Valentin said.

The kid gave a wink and a nod. "Righto."

They went outside. Beansoup strolled off to Basin Street. Valentin walked to the corner of Bienville Street and turned south, taking the long way down to the *Daily Picayune* building.

He just missed seeing Justine, wrapped in her flowered shawl against the cool of the night, hurrying down Basin Street to catch a Canal Loop to the St. Charles Line car and her appointment in the basement of the building at the university.

She found herself eager to go to a place where she became someone else, her body put to use for something other than some well-to-do white man's pleasure. It would be as silent as church in the cavernous room, save for the scratching of the pens, the rustling of clothes, and the whispers of the instructor as he reviewed the work of his students. She would give the young fellow who had shyly handed her his drawing the sweetest smile of thanks that a figure model could afford. She imagined he would dip his innocent brow with pleasure.

Later, when it was over and she had dressed, collected her pay, and stepped out into the night, she wouldn't want to come back to Basin Street at all.

Joe Kimball let him in the alley door, smelling of Raleigh Rye and rancid cologne, the mixture akin to the reek of a funeral home full of dying flowers. Kimball wouldn't notice, his senses now pickled by years of soaking in alcohol; either that or he knew exactly the effect he was having and was using it as a way to keep unwanted visitors out of his domain.

He fixed Valentin with a delighted eye. "You got that fucking Dodge all in a fit. He got into all kinds of trouble for talking to you." He winked and let out a coarse laugh. "Seems there's a policy about sharing confidential newspaper information with a private investigator."

"There's more to it than that, Joe."

"I know. You're sticking your nose in Henry Harris's business."

Valentin's expression was only slightly surprised. "I'm beginning to butt into him every time I turn around."

Kimball slapped his back shoulder blade and chortled as he waved the detective to follow him. Once they reached his office, he poured drinks and they put their feet up on opposite sides of the desk. They could hear the traffic on the street through the two tiny windows above their heads. They drank and talked about this and that, and Valentin regretted having to get to business.

"I just came across some interesting information," he began, and related what Vernel had divulged about the secret business with Henry Harris, John Benedict, and Charles Kane as partners.

Kimball put down his glass, his eyes widening. "I never

heard about it," he grunted. "I know these goddamn pirates do it all the time though. It's easy enough. Just pay for the legal notice, come up with a charter...I don't even think you need an address, just a box at the post office, is all."

"Why keep it secret?" Valentin said.

"Because they didn't want people to know about it, Mr. Detective." Kimball grinned broadly. "I guess you need to find out why." He sipped his whiskey. "What else you got?"

Valentin told him about the ring. He described the inscription, hidden deep beneath the stone. He paused for a moment, his brow furrowing. "I wonder..."

"If maybe Kane and Harris would own one, too?" Kimball said. "You think they're the three V's?"

"Why V's, though?"

"And why hide it?"

They drank in silence for a few moments.

"Whatever else you know about him, Henry Harris is a strange character," Kimball said presently. "I think a lot of these rich fucks are that way. They all have something missing in their heads. Him and all that racial-purity business. Who knows what he's up to?" He mused a little while longer. "I'll have a look and see what I can come up with," he said. "You want another drink?"

"One more short one," Valentin said. He finished the whiskey in a couple quick swallows and got up to leave. "I'll come around tomorrow night," he said. "But if you find something before, just call over to Mangetta's."

"Oh, I will," Joe Kimball said, raising his glass. "Find something, I mean."

It was after 1 A.M. when Valentin passed by Antonia Gonzales's mansion and glanced up at the second-floor windows. He knew a dove as pretty and as skilled as Justine would claim the best room in a house, the front corner. There was a low light in that window, and as he looked up, he saw a shadow pass by. It gave him a start, and he quickened his steps along the banquette.

Justine had just come to the window and peeked out to see someone who looked much like Valentin moving away down the line. Though the lights were golden bright, the street itself was pocked with shadow, and she couldn't be sure it was him. As she let the curtain fall back, she saw another man emerge from across the street at a stalking gait and follow in Valentin's path. She let the curtain close and didn't see the second fellow who came along twenty paces behind the first.

Valentin sensed someone following him as he turned off Basin and onto Bienville. Fifty paces on, he felt the movement around the corner, a man skulking like a dog tracking prey. It wasn't Picot's man; this one was a slicker operator. Valentin was a little surprised and much relieved that he could still discern the way the air moved on a quiet street and what it foretold. Tonight it meant he was being tracked by someone with bad intentions.

Earlier that day he had opened his top drawer and dug into the back. He put his whalebone sap in his pocket and strapped his stiletto knife to his ankle. He decided to leave his pistol, though; now he wished he had brought it along.

He could still turn the dark street to his advantage. Mangetta's Saloon faced a taller building that blocked the silver light of the moon when it was hanging low in the night sky, as it was this night. Just as he was about to cross over to Mangetta's, he heard the click of a hammer being drawn back and stepped into a shadow, then sidestepped into the doorway facing Mangetta's.

In that quick second, the man on his tail lost him. In a small panic, the fellow raised a pistol, pointing blindly into the darkness. Valentin's sap whipped out of the shadows and down across his wrist. He let out a shriek of pain and the revolver went flying, then clattered on the cobblestones. Valentin used the same fist that gripped the sap to shove the stalker against the wall of the building as he swept his free hand down to come up with the stiletto. He pushed the point under the man's chin, freezing him in place. The fellow's eyes, black with dirty whites, rolled around. The detective moved a half step to the right to get a better angle and see if he recognized him.

Just as he made that move, he sensed someone behind him. Before he could turn around, cold steel cracked hard on the bone behind his left ear. Blood went trickling down his neck.

"Put the fucking blade down," a voice growled. Valentin didn't move. "I said drop it!"

The detective drew the knife away and let it fall onto the banquette. The man he'd pinned against the wall snickered, knocked his hand off, and grabbed his collar, returning the favor. Then he cracked him a good one on the cheekbone.

"You're gettin' out of this business with these here white folks," he said. His breath stank of sour whiskey. "And just to make sure you do, we're—" His gaze shifted, his eyes going wide, and he uttered a startled, "Hey!" Valentin heard a thump and a grunt, and the cold barrel of the pistol abruptly dropped away from his ear.

He jerked back, breaking the first man's grip, and was greeted by the bizarre sight of Frank Mangetta standing there, gripping a saxophone in his hands like a crooked baseball bat. The man who had had the pistol on him was on the banquette, holding his bleeding head and groaning.

In that confused moment, his companion snapped a Liberty .22 out of his pocket and held it on the two men who were still standing.

"Smiley, can you move?" Smiley, the man on the banquette, grunted a curse, and then started to crawl. "Come on, then, goddamnit!"

Smiley lurched to his feet and staggered away. His companion kept the pistol pointed and the two backed off until they got to Iberville Street. Then they ran north in a flit of jagged motion.

Frank, watching them go, said, "Shit! What the hell happened?"

"I caught the first one. I didn't count on the second."

"What was they after?"

"I think they had a message for me." He looked at Mangetta, standing there in his trousers, shirt, and suspenders, holding the battered horn in his hands, and started to laugh. "That's some weapon, Frank."

Mangetta held up the saxophone and inspected the dented bell. "I was cleaning up and I looked out the window and I saw you put that one against the wall. I went for the door. Then I saw the other one." He hefted the saxophone. "This here was lying on the table. First thing I could grab."

"Well, you got him good."

"I think it's Bob Camp's. He's gonna be mad."

"Tell him I'll pay to get it fixed."

They started back across the street. "What message?" Mangetta said.

Valentin shook his head. "He never got around to saying." He didn't know if Frank believed him, but there was no point in putting him in the middle of something.

They reached the other side of the street and Valentin held the door of the saloon open. "I'd like to buy you a drink," he said.

"*Grazie,*" Frank said. "I think both of us could use it."

NINE

Justine woke up thankfully alone. She lingered in the warm bed, letting her drowsy thoughts drift this way and that. She had just risen out of one of the dreams that took her back to the bayou where she was born and raised. Though terrible things had happened there, her reveries were for the most part kind. Mostly because she made herself recall the special things, like the way the sunlight would come through the green trees and dapple the brown dirt in the afternoon. In that same corner of her mind, she cradled the smells of woodsmoke, the feel of cool earth under her feet, the sight of the wildflowers that blazed like flames on the banks of the green water.

These thoughts led to a conjuring of the faces of her brothers and sisters, now lost to her. She prayed that they were safe; or at least safer than they would have been back on the bayou.

Sometimes she tried to imagine what each one in turn might be doing at that moment. Raising their children, going to work, laughing at life's joys. What more could anyone of color hope for? She and her older brother had rescued them and gave them a chance for decent lives, but at a sad price. She had made a devil's bargain, and it wasn't the only one. Lying there, thinking about that, she felt a tear well in her eye and run down her cheek.

She sat up, wiped her face, propped the pillows, and leaned back again, gazing out her window to see the sun poking long rays through puffs of rolling clouds. It looked like rain blowing in from the Gulf. She was ready; it would suit her mood.

As her thoughts cleared, she remembered that she had taken the step to send a message to Valentin and felt a small throb of panic. It was too late to do anything about it now. Beansoup had no doubt rushed to find the Creole detective, so whatever had been standing between the two of them would fall that day. Though she could always cancel it.

She let out a frustrated sigh. She was feeling foolish, like some schoolgirl who couldn't make up her silly mind. So she fixed her thoughts back to Mr. George's story of the crime that had occurred in the French Quarter, and the mention of a detective who had been hired by the victim's daughter.

She stopped to wonder if the rumors might be true, and he had been smitten by the young white miss. She didn't believe it. More likely the other way around; if he put his mind to it, Valentin could wrap even a genteel American lady around his finger. She was creating a little scene about the two of them in her head when a knock on the door interrupted her. If it was Mr. George, back again, all fussy and scared like some old woman, she swore she'd—

"Justine?" Miss Antonia called to her. "Open up, please. Something happened to Valentin on Marais Street last night."

Justine bolted from the bed and threw the door wide, her heart drumming. "What happened? Is he all right?"

Miss Antonia saw the look in her eyes and said, "Yes, he's fine." She pursed her lips in reproof. "Two fellows tailed him to Marais Street and had him cornered. But Frank Mangetta saw and came running out." Her eyes got merry. "The word is Mangetta laid one of them out with a saxophone! Jane the maid said he's been strutting around his grocery store like a dago rooster, telling everyone who'll listen and showing off the horn."

Justine stood there in a fixed daze as she recalled last night and the man who looked like Valentin being trailed across Basin Street and deeper into the District by a shadowing figure.

"But Valentin wasn't hurt?" she asked the madam.

"He was lucky," Miss Antonia said. "This time."

Justine murmured a thank-you for the information. The madam walked back along the hallway, wondering frankly if she was now going to have to tie the girl to the bed to keep track of her.

Anne Marie went to look in on her mother and found her still sleeping, the leaden slumber that came from the small apothecary vial by way of a hypodermic needle. She slipped out again, closing the door behind her. It had been her intention to talk to her or her doctor and get her to stop with the medication. She didn't need it. There was nothing wrong with her, except for lingering grief and the general emptiness of her days.

She hadn't done it yet. There was too much on her mind and, truth be told, she wasn't ready to face the monster that would surely appear if they tried to take the medicine away.

Betsy was in the kitchen, drinking coffee and perusing a copy of the *Mascot*. The headline had to do with a house that was reputed to offer women for the pleasure of customers of their own gender. The drawing that went along with the piece was appropriately lurid, with two sporting girls entwined in an embrace, one in her camisole, the other in a dress that was half undone. Anne Marie noticed how entranced Betsy looked as she struggled over the text. She wasn't surprised. Betsy's eyes often raked her when she was coming out of a bath or in the middle of dressing.

She let out a feigned huff of annoyance, and the maid quickly closed the newspaper, got to her feet, and went to the stove. She brought a cup of coffee to the table, then stepped away to start on breakfast.

"Wait a minute," Anne Marie said. "Sit down, please." Betsy

took a chair at the big table, looking perplexed and a little anxious. Anne Marie sipped her coffee, then put the cup down. "You and I are going to take a trip today," she said.

Since the Benedict case had begun, Lieutenant J. Picot couldn't keep his mind on his work and found himself at regular intervals staring out the window and muttering quiet curses. The man he had sent to dog St. Cyr had been hopeless, unable to keep pace with the movements of his subject, then unable to deliver any worthwhile information when he did. So he pulled him off and sent him to guard something. The lieutenant could only imagine what was going on as the detective wandered from point A to point B. All he knew for sure was that his life was about to get complicated again, thanks to one son-of-a-bitch Creole.

He was still mulling and muttering when the desk sergeant came knocking on his door. Picot waved him inside.

"That fellow St. Cyr?" the sergeant said.

Picot glowered, wondering if he'd been thinking out loud. "What about him?"

"He was attacked on Marais Street last night."

The lieutenant felt his pulse start to lope and came halfway out of his chair. "What happened?"

"He got jumped on by two fellows."

"Is he dead?"

"Naw, nothin' like that," the sergeant said. Slowly, Picot sat back down. "From what I heard, they had him good, but then that dago Mangetta got into it and they run them off."

"Was it a robbery?"

"Ain't no one said."

"How did you hear about this? Did he make a report?"

"No, Mangetta's got a big mouth. He was crowin' about it in his store, and the word's all over the District."

"I swear that nigger's got nine lives," the lieutenant muttered.

The sergeant said, "Sir? Which nigger is that?"

Picot chopped an annoyed hand in the air. "Nothing, never mind."

The sergeant backed out of the door, leaving the lieutenant sitting at his desk with his face all dark and pinched in frustration.

By the time Valentin got downstairs, it appeared that everyone in uptown New Orleans knew what had happened on the street the night before.

Valentin stepped into the grocery, took one look at Frank huddled with a couple of his *paisanos,* and understood. The saloon keeper had told one person, a mere whisper, and the word had gone out from there. For all his Sicilian reserve, Frank couldn't resist telling a good story, and when the first person came around asking if what he had heard was true, the tale was retold. And so on.

If Valentin had any doubt that this was what happened, it was washed away with the glance that Frank cast over his shoulder when the detective walked into the grocery.

He went into the saloon, and Frank came along a few seconds later, looking distinctly like a dog about to be whipped. Still, there was no way Valentin could get angry over it; the man had saved his life. Exasperation was as far as it went. "What the hell are you doing, Frank?" he asked.

"What? They already knew."

"I wonder how that happened?" He frowned. "Where's the saxophone?"

Frank hoisted a limp thumb in the direction of the grocery. Valentin threw up his hands.

"You ain't ate yet," Frank said, and hurried off to the kitchen. "I'm gonna go fix you a nice breakfast."

An hour later Valentin was ringing the bell on the downstairs door of the address on Ursulines. When nothing happened, he rang again. He heard the balcony above his head let out a soft metallic creak.

"Who's there?" The voice was low, without inflection.

The detective stepped back to the edge of the banquette and looked up. A woman in a soft cotton shift had stepped onto the balcony, her hands gripping the iron railing. She was tall and willowy, with smoothly angled features that marked her as Caucasian. Her milky brown skin marked her as something else. Her hair hung about untied, a mess of dark ringlets. Her eyes, large and liquid ebony, peered down with an odd distance, like she was looking at something past him. She didn't seem very surprised to find a stranger at her door. She also didn't seem to care that she was on her balcony in the middle of the morning wearing only a shift that was too loose for modesty.

Valentin enjoyed the view for another moment, then introduced himself and said, "I'm investigating the murder of John Benedict."

She tilted her head to one side. Now she noticed him. "Who sent you here?" she asked.

"I'd like to talk to you about Mr. Benedict's murder," he said.

Her beautiful deep eyes studied him with a faraway calm. "All right," she said. "Come up, then."

Her apartment reminded him of the one Justine had taken for a short while in her failed attempt to be a rich man's mistress. It turned out she was too unruly for that life and she quit him. Those rooms had the same kept look: pricey furnishings, expensive wood furniture, Persian rugs on the floor, good paintings and other adornments on the walls, all harkening to the privileges of wealth, more like a display than a home. He knew the bedroom in back would be even better appointed, with a huge brass or four-poster bed at its center. Indeed, there would be rooms like this all over downtown New Orleans, as part of one of the city's oldest traditions, the taking of quadroon and octoroon mistresses by married men of the moneyed classes.

Sylvia Cardin made her way around the perimeter of the room, her movements languid but still wary, like she might bolt at the first sharp sound. Valentin studied her more closely. Her face was a long and perfect oval, with high cheekbones, a round and pert nose, and those obsidian eyes with lids that were slightly hooded. Once she uncurled, she would be an inch or two taller than him. All in all, she was a presence that couldn't be denied and a prize for the man who could afford her.

At the same time, there were rough edges. Her eyes stayed cool, her lips were pressed tight, and her nostrils flared slightly, a predatory cat. Valentin could tell from her expression that his visit was not welcome. He didn't mind; it gave him something to work with. She was acting that way for a reason.

She performed a small ballet of arranging herself on a divan and waving him into the tufted armchair opposite. She opened a silver-plated box from the end table and took out a long French cigarette in creamy white paper. Valentin saw the strike box on the table and reached for it. She was ahead of him, though, snapping it up and catching the flame herself. He got the message and sat back.

"Thank you for inviting me into your home," he said, as he took out his notebook and pencil.

She gazed at the pencil poised over the page. "How did you find me?"

"Mr. Delouche gave me your address." He didn't mention the attorney's icy, injured silence and that he gave up the information as if it was being torn from his very flesh with pliers. She watched him, smoke swirling before her face.

"I asked who sent you here," she said abruptly. He decided it would be her last question.

"I've been engaged by Benedict's daughter to in—"

"Anne Marie."

"That's correct."

"He talked about her." Miss Cardin's voice was blank. "Now she wants to know what happened to him, after he's gone. Well, it's too late now, isn't it?"

Valentin took note of the strange turn in the conversation and went on. "When was the last time you saw him?"

"It was... over a month ago, I believe."

"Over a month?"

"That's right."

"Was it usually so long between your meetings?"

"No."

"Why this time?"

"Because that night I told him I didn't want to continue our... arrangement any longer."

Valentin noted the time interval. "Why was that?" he asked evenly.

"Because I didn't wish to be with him anymore." He glanced up, saw that her expression had turned hard, as if she was bolstering herself against something. His next question was forming when she sat forward and said, "When I was fifteen years old, my mother sold me to a man old enough to be my grandfather for one hundred dollars in gold coins. He was sickly and he didn't last. Then there was a wealthy gentleman who made promises to me. He went to California and never came back. After that, I met John Benedict. I'm not a harlot, sir. I'm no one's slave, either."

Valentin met her gaze for a moment. Then he put the strange diatribe away and went back to his question. "How long did you know Mr. Benedict?"

She hesitated, then settled again. "For seven years."

"That's a long time."

"It's seven years."

"Are there any children between you?"

"Why do you ask that?"

"I'm curious."

"Do you see any?" she said. There was a sudden crisp light in her eyes as she held her cigarette before her like an upended sword and met his gaze with her black stare.

"So the last time you saw him would have been three weeks before he was killed."

After a moment she nodded.

"Do you know the details of his death?"

"Yes," she said, and her voice got quieter, darker. "I heard all about it."

"Do you have any idea why he went to Rampart Street that night?"

"No, I don't."

"Did he ever go there before?"

"If he did, he never told me about it."

"You know what it's like out there?"

"I've heard."

"It doesn't make sense, a man like him, alone on Rampart Street."

She was sharp enough to notice that it wasn't a question and said nothing as she watched a curl of smoke rise up to the ceiling.

"Do you think he might have gone there after a woman?"

He got her attention with that one. She lowered her gaze to regard him calmly, not taking offense, a cool smile lightening her face.

She straightened her spine and pushed her chest and hips toward him in one curving motion, like a wave coming in, and at the same time lowered her brow very slightly, so that she gazed at him from the tops of her hooded eyes. It was an animal motion, flush of the force of her beauty, and she did it so well that it froze him for a moment.

She brought it on, casting a heated glance at him and making movements that somehow stirred a primitive scent of mating. Subtly, in one motion, she also pulled her shoulders back and spread her knees a few inches. Valentin felt a tiny electric tingle shoot up his spine.

"What do you think?" she said in a silky voice.

He pulled his eyes away with an effort and stared down at his notebook, moving his pencil in aimless circles. It was some show, a mere few seconds of energy that would still bring any man with a pulse running, perhaps right to his bloody end. And she would somehow make it appear worth the agony. He didn't know if he'd ever seen it done better.

But when he glanced up again, he saw that the effort of mounting the carnal display had been too much for her. As quickly as she had struck the pose, she slouched back into the cushions. Her face fell. She didn't look so striking anymore, still beautiful, but in a forlorn way.

Valentin lingered on the image, then pushed himself back to the business at hand. "Are you aware of any problems he was having? Any threats to his person?"

She shrugged. "He didn't say anything to me."

He glanced at his notepad. "Do you know anything about the ring he wore on his right hand?"

She paused. "He never wore a ring, except his wedding band," she said. "And he took that off when he was here."

"You never saw him wearing a ring with a heavy gold band and a dark blue stone?"

Now she looked perturbed. "That's what I just said, isn't it? Why do you keep asking the same question?"

He dropped that line and picked up another. "Do you know the name Charles Kane?"

"No, I don't know that person."

"He died over the weekend. Drowned in the river."

Sylvia kept her eyes steady.

"He was also in the shipping business. He was a partner in a business with Mr. Benedict." He paused. "And with Henry Harris."

If he hadn't been watching her, he would have missed the tiny flick of light in her eyes. And that when she put the cigarette to her lips, she missed the mark by a fraction of an inch.

"You do know him?"

"Know who?"

"Henry Harris."

"Everyone knows who he is," she said.

"Did you ever meet him?"

She paused, then shook her head again, now with a petulance that seemed more like she was refusing something that had been placed before her. "I think..." She considered for a moment. "John introduced me to him, at a dinner. It was years ago."

"That's all?"

"I was his mistress, not his wife," she said. She came up with a strange and unreadable smile. "I didn't go to many social events that Mr. Harris hosted. Because I don't believe he cares for being around colored folk. That's what he says all the time, ain't it?"

He could tell she was getting tired of him and his questions, and he didn't want to drag it out too long and lose her for later. He took a last look about the rooms, closed his notebook, and stood up to leave. "Thank you for your ti—"

"It was terrible what happened to John," she said, cutting him off. "He didn't deserve to die that way. But he was stubborn. You couldn't tell him anything. He wouldn't *listen*." She shook her head grimly. "I didn't want to stay in this arrangement with him. It was just time to stop. And now he's gone. We all need to leave it alone." She stubbed her cigarette out in the crystal ashtray.

Valentin looked down at her. "Miss Cardin?" It took her a moment to look up. "Did you have anything to do with his death?"

Her eyes took a set. "I'm not answering that," she said.

On that distracted note, Valentin went to the door and opened it. "If you think of anything you've forgotten, you can get a message to me at Mangetta's," he said. "It's in the District, on Mar—"

"I know where it is," she interrupted, her voice wavering oddly.

"All right, then. Thank you for your time," he said.

She was watching him. "What happened to your head?" she asked.

"It's nothing," he said. "An accident."

"You should be more careful."

He left her there, her beauty half hidden behind the gauze of smoke from her French cigarette.

When Tom Anderson arrived at the Café, he was greeted by the news about Valentin getting assaulted on Marais Street. He listened to the details, then went up the back stairs, pondering what in god's name he had started. He had thought he was doing a small service for a local politician and giving St. Cyr a chance to get back on his feet, all in a nice little package. Now his nice little package was blowing up as if it had been packed with gunpowder. The whispered word that there might be something more than a professional arrangement between the detective and his client was less surprising, though no less troubling.

Anderson had already had Chief of Police O'Connor, the family lawyer Delouche, and the city alderman Badel taking turns scolding him over it. Because it wasn't such a simple case, after all. Because it was now revealed that Benedict and the second victim, Kane, had both been in the shipping business, shoulder to shoulder with Henry Harris.

The name had as much weight as one of the many ten thousand–ton ships his factories built. Harris wasn't on the level of Pittsburgh's Carnegie, Detroit's Ford, or New York's Vanderbilt or Rockefeller, but he could sit at the next table. Anderson was not above standing in awe of Harris and his wealth and influence. Especially since Harris had not had it handed down to him, like so many lords of the affluent class. Like Anderson himself, he had built an empire out of almost nothing.

He had constructed his fortune on the ashes of the war, snapping up companies along the river from those once-proud and now-penniless defenders of the Confederacy. Harris was not a Southerner—he had claimed a bland midwestern heritage—and so he could take contracts denied to natives. He quickly amassed a small fortune, then a larger one, though he was still a dwarf when compared to the true robber barons of the cities in the North. He was good at business, better at warfare. The newspapers cast him as a gruff patriarch and a hero who had brought much wealth to the city. Even Bas Bleu, that impertinent newspaper wag, wouldn't touch Harris's exalted self.

Other gossip painted a picture of a tyrant, a man who indulged petty spites, even displaying signs of mental unbalance when he strayed away from making money. He gave to the church and all the correct charities, though he cared little about them. That was all his wife's doing. Anderson had seen photographs of the man who never smiled for anyone, much less the photographers. In truth, for all his public influence, Harris was said to be unnerved by even small crowds and the eyes of cameras, which these days were poking about everywhere.

He had for a time been a state senator like Anderson, though only for one term, to see if he wanted to run for a higher office. He decided that he despised local politicians along with the sluggish masses they represented. With his money, he wielded more power in a day than an elected local official could employ in a lifetime.

Anderson remembered him from those days in the state senate as an elegant and utterly unpleasant man. When he bothered to show his face, that is, which wasn't often. Though the two represented the same part of the state, Harris regarded Tom Anderson as a crude pimp and fixer, and spoke to him only through intermediaries.

On the rare occasion that Harris made an appearance in Baton Rouge, it was not for the people's business, but to propound certain views, railing on the senate floor like the worst of the Know-Nothings. When he quit the body, it was mostly from exasperation that so few local politicians shared his rabid opinions. Anderson hadn't heard much about him in years. His companies thrived, growing more prosperous and stretching out to engulf all sorts of ancillary businesses along the river. The word was he visited his office rarely, spending his time on his hundred-acre plantation at Nine Mile Point, along the Mississippi just north of the city, pondering a U.S. Senate campaign. It was said that he craved the power that only Washington could offer. Though he could certainly buy himself a seat, he still had to go through the tiresome motions of getting elected.

Simply keeping his ears open, the King of Storyville had learned other, more private information about Harris. He knew, for instance, that along with a wife and a litter of slothful and profligate children, Harris had kept a string of whores at his beck and call, all willing and able to endure certain unique kinds of pain.

As tasty as it was, Anderson would never use this information. In his most honest moments, he had to admit that he harbored a fear of Harris and men like him, who drew power from a source he could never summon. He knew that his name would be lost to history while Harris and his ilk would be revered for a century.

Now, thanks to Tom Anderson, a certain Creole detective was rousing the wrath of the Crescent City dragon.

Anderson knew that the attack on St. Cyr wasn't a robbery any more than Benedict's murder was. The Creole detective had little worth stealing and rarely carried more than a dollar or two in his pockets. No, this was something else. Anderson could envision the long arm of Henry Harris reaching out, and it didn't surprise him. Every time Valentin was turned loose on a case, the same thing happened. Doors that were closed flew open, loosing pandemonium. Anderson had imagined that this time it would be different, but again, St. Cyr had turned it right around. He let out a sigh of frustration as he stopped to wonder exactly how long it would take for the next body to appear.

It was the first time since just before her father's death that Anne Marie had wandered beyond the blocks around their house. For some reason, she felt like it had been much longer since she'd been away from the city.

She had picked a good day for it. The sun had come up a rosy pink through the morning mist and the branches of the live oaks with their new leaves. A light breeze carried scents of magnolia, oleander, and sweet apple. It was still cool, which meant that Anne Marie could wear a hat with a veil. Even better, clouds were coming up from the Gulf, bringing rain. They'd have use for an umbrella and that suited her purposes all the more this day. She didn't want anyone recognizing her.

She had decided it was time to make a foray into the devil's backyard, with Betsy as her guide. The Creole detective was prowling ever closer to her family affairs and she told herself it would be smart to step onto his territory for once. Of course, there was more to it. She had developed an insatiable curiosity about his sordid world. And, quite simply, she wanted to get out of the house and the neighborhood and be someplace *else*.

Once she explained it, Betsy was ecstatic, falling to the task with such zeal that Anne Marie had to tell her to settle down. The maid began by sending Anne Marie back upstairs for a day dress that was slightly fancy, the kind a higher-class Basin Street sporting girl would wear before dark. She herself would pose as the trollop's maid. The whole fiction was fantastic and silly and exciting.

The next problem was transportation. Neither of them could drive Mr. Benedict's big Oldsmobile, and it would be too obvious in any case. They decided to slip out the back and move through the alleys until they got to Esplanade Avenue, where they could catch a streetcar. Anne Marie trusted Betsy on this; she had seen her slip off this way a dozen times.

Before they left, she went upstairs, knocked lightly on the door, and went into her mother's bedroom. She found her propped on her pillows, a book open in her lap. It was the same volume that had been on the nightstand for months.

Anne Marie sat down on the edge of the bed. "We're going out," she said. "Betsy and I."

"Out where?"

"We need some things. We'll go to Mayerof's and some other stores. Is there anything I can get you?"

"No, I have all I need right here." She turned her head to the curtained window. "I used to love to take the air," she said. For a moment Anne Marie thought she was going to ask to go along. Then she felt ashamed. The poor woman never left the house. Since her husband's death, she had become all but paralyzed by the blend of grief and morphine.

"You have a lovely time," Mrs. Benedict said. "I'll be fine right here."

Anne Marie kissed her pallid brow and slipped out the door.

Betsy was waiting at the bottom of the stairs like a filly ready to race. They went through the rooms to the kitchen. Anne Marie's hat was on the table, and she put it on while Betsy opened the back door and stepped out onto the gallery. There was no one working in the gardens of the properties on either side. Anne Marie dropped the veil to cover her face and followed the maid along the path to the back gate. They were giggling like schoolgirls. As they made their way along the alleyways that were deep in shadow from the overhanging branches, Anne Marie's breath came shorter.

They would be switching cars twice, from the St. Bernard Line to Broad, then to the Canal Belt. These were busy routes and it would be all the easier to get lost in the crowds. The hardest part would be the last part, getting off the streetcar on the corner of Basin Street and crossing over into Storyville's infamous twenty blocks. When she put a foot on the step of the car at the corner of Mirabeau Avenue, Anne Marie felt as if she was about to shed her skin, even though it was only a simple ride into the city.

Valentin was never in the mood to wander down the more disreputable streets of the District, whatever the reason. The farther north from Basin Street, the meaner the neighborhoods grew, right back to Robertson Street, which was mostly taken up with row upon row of narrow cribs, just large enough for an iron bed with a lousy mattress and a washstand. With their Dutch doors, they always reminded Valentin of horse stables. The cheap, drunken, and brazen whores who wandered those streets would perform an act with anyone or anything for a half-dollar or less.

What was commonly called the Jew Colony, located along the farthest block of Bienville Street, was a considerable step up from this state of affairs, but it still gave Valentin morbid pause. The small houses were generally tidy, the women mostly clean and rarely abused of drink and narcotics.

He knew the landlady of the cleanest house on the street, and it was to her establishment that he went first. Belle Golden—at least that was the name she used—was the type of madam who was more akin to a mother hen to her chicks.

She met him in the foyer, and he asked after Sophie Solomon. She in turn questioned her girls until one of them remembered that she was at Ruth Grossler's, or at least had been the previous week. The girl knew because there had been police trouble that involved Sophie. Something about a customer getting robbed.

He thanked the girl and the madam and went out on the banquette. He thought about going back downtown and telling Solomon that his daughter was alive and that's all he knew. He only owed the man so much.

They were a common-enough sight, the young American miss and her Negro girl, and could have been on their way to shopping at the department stores on Canal Street and Broad Avenue. Betsy kept casting significant glances Anne Marie's way as the car rolled south; then it came to a stop and they stepped down. The car rolled off again and suddenly Basin Street was on display. It had started to rain, a light New Orleans drizzle, and they stood there under their umbrellas for a few minutes, until Betsy touched Anne Marie's elbow and they crossed over.

They passed a couple drinking establishments, the Terminal Saloon and Fewclothes Cabaret, between Canal and Iberville streets. Storyville began in earnest there, with the famous Anderson's Café and Annex like an anchor on the corner, followed by a row of grand mansions. Anne Marie felt a sense of unreality as she watched proper gentlemen mount the steps to the galleries to be greeted by young women, who escorted them inside, there to engage in all manner of debauchery. It made her want to laugh out loud. She saw other gentlemen being sent on their way by other young ladies, the men carrying a look of satisfaction from a job well done. Windows were open all along the street, and the music of pianos and Victrolas came wafting from the parlors. She saw the shapes moving by the windows, heard the gay laughter. She let her gaze roam to the second floors and thought about what might be going on in those rooms at that very moment.

They crossed Bienville Street, and halfway down the block, Betsy pointed to a large mansion and whispered in Anne Marie's ear, explaining that on one side was a French house and the ground floor of the next door was the Circus, both run by Emma Johnson, a black-hearted witch of such debauched tastes that she disgusted even the most jaded bawds on the street.

Anne Marie knew what "French" meant, though she wasn't completely clear on all the mechanics. Or what was involved in this "Circus." Betsy was only too happy to explain.

"All these fellows pay to get in. I'm talking about rich men, judges, doctors, all like that. And they got this big room cleared out by knocking down walls. Big as a barn. And they turn out all the lights except on this here stage and they put on a show."

"What kind of a show?"

"They got men up there doing it to women," Betsy whispered. "You know, fucking. And they'll have a woman sucking on this other fellow's yancy, must be a foot long. They got dyke acts, with two women on each other. They got a guy named Joe the Whipper, who gets all dressed up like a magician, and then they tie these girls down and he beats on them. And they like it. Sometimes they come. Or at least play like they do." Her eyebrows hiked. "And then there's the pony."

Anne Marie, already aghast, said, "What pony?"

"They got this here pony and this one whore comes out and gets him all excited, and then she slides on under him and..."

"Oh, good *god*!" Anne Marie moaned, feeling a little like she might get sick. Then Betsy said, "Course, the kids, the trick babies, in the daytime they get to ride the pony out in the backyard," and she shrieked out a laugh.

They kept walking until they reached Conti Street and were looking across at St. Louis Cemetery No. 1. Anne Marie wanted to go in and wander the city of the dead, but Betsy said it wasn't safe without a guard, even during the day. She instead suggested they tour the rest of the District and promised a saloon that had a back room for unescorted ladies. Who knew who or what they might see along the way?

Valentin stated his business, careful to mention Tom Anderson's name, and dropped a Liberty half in the madam's hand. He mounted the steps, went down the hall, and let himself into the third door on the right.

Sophie was lying facedown on the bed, fast asleep. She was wearing a camisole, hiked up so that her round bottom was on display. Valentin tugged the sheet to cover her as he went to open the French doors. After a minute or so, fresh air and noise from the street roused her. She groaned a little, then looked over her shoulder with one dark eye open.

He said, "Hello, Sophie."

"Who let you—?" She recognized him and the eye closed. "God. What do you want?" She pushed her face back into the pillow. "What day is it?"

"It's Wednesday," he said. "Afternoon."

There was a chair in the corner, and he dragged it over to the side of the bed. When Sophie's eye opened the second time, it was baleful. "What do you *want*?" She sounded like a whining child.

Valentin looked her over for a moment. When she had first come into Storyville, she was a fair-looking sporting girl, with her head of dark curls, her full mouth and black eyes, her dark olive skin. She had a buxom figure, pinched at the waist and full in the hips and bust. She quickly gained a reputation. When sober, she was wickedly entertaining. When she was drunk or whiffing cocaine, she went right out of control. She liked to show off and might have ended up as part of French Emma Johnson's Circus, except that only good Christians were allowed to debase themselves for the entertainment of the crowds that gathered at that address.

Once she set up shop in the Jew Colony, she began to spiral downward. She hadn't yet hit bottom, though not for lack of trying. She was well known to the local coppers. She had been thrown out of a half-dozen houses. Valentin himself had bailed her out of the women's prison. After which she went right back to her outrageous behavior.

Sophie was a sturdy girl and so far had taken what the streets dished out, following in the footsteps of the tough harlots of old, vicious bawds like the legendary America Williams and One-Legged Mary Duffy, also known as Bridget Fury. No matter how fierce their reputations, though, they finally met their matches, dying grim, bloody deaths. As Sophie likely would one day.

"I'm not coming with you." Her voice was muffled.

"Didn't ask you to," Valentin said.

She turned around and pushed herself up on one elbow, un-mindful that her left breast had fallen completely free of the sheer fabric of her camisole. "Then what are you doing here?" she crabbed. "I'm not going back. So why do you come around here?"

"For your father. He worries. He cares about you." His voice hardened. "He wants to save your life."

She shook her head in annoyance. She happened to look down and notice she was uncovered. She took her time hooking a finger along the top seam of the camisole and pulling it up over the mound of her breast.

"There, that's better," she said. She gave him a coy look. "Or did you like it the other way?" She cackled dryly.

"You know, I would really like to break something over your head and drag you out of here." He held her gaze. "I won't, though. Because you'd just come back, wouldn't you?"

"Yeah, I would," she said. "Of course, I would. So fuck you, Mr. Valentin."

"Your father wants you to go to synagogue."

She laughed darkly. "He needs to forget about me."

"You won't let him. You hurt him. You make scenes and get arrested. You're killing him."

"Did you come up here for a fuck?" she demanded abruptly. "Because if you didn't, we've got nothing to talk about. And I'd like you to leave."

Valentin said, "I will. But there's something else I need to tell you."

Sophie's mouth pinched in annoyance. "Tell me what?"

"You need to keep an eye out for a tall man named Nelson. He might come around. He means you harm."

"Why?" she said dully.

"To get at your father. For helping me."

"Nelson, huh?" She laughed shortly. "Well, I'll keep an eye out."

"This is no joke, Sophie."

She gave him a look of resentment. "Did you hear me say you need to leave?"

Valentin stood up and hoisted the chair, placing it back in the corner. He could feel her eyes fixing on him. "People talk about you," she said, her tone accusing.

He gave her a sidelong glance. "What people?"

"Men who come to visit me. People in the saloons. I hear them say your name."

"And what do they say?" he asked, curious despite himself.

"They say you're a *malekha*. You know what that is?"

He looked over at her now. Her face was cleaved into light and shadow and the eye on the dark side gleamed. "It's what Jews call an angel of death," she said. "Everywhere you go, people end up dead. You've got a mark on you. You always did." She looked away from him.

"I'll be around again in a week or so," he said.

"Don't!"

"You stay out of trouble," he said. "Or I'll make sure the next time you get sent to the women's prison, you don't get out." It was an empty threat, but it was all he had.

"Go *away*."

Valentin stood in the doorway. She was up now, looking beaten and broken, a rag doll, and her day had just begun for her. He closed the door and walked down the hall, down the steps, and onto the street. He gave her another year at the most, and her father could visit her, in peace at last, in the Hebrew Rest Cemetery on Saratoga Street.

They had seen everything and were enjoying a glass of whiskey in the back room of the Poodle Dog Café on Liberty Street. The place was a regular daytime watering hole for sporting girls, and Anne Marie, ensconced at a corner table with Betsy, was able to take off her hat and veil and view a parade of harlots of every color from Irish white to au-lait brown.

"You watch how they drink and that's how you know if they got any class to them or if they's just low-down sluts."

Anne Marie perused the dozen sporting women.

"They got rooms upstairs, you know," Betsy said, tilting her head toward the ceiling.

"Rooms for what?"

"What do you think? That door over there could open any second, and some fellow will walk in and take a look around and point to one of the girls. And off they go." She chuckled. "Sometimes the bartender will go *shhh* and everyone gets quiet and you can hear them goin' at it up there."

Anne Marie said, "Some man might just walk in and pick out a girl?"

Betsy nodded slyly. "Maybe you."

Hearing that, Anne Marie drank off her whiskey and asked if they could leave.

"Is there somethin' special you want to see?" the maid asked.

"Yes, there is," Anne Marie said.

Betsy took her arm and led her back out into the rain.

———

Valentin had taken care of everything for the afternoon except for the most awkward task. He had saved it for last, hoping that perhaps a tidal wave or hurricane would come along. No such luck; rain had been brewing through the day, and now the city was getting a drenching, the gutters running in rushes of brown water.

It didn't help that his mood had grown more somber after dueling with Sylvia Cardin and then fighting with Sophie Solomon. He thought for a moment how pleasant it would be to have a place to go where someone would be waiting for him. A place that would be quiet and safe. It was often that he longed for such a refuge. He knew the feeling would pass.

He ducked his way along the banquettes and stopped at a workmen's diner on Common Street to eat a quiet early meal of rice and beans and drink a glass of beer. Afterward he headed up Canal Street and turned onto Basin. He stood directly across the street from Antonia Gonzales's. There was a break in the traffic and he crossed over.

Just as they turned the corner from Bienville Street, Betsy grabbed Anne Marie's arm to stop her. "Lookit that!" she hissed. "There he is right there!"

Anne Marie saw him, too, making his way across the wide street and stepping onto the banquette halfway down the block. It was so odd seeing him, there in his own element, that she could only gape. She was aware of Betsy turning away, in case he looked their way.

It didn't matter. He glanced neither left nor right as he mounted the steps to the gallery. Anne Marie wondered if he was about to go inside and enjoy one of the women there, maybe the café-au-lait dove she had wanted to see. For some reason, the thought gave her a moment of pique.

Betsy was tugging at her elbow again. "It's getting late," she said. "We need to go."

Anne Marie shook her head and said, "No, let's wait. Just for a minute."

Valentin stood on the gallery of Antonia Gonzales's mansion, thinking seriously about walking away before someone answered the bell.

Courtesy would have had him send Beansoup ahead to let her know he was coming. Instead, he had just come knocking unannounced. The girl who answered the bell gave him a quick nod of recognition, though, as if she'd been told to expect him. She let him in and asked him to wait there in the foyer.

After he had saved Justine from the imprecations of a drunken boss, and before moving her to his rooms, he had visited her dozens of times in this same house. He had been such a regular guest over those months that Miss Antonia began asking him for small favors, which he was glad to oblige. Her mansion had been a comfortable place for him, other than the fact that the sporting girl he was coming to visit was selling herself to a series of sports who happened to be flush. As a proper rounder, he put on a show of indifference, and he knew that Justine had always considered this a treachery. She thought he should have realized that she cared for him and claimed her. And yet it was only when he feared for her safety during the Black Rose murders that he had taken her away.

He remembered specifically that it was in her upstairs room that Miss Antonia had appeared one morning around the break of day to whisper in his ear. An hour later he and the madam had arrived in black Storyville, and he was gazing upon the dead body of a young black girl. And so began his descent into the case that still shook him to this very—

"Mr. Valentin."

She was standing at the top of the stairs, wearing a day dress of soft cotton, off-white, with wide shoulders, buttoned to her neck. He let out a thankful sigh that she had not done herself up to torture him, with rouge and mascara and one of her working gowns that was tight over her figure and could be removed by unhooking a few stays to display her in one of her thin camisoles. She had done him that courtesy.

Still, she presented such a picture that he felt a pang in his chest, like something sharp had been planted there. Her face still looked girlish, though her face and body had filled out, just enough for him to notice it. Her hair was as he remembered it, the loose curls pulled back in a bow.

For her part, she was gripping the banister as if she needed the support. After taking a moment to compose herself, she lifted her skirt and started down the stairs.

As she drew closer, she saw how gaunt he looked, the angles of his face sharper and darker. Or maybe he had been like that before. She didn't really remember; she'd been in such a fog much of the time, courtesy of a willing doctor and New Orleans' well-stocked apothecaries.

She stopped on the second step from the bottom, which put them on eye level. Their gazes met, then scattered. They were both acting shy, like they were meeting for the first time. She noticed the bruise on his cheekbone and said, "Did you get that last night?"

"You heard about it?" He didn't know why he was surprised.

"It's going around. Are you all right?"

"I'm fine."

"Do you have any idea who the men were?"

"Not yet, but I will," he said quietly. He made a tense half turn toward the front door. "Can we?"

"I'll get a wrap," she said, and came down the last two steps. She went to the tree where the coats and such were hanging, took down a silk shawl with an ornate floral pattern, and draped it over her shoulders. It looked familiar and it took a moment for him to realize that it was one he had bought for her after seeing it in a store window. Had it really been three years ago?

He took one of the umbrellas from the stand in the corner.
She opened the door, and as she passed by him, he reached out
and took some material that had folded under at her neck and
set it right. Their eyes met for an instant, and she gave him a
small, sweet smile and stepped out onto the gallery. He could
still see the scar when she turned a certain way, a small, curved
indentation above her temple. It was his fault it was there and
she'd carry it for the rest of her days.

He led her down the banquette and then across Canal Street.
It was a busy walk, both of them dodging pedestrians, street
traffic, and the steady drizzle. She didn't take his arm, and they
didn't have to speak until they reached the other side of Canal.
He led her to a café where he knew the owners would permit
him to bring a woman of color inside. They found a table by a
window and sat down, facing each other.

They sat in an embarrassed silence until the fellow came out
from behind the counter to stand by the table. He greeted
Valentin with a wink and asked what the lady was having. She
asked for jasmine tea. Valentin just shook his head and the waiter
went away.

She treated him to a small glance. "You've lost some weight."

"And you got some back," he said. "I mean it's good."

"I know what you mean." She gave him a small smile. "You
never liked women too thin."

There was another silence. Valentin tried to think of something polite to say and came up blank. He shifted in his chair.
"So what is it you wanted to talk about?" he asked her.

She fingered her napkin for a musing moment. "I have a gentleman friend," she began, and immediately saw his eyes settle,
like he was watching her from a hundred yards away. She knew
the look, had expected it. Still, it wounded her, and she bit down
on her dejection before he stopped her cold.

"He came in early Sunday morning, all upset," she said.
"And he had some story to tell."

She knew that would get him. She saw his eyes widen the slightest bit. She related the tale Mr. George had told her. She drew it out, taking a good long time to paint a picture, and noted with satisfaction that he came to her just a bit, drawn in by the tale. She could almost hear the gears turning in his head as he tried to connect it to his case. It took her back to their kitchen table on Magazine Street, where he would talk to her about his investigations, replete with vivid descriptions of the bloody little dramas of ne'er-do-wells on both sides of the law. That had been some time ago and so much had happened since.

The waiter arrived with her tea. Valentin watched her as she stirred in some honey from the pot, her hand moving in a gentle rhythm.

He wanted to digest the information Justine had brought him, but his mind wouldn't engage. Being there with her had him twisted in knots and he couldn't think. As long as he was sitting across a café table, dazed by the sight of her face and the curl of her figure, by the sweet common smell of her flesh, it was hopeless. After a moment he gave a benumbed shake of his head, wondering again what had happened to the rounder that used to walk around in his body.

Justine knew most people could not read Valentin at all. She could, though; and she saw him come up to the brink, his eyes deepening and darkening, and wondered if he was going to say something that mattered to her and make the awful barricade between them evaporate. Then his gaze flattened again.

"What's his name?" There was only the slightest catch in his voice.

"George Reynolds," she said quietly.

"Did Mr. Reynolds know John Benedict?"

"He did. He had worked for Mr. Kane." She paused. "He believes the deaths of the two men are connected."

"Did he say why?"

"He didn't say at all. I can just tell."

He believed her. She had learned some things from him.

"Whatever it is, it's got him scared," she said.

Valentin gazed out the window, mulling the information. "Does he...does he know about...about you and me?"

"All he knows is that there's someone on the case," she said. "He doesn't know who you are. Or that I know you."

In the silence that followed, she saw the shadow return to his face. "Do you want to talk to him?"

"I'll have to," he said. "Can you get him to come to Miss Antonia's tomorrow?"

"I think so," she said. "I'll send Beansoup around to tell you when."

He nodded. She decided to have mercy on both of them. She gave him a quiet smile and said, "I can drink my tea alone, you know." She paused. "Actually, I'd like to."

He hesitated, then got up from his chair, mumbling something foolish about having to get back to work on the case. He gave her the briefest glance and walked away from the table. He dropped a Liberty quarter in the waiter's palm and escaped out the door in the rain and the falling light of the New Orleans evening.

Joe Kimball's brain was as much a mystery to its owner as it was to those who encountered it. He had maintained a savage thirst for alcohol that went back into a murky, muddy past. He had no recollection of that faraway moment when he'd had his first taste. Only that ever since that point in time, the days of his life had been a besotted blur, defined by the bottles that nestled at various cubbyholes and between certain volumes all around his little warren.

So his mind was so much mush, except when it came to his files. He had once read about a Negro in Georgia, a blind idiot who could not tie his own shoes but was a pure wonder at the piano. So Joe Kimball had one room in his brain that was unpolluted by liquor where he stored copies of the cabinets and boxes and bound volumes that were laid out around his workplace. He often startled himself with his ability to find the information someone was searching for, targeting names and dates like a machine. He could spout arcane details, stunning himself all the more, because of the way they just popped out from someplace in his brain as if he had stuck his fingers in and collected them.

Because of this astonishing facility, most of his work was mundane. He could handle it in his sleep or, more accurately, blind drunk. The rare exceptions to this were the times St. Cyr came by. The Creole detective usually had something delicious working and Kimball delighted in helping him ferret out some piece of information that was a piece in a puzzle that would eventually be solved.

So he was glad the detective was back in town and all the more delighted to push other business aside to attack the question that had been laid in his hands. And, he muttered to himself, the hell with what anyone upstairs thought about it.

He stared at the letters on the slip of paper St. Cyr had given him for a long time: VVV. He drank from the pint flask he always carried and stared some more. A tiny light went on in the back of his mind, then became bright and steady. He stood up, his gaze blank. He had it.

He walked away from his desk like he was in a trance, marching directly to the north corner of the room and a row of file cabinets. He went directly to the third from the left and the second drawer from the top. He pulled it open and let his fingers trip over the file tabs, his whiskey-scented breath coming short.

Within a few seconds he lifted a file folder from the drawer and started back to his desk. He heard a scrabbling noise on the opposite side of the room, and he shot a bleary glance that way. They hired a man to clear out the rats, but they always came back. Joe sometimes fell into a snoring sleep, only to be awakened by one of the filthy creatures brushing by his leg. Other times, he could see their little red eyes shining in the shadows. Or maybe it was the whiskey doing that.

Just as he reached the door, he heard the scratching sound again. Something was moving and it sounded big.

"Rats," he snarled. "Rats, rats, fucking rats..." They were everywhere. He told himself to remember to call upstairs and get the rat catcher back first thing in the morning. And this time get rid of them once and for all.

He sat down, took a pull from his flask, and opened the folder. He read through the news story, though it was hardly necessary. He knew what the lines said. What jumped out at him were the letters <u>VVV</u>. There was a faded photograph to go along with the story. Studying it, Kimball laughed blearily. St. Cyr was going to love it.

He heard another sound and glanced up to see a figure standing in his office doorway. He gave a start, caught his breath, frowned, and said, "What do you want?"

Eyes fixed on him glowing red, like the rats that only came out at night.

"I said, what do you *want*?"

The red eyes fell on the papers in Joe's hands. Followed by a snarling smile of yellow teeth.

An hour later Valentin came around the corner of the building and down the short set of steps to find the door open. He drew back. He had never before found it standing ajar or even unlocked. Kimball was too fixed on being left alone. If he wasn't in the mood for visitors, a thunder of pounding wouldn't rouse him.

The only thing Valentin could think of was that Joe had gone out and had been too drunk to remember to lock up. That's what he wanted to think. He had visited that basement too many times and knew better. Something was wrong.

He pushed the door open. The front room was in shadows, the only light coming from Kimball's office far in the back. As he moved to the doorway of the second, larger file room, he heard scrabbling feet along the baseboards. He waited there for a moment, heard nothing.

"Joe?" he called out. "Joe Kimball!" All he caught were echoes.

He crossed between the file cabinets to the other side of the room. As he came upon the office door, he saw a silhouette on the wall just inside and stopped. With a sinking sense of dread, he stepped into the doorway.

Joe was at his desk, his head tilted forward as if he was dozing or looking at something that had settled in his lap. In the dim amber light from the lamp in the corner, Valentin saw the splatters of blood that had joined the splatters of whiskey down the front of his shirt. He looked closer, saw another dark pattern on the wall behind.

"Joe," he said, his voice cracking. "Oh no..."

It took an effort for him to step to the desk, place his hand under Kimball's chin, and lift it. The hole, round and neat, probably from a .22, was centered on the forehead, an inch above the red tufted brows. The eyes were open and still bloodshot, gaping at the other side. Gently, Valentin let the head droop forward again.

He stared at Joe for a half minute, quelling the awful sickness in his stomach. From the looks of the graying flesh, the killer had been gone for a while.

He went to the office doorway, to get away from the sight of his friend and to get a breath of air. He thought for a moment about running out the door and to the nearest church so he could fall on his knees and confess all his failings, his pride and selfishness, his armor of cold indifference. Then he thought it would be even better if he walked out of those dark rooms and directly to the Union Station yards in order to jump the next freight train smoking. And this time never come back.

He put a hand over his eyes, and as he did, he heard Picot's voice in his head. The lieutenant had said it a dozen times: people who got tangled up with him got hurt. Some ended up dead, like Joe. He was right back to assuming his place as the local angel of death, Sophie Solomon's *malekha*.

Now he had led another poor victim to slaughter. Though he had little doubt Kimball would have been killed even if he had handed over what he'd found. He couldn't be allowed to walk around with damaging information, no matter how sodden his brain. It was Valentin's fault. He had put him in that spot and left him unprotected. It wasn't the first time for that, either. And for what? To capture the killer of a rich white man who meant nothing to him.

He walked to the basement door and stared out into the dark alley. A small shape darted along the gravel and he gave a start. It was only a rat.

Valentin knew running away would only make things worse. He'd have to face the blame for what had happened to Joe. Then he'd have to find out who had murdered an innocent man with such cruel deliberation, and all for a few lines of information.

He went back to Joe's office, pushing the moment's grim reality out of the way, knowing it would be waiting for him when the sun came up, and just as surely. For now, he owed it to Joe to put the detective side of his mind to work.

He stood back, fixing his attention on the scene from wall to wall, scouring for clues. He saw nothing of value, no hand marks, no spent cartridges. Joe had a file folder open before him. It was empty. Then he saw the trail of newspaper clippings that were strewn over the desk and onto the floor, making a trail leading to the door. The pages had been rifled until the one that mattered was found. The one with information that couldn't get out.

Valentin went around the desk to gently push the chair and the body it held back to the wall. The old casters squeaked and the springs groaned. Valentin looked about on the floor, saw only a layer of dust, scraps of paper, two empty pint bottles, and the usual useless clutter.

He opened the desk drawer, poked around, saw nothing of interest. He found lucifers there and struck one, then went to his knees and put his head under the desk. There was nothing lying about that Kimball might have dropped on the floor. When the lucifer burned his fingertips, he tossed it and struck a second one.

In the flickering light, he twisted his head upward and saw, on the underside of the drawer, the place where the soft wood had been scratched. From the light color, the mark was fresh. The second lucifer burned down, and he tossed it away and struck a third. Holding it close, he discerned the scrawled lines of the single letter K. There was nothing else. He dropped the lucifer on the floor and crouched in the shadows, realizing what it meant. In the moments before he died, Kimball had managed to keep his killer talking long enough to leave a message. It was an astonishing act of courage, and it brought a sharp ache in Valentin's chest.

He crawled out from beneath the desk and wheeled Joe and his chair back to their original positions. He glanced at the telephone and thought about calling the coppers, then decided it wouldn't do any good. Someone would find Joe soon enough; and it seemed only proper to leave the man among his files for a little while longer.

He made his way through the rooms and out the door, pulling it closed behind him. He slipped down the alley and into the dark shadows of the New Orleans night, feeling an old, familiar weight dragging at him, as another corpse joined the parade.

TEN

It wasn't until 8:30 that anyone had a need to visit the newspaper's morgue. A young copyboy was sent down the stairwell to face Joe Kimball's morning-after wrath in order to gather background on two Garden District families in preparation for upcoming nuptials. It was well known how much Kimball hated even pointing anyone in the direction of background for the society pages. More than once, he had been caught slipping certain bits of delicate information into a story, arrest records and the like, in order to embarrass the parties mentioned. He thought it was funny. He knew he was too valuable to be fired, no matter what he did.

So by way of initiation, the most junior of the copyboys, a fourteen-year-old with the unlikely name of Richard Ricárd, was sent down to the depths to poke the monster who dwelled there.

Young Richard found the fearsome figure slumped in his chair. The boy cleared his throat and waited. Then he spoke Kimball's name, very politely. He waited, spoke it again, waited some more. It was gloomy in those dank rooms, and Richard did not notice that the man's flesh had gone to a sickly gray, despite being pickled in whiskey. Or maybe he thought anyone who lingered underground looked that way. He stood fidgeting for another minute before stepping closer to the desk and bending down to see if he could rouse Kimball from his nap. It was then that he noticed the neat hole in the middle of the bloodless forehead and the eyes open and staring downward, as still as glass.

Richard Ricárd let out a strangled shout, jumped back, and lurched dizzily for the door, stumbling over stacks of newsprint along the way and trying to keep his breakfast in his stomach.

Upstairs, the reporter who had sent the boy to the morgue started cursing as soon as he saw that he had come back emptyhanded. Richard could only point a shaking finger at the floor and sputter, "He's...he's..." It took a few minutes for someone to decipher his bleats. There was a noisy rush of bodies down the stairs.

Within a quarter hour, two patrolmen arrived and secured the scene. Then came two detectives, and lastly Lieutenant J. Picot showed up, a squat figure under a derby hat, plowing through the misty rain like a tugboat at sea.

Picot surveyed the basement room and listened to the reports from the detectives. Then he pulled one of them aside to whisper in his ear. It didn't take long for the detective to return with a scribbler named Robert Dodge. The reporter was led into the low-ceilinged morgue, sweating, his hands shaking as a nervous tic animated his round face.

Picot asked him about Kimball. The reporter had a loose tongue and babbled about the editors at the paper grumbling over the victim's friendships with Pinkertons and the like, and the way he gave them information from the paper's files. Picot already knew that Kimball traded in information. He had sent his own officers to visit the morgue dozens of times. Kimball was useful in more ways than one. Hints planted in his ear would bloom and then appear in print the next day. Still, it irked him to be reminded that St. Cyr and other detectives did the same and likely got better service.

The air in the basement was close, and Dodge did not look well. He had developed a shiver, and his face had taken on a greenish cast. The lieutenant invited him back outside to get some fresh air. At the top of the stone steps, Picot cadged an umbrella and once he and Dodge were huddled under it, he offered one of his cigarillos. Dodge smoked badly, and the cigarillo quickly shredded in his nervous fingers.

The lieutenant wasted no time in asking about St. Cyr and grunted when he learned of the detective's visit of the previous Monday. In fact, he said, it was Kimball who had sent the Creole detective to see him.

"Did he come to talk to you about John Benedict?"

"That's what he wanted."

"Were you able to help?"

"I refused. I told him to look elsewhere." Dodge's eyes glistened. "In fact, I told him to come back down here and see his *friend.*" He stared back into the basement, frowning. "Say, you don't think he did it."

"I doubt it," Picot said wistfully. He, too, gazed toward the door of the morgue. "I wonder what could have been so important that it cost a man his life," he mused. "What the hell could it be?"

Dodge thought about it, then cleared his throat. Picot listened, his eyebrows arched politely, as the reporter spoke in a low, loose voice. Amid the garbled aside was the name "Henry Harris." When the lieutenant didn't look at all surprised or impressed, the reporter's voice trailed off.

Picot said, "I'm wondering if you might have a look around the scene in there." He saw Dodge blink and go pale. "After we move the body, of course."

"Oh, well...I wouldn't be of much..." He saw the look on Picot's face. "Well, of course, if you need my help."

"You'll earn the gratitude of my office," the lieutenant said smoothly.

Dodge performed something like a subservient bow and shuffled off to wait his call to duty. Picot stifled an urge to guffaw at this bizarre performance. Then he got serious again. He doubted the reporter would find anything worthwhile. If St. Cyr had been there, it would be a waste of time. The Creole detective was far too skilled at covering his tracks. Still, he'd gotten a friend murdered and that was worth something. Picot didn't want to waste any time before cashing it in.

Frank Mangetta hadn't seen Valentin all morning. He hadn't come downstairs for breakfast, only the second time that had happened since he'd been back in New Orleans. Frank didn't know if he was still in his room and wasn't about to go knocking on his door. He ate some eggs and peppers, drank his coffee, and read the newspaper alone, wondering idly what might be keeping his boarder.

He got an answer in another hour, after he had helped the cook and the dishwasher get ready for the lunch crowd. He had taken a moment to slouch in the archway between the saloon and the grocery for a few moments' rest. The cook, a thin, quick-tempered Italian, knew his boss enjoyed a smoke now and then, and had offered him a cigarette, hand-rolled with Half-and-Half, or *mezza-mez'*, as the Sicilians called the rough tobacco brand. Frank puffed away, nodding greetings to the customers in the grocery.

A police automobile pulled to the curb outside, and a few seconds later Lieutenant J. Picot stepped inside, followed by two patrolmen. Picot ambled over to one of the clerks and asked gruffly for directions to the second floor. The clerk looked at Frank and received a tiny nod.

The lieutenant left one of his men there and took the other one with him into the storeroom. Frank heard their footsteps thumping up the stairs.

———

They stopped at the door. Picot jerked his head and the patrol-man rapped his nightstick twice on the jamb.

"St. Cyr!" the lieutenant called. "I want to talk to you about Kimball. I mean now."

A few moments passed, and there was movement from inside. "I'll come downstairs," St. Cyr muttered from the other side of the door.

As they turned to walk back to the stairwell, Picot glanced along the hall at the door of the other room. He remembered hearing that it was a Sicilian who kept it, another of those stone-faced dagos who appeared off a ship one day, worked like mules, then took their savings and disappeared back to their homes in Italy. Maybe, he thought, one day one of them would do him a favor and take St. Cyr with him.

Picot was sitting in one of the booths, his derby on the table and his hands in the pockets of his jacket, when the Creole detective came through the archway from the grocery. Mangetta was wiping down the bar, and the two men exchanged a glance. Instead of sliding into the booth across from the lieutenant, Valentin took a chair down from the closest table. Picot got right to the point.

"You're in trouble," he said. "You were in the morgue at the *Picayune* last night. You didn't report that there had been a felony committed."

Picot hadn't been completely sure that this was true. St. Cyr's silence confirmed it.

"Did you come to arrest me?" Valentin said.

The lieutenant moved his derby three inches to the left and folded his hands before him. "Who murdered Kimball?" he said.

"I don't know."

"You know why, though, don't you?"

Valentin hesitated. He and Picot seemed destined to do some version of this dance. They were bound together by terrible secrets, and it had put them on equal footing. So he wasn't about to waste time in evasion.

"What I know is that I asked him to find some information for me," he said. "Someone didn't want whatever he found getting in my hands."

"Which was what?"

Valentin didn't answer.

"So somebody followed you there. Somebody who knew what was going on." Cold humor danced behind Picot's eyes. "You didn't know you had a tail? After what happened on Marais Street?"

"I…I missed that," Valentin admitted. He looked at the copper. "But, of course, he wasn't one of yours."

Picot's lips twisted. "No, he wasn't," he said. "This one was a goddamn murderer, and he shot your friend in the head. What I want to know is why."

Valentin said, "I don't know what he found, Lieutenant. I didn't take anything out of there. And you didn't find anything, either."

"Well, I guess it was something pretty damn fresh," the lieutenant snapped back. "Because it cost the man his life." He glowered and dropped his voice another notch. "If you know who did this, you better say."

"Maybe it was Ten Penny," Valentin said. "You should check his whereabouts."

"I'm not playing with you, St. Cyr."

Valentin said, "You don't want to know what this is about."

Picot raised his head, his eyes narrowing. The Creole was doing him a favor, and he didn't like it.

"Oh, is that so?" he said out of sheer annoyance. "Well, then…" He sat back. Maybe St. Cyr had carried something out of Kimball's office and maybe not. For all his bluster, the nervous scribbler Dodge hadn't found a thing after an hour of fumbling around and was sent away. Picot knew the Creole detective wasn't going to give him a thing, no matter how aggrieved he felt over his friend's death. He was wasting his time.

He snatched up his hat and pushed himself out of the booth. Looking down at the detective, he said, "Kimball was a damn drunk, but he wasn't a bad fellow. Now he's dead, because he was helping you. You must feel like shit. You must be feeling like getting the hell out of here and never coming back. I know I would." He centered his derby on his head and walked out of the saloon and into the grocery, his two patrolmen trailing behind him. The street door banged open and closed.

Frank stood in the kitchen doorway, looking at Valentin, who sat unmoving at his lonely table, his eyes fixed on the floor. Within the minute Beansoup came in, spotted him, and walked over to the table to hand him a slip of paper. Valentin didn't look up. Frank ducked into the kitchen, and when he came out with the fresh cup of *caffè anisetta,* the kid and the detective were both gone. So he drank it himself.

Picot's parting words had gouged the wound. Poor Joe; he had only wanted to help, then sit back, satisfied, and drink to a job well done. Look what had happened.

When Beansoup came up to the table to hand him a piece of paper, he didn't look at it and didn't speak, and the kid went away. He heard Frank puttering around in the kitchen and knew that if he stayed there, he'd have to face his kindness. So he put the paper in his pocket, got up, and headed out the door.

He walked up one street and down the other, leaving a scrambled trail that he dared anyone to follow. After an hour, he had circled and crossed the District two times over. Near the end of this amble, he had the abrupt feeling of stepping out of a fog, the kind that filled the streets when a warm day was dawning. He saw a pattern appear like a pale sketch in the air before his eyes, lines that led from the evil fuck who had put a .22-caliber bullet in the brilliant brain of his friend—for nothing but what was printed on a piece of paper—to Nelson, then to William Little or some other callous underling, and finally to Mr. Henry Harris himself. On the periphery stood Anne Marie Benedict. His gut told him that she was no innocent with a simple desire to have her father's murder investigated.

Piece by piece, his detective's sixth sense was coming back, and he was now almost certain that she was in deeper than that.

Why was John Benedict killed? Maybe Anne Marie knew. Maybe Joe Kimball had known, but now he was dead. Whatever either of them were holding didn't signify; it was Valentin who had put Joe on his last fatal road. Case or no case, no one else would seek redress for the loss. It was on him now.

He crossed over Basin Street into the north end of the Quarter. Another ten minutes brought him to the door in a back alley. He rapped a knuckle and waited. Sensing a presence on the other side of the door, he said, "It's Valentin, Papá."

The door scraped open. Bellocq's figure, looking to Valentin's eye more hunched and crabbed than before, moved away, placing a stilted arm on the wall for support. The detective stepped inside.

Bellocq eyed him. "Did I hear right? Joe Kimball got shot dead?"

"He did," Valentin said.

The little man said something the detective didn't catch. He went silent for a few seconds, and then said abruptly, "He had a lump behind his ear."

Valentin stared at him. "Who did?"

"The one they pulled from out of the river," Bellocq said. "Kane. He had a lump behind his ear. I saw it."

"How did you know that's what I came for?"

Bellocq almost smiled. "What else?" he said. "Nobody pays me no mind for six months. Maybe more. Then a copper comes round, says I got to go downtown and look at a body. Mr. Kimball's dead. And now you're at my door. After, what, two years?"

Valentin heard the cranky note of recrimination in the Frenchman's weird voice. "It's been eighteen months," he said.

"Don't matter." Bellocq raised a hand and tapped a crooked finger on his skull. "He had a lump. He got hit there."

"That could have happened when he went into the water."

"Maybe so," the Frenchman said. "That's probably what everybody think." There was a cunning glimmer in his eye.

"But you don't."

Bellocq came up with one of his weird smiles. "You carry one of them saps, *non*? You want to take someone down, where you hit them at?"

"The back of the head."

"This here one was above," the Frenchman said. "Close enough."

"So someone knocked him cold and then dumped him in the river?"

"Why you ask me? Ain't you the detec*tive*?" He put the emphasis on the last syllable, a rare display of humor from the little man.

"You knew Kane from the docks?"

"That's right."

"Do you remember anything about him?"

"He was one of them loud, stupid men," Bellocq said. "The kind you wonder how they got to be where they at. Go ordering people around, then start yelling if they don't move fast enough." One china blue eye flashed. "After I was done with his picture, he told the man next time get someone else do this. 'This cripple's too goddamn slow.' He said that while I was still in the room. 'This cripple's too goddamn slow.' That's what I remember about him." He smiled, displaying a row of small yellow teeth. "But he didn't look like such a *boss* laying there on that cooling board, *non*. He just look like another dead man to me."

Valentin thought it over for a moment. "I want to show you something," he said. Bellocq waited while the detective took a pen from his pocket and drew the three V's with the underline on a piece of scrap paper. He held it up.

Bellocq peered. "What's that?"

"I don't know. I'm trying to find out. Any ideas?"

The Frenchman studied the letters, then gave a Gallic shrug.

"Three men have died now, and it has something to do with this right here." Valentin rattled the paper.

"That don't make me know what it means," Bellocq retorted. "I can't help you."

The detective put the paper away. There was a silence between them. Bellocq kept his eyes averted.

Valentin noticed and sighed quietly. "Papá, I'm sorry I haven't come round to see you."

"You just did," Bellocq said.

The detective understood that his apology had been accepted. He made ready to leave.

"I'm sorry that happened to Kimball," the Frenchman said. "He was a good fellow."

"Yeah, he was."

Bellocq lifted his chin and smiled inquisitively. "So what's her name? The American girl on Esplanade."

"Jesus, you know about it, too?"

"It ain't a very big town, is it?"

Valentin shook his head, confounded. "Anne Marie. Benedict."

"So what now?" Bellocq said.

"Now I have to finish it. Whatever that means."

"It means you gonna be knockin' on the devil's door."

"That's funny," Valentin said. "It sounds like..."

"Like what?"

"Nothing. It doesn't matter."

"You askin' for a lot of trouble, Valentin."

"I'll keep you out of it."

Bellocq's eyes widened. "Oh, you will?"

The detective shrugged and waved a hand at a disbelieving Bellocq, went to the door, and let himself out into the air of the spring afternoon.

One of Miss Antonia's girls led Valentin through the house to the kitchen. Justine was sitting at the big table. A man in his forties was leaning against the counter near the door, folding and unfolding his arms as he tried to appear at ease. He was pink-faced, a once-sturdy sort now going to flab, and well-attired, though there was something a little coarse about him. He sported a trimmed beard and his brown hair was slicked. This was Justine's gentleman friend, George Reynolds.

After a first tense glance, Reynolds wouldn't meet Valentin's eyes. He kept casting furtive glimpses Justine's way. If the man had any sense, he would have been alert to signs that there was much unsaid between the Creole detective and the sporting girl. He seemed too agitated to pick up on anything.

She introduced him as "*Mr.* Reynolds" and said he might have something of value in regard to the murders of John Benedict and Charles Kane. Valentin did not fail to note the more formal appellation, rather than the casual "Mr. George" that she no doubt used when they were alone. It was a small gesture toward sparing his feelings.

Justine started by saying, "I heard about what happened at the newspaper. I know he was a friend of yours."

Valentin nodded soberly. He really didn't need to fall into that pit right now. He wanted his wits about him; and so he was glad that he had somewhere else to focus his thoughts. Still, he didn't fail to notice how Reynolds had tensed when Justine delivered her sympathies.

Settling at the end of the table, he took his five-cent notebook and a stub of pencil from his pocket and addressed Reynolds directly. "You worked with Mr. Kane, is that correct?" he asked.

Reynolds gave a tense bob of his head. "Worked for," he said. "I was his assistant. His second-in-command."

"This was in a shipbuilding company?" the detective inquired.

"Actually, we outfitted the ships, after major construction."

"What was the name of your company?"

"Dixie Star."

"And what about Mr. Benedict?"

"He owned and managed White Cross. They built ships. Small freighters, mostly."

"What did Henry Harris have to do with these companies?"

"They supplied each other. Parts and so forth."

Valentin nodded. The windows were open, and they could hear the Basin Street traffic. He let the pause hang, a way of putting the subject just ill at ease enough to move the way he wanted. He sensed that there was something that Reynolds wanted to tell him. He just needed to be pressed on it.

"So the only connection between Benedict, Kane, and Harris was that they all ran shipbuilding companies?" the detective said.

Reynolds looked at Justine for a moment, as if for approval. "No," he said. "That's not all." He shifted his weight. "They formed a separate company. A partnership."

"To do what?"

"Import and export. Handling anything that landed on the wharves."

Valentin stared at him until Reynolds fidgeted.

"What was the name of that company?" Valentin said after a moment.

"Three V."

Valentin jotted the letters in his book as if this was new information. "What exactly did Three V mean?"

"I don't have any idea. Something they invented."

"Because no one's name starts with a V."

"I said I don't know." Reynolds gave an impatient shrug.

"Were they successful?" Valentin said.

"Oh, yes, very successful. They've had all the produce business for the past twenty years."

"What happened to the former owners?" Valentin asked, and felt Justine's stare on the side of his face.

"I believe the—"

"They were forced out, weren't they?"

Reynolds gave a start at the detective's sudden rancor. "I don't know that," he said. "I'm just telling you what happened. I didn't have anything to do with it. It wasn't my place to ask questions. We're talking about Henry Harris, for god's sake!"

"You worked for Kane," Valentin said in a quiet voice.

"Actually, before all that happened, I was offered another position at Gulf Shipping and I left Dixie Star, so I didn't..." As he trailed off, he looked at Justine, only to find her gazing at the detective.

It didn't surprise Valentin a bit that this white man was hedging. Everybody had an angle to play. He glanced down at his few notes, then moved on. "You were with Kane the night he died."

Reynolds took a breath. "I was."

"Why?"

"Why?"

"Why were you with Mr. Kane? Was it a special occasion?"

"No, we just..."

"Just what?"

"Did that now and then. He invited me and I went."

"And he was your former superior?"

"That's right."

"All right, you went out for drinks. What happened?"

"What happened was afterward he was walking to find his automobile, and I saw somebody grab him off the street and drag him away."

"Can you describe this somebody?"

Reynolds told him about the shape the figure took, the

duster or cape, or even something that looked like a wing. As time passed his memory was changing on him, and he felt no less foolish than the first time he related it. When he finished, Valentin considered for a moment, then said, "What were you doing before this occurred?"

"We were drinking at the Napoleon House," Reynolds said. "Charles had too much, as usual. We left and walked through the Quarter. His automobile was parked on St. Peter."

"He was drunk?"

"Oh yes."

"Drunks get loose about what they say. Did he say anything?"

"Well, we were talking, and he—"

"I mean anything unusual."

Valentin saw the shifting in the white man's eyes.

"Mr. Reynolds?"

"He talked about John Benedict," Reynolds said. "He said that John had it coming. That's what he said. 'He got what he goddamn well had coming.'"

"What else?"

"He said some other things but I can't be sure what. He was muttering some awful things."

Valentin sat back, tapping his pencil. So Kane had known who had murdered Benedict, and why. He jotted a note, then looked up. "It sounds to me like Benedict was going to talk. Talk about what?"

"I don't *know*." Reynolds's whole body seemed to take part in the lie. His gaze roamed and his thick frame deflated and he dropped his chin like a schoolboy. It was so blatant that Justine rolled her eyes.

The white man was getting perturbed, no doubt wishing he hadn't agreed to this. He folded his arms across his chest in a posture of disdain. It didn't work, though, and he found the Creole detective gazing at him with a blank curiosity, as if there was something on his face. He fidgeted, coughed, shifted his balance.

"Something else on your mind, sir?" Valentin asked momentarily.

"I just don't want to get blamed for…" He stopped to catch a breath. "I don't want someone coming after me. I wasn't part of it! I didn't do anything!"

For a moment Valentin thought Reynolds was going to burst into tears. He saw Justine regarding him with a lopsided frown, her eyes narrowed in disgust at the display. He put his notebook and pencil stub away. "That's all I have," he said. "Thank you for your time." He looked at Justine. "And thank you for your assistance." It was all very polite. He gathered himself to leave.

"Wait just a moment," Reynolds said in a shaky voice. "What about me?"

"What about you?" Valentin said.

"I'm going to be needing protection."

"I can't help you with that." He treated Reynolds to a cursory glance. "You can find a man in any saloon in the city. But I wouldn't worry. I don't think you're in any danger."

"You don't *think*?"

"You don't know anything, isn't that what you said?" Though the detective kept his voice even, Reynolds's broad face still flushed red. "If something important comes to mind, something you've forgotten, please send a message to me at Mangetta's on Marais Street."

Reynolds turned to Justine, as if expecting her to say something.

"I think we're finished," she murmured, with a tiny note of contempt in her voice that warmed Valentin's heart. He nodded to her and walked out of the kitchen.

Outside on the banquette, he let out a breath, as if he was coming up from underwater. He had survived seeing her with the man who was currently paying for her body. It was good, then, that Reynolds threw some things out that he could fix his mind on.

Henry Harris had, along with Benedict and Kane, created a company and named it Three V, the same as the inscription on the rings. He still didn't know what the letters meant. It had to matter, or why hide the inscription beneath the stone?

That likely was what Joe Kimball had uncovered. And in his last moments, he had tried to provide another piece of the puzzle by scratching the letter K or something like it, under the drawer. It might have stood for Kane, though that didn't really go anywhere. Something about the letter was nagging at the edge of his mind, as if it was just below the horizon, not yet clear enough to discern. It would come to him eventually. He hoped it was sooner rather than later.

He got to Esplanade just as a streetcar was pulling up, its wires crackling noisily overhead. He put his foot on the step and hopped on.

Anne Marie had spent much of the morning replaying her adventure of the day before. She felt like she had spent an afternoon in a strange land or had crossed into enemy territory, like Belle Boyd or some other famous spy. Except that she now had the disorienting feeling that Esplanade Ridge was the alien territory.

She had seen St. Cyr, too, and then the dove from the house on Basin Street. She and Betsy had followed them through the drizzling rain to Canal Street and watched them cross over. By then it was late and time to get home. Her mother had been alone all afternoon. When they got there, they found her wandering about in her nightdress, looking for something she couldn't name. Betsy took her back upstairs and got her a bowl of soup for dinner, which, to their surprise, she wolfed down, then asked for more.

Anne Marie had come awake with a vision of Valentin on a rainy Basin Street crossing her mind. The image stayed with her through the morning. She puttered aimlessly, feeling nervous and a little frightened, as if something dire but unknown was about to happen. Then Betsy came back from making market with the report that two evenings ago St. Cyr had been attacked on Marais Street and had barely escaped with his life. The maid followed this with the news of the detective's friend at the newspaper being shot to death.

Anne Marie turned away to hide her shock and hurried out of the kitchen, startling and puzzling Betsy. She went into the study and closed the door behind her. She sagged against the wall in the dark room, trying to get a fix on what had happened. The Creole detective had almost died and his friend was dead and she couldn't shake the feeling that it was her fault. She should have left it alone. But she couldn't. She couldn't.

She guessed that he would come on all the more fiercely now, determined to find out what happened. It never occurred to her that he might quit. He wasn't the type.

With that thought, she went back out into the foyer, then up to her room for a glass of brandy.

She was standing by her window, trying to decide whether to send Betsy to fetch him when the maid hurried in from the front gallery where she had been sweeping, banging the front door. She raced up the steps all excited and burst in to tell her that the Creole detective was coming up the banquette that very moment!

"Can you knock, please?" Anne Marie said, working to keep her face stern.

They heard him rapping at the front door.

"I'll see him in the sitting room," she told the maid.

"You ought to see him in this *here* room," Betsy said.

Anne Marie said, "Betsy, I swear, you—" The doorbell chimed, interrupting them. The maid hurried out the door and down the hall.

Valentin was pleased when Betsy brought coffee. He needed it. He added his usual cream and a bit of sugar while Anne Marie waited, fidgeting distractedly. She wasn't partaking this afternoon. He could feel her nervous gaze on him as he stirred his cup and took a sip.

Anne Marie thought he looked somber, not at all happy to see her, and it gave her pause. She wondered what was going through his mind, after the attack he'd suffered and the murder of his friend. He wasn't giving any clue at all and sipped his coffee until she said, "Well, then?"

He put his cup down and went about recounting his past forty-eight hours. On Tuesday night he had gone to visit Joe Kimball at the newspaper in the hopes of getting background information that would help. He told her about visiting Sylvia Cardin the previous morning. He did not mention meeting his au-lait dove at all. Late the previous evening, he finished, someone went to the newspaper morgue, cornered his friend Joe Kimball, and shot him to death there.

"Was it because of this investigation?" Anne Marie asked in a hushed voice.

He looked at her directly for the first time. "There's no other reason."

"I'm so sorry," she said, sounding sincere.

He took a moment, and then said, "I have something of your father's. It was taken from him on Rampart Street."

She raised her eyes to meet his gaze. "What is it?"

He went into his pocket, produced the ring, and held it out between them. She stared, making no move to take it.

"I don't remember ever seeing that."

"Charles Kane had one, too. Exactly the same."

She gazed at the ring for another moment. Then her eyes shifted. "How long have you had it?"

"Since Saturday."

She studied him for a moment. "Why is it important?"

"I don't have any idea." He paused. "If you don't know anything about it, I'd like to ask your mother."

Now her eyes took a cool set. "I told you, no. She's indisposed."

Valentin stared at her, feeling something rising in his chest. His gray eyes glittered hotly.

"She's *indisposed*?" he said. "A friend of mine named Joe Kimball is *indisposed,* too. Permanently. He's dead. Because he was helping me on this goddamn case."

She stared at him, swallowing, her face paling as her hands gripped the arms of her chair. He knew no one talked to her that way. He didn't care. She started stuttering, "I don't...I..."

"Whoever murdered your father murdered Charles Kane and Joe Kimball," Valentin said in a calmer, though no less icy voice. "I'm pretty sure they want me dead, too. So I'd like to find out who's behind it and why it's happening. I want to talk to your mother."

"All right, then, I'll see if she'll speak to you," she said, though he could see she was troubled over it.

He placed the ring on the end table, on the doily that was under the tasseled lamp. Anne Marie wouldn't look at it or him.

He changed his tack. "I have something else to ask," he said in a quieter tone. "I'd like to look through any papers your father may have left behind."

She turned her head to meet his gaze. "What sort of papers?"

"Records. Having to do with his business. Did he keep anything here?"

She nodded, now looking a little dazed, as if trying to catch up. "In his...his desk. In the study."

"I'd like to see them."

Anne Marie said, "When? Now?"

"Not now. I'll come back tomorrow. Unless you have an objection."

"An objection..." She was regarding him with her mouth slightly open.

From the doorway, Betsy came to the rescue. "Will you be around for lunch, then?" she asked.

Tom Anderson was surprised to find Alderman Badel seated at the table at the end of the bar. *His* table, the one he used for most of his business. It was all the more brazen a move because he had taken Anderson's choice of chairs, too, the one facing the door. It was akin to sitting in the King of Storyville's throne.

Whatever Badel's intentions, it dawned on him that he might have blundered when Anderson stopped halfway down the bar and rapped his knuckles on the polished surface. The crack echoed through the quiet room. The bartender who was setting up for the day quickly placed a short brandy before him. Anderson didn't say a word, but kept icy blue eyes on the alderman as he took a sip from the glass. He didn't move until the alderman flinched and got up from the chair with a small hiss of impatience. Badel swaggered to the bar and stood before the King of Storyville. Apparently, he still didn't understand what a gaffe he had committed for he, too, cracked a knuckle on the marble. The bartender looked at the proprietor, who took a moment before nodding slightly. A second glass of brandy appeared.

Badel took a healthy sip. "That's a decent vintage," he said, as if Anderson might have served the cheap stuff.

"What can I help you with, sir?" the King of Storyville asked him, the edge in his voice belying the cordial words.

"We've got a serious problem," Badel said.

"What would that be?" Anderson said, though he already had an idea.

"Not what, *who*. St. Cyr."

The King of Storyville flipped a hand. "He doesn't work for me any longer. I put him off the payroll."

Badel smiled tightly. "He's still your man, Tom."

"Not so much," Anderson said, bridling at the familiarity.

The alderman took another sip of brandy. "Well, one way or the other, he's still a problem." He glanced at the bartender, who was working a few feet away.

"Would you rather talk in my office?" Anderson offered.

"No," Badel said. "This will do fine."

Anderson understood. The last thing the alderman wanted to do was climb the steps to the second floor. It wasn't just the man's unwieldy bulk; it appeared that the glass in his hand wasn't the first he'd had that afternoon. He was halfway to drunk. Apparently, he'd needed extra fortitude for this mission.

Anderson caught the bartender's attention and raised an eyebrow. The young man, used to this gambit, dropped what he was doing and found some work to do farther down the bar.

"All right, then," Anderson said, turning back. "What is it?"

"You've got to get rid of him," Badel said.

"Of who? St. Cyr?" The alderman's answer was a shift of small eyes. "I told you, he's not working for me anymore."

Badel's mouth tightened into a grotesque excuse for a sneer of command. "I mean it. You have to get rid of him, Tom."

The King of Storyville stopped, then cocked his head like he hadn't heard right. His gaze settled on the alderman's fat, florid face. "Who sent you here?"

Badel drank some more of his brandy. His hand was clumsy and the glass clinked heavily on the bar. "Nobody sent me," he stated. "I've got ears. I hear what's going on. How people are talking. You want all this landing in your lap?"

"You better say it plain, Alderman."

Anderson loomed as if he was gaining substance by the second, and Badel started to quail. "I did my part. I'm not saying no more."

He drained off the rest of his brandy, pushed the glass aside, and started to move past. Tom Anderson grabbed hold of his lapel in one heavy hand. His grip was like iron and Badel froze. The

King of Storyville's glare was fierce. "Tell the person who sent you he can come face me anytime he wants. You pass that on."

"I can't!" the alderman said, just shy of moaning. "I can't..."

The alderman drew away like he wanted to bolt, but Anderson held him fast. "You're in this deep, Badel," he said. "You're the one who started it. Even if you were just running an errand." He let go of the lapel with a small, rough shove. "I'd leave St. Cyr alone if I was you," he said. "He's not as polite as I am. And he's been having a bad time lately."

Badel walked a swaying circle for the door. Anderson fumed for a moment, sipping his brandy in angry little snaps. Then he put his glass down and crooked a finger. Beansoup, who had been lurking in the far corner of the room, hurried over.

"Go find St. Cyr." The King of Storyville's blue eyes were blazing with anger. "Get him over here, and I mean now."

Once the bartender had been directed to move away, Anderson and the alderman forgot about him, and he was able to linger just close enough to pick up a word or two of the heated exchange. He didn't know what it meant, only that it might be worth something. The bartender, whose name was Jakes, nurtured a lust for girls who were far too young for even the broad bounds of Storyville, and when he got caught about to corrupt such an adolescent, a police lieutenant made him a proposition. The entire matter would be dropped, and he would face neither the wrath of the law nor that of the girl's brothers, a far more dire fate. It would, in fact, not go beyond the walls of the interrogation room, provided that he never have anything to do with a girl that young again, and that he report back about goings-on at Anderson's Café.

Jakes balked. Jail was no treat; a beating at the hands of the girl's brothers would be worse. Getting caught spying and informing on Tom Anderson would mean the hospital, then jail.

On the other hand, if Anderson learned about his crime with the girl, he'd be out of a job. He was in a rough pinch.

"It's up to you," the copper had said, breaking into his frantic thoughts. "You can do the police a service. Or we can turn you over to the family. We'll collect whatever's left of you when they're finished, and the next stop will be Parish Prison." Then he smiled.

A few minutes after the alderman had gone stumbling out the door and Anderson had settled back at his table, Jakes made an excuse about an errand and hurried out the door, across Basin Street, and downtown to the police precinct at Parish Prison. He stopped at the desk and sent a message that contained a particular word upstairs. Then he walked to Jackson Square and sat down on one of the benches. Within ten minutes, a familiar figure appeared. As usual, he was carrying a copy of the *Picayune*. He sat down on the other end of the bench and opened his newspaper.

"So," Lieutenant Picot said, careful to keep his tone casual, "what's new this day?"

Beansoup got the word from Frank Mangetta that the detective had probably gone off to Esplanade Ridge again, but that he might be back any minute. The kid skittered around the saloon and the grocery, then out on the street, clearly agitated that his errand for Tom Anderson was taking so long. He blew his harmonica out of sheer nerves.

He hurried back inside and asked to use the grocery telephone. A few moments later, he was whispering into the mouthpiece. When he came back into the saloon, he was all settled. He went to sit at the bar and drank the sarsaparilla Mangetta poured for him, glancing occasionally at the clock on the wall. He finished his soda, thanked the saloon keeper, and stepped out onto the banquette. A few minutes later Valentin appeared, as if the kid had known exactly when he was going to arrive.

Frank stepped to the window in time to see the two of them disappear around the corner of Iberville, heading for Basin Street.

That Beansoup was acting on behalf of Tom Anderson seemed to give him no end of delight. Valentin had to spend a moment pulling him down from his lofty perch so he could actually receive the message.

"You gotta hear this," he said. "You know that alderman named Badel?"

Valentin slowed his steps. "What about him?"

"He showed up at the Café a little while ago. He was drunk." Beansoup glanced around and lowered his voice. "He told Anderson he better get rid of you."

"Is that right? What did Mr. Anderson say?"

"He run him the fuck off." Beansoup snickered. "Told him he better get the hell off of you, too. I thought he was going to pick him up and throw him out the door!"

Valentin gave him a wry look, and Beansoup snapped back to business. "Anyway, Mr. Tom says you need to come by. And he said go round the back way. Don't let nobody see you."

The detective noticed how Beansoup was taking himself. It seemed that just a few days ago, he was a snot-nosed street Arab, running messages and errands for dimes and quarters. Now he was a player, on the fringes, but still on his way to becoming a rounder. Tom Anderson trusted him with important matters. On his own, he'd made himself that useful.

As if to punctuate that thought, the kid took the opportunity to switch to the subject of the third of the three witnesses that had come up on Ten Penny and John Benedict that night. The one who had seen the stranger in the duster.

"I went back to check on him," Beansoup said. "Got that butcher he works for to tell me where he lived at. A rooming house off Decatur Street. I went over there and the landlady said he moved out. Said something about going to Memphis, but she couldn't be sure. Could have been Mobile. He's gone."

"And we'll never find him," Valentin said. He mulled the information for another few moments, then went into his vest pocket for a coin.

Beansoup held up a hand. "I don't need none of that," he said. He winked and waved a hand in the air.

"Where are you off to?" Valentin asked.

"Go find Charley," he said. As he strode away, he pulled out his harmonica and began playing a reedy melody that trailed him down the narrow street.

Valentin pushed through the swinging doors of the kitchen and into the Café. Anderson was at his usual table, and he waved the detective into the opposite chair.

"You want a drink?"

"No, thanks," Valentin said.

"Well, then," Anderson said. "I had an interesting visit today. I'm going to guess you already know about it."

Valentin smiled. "The kid's getting better all the time."

"That fucking Badel," Anderson muttered. Valentin could see the anger flashing in his eyes. "He must be crazy, coming in here like that."

"Or too scared not to."

The King of Storyville nodded somberly. "You'll have to watch out," he warned. "I can't just fix this."

"I understand."

"Those two fellows the other night were stupid. It won't be a couple of clowns like that the next time. Do you understand that?"

"I do," Valentin said.

Anderson gave the detective a long look. "Listen to me. You can't go after a man like Henry Harris, Valentin. It's just not possible. There are certain things you have to accept."

"And I can't just let it go, either," Valentin said. "He murdered Joe Kimball."

"He didn't do any such thing."

"He was behind it. He's guilty, Mr. Anderson."

"Everybody's guilty!" Anderson said, his voice rising. "It's the way of the world!"

"Joe Kimball wasn't guilty of anything," Valentin said stubbornly.

The King of Storyville sighed and sipped his drink. "It's not too late to stop it," he said.

"I don't want to stop it," Valentin said. "I want to finish it. And I will."

"Oh? And what if he decides to pick off someone else next? Maybe Beansoup. Maybe Justine."

"Or maybe he'll come after you," Valentin said.

Anderson almost smiled. "I'll have to keep an eye out."

"No," Valentin said with a slight shake of his head. "I'm the one they want. You and everyone else can stay out of the way."

"I'm not afraid of Henry Harris," the King of Storyville said.

Valentin paused over that, then offered a quiet thank-you and walked out the way he had come in.

George Reynolds spent the rest of the afternoon in his office without getting any work done. He did his best to keep busy with the papers his secretary put before him, and yet as hard as he tried to concentrate, he found his mind drifting. He gazed fretfully out his north-facing window, across the rooftops. A half-dozen times he heard his name called and snapped out of his blank reverie to see his secretary standing there, her brow knit with concern.

"Are you feeling all right?" she'd asked him.

The hours dragged and he was grateful when the streetlights finally began to come alive all at once. Farther back-of-town they still employed gas lamps, and those glowed in a slow sequence as city workers made their way from street to street. George sat in his chair and watched their progress, hoping the sight would calm him.

It did not. Over the past week, a monster he thought was long buried had raised its ugly head.

He remembered the excitement when Charles Kane announced that Henry Harris himself had asked John Benedict and him to join in a business venture, a new company that would be a major operation on the docks.

George knew the story in the most general terms. Kane had described it in detail. Harris had looked down from his office window and saw the busy activity on the wharves, with ships loading and unloading produce around the clock. The longshoremen were like ants in their scurrying, and as he stood there, he imagined not fruits and vegetables being toted, but bags of money. New Orleans was a major international port, so it had to amount to millions.

He also couldn't fail to notice that most of the names on the shingles hanging over the doors of those businesses ended in vowels. That's all he needed to see to move forward.

He couldn't very well go down to the docks and commit wholesale murder in order to take over. But he knew the Sicilians were quite good at that themselves, and so he went about fomenting what was later called the "Orange Wars" by throwing fuel on a small feud between two families that had business on the waterfront. It culminated when one group of Sicilians was framed for the murder of the chief of police, and eleven innocent men were lynched in the yard of Parish Prison. After the dust settled, Henry Harris looked around and was stunned to see that like barnacles, the Sicilians were still clinging to each other and to the docks.

A wave of protest about the murder of the Sicilians came from as high up as the king of Italy himself, directly to President Roosevelt, so a repeat performance was out of the question.

Grudgingly, Harris decided to do what he should have done from the beginning, which was to form a shipping company and simply buy up the businesses he had tried to usurp.

He chose two like-minded businessmen, Charles Kane and John Benedict, to join him in this venture. They formed their partnership in secret, so as to avoid any questions of a trust. They made reasonable offers to the owners of the businesses, but to the partners' disbelief, every one of the owners refused politely. A slightly more generous offer was tendered. The response was the same. The Sicilians didn't want to sell their businesses at a fair price at all. They were successful and happy, and they were bastions for the burgeoning Italian community.

Furious and not to be denied, Harris sent thugs to offer a more direct inducement. The men all ended up in the river. One came back with a message that the next crew wouldn't be able to swim out again.

Henry Harris had gone into a rage. This was exactly what he had been talking about for years! These people were defying him and they weren't even Americans!

George Reynolds knew about what had happened next. After it was over, he was relieved to be able to leave Dixie Star for a position that, over the years, advanced him to the presidency of Gulf Shipping. He thought it was history, that he'd never hear of it again.

He didn't escape, though; Charles Kane had stayed in touch all that time. Odd, until George realized that Kane was making sure he kept his mouth shut. Not that he ever wanted to speak about it.

He finally did, though, letting his lovely Justine persuade him to talk to the detective in the kitchen of the Basin Street mansion. St. Cyr had listened absently at first, as if he wasn't much interested. He came around when George got to the end of the tale.

All throughout, George couldn't fail to notice how Justine seemed to move closer to St. Cyr, even as she sat in the same chair. She wasn't on his side any more than the detective was. It was then that it began to dawn on him what a mistake he was making and ran for cover. The way she looked at him: like he was a coward, all but begging for the detective to offer him safety. She didn't know what he knew, though, and she wouldn't under—

"Mr. Reynolds?"

He came out of the brood and swiveled the chair around. His secretary was holding his scarf and hat.

"Your car's downstairs," she said.

With a nod of thanks, he put on the hat and draped the scarf over his shoulders. He offered the girl a good-night and went out the door and down the steps.

The Maxwell was idling at the curb in the cooling air of the falling night. The driver in his long driving coat, slouch hat, and goggles sat tapping his fingers on the wheel. George didn't know the man—nothing unusual. The company provided drivers from a pool as a courtesy to executives. He stepped into the backseat too distracted to notice the usual admiring looks that the workers coming out of the gate cast in his direction. Actually, it was the Maxwell that received the stares. A few of them, discontented types, would be thinking that the fine machine was bought at the cost of their sweat. Which, in a way, was true.

George pulled his scarf around his neck as the automobile swung away from the curb. They puttered west along Thalia, then turned south on Dryades. George thought that the car was moving a little fast for the traffic but didn't say anything. He was still deep in thought over what he'd told St. Cyr.

So much so that when they reached the Dryades Market, it took him some moments to realize that instead of going straight, they had turned onto Melpomene and were now zooming west on that wide boulevard, passing automobiles and carriages alike.

"Why didn't you turn?" he called to the driver. The fellow didn't seem to have heard. The motor was making a racket as they picked up speed.

George cupped his gloved hand around his mouth. "Driver!" he yelled over the wind and road noise. "You missed the turn back there!" When the driver still didn't respond, he leaned forward and poked him with a gloved hand. The fellow gave a jerk of his shoulder, brushing the hand off, and pushed the accelerator lever forward another half inch. George, first startled by this insolence, felt fear shoot through his bones like an electric shock. He wanted to yell for help, but his mouth had gone dead dry, and no one would hear him for the roar of the racing engine, anyway. The pedestrians on the banquette snapped by in a series of blurs.

The Maxwell swerved wildly to avoid a horse-drawn hack at the intersection of South Franklin Street and went flying past the Leidenheimer Bakery and into the dark recess beyond, where the gas lamps had yet to be lit. George felt the clutch in his guts as it dawned on him what was happening. Kane had been snatched off the street, too. Now it was his turn.

The driver turned so sharply off Melpomene that the right-side tires almost came off the boulevard. He cut down a gravel alley between two warehouses, where he threw the Maxwell into a skidding stop. He cut the ignition switch and the four cylinders rattled into silence. Before George could open his mouth to protest, the fellow at the wheel turned around with a pistol in his hand. The goggles and hat stayed in place, and his collar was turned up so the details of his appearance were concealed, though George was so terrified, he likely wouldn't have remembered them if they'd been in full view.

With a smooth motion, the driver laid the barrel of the pistol to rest on George's brow, right between his eyes.

"If you call out, I'll kill you." The voice was muted, not much above a whisper, barely threatening. Still, George had no doubt that he meant what he said, and he willed his shaking limbs to be still.

"You know what I want," the driver said.

"What—" George's teeth went to chattering, as if he was chilled. "What about—?"

"You want to stop that," the driver said. He waited a moment. "Now, let's hear it."

"Hear what?" George sucked in a loud breath. "I don't know anything. I'm not—"

The driver pulled back the hammer on the revolver. "I can ask someone else."

"All right, all right!" George's voice went up another notch. "Benedict was going to talk. I think so."

"About what?"

"About Harris and Kane and that business on the docks. About that damned company they formed. Benedict was going to talk, and Kane knew it, too."

"And you were part of it."

"I wasn't! I only heard about it from Kane. My god, it was almost twenty years ago!" George swallowed, tasted bitter bile. "Please don't do this! I didn't have any part in it!"

He felt the driver staring at him through the lenses, probing for a lie. Then the gloved hand released the hammer. "From here on, you keep your mouth shut about this or you'll end up like those others."

George nodded, or at least made a semblance with that cold steel barrel pressing into his forehead.

In the next motion, the driver withdrew the weapon and dropped down from the seat. "Hope you can handle this thing," he said with a short laugh. "You're a long way from Russell Street." He backed away, keeping the pistol pointed. Not that George was about to challenge him.

Then, in a sudden swirl, he was gone, melting into the shadows cast by the backs of the buildings like some scrap of a rag that had been whipped away by the evening wind, leaving the alley still and silent. George was startled. It was the kind of swooping movement that had carried Charles Kane away, yet just a little off. This fellow seemed sleeker, more nimble. Or maybe he was seeing things again.

He clambered from the backseat, holding on to the side panels for support. Now the fear he'd forced down came up in his guts like a wave, and he had to clench his bowels to keep from soiling himself. That wouldn't do for his stomach, though, and he bent his head to vomit, splattering the front of his coat, his shoes, and the Maxwell's bright yellow wheels. He drew a handkerchief from his pocket to wipe his mouth, then leaned against the fender, sweating in the cool air and gasping for breath.

Sick fear wrenched his gut again, and George heaved himself into the front seat. Though he had only driven the car once or twice and the controls were all a blur, he managed to advance the spark, close the choke, and turn the starter. The Maxwell's quartet of cylinders coughed to life, then sputtered and stopped. The air reeked of gasoline. He had forgotten to open the choke. He waited for a trembling ten seconds, shooting fearful glances up and down the alleyway, then tried again. This time the engine caught and settled into a slow idle. He engaged the clutch and pushed the accelerator handle with an unsteady grip. The motorcar rolled away toward the blessed amber gaslights of Claiborne Avenue.

There was a ruckus outside Miss Antonia's mansion. The piano man stopped playing, and the girls hurried to look out the front windows. A green Maxwell touring car had come to a shuddering, piston-rattling stop and sat at a crazy angle in the street, with one tire perched on the banquette. As they watched, George Reynolds clambered down from behind the wheel like some drunkard and hobbled up the steps to the gallery.

One of the maids went running to find Justine, who swore a mild curse. Then she went down the stairs.

He looked bad and smelled worse, and he swayed like he was about to topple over at any second. The girls who had gathered round stood back, curling their noses, though it wasn't the first time they'd seen such a spectacle.

They scattered like startled birds when Miss Antonia bustled out of the parlor, where she'd been entertaining. She called for one of the toughs who lingered on the back gallery, ordering him to go move the motorcar that was hiked on the banquette. Then she and Justine helped Mr. George up the steps.

Once they had maneuvered him into the bathroom at the end of the hall, the madam went to a special closet and picked out some articles of men's clothing that were kept there. She left the clothes hanging outside the door, then went downstairs to see to her other girls and their guests.

Justine meanwhile undressed Mr. George down to his undershirt and drawers. She wiped his face and neck with a damp cloth. Once he was cleaned up, she guided him to her room. She offered him a drink, but worried that he couldn't keep it down, Mr. George refused. She gave him a few moments to calm himself. Then she asked him what had happened to upset him so. Had someone else died?

Well, *he* almost died, he told her, and as he went about relating the story, his face went white and she rushed him to the bathroom. She stood outside listening to him heave.

Once back in her room, he finished the story. They sat for a little while, then Justine went out in the hall to the top of the stairs, where she beckoned one of the maids. When the girl came up, she whispered in her ear to go find the street Arab named Beansoup and ask him to fetch Valentin St. Cyr.

When Beansoup got the message, a half hour or so later, he was strolling along Canal Street with the girl, showing her the sights and talking like he owned the place.

He went to work immediately, all ready to show her what a rounder like him could do. But of all the times for it to happen, he couldn't locate the detective anywhere. He went up and down the street, asking all the regulars if anyone had spotted him. He checked some of the watering holes where they played jass. Then he went to Marais Street, left the girl on the banquette, and went inside. No one had seen St. Cyr at Mangetta's, either. He went up to the second floor, just in case. He knocked on Valentin's door, got no answer. In his desperation, he went down the hall and knocked on the neighbor's door. He was turning away when the door cracked open, startling him. A rough-looking Italian stood staring at him, his eyes shining like opals.

"I'm looking for..." Beansoup made a vague gesture toward St. Cyr's room. He started to ask if the Italian had seen his neighbor, but the door closed as abruptly as it had opened.

When he came back outside, the girl took one look at him and said, "What's wrong?"

After another hour making rounds, Beansoup decided that if the Creole detective wasn't around, it was because he didn't want to be found.

They went back to Miss Antonia's mansion. They wouldn't let him in to see Miss Justine, so he told the girl at the door to pass the message that Mr. St. Cyr couldn't be found this night. After that, he walked his companion down Basin Street so she could catch a car home.

Walking away from the corner, he threw up his hands in exasperation, thinking about how his night might have ended if he had found the Creole detective.

Cole and Smiley spent the last hour of their lives arguing over whose fault it was that St. Cyr had gotten away clean. Smiley said Cole should have moved in sooner, and Cole told Smiley that it wasn't his idea to taunt the detective instead of just doing the job. Smiley suspected that his partner had put him there, expecting the Creole detective to pull a trick. He had been the goat, in other words, though there was no way he could prove it. The pair had pulled other jobs before, and it occurred to Smiley that he was always the one getting hurt. Though he could never quite figure out how it happened that way. He guessed it had something to do with Cole going to school as far as the second grade, when he hadn't gone at all.

Cole bemoaned the job and money lost. He said they wouldn't get any more of that kind of work unless they fixed this one. Smiley waited for two days for Cole to come up with another plan. Finally, Cole said they'd take the simple approach and go to Marais Street and hide until St. Cyr appeared. He'd have to show up sooner or later, and they'd jump him, finish what they started, collect the money, and be back in good graces.

Smiley asked if they could add the dago Mangetta while they were at it. He still had a lump where he had been cracked, and with a saxophone of all things. Cole grinned every time he looked at his partner. Smiley didn't see the humor.

They stumbled out of the Robertson Street saloon, cut through the alley between Villere and Marais, and found a darkened warehouse doorway, where they could lurk to see what happened. After an hour had passed, Smiley decided it was another stupid idea. They were fishing in a pond that might be empty. Who knew if the Creole was even going to pass that way? He wanted to go to his room and sleep. The liquor was leaving him, and the music from Mangetta's was giving him a headache.

He was just about to suggest they leave when he heard a click of a pistol hammer being pulled back. He and Cole stared at each other. Cole was opening his mouth to say something when the side of his head came apart to the roar of a shot. He spun around and crumpled to the bricks. Smiley gaped in shock, then turned to see a shape in a dark duster standing ten paces away. He put his hands up and started to explain that it was Cole's idea, it was *always* Cole's goddamn idea, when the pistol barked and he felt the slug slam into his chest. He fell backward and found himself staring up at the stars that blinked over Story-ville. After another second his sight went, but he could still hear the footsteps coming closer. He felt the pistol pressing against his temple. There was a second of light and heat brighter and hotter than the sun, and then it all went dark and cold.

Frank Mangetta was closing up, dragging his weary shoes back and forth across the floor, when he was startled by a police wagon racing up Marais Street from the direction of Canal, the team's hooves clattering in crazy staccato on the cobblestones and the siren in full wail. The shrieking got louder, and the wagon appeared suddenly outside his window. The driver pulled the nags to a halt and jerked the reins to drive them into the alley alongside the saloon. The copper who was turning the crank on the siren let it drop, and the alarm wound down to a sob and fell silent. The hooves clopped and the wheels creaked along the alleyway. Momentarily, he heard gruff voices calling back and forth.

After a minute went by, the saloon keeper heard the chugging of a gasoline engine. One of the police department's automobiles came to a skid on its tall balloon tires out front, then followed the wagon into the alley.

Frank unlocked the door and stepped outside. Buttoning his jacket against the predawn chill, he walked around the side of the building to see what all the commotion was about.

Halfway along the alley to Claiborne Avenue, the police were setting up portable gas lanterns. Keeping to the shadows, Frank stepped around the parked motorcar and the wagon and team. One of the horses had just dropped a small mountain of wet manure, and he went around that, too.

When he got up close, he saw two bodies sprawled out on the gravel, each one floating in a pool of dark blood. He stared grimly. He couldn't mistake the two dead faces, like wax in the pale yellow glow of the lamps. The one he had hit with the horn—Smiley, as he recalled—lay with arms flung wide, a hole the size of a Liberty quarter in his chest. His shirt was soaked maroon as if it had been made that way. The other one, the one who had done the talking, was missing a chunk of his head on one side. He would carry his startled stare into eternity.

There were three coppers in uniform and two detectives milling around, muttering and shining lamps about, looking for evidence. None of the coppers had noticed him, and before one of them did, he slipped off the way he had come.

He went back into the saloon and, despite the hour, poured himself a quick glass of grappa. He drank it down, gazing fretfully at the ceiling and wondering if he should wake Valentin to tell him. He finished the drink and stepped through the archway, through the back room of the grocery, and up the narrow staircase that was lit by a single gas jet. He went down the hall and knocked lightly on Valentin's door. A second passed. Then the detective said, "Come in, Frank."

Frank used his passkey and found the detective sitting on the dark windowsill, watching the scene in the alley. The saloon keeper came around the foot of the bed to lean against the jamb.

"Hell of a way to end a night," he said.

"Did you hear the shots?" Valentin said.

"We had a band playin'."

They watched in silence for a few moments. Then Frank told him that the kid Beansoup—the Sicilian called him *fagiol'* from the popular bean dish—had been around last night before and all in a fit.

"What did he want?"

Frank said, "He had a message for you. From Miss Justine. He wouldn't say what it was."

Valentin kept reading. "That's all?"

"No, that ain't all." Valentin heard something in the Sicilian's voice and glanced up to see him grinning, his teeth white below the black mustache. "He come upstairs to look for you. And the damned *ragazzo* went and knocked on Angelo's door."

The detective turned his head, half smiling.

"I thought he knew better," Frank said, chortling. "You wasn't there, so he knocked on the door. And he was in there."

"What happened?"

"All I know is when he came back down, he was whiter than he was when he went up. And that's pretty white."

Valentin shared a laugh with the saloon keeper. Then he said, "He wouldn't tell you what Justine wanted?"

"No," Frank said. "He was acting the big cheese." He winked. "He had a young lady with him. I saw her standing outside, peeking in through the window. She was waiting for him."

"Was this a Negro girl, short, kind of pretty?"

"That sounds right. Why, you know her?"

"I do," Valentin said. A moment passed and his mouth tilted into another slow smile. "He knocked on Angelo's door?"

Frank shook his head, bemused. "Poor kid. I thought he knew."

Valentin was quiet for another moment. "You think he might want to talk?"

"Who, *fagiol'*?"

"Angelo."

Mangetta chuckled. "The *paisan* barely speaks English. Talk about what?"

"I don't know. You don't think he's..."

"What?"

"Kind of lonely in there?"

"No, I don't think so. Not that one." He paused for a thoughtful moment. "You ain't never been to Sicily. So you wouldn't understand a fellow like that. He don't get lonely."

"Someday you'll have to tell me the story, Frank."

"What story?"

Valentin tilted his head slightly in the direction of the doorway down the hall.

"Oh...," the Sicilian said. "Yeah, someday I will."

Valentin watched the scene in the alley some more. Momentarily, he let out a snicker.

"What is it?" Frank said.

Valentin pointed. "Picot."

Lieutenant Picot had looked up to see what could only be St. Cyr's form folded in the open window. Another dark shape lurked there with him—his dago friend Mangetta.

He muttered a quiet curse. Once again he had been dragged from a soft bed to an alley in the predawn to stand over cooling corpses. Staring at the two dead men, he was completely convinced that it was all somehow St. Cyr's doing, even if the Creole hadn't pulled the trigger.

Picot knew the victims; another couple worthless tramps of the army of dirt white rodents who infested the city, living by stealing most of the time, though always available for other kinds of vile work. Now they were dead—no loss. The lieutenant wondered if the slugs were of the .32-caliber variety, like those that nestled in the chamber of St. Cyr's Iver Johnson revolver. He peered closer. The gaping holes in the victims' bodies announced a heavy caliber, probably a .44 or .45. The same as the one that had felled John Benedict.

He glanced up at the second-story window and saw that the dark figures were now gone. With a grunt of annoyance, he took out his leather-bound notebook and a pencil and went about the useless task of collecting information on the homicides of Messrs. Cole and Smiley.

Frank had left Valentin sitting in the window, watching the proceedings in the alley. Out in the hall, he glanced at Angelo's door, saw a light underneath, and wondered what the *signore* was doing in there. The noise outside may have woken him. Or perhaps he was just saying his morning prayers.

Frank went down the stairwell, thinking about what had happened, with an odd sense that the last act in the story had just begun.

ELEVEN

Reporters for the *Daily Picayune,* the *Sun,* and the *Mascot* had made it to the scene of the crime just in time, each with a photographer in tow, though only the *Mascot* would eventually publish the pictures of the murdered men. When the reporters tried to interview Lieutenant Picot, he told them he'd have nothing to say until his investigation was complete, and then had one of his officers run them off.

The last of the coppers were gone by first light. Before they left, every patrolman who worked the streets of Storyville was taken aside and given orders to find anyone who might have seen the Creole detective St. Cyr around the time of the shootings and pass the information along to Lieutenant J. Picot immediately. The lieutenant had gone off to his office to busy himself with paperwork and wait, and was not surprised that the rest of the morning passed with no reports. Maybe someone would come forward, though he doubted it. The Creole detective had once again gone invisible. This time he appeared out of the shadows to perch on his windowsill and enjoy the follies in the alley below.

By noon everyone who was awake had heard the news that two men had been shot dead in the alley alongside Mangetta's Saloon and Grocery. Though few details were available, there were nods and winks aplenty. Whispers followed, to the effect that they were the same pair who had gone after Valentin St. Cyr two nights before.

The madams down the line found out about it, thanks to the busy network of spies and gossips. That St. Cyr was in the middle of something surprised no one; he had always drawn trouble like a magnet. That much hadn't changed. Though not a few of the madams entertained the private thought that he wouldn't be in such a fix if he had paid them the respect they were due and stayed where he belonged.

Beansoup heard about it shortly before breakfast when he passed a couple sharps who were talking in front of a Franklin Street café. By the time he arrived in the alleyway, the coppers had left, taking the bodies with them. All that remained of the crime scene were the dried puddles of blood, now turning into black stains. A handful of curious citizens were lolling about, and Beansoup paced around like he had business there, feeling the eyes of the bystanders on him. He was the one who then went on down the line spreading the word, tootling his harmonica along the way.

Miss Antonia Gonzales heard it from him and told Justine when she came down from her room. The madam took the opportunity to ask after Mr. George. Justine's averted eyes and blank response told her not to be surprised if she didn't see that free-spending gentleman again. Miss Antonia gave a loud sigh of vexation. She should have known; once Valentin St. Cyr came back to town, it was only a matter of time that he'd get to her.

Tom Anderson was enjoying morning coffee and pastries in the private dining room at Gipsy Shafer's mansion when Billy Struve, his own most able informant, showed up to relate the news. Anderson chased away the girl who had been serving him, upstairs and down-, in bed and at table. After Struve repeated the details, he wondered for a moment if St. Cyr had shot the two men, then decided it wasn't likely. The Creole wasn't an assassin. Anyway, he could well guess who might have executed that bit of dirty work.

When Anne Marie stumbled in for her breakfast, Betsy jumped up to tell her about the same two men who had attacked Mr. St. Cyr on Marais Street getting shot down in the alley next to Mangetta's Saloon.

"Who were they?"

"A couple low-down rounders," Betsy told. "No good sons of bitches, that kind."

Though no one else was about, Anne Marie lowered her voice. "Do you think he did it?"

"I don't know about that," Betsy said, and went to fetch Anne Marie's eggs and coffee. The women were quiet for a few moments. Then Betsy said, "He goin' to be coming around today?"

"How would I know?" Anne Marie said. Betsy heard the odd note in her voice and turned around. Anne Marie had her hands clasped before her, and she looked like she was about to start weeping. "I did a terrible thing," she said.

Betsy, puzzled, placed a china cup of coffee on the table. "What are you talkin' about?"

"I'm afraid of what Mr. St. Cyr's going to find out."

"About what? What is it?"

"I can't tell you, Betsy. I'm sorry. It's not because I don't trust you. I do. I just can't."

"It's all right." Betsy watched her for a moment. Then she said, "I don't believe he's out to hurt you." Anne Marie heard the kindness behind the words and began to weep into her hands. Betsy hesitated for the briefest second, then put her arm around the heaving shoulders so Anne Marie could sob against her. In the seconds that followed, she mused over what that Creole detective had brought to their door.

"What have I done?" Anne Marie whimpered.

Betsy let her go on some more. "Everything's gonna be all right," she murmured.

Anne Marie caught her breath and wiped her eyes, trying to regain her composure. The moment passed and Betsy's arm went away, as she stood back. "Thank you," Anne Marie said in an impossibly soft voice.

She got up from the table. A few minutes later, as she was sweeping the floor, Betsy heard Miss Anne Marie on the telephone in the foyer. She crept into the dining room to see if she could hear, but her voice was too low, the kind of voice people used to tell secrets.

The telephone call ended and Anne Marie's steps padded up the stairs and down the hallway above. Betsy waited until she heard a door squeak open and closed. Then she went to the foyer and stood at the telephone desk.

Right there was a piece of paper and on it was a four-digit telephone number. Betsy selected a pen and copied it over on another scrap. She stopped to listen. There was not a sound from upstairs. There was a stack of mail on the desk and she went through it. There was nothing of interest. She closed the drawer and went back in the kitchen, attending to her domestic duties.

Valentin and Frank Mangetta ate a late breakfast that was actually an early lunch, trading sections of the *Picayune* without exchanging a word. The news of the killings in the alley would not make it into print until the evening editions, though no doubt with every bloody detail. As for a suspect, the police would not go corralling some innocent like Ten Penny this time. No one cared enough about either victim. And Lieutenant Picot wanted to make sure the suspicions about St. Cyr lingered for as long as possible.

Valentin finished and stood up to carry his plate to the sink in the kitchen. When he came out and sat down again, he found that Frank had laid his section of newspaper aside. The saloon keeper reached for the toothpick that was next to his coffee cup and regarded the detective fixedly as he poked about with it.

"That was strange business with those two in the alley," he said after a few moments.

The detective smiled dimly. "You didn't kill them, did you, Frank?"

Mangetta tilted his head toward the bar. "All I got is that sawed-down *lupara* back there. What about you? You're the one they was after."

"Then I guess someone did me a favor."

"Maybe it was that American lady," Frank said, smirking. "Maybe she decided you needed some protection."

"I wasn't the one who got protected. Someone wanted them shut up before they ratted."

"That's probably it, all right."

Valentin went back to perusing his newspaper. "You ever have to use it?"

"Use what?"

"Your shotgun."

"Just once. And it was not a pretty sight." Frank collected the coffee cups. "But I'd do it again," he said, and walked to the kitchen.

The exchange was still on Valentin's mind when he got back upstairs. He cast a cursory glance at Angelo's door. As usual it was shut tight, and there was no light through the space at the bottom. He pictured poor Beansoup, standing there, quaking in his worn and dusty shoes after rousing the Sicilian.

In his room he stood at the dresser, opened the drawer, and dug out his sap and stiletto. Then he unfolded the oily cloth and hefted his Iver Johnson revolver. After what had happened in the alley, he had no choice but to carry it again.

Though he didn't like the idea much. He had seen how toting a pistol changed some people. He knew for a fact that more cowards than brave men carried one. A weapon gave them an authority they hadn't earned and didn't know how to use, and too often some innocent soul ended up dead.

That was the finality. A stab wound, a blow from a whalebone sap, and, sooner or later, the victim would likely walk away. A pistol was a different matter. There was a brief second of roar and smoke, and a life evaporated. He knew too well about that. And so he hated carrying that extra weight.

It didn't matter; he was back in dangerous waters. So he took the pistol along. Since he never wanted to get used to it, he tucked it in a pocket rather than a holster. This meant it took an extra heartbeat to draw it out, and that was fine with him.

Anne Marie led him into her father's study, which was on the other side of the foyer from the living room and on the front corner of the house. There was a curtained window on each outside wall. The inside walls were taken up by a bookcase filled with volumes that likely had never been read. In the center of the heavy carpet was a large oak desk with a blotter holding a set of pens and an inkwell, also looking unused for some time. Double-wicked study lamps of polished brass had been placed on either side of the blotter.

They both stood quietly for a moment. Anne Marie was clearly nervous, her eyes flitting, and he guessed that she was regretting her decision to allow him access to her father's papers. Valentin wondered if she was going to tell him to leave.

To ease her mind, he didn't go to the desk to start opening the drawers and rummaging. Instead, he stood at arm's length from her side, waiting for a signal.

Momentarily, she said, "I want to tell you again how sorry I am about your friend at the newspaper. And about what happened to you on the street. I know it's because of this case." She looked into his eyes, then looked away. "I didn't know I was going to put you in any danger."

"Somebody sure wants to stop me," he said.

"Do you know who it is?"

"I believe it's Henry Harris. Or someone acting on his behalf."

She gave a small start of alarm. "You can't stand up to someone like him."

"That's what I keep hearing." He shrugged. "But I can't stop now."

"Why not?"

"Because I already spent some of the money you paid me."

"I don't think this is funny," she said. "I mean it. You can stop if you want. I would understand you making that choice. I never knew it was going to lead to this."

Valentin gave a slight shake of his head. "I'll finish it," he said. "I have to. For Joe."

Anne Marie watched him closely and nodded.

In the silence that ensued, she became aware of how small the room felt. It was cloudy outside and the gray light was even more muted by the heavy curtains. The house was quiet. Her mother was napping, and Betsy hiding somewhere close by. Meanwhile, the Creole detective seemed to have fallen into his own reverie. He didn't move, totally relaxed, gazing at the objects on the top of the desk as if his mind was miles away.

She caught a scent from his skin, something smoky with a slight musk beneath. She knew it was the fashion for men to douse themselves with various reeking potions. Not quite as bad as the ladies, but close. Not him, though; he smelled like an ordinary man.

She could trace his profile out of the corner of her eye, and she realized that from where she stood, all she had to do was lift her arm and she'd be able to touch his face. She wondered how it would feel. She had handled a snake once at an exhibition and was mesmerized by its sleek skin, like the finest leather.

He turned his head toward her, and she saw curious gray eyes that were knowing in some way, as if he could read her thoughts. It made her feel a little dizzy, and she heard someone laugh, then realized that it was herself. The detective smiled quizzically. She coughed and covered her mouth, all the while thinking she must be going completely out of her mind. He was waiting.

She raised a hand as if to steady herself on some invisible support and found her voice. "Well," she said, letting out a low breath. "This is…that's his desk."

He nodded. "Could you light the lamps please?"

She went to the desk and rooted through the middle drawer until she found a box of lucifers. She lit both lamps, casting an even glow. She left the flames down low.

As she stepped back, she raised her eyes to look at him. She was wearing a strange expression, her face soft and her gaze dark in the shadowy room. Valentin reached over to turn up the wick on the lamp that was nearest to him. The room took on a cheery glow and the spell was broken.

"Well, then," she said. "I'll leave you alone."

He waited like a gentleman until she stepped away. Then he pulled out the big leather chair and sat down. She stood in the doorway, looking back at him as he went about his work. At one point she seemed about to say something, and he waited until she said, "It's nothing." The next time he glanced up, she was gone.

He spent an hour and a half going through accordion files stuffed with papers without finding a single page that had any relevance to the case. Most of what he read was legal and financial and was on the White Cross letterhead. He came across numerous documents related to the house. He learned how much it had cost at purchase and that Mr. Benedict had paid cash for it. He knew how much insurance was carried in case of fire or flood.

In another packet he came upon Anne Marie's birth certificate and the Benedicts' marriage license. He learned more that he didn't care about. He didn't mind. After all the excitement of the last few days, the blood and violence, the quiet study was a refuge.

In more ways than one. As he paged idly through the files, his thoughts drifted off to Joe Kimball's wake, which would be starting just about that time. It would likely be a rowdy event, with a lot of wild-eyed, whiskey-fueled paeans to the great man. Valentin couldn't recall if Joe had any family nearby, but he had more than enough cronies to make a crowd. As much as he wanted to be there, he knew he couldn't go. It would ruin everyone's good time. And with all the drinking, someone was sure to point a finger and blame him, and the guilt would be too much to bear.

He stopped working and played the narrative leading up to the scene in the basement of the newspaper over again. He should have seen it coming. Powerful people didn't like their secrets revealed. He should have *known* that. His mind went around this circuit, time and again, and so it was a relief when Betsy appeared in the doorway to tell him she had lunch prepared.

He took a seat at the maple table while she went to the stove to fix his plate. There was only one place setting, which meant that Anne Marie wouldn't be joining him. He didn't ask why, and Betsy didn't offer an explanation.

She came from the stove with a plate of chicken and rice, done up Creole style, with tomatoes, peppers, and filé spices. He took a sip of lemonade, broke off a piece of bread, and went to

work. Betsy took a glass of lemonade for herself, sat down, and
watched him eat for a moment.

"Guess it's all right, then," she said.

"You're a good cook," he told her.

"That I am," she said.

He reached for his glass. "I know I've seen you around somewhere before this, Betsy."

"Is that right?"

"Where did you work before you came here?"

"I was in service."

"What kind of service?"

"You want some more lemonade?" His glass was still almost
full. He shook his head, keeping his gaze on her. To deflect him,
she said, "You got any idea who shot your friend?"

"I'm not sure. It could have been one of those fellows who
were shot in the alley next to Mangetta's."

"I heard they was the ones that come after you couple nights
ago."

"Heard where?"

"I heard it on the street."

"Which street?"

She stared at him.

"I know you haven't been going to Storyville to make market," he said. He worked on his lunch for a few moments. "You
happen to know a fellow goes by the name Beansoup?"

She looked away from him.

"Betsy?"

"He don't like being called that."

"Oh, no? What then?"

"He's been thinkin' about 'Little Junior.' So it'd be Big
Charley and Little Ju—"

"Did Miss Anne Marie send you over there?"

She sighed and said, "Yes, sir. She sure did. She wanted to
know about you. What she was getting herself into."

"It's all right," he said. "I already figured it out." He took another bite of his chicken.

Now she was watching him, looking bothered. "He in trouble with you?"

"Who, Beans—" He caught himself. "Emile?" He shook his head. "No, I don't think so. You're a pretty and charming young lady, Betsy."

She smiled, pleased. Though her skin was dark, he could detect the blush.

"So now maybe you can help me," he said.

"How's that?"

"Do you know anything about it that I could use?"

"No, sir," she said. "I ain't been keepin' nothing from you." She stole a glance toward the door. "The only thing I know is that she's hiding something," she whispered. "I ain't sure what. But I think you might be close to finding it."

"And that's all?"

Betsy hesitated, then went into the pocket of her apron and pulled out the slip of paper from the telephone stand. She handed it over. "She called this number and she didn't want me to hear."

He took the paper, put it away. "What else?" Valentin said.

"Nothing else that Miss Anne Marie ain't already said." She poked at her food with her fork.

"I'm going to guess Franklin Street," he said.

She came up with a cool look. "What's that, now?"

"Franklin Street is where I saw you last. But it's been a while."

She sighed impatiently. "Why are you worryin' me about this? Why dontcha leave me alone?"

"Because we're friends, Betsy."

She rolled her eyes. "Finish your lunch," she said. "You look like you need it."

———

He thanked the maid for the meal and got up from the table. She glanced over her shoulder at him as he walked out.

As he passed through the foyer, he peered up the staircase and cocked an ear. There was no sound coming from the upper floor. He went into the study, sat down at the desk, and opened another drawer, wondering frankly what he was doing there. He hadn't found a thing. He closed the drawer. This was getting him nowhere. This was a Pinkerton's job, perusing documents for clues, and not to his taste. He preferred the street.

The front door opened and closed, and he heard footsteps on the gallery. It sounded like Betsy had gone off on an errand.

Since he was there, though, he decided to finish what he had started and pulled the other drawers open, one by one, and glanced over the contents. He went all the way around and was closing the last one, the bottom right, when he noticed the corner of a legal document with a seal and bloodred ribbon attached. He took it out of the drawer. In florid script at the top of the first page was the word *Charter.* The first paragraph stated that it was a binding agreement for partnership in a company to operate under the name Three V, Ltd., to be licensed by the city of New Orleans. The principals in the company were identified as John L. Benedict, Henry C. Harris, and Charles M. Kane. The paragraphs that followed on the attached pages were filled with arcane legal language, what appeared to be a standard partnership agreement. He flipped to the last page and saw the signatures of the three principals and the date.

It was the legal verification of the arrangement George Reynolds had described and so not of any real value. Now he stopped again to ponder something that had been nagging at him: Why bother with partners at all? Certainly, Harris wouldn't need the money the others could invest. There was some other pernicious reason that he couldn't put his finger on. He'd ask Anderson when he got a chance. The King of Storyville was an encyclopedia of devious ploys.

He was flipping through the rest of the contract and finding nothing of value, when a single page slipped out and glided to the floor. When he bent down and picked it up, he realized that it wasn't part of the partnership charter at all, but a separate sheet, a letter on a heavy cream-colored paper.

He held it under one of the lamps and began to read. It was on the letterhead of the Henry Harris Companies, Ltd., and was addressed to Messrs. John Benedict and Charles Kane. It was dated the same day as the partnership agreement.

There were three paragraphs, and as he read down through them, he felt his face getting warm and his heart begin to race. He was pinching the paper so hard between his fingers that he was in danger of ripping it in half. Just as he reached the last paragraph, he jumped at the sound of footsteps on the stairs.

He quickly folded the letter and slipped it into the pocket of his jacket, which was hanging on the back of the chair.

A few seconds later, Anne Marie appeared in the doorway. She stood there for a moment, then said, "I want to see if...Did you find anything?" She was watching him, her eyes liquid.

"Nothing helpful," he said.

She stepped over to the desk, glanced at his face, and frowned. "Is something wrong?"

"I just...I think I could use some air." He took his jacket off the back of the chair. "I didn't find anything of use, anyway." He went about turning the lamps down low. When he stood up, she took a step back, out of his way. She licked her lips nervously, and her eyes raked the desk.

"Thank you for the courtesy," he said. "I'll come back when I have something more to report."

When he walked past her and out the door, she raised a hand and opened her mouth as if to say something. She let him go, though, without a word.

He waited until the streetcar crossed Miro Street to go digging into his pocket for the letter. For some reason, stealing it had made him uneasy, and he looked around the car, just in case someone was watching too closely. He didn't see anyone who looked at all suspicious, just a few maids and workmen heading home at the end of their day serving American New Orleans. Still, he had no doubt he was being watched, probably from some small distance. An automobile might be puttering along behind the car at that moment.

They couldn't see him and that's all that mattered. He unfolded the letter and was surprised to find his hands shaking as he read it again.

At the top, beneath scrolling letterhead, was a greeting,

My Friends,

Ours is an important task. Millions of patriotic <u>Americans</u> are counting on us, not the least of whom are our own families. The secrecy of our task is of the utmost importance. Therefore, once you've read this letter, please destroy it in the most complete fashion.

Valentin stopped there, gazing out the window at the park they were passing, the trees in their first bloom of spring. John Benedict had kept the letter, in spite of the instructions.

We lost a battle. We can lay down our arms and surrender or we can answer the call to remove a scourge upon our city and our country once and for all. In so doing, we will regain control of a commerce that is rightfully ours and reap its considerable profits. There is no iniquity in utilizing one to affect the other. Indeed it is our duty! We are joining as partners in the Three V Corporation to do precisely that.

This chance will likely never come again. Though the justifiable rage over the Hennessy case has faltered, we will not. It is time for us to strike our own blow in our own way. Let it never be said that we stood by and let the alien hordes claim victory in New Orleans, and most especially along the mighty Mississippi.

Valentin stopped, caught a breath, and went on.

As its rightful proprietors, we will take back our river and its riches. Once again, let those who are not Americans find their livelihood elsewhere. Indeed, let them all go back where they came from and if not, let them all go to Hell!

The paper rattled in his fingers and Valentin drew his eyes away for a few moments as the full import of what he was reading began to sink in. He forced himself calm, then went back to finish the final words.

We will marshal our forces, our acumen as businessmen, and the able support of those in the government who can grasp the full import of this quest. From this day hence, the invaders will not be able to buy food, fuel for their furnaces, light for their homes and shops, medicines for their maladies, or any of the staples necessary to continue the livelihood which they do not deserve.

Any company that provides any supplies or provisions to any of the families or businesses we are discussing will have their contracts with Henry Harris, Ltd., canceled. I have your agreement that the same will be in force at White Cross and Dixie Star. In this manner, we will reclaim what is America's for Americans!

Remember, we are part of something larger and grander. Let Three V be our banner as we march to victory!

God bless this great nation!
Your friend in Christ Our Savior,
Henry Harris, Esq.

Valentin sat unable to move as the car rolled west on Peters Street, the letter in his hand. He looked out the window at the pedestrians streaming by and wondered if any of them had been there at that terrible time. If any of the poor Italians or Greeks or blacks had seen their families affected. Then he noticed a white gentleman of some years, portly and in fine mettle, standing at the doorway of a hotel, waiting, no doubt, for his chauffeur, and he wanted to rush off the streetcar while it was still moving, rush up to the man, and strangle him where he stood.

The heated moment passed and he calmed himself, marveling that such an old wound could spring so fresh. He read the letter once more, this time forcing his mind to take it apart line by hateful line. It was an impassioned clarion call, a rationale for the mission of Three V, which was to starve out the importers, after which the company would accept the responsibility of taking over the trade.

Valentin saw what was lurking behind the florid language. Though Harris seemed sincere in his vitriol, animated by the same raw animosity of the Know-Nothings and other political movements that took their energy from racial hatred, the detective noted the elements of an elaborate sham, a high-blown excuse to steal. He understood why Harris wanted partners. Partly, it was a politician's cowardice; he didn't have the fortitude to carry such a plan forward by himself. Just as critically, he would have two scapegoats if it all went wrong.

As the car approached the corner of Canal and Marais streets and the Storyville rooftops appeared, Valentin felt a sudden and fervid relief that he was on familiar ground again. He bolted from his seat and was off the car before it rattled to a stop, ducking his head in the rain.

He leaned on the bar across from Frank Mangetta. "I need you to tell me something, Frank."

"Tell you what?"

"What happened after I went to live in Chicago."

Frank eyed him. "You mean about your mother?"

"No, about the Sicilians on the wharves. After the Orange Wars."

"What for? That was, what, twenty years ago."

"You were here. I need you to tell me what you remember."

The saloon keeper let out a reluctant sigh, then said, "What I remember is it started quiet. There was some talk that the ship-pers couldn't get supplies. They had men take wagons all the way to Mobile to find what they needed. They just couldn't keep doing it. So they couldn't get oil, couldn't get parts for the steam engines that ran the hoists and all that..." He smiled. "So they just did it all by hand. They figured out a way to load and un-load the ships with muscles and their mules. That only lasted a little while. Then the word came down—don't let no Italians un-load your ships. Only Americans. So every morning there was crews waiting at the gates. Our *paisanos* just had to stand there and watch..." At this, his face flushed a little and his jaw trembled with emotion.

"And the people who owned the ships went for it?"

"Enough did. It hurt them. But they still hung on. Then they went after the families. One by one. They told the stores not to sell them nothing or they'd make a... *come se dice*... boycott? Is that right? They couldn't feed their families. And one by one, they had to give up and leave."

"What about after?"

"After, they went this way and that. Some stayed here and did other business. Others left town, went to Houston, St. Louis...some went back to the old country." He shrugged. "That was the end of it." He took a sip of his coffee.

"No vengeance?"

Frank said, "Against who? Harris had an army. You know about Parish Prison." He paused. "And you know what happened to your father."

Frank glanced over his shoulder toward the kitchen, where even now the voice of his hot-tempered day cook was rising to a sputter of Italian curses. His face had gone dark with melancholy.

Before Valentin could press him any further, there was a clattering of pans and another rude shout from the kitchen.

"*Managgia!*" Frank smacked an irate hand on the table and got up from his chair. "These fucking guineas are gonna be the death of me!" Looking relieved, he headed to the back to try and calm the raging cook.

Valentin sat for a moment, then took the letter out of his pocket and read it again. The final passage caught his eye: "Remember, we are part of something larger and grander. Let Three V be our banner as we march to victory!"

He stared at it until Frank came out of the kitchen, rolling his eyes. "And I leave him back there with the *coltellos,*" he said.

Valentin decided he needed a drink, and asked for a glass of whiskey. The saloon keeper didn't hesitate to snatch up a bottle of the good blend and two glasses. He looked like he needed one himself.

"I know why Benedict and Kane were murdered," Valentin said as the glasses were poured.

The Sicilian's thick eyebrows hiked. "Why?"

Valentin unfolded the letter. Frank glanced at it. "What's that?"

"It says that Harris and Benedict and Kane became partners to do exactly what you just said."

Frank frowned. "Why? Just for the money? They wasn't rich enough already?"

"Yes, for the money," Valentin said. "But there was this, too..." He took out his notebook and his pencil, then tore off a sheet of paper and drew the VVV insignia. Then he made a small adjustment to the letters and pushed the page under Mangetta's nose.

"*Gesù Cristo*," the saloon keeper said out loud. "*È vero?*"

"Yeah, it's true," Valentin said. "Joe Kimball told me so. Three days ago. It took me this long to figure it out."

He folded the letter again and sat back to finish his drink.

When Valentin got to Russell Street, he found the green Maxwell parked at the curb, a ruddy-faced driver strapping suitcases on the back and the running boards.

Valentin walked over to him. "Somebody moving?"

The driver—short, white, with a spare mustache and grimy mechanic's hands—glanced over his shoulder. "Family's leaving out, that's all I know. A vacation."

"To where?"

The driver shook his head. "Nobody's said. They just told me to show up ready to drive."

Valentin started up the walk. George Reynolds, looking flustered, hurried through the open doorway to intercept him. "What are you doing here?" he demanded.

A woman, Reynolds's wife, passed by the front door. She stared at Valentin before turning her attention to the bags that were arranged at the bottom of the stairs.

The detective said, "Henry Harris had my friend murdered. And your friends Benedict and Kane."

"They weren't—"

"And those street rats who came after me, too. Everybody that crosses him ends up the same way."

"And that's why I'm leaving," Reynolds muttered.

"You haven't done anything."

"I talked to you."

"That's true, you did," Valentin said. "I don't think anyone knows that." He paused for a short beat. "Not yet, at least."

Reynolds drew himself up and squinted. "What do you want here?"

"I want you to get a message to him," Valentin said, keeping his voice low.

Reynolds looked baffled. "Do what?"

"Get a message to Henry Harris."

Reynolds looked stunned. "I'm not doing anything of the sort," he said. "Even if I knew how, I wouldn't do it."

"And you need to do it before you leave."

Reynolds studied the detective for a few seconds, then laughed indulgently. "You're out of your mind. You go after a man like him and all you're going to get is dead. You'd have an easier time shooting the president."

"I don't want to shoot anybody," Valentin said. "I just want to talk to the man."

"Well, I can't help you," Reynolds said absently. He stood waiting for the detective to go away.

Valentin's gaze roamed over his shoulder to Reynolds's wife, who was standing by the door, fussing at the colored maid about the packing. She looked to be in a bad humor. He didn't blame her. "Does Mrs. Reynolds know about Justine?" he inquired.

Reynolds glared. "You can keep your mouth shut about that."

"I'll tell her right now," the detective said. When Reynolds didn't flinch, he turned away and took a step in the direction of the front door. "Ma'am?" Mrs. Reynolds straightened, regarding him uncertainly. Reynolds hissed something under his breath. "Never mind," Valentin said.

"All right, damn it!" Reynolds muttered. "I'll see what I can do. What's the message?"

"I want to see him. I want to meet him, face-to-face. One time. That's all."

Reynolds shook his head. "Why the hell would he agree to that?"

Valentin went into his pocket, withdrew the letter, and handed it to Reynolds. He read it through, shaking his head, then muttered as he handed it back to the detective.

"Tell him I have this," Valentin said. "Tell him I said he might be a powerful man in New Orleans, but somebody somewhere else is going to see this. Tell him one more thing. The name of a Sicilian, one of those who worked on the docks. Antonio Saracena. Can you remember that?"

"Yes, all right. My god!" He gave Valentin a grudging glance. "Are you done now? Because you need to go. In case you haven't noticed, you don't belong in this neighborhood."

"And you don't belong in Storyville," Valentin retorted.

"Excuse me?"

"I'll tell her you sent your regards before you left." He nodded toward the open door. "I think your wife needs your help," he said, and went down the walk to the banquette.

On his streetcar ride back to the District, he told himself that he had no business meddling in her affairs. Justine would be furious if she thought he'd scared him off of her. She'd just have to find herself another rich gentleman. She'd never had any trouble before.

When he got to his room, he took down his black suit, the other one he'd left behind. It was wrinkled, the cuffs were frayed a bit, and it smelled a little musty. It would just have to do. Joe wouldn't mind. It was good that it had started raining. It meant he could borrow one of Frank's umbrellas and crouch beneath it to escape the accusing stares.

Joe Kimball had told one of his friends that when he went, he wanted to be laid to rest as the sun was going down. It seemed somehow fitting. He no doubt expected to wake in the morning ready to start drinking his way through eternity.

There was no sun this evening. The sky was gray and the rain was coming down steadily. All agreed that Joe wouldn't have minded that, either.

So, by the appointed hour of six o'clock, the umbrellas were huddled like black flowers on the banquette outside Gasquet's Funeral Parlor on Gravier Street. There was a band there, as the tradition demanded, though it appeared to be less an organized first line than a gaggle of Kimball's friends, all deep in their cups, who had brought instruments from closets at home. Every musician had a partner who held an umbrella over his head, at least part of the time. They were mostly too besotted with whiskey and grief to notice that they were getting soaked.

Valentin sidled up just in time for the bass drum to start thumping, announcing that the parade was about to begin. Because of the weather, they went in a straight line along North Rampart Street and turned at Conti. The music—a bizarre-sounding gumbo that came from too many drunks playing too many different tunes—made up in spirit and volume what it lacked in finesse, and Valentin figured that Joe would be delighted with the raucous noise. Though it had likely been decades since the late Mr. Kimball had seen the inside of a church, the detective spotted a priest who appeared to have been hired for the event, a red-nosed old fellow who had shown up for a Liberty dollar and the free liquor.

As they passed through the cemetery gates, word went along for the instruments to be still, and the cacophony of brass and drum dropped into a silence that was broken only by the hiss of rain and the shuffling of shoes.

Though the borrowed umbrella allowed Valentin to hide, the other umbrellas made it hard for him to spot anyone of interest. The parade crept along the pathway and deep into the city of the dead, because all the bodies were placed in biers above the wet earth. As such, there were mansions and there were hovels, and Valentin had known people who had ended up in each. They passed by the fancy vault occupied by the madam named Florence Mantley, one of the Black Rose victims. Valentin was gazing at the ornate stonework and thinking about her funeral when someone pushed in close to him.

"Mr. St. Cyr?" It was Reynard Vernel, whispering. "I thought we had an agreement." The expression on Vernel's young face was reproachful.

"You can't be seen with me," Valentin said. "It's getting too dangerous." He saw the young man flinch and he lightened his tone. "Tell me how I can find you."

"I have a room in a house on the corner of Carondelet and Perdido."

Vernel nodded quickly and slipped back into the crowd.

The service was mercifully brief. The rented priest didn't know the man in the stone coffin and so he read blessings out of a Bible, made the sign of the cross, then folded his hands piously and stood by while the pallbearers slid the coffin off the wagon and into the bier. Later a mason would come to place a block of stone with the name and the span of his life, thus performing the final act in Joe Kimball's time among the quick.

The crowd was ambling along toward the gate when Valentin spotted Robert Dodge ahead. He caught up with him.

"Mr. Dodge!"

The newspaperman turned, blinked, then gave a start. Valentin offered him a thin smile and said, "Did you hear that a couple characters tried to put me back there with Joe? And now they're at the morgue."

Dodge looked flustered, his mouth working soundlessly. The detective leaned closer, winked, and said, "Keep an eye out over your shoulder from now on." He turned away, ducked to avoid a couple people, and half trotted ahead to the gate.

He reached the Conti Street banquette and slowed his steps. He had nothing he wanted to do. He walked along the banquette for a half block and crossed Liberty into Eclipse Alley. There was a saloon there, a dark and narrow cavern called the Blue Cat, a regular hangout for petty criminals, where everyone minded his own business.

He found only three customers inside, and not one of them looked up when he walked in. It was that kind of place. He stepped up to the bar and asked for a glass of Raleigh Rye, Kimball's elixir of choice. The bartender, a rough-looking Creole, served the drink, then waited wordlessly for Valentin to lay a Liberty dime on the bar. The detective sat staring at the amber liquor for a half minute. Then he lifted it in a silent toast and drank it off.

It was dark when he got back to Basin Street, and he found it lit up like the carnival of flesh that it was. He stood on the corner of Canal and gazed down the line. The mansions were busy, carriages and motorcars pulling in and pulling out, men stepping up and stepping down, mounting the steps to galleries or descending them. Windows were open and he heard pianos tinkling gaily from parlors and the rowdy sounds of jass bands from the doors of the saloons.

He could tell that Anderson's Café was crowded, and for a moment he missed the jovial heat of all those bodies, the drinks being poured, the silver coins flashing as money was lost and won, the bands playing for dancing. It was like a certain kind of heaven, all intended for the pleasure of men. Except that the sun would come up in the morning and reveal tawdry bones underneath the sordid artifice. The same sun would light the whitewashed walls of St. Louis Cemetery No. 1 as stolid and unmoving as the final truth they contained. Those who remained in Storyville knew when they would end.

Valentin let out a short laugh at his own foolishness. He had tried escaping and Storyville had drawn him back. He had quit as a detective, only to find himself up to his chest in another case.

What had it been, just shy of two weeks? And in that time, another congregation of actors had accumulated around him: Justine, Anne Marie, Betsy, Bellocq, Vernel. And then there was an assembly of the dead: Benedict, Kane, Cole, Smiley, and Kimball, the only one he cared about. Valentin knew he'd be paying for that one for a long time.

It was the end of a long day. He didn't know what tomorrow would bring. There was no telling what Harris would do or how far he would go once he received the message that contained a silent threat. Without thinking, Valentin glanced over his shoulder but saw nothing except more shadows.

TWELVE

As he walked along the alley toward Marais Street, Valentin glanced down at the place where the two miscreants had fallen and said a quiet thanks Little or Nelson or whoever was in charge hadn't sent better assassins.

The grocery had been open for two hours and Valentin glanced in through the window to see Frank's two helpers hurrying about, waiting on the Saturday-morning crowd. It appeared that the proprietor had taken the rare privilege of coming in late.

Valentin knew how late Frank had been up because he had spent the evening in the saloon, something he hadn't done since he'd gotten back to town. He told himself it was a tribute to Joe, the kind his friend would have appreciated. Frank had a jass band playing, with a trumpet, clarinet, bass fiddle, a guitar that was handled in a way that reminded him of Jeff Mumford, and a bass drum and snare, which was unusual for a small ensemble. The two Negroes, two Italians, and one Creole played clean and sharp, and the room shook with the feet of the dancers and the pounding of the drums. Valentin let Frank park him at a table in the front corner, and he nursed a couple whiskeys. Some rounders and sporting girls he had known from the past were surprised to see him there and sat down to chat. He was relieved that no one wanted to ask him about what had happened in the alley and no one mentioned Kimball. They just wanted to have a good time. Into his second whiskey, Valentin thought it was almost like it had been before, and it took his mind off his troubles for a little while. He smiled, thinking about an old Negro he'd met calling it "chasing the *blues*."

Speaking of which, round about midnight, Beansoup walked in with Charley, who was carrying his six-string banjo. Charley didn't look too happy to be there, but then he never looked too happy to be anywhere. He was just that kind of man. Beansoup saw the detective and gave a little start, but Valentin smiled and nodded, and the kid's face went pink with relief, and he stood aside. That's when Valentin saw Betsy standing there looking shy and pretty.

When the band took a break, Frank waved a hand and Charley and Beansoup got up on the low stage and played three songs, the first a mournful gutbucket lament about a woman named Delia, another one of those that was taken from a true story. Then came a fast, wickedly funny song about a place where "babies cry for whiskey and birds sing bass." The finale was a bouncy rag. Though still rough at the edges, Beansoup managed to hold up his end. Some people in the crowd started grumbling about wanting the band back so they could dance, and Frank hustled the duo off, putting a Liberty dollar in each musician's hand.

Charley decided they were done for the night and went off to spend his dollar on a pint and a crib girl. Beansoup and Betsy brought their drinks to Valentin's table. With the first fast tune, they got up to dance, Betsy in an expert bounce, Beansoup with a clumsy display of flailing arms and legs. He came back to the table huffing with happy exertion.

When the band stopped around two, Valentin, Beansoup, and Betsy were still at the table. The crowd thinned and Frank came over to join them. Valentin had gotten just a little tipsy, and he looked around the table from face to face, feeling a sort of languid peace come over him. It had been a long time since he had felt anything like that. He had slept pretty well afterward, too.

Now he stood on the Marais Street banquette watching the rain wash the cobblestones, realizing that the evening's interlude was over, and the light of day meant it was time to finish what he'd started. He sauntered off in the direction of Canal Street to get a bite to eat before he caught a streetcar north.

He stepped off the Esplanade Line car at one o'clock and walked through a light rain down Rendon Street to St. Philip.

He opened the Benedicts' front gate and stepped onto the gallery. Betsy didn't appear after he knocked and waited. He turned the doorknob and found it unlocked. He went through the rooms and into the kitchen. From what he could tell, the maid was not on the premises, probably making Saturday market. Or maybe she had found a place to hole up with Beansoup. Or Emile or Little Junior.

When he got to the kitchen and looked outside, he saw Anne Marie standing in the garden, still and a little dazed, as if she had wandered out there and gotten lost. She was wearing a simple white day dress with short puffed sleeves. Her hair was woven in one long braid down her back.

She turned when she heard the door open. It was very quiet, and with the drops of rain from the tree branches pocking the soft earth and the mist rising around her, she looked like a figure in an old painting. Valentin stepped down off the gallery and along the flagstone path.

They looked at each other for a long moment. "I found the letter," he said. "But I could have missed it. I almost did."

"I'm sorry," she said, her voice breaking a little. "That was foolish."

"Did you reach Henry Harris?"

She shook her head somberly. "No. He wouldn't speak to me."

"What were you trying to do?"

"I don't know. Accuse him. Make him say something about my father. It was stupid. I know that." Her shoulders shook and, standing there in the rain, she began to weep pitifully.

Valentin took her arm and steered her to the gazebo. There were two wrought-iron benches, painted white, and he settled next to her on one of them. The rain was coming down a little harder now, and the house faded into a blur as the sky went from blue to slate. He watched her and waited.

She took his hand in hers and spent an absent moment caressing his skin, as if it was something exotic. He was just a little surprised by this sudden immodesty, but she seemed content to stay like that.

"I need you to tell me," he said presently.

With a little sigh of regret, she released his hand. Then she took a breath to steady herself.

"I found it over a month ago," she began. "I was looking for something else and there it was. I didn't understand it. How could it be that my own father would be a party to something like that? So I showed it to him, and he told me the whole thing." She stopped, swallowed. "He told me that they broke those people so they could do what they wanted. He said they made it so they couldn't feed their families. He didn't make any excuse. He admitted it." She took another shuddering breath. "He saw how ashamed I was. How ashamed of him."

"And he decided to do something about it."

"I guess he did," she said. "He came to me a few days later and said that he'd told Kane they had to make things right. He also sent a message to Harris. He told them if they didn't do something, he'd give the letter to the newspapers."

"What did he expect them to do?"

"Find those people, if they could, and pay them for their pain and suffering. That's what he wanted to do. Then he got all secretive. The phone would ring and he'd whisper into it. There was something going on, but he wouldn't tell me what it was." She stopped for a moment. "Then that Monday morning, the police were at our door. His body had been found on Rampart Street." She let out a sudden sob. "It was my fault! If I hadn't accused him like that, it never would have happened!"

"It's not your fault," he said, leaning closer. "He wanted to do the right thing. When Harris found out, he had him murdered. You can't be responsible for that. Do you understand?"

She began to weep harder, her sobs deep with grief. He guessed that she might be embarrassed to act this way in front of a stranger and prefer to be alone with her sorrow.

"I'm going to do something about this," he told her.

"Do what?"

"I'm not sure. And I wouldn't tell you anyway." He waited for a moment to let her weeping subside. "I should go," he said gently.

She raised her eyes. "Don't," she said. "Don't leave." She used her wrist to dab the tears. "I don't want you to." Her voice was forceful. She reached up and laid her fingers on his cheek. Her gaze floated over his face, inch by inch. Then something seemed to fall loose, and she closed her eyes and kissed him on the mouth for lingering seconds. She put her lips to his ear and whispered, "I want you to come into the house now. Please."

He held himself still, feeling the pounding of his heart.

"I'll be waiting for you upstairs."

She watched his face for another moment, kissed him lightly again, stood up, and slipped out of the gazebo and into the gray drizzle. He could barely make out her shape as she made her way along the walk to the back gallery. When she got to the kitchen door, she stopped and he could discern her profile. She went in, closing only the screened door behind her.

Valentin looked out the other side of the gazebo, through the mist toward the back gate that led to the alley, his route of escape.

She had told him everything he needed to know. As much as he might have wished for one, there was no reason for him to stay. She was in a delicate state, and if he went into the house, they both might well regret it.

With that thought, he stood up and stepped from under the cover of the gazebo.

He hadn't been with a woman since Christmas Day, when he'd heard weeping through the thin slat walls of the hotel in the dusty New Mexico town. He went to knock and the shy half-breed Navajo, sad and alone, let him in.

Now he pushed open another door to find Anne Marie standing at the foot of her four-poster brass bed. She had turned back the covers and had let down the shades and curtains. Her feet were bare. She treated him to a steady look, her aquamarine eyes liquid and her mouth slightly open, and he knew it was a last chance to beg off and leave.

As he closed the door behind him, he glanced toward the window, an old habit. The roof of the back gallery was outside, just in case he needed to bolt in a hurry. Then he remembered that there was no husband, father, or brother to come pounding up the stairs.

He went to stand behind her. She closed her eyes and in-clined her head. He reached up to the back of her neck and undid one button at a time, working his way down to her tail-bone. When he got them all undone, she leaned forward a little and the garment came loose and fell to the floor. Underneath, she was wearing a silk camisole of pale ivory. She stepped out of the dress, then turned around, sat down on the edge of her bed, and reached for him, her face infused with a secret light.

Twenty minutes later she was curled into him, letting his body envelop her. She didn't say anything, keeping her face turned away and her eyes closed. Gradually, he sensed something in the way she pulled herself tighter and she started to weep again, though now with a kind of release. He raised himself on one elbow to see that she was shielding her face. Tears trickled from under her hand and onto the sheet.

At first he thought it was because of what had just happened, though in the moment, she'd been anything but reluctant, spreading her legs to draw him into her and frolicking with spirit once she got past the clumsy part and the moment of wincing pain. She had huffed and gasped and spoken his name in breathy whispers.

Now she was sobbing, though, and he began to fear what might be next. If she claimed that he'd raped her, he'd be finished. He'd have to run and never come back. Warrants would be issued for his arrest. That his case would be finished would be the least of his troubles.

She began to breathe in slow, peaceful sighs. Or maybe in her shame, she was only pretending to fall asleep. He watched her for a few moments more as she drifted off. He knew that he should get out of there, but it was so peaceful and quiet and she was so warm. Telling himself that he'd only linger for a little while, he curled behind her and closed his eyes.

The thump of the door closing woke him. He didn't know how long he had been asleep; more than a few minutes, to be sure. Through the space between the curtains, he saw that the sky outside the window was a darker gray. Anne Marie slept on, hugging a pillow tightly.

It was past time for him to go. He lay quietly for another few minutes, and then separated from her, an inch at a time so as not to wake her.

He dressed in silence, wondering what was going to happen now. Especially when she came awake and realized that she had been ruined by a colored man, and that there was a dark stain on the mattress to prove it. He grimaced over that.

He had not meant for it to happen, and it was not something he could undo. He'd be living with the consequences, sooner or later. He finished dressing, then slipped out the door and down the hall, carrying his shoes in his hand.

As much as he wanted to go, he thought of something he needed to do. Stopping at the next door, he turned the knob and opened it. Mrs. Benedict was sitting propped on her bed. She was wearing a nightgown and her face was blank and dull, as if she had been woken from a deep sleep. The look she gave him was without surprise or even much interest, as if strange Creole men carrying their shoes wandered into her bedroom regularly.

"I'm sorry, ma'am," he said. "I opened the wrong door."

She gave him a sidelong glance that hid a cunning smile. "Yes, you did," she said. "Now what are you going to do about it?"

He wasn't sure what she meant. The one he had just come through? Her daughter's? Or the one that led to her husband's murder?

"They were the worst kind of thieves," she said suddenly, in a dark and plaintive voice. "What did they think was going to happen?"

Valentin watched her gaze roam.

She sighed and said, "My John was a weak man. He was weak to get involved in the first place. And he was weak at the end. He wanted to make it right for Anne Marie. But he just wasn't man enough for it. You can't fix something like that, can you? Not after all this time."

"No, ma'am," Valentin said. "I don't think you can."

She shook her head slowly. "No...you can't." She fell into another musing silence. "They were *thieves*," she repeated. "If it had just been money...That damned Harris didn't care. He had to have it all." She smiled coquettishly, her attention shifting. "Everyone assumed that John was in that terrible place because he was after some low-class whore, when all the time he was trying to do something good."

She sighed as her thoughts turned inward. Momentarily, her

eyes wandered to the leather kit on the side table. She reached over to open it with one hand. Inside there was a brass syringe and a small vial of liquid.

"You'll have to excuse me," she said. "It's time for my medicine." She looked up at him. "Please stay if you like."

He shook his head. "Thank you, ma'am," he said. "I'll be going now." He went to the door and let himself out.

He was halfway down the steps when Betsy bustled into the foyer. The maid glanced up to see him standing there, shoes in hand, looking like a boy caught in mischief. She stopped, her mouth dropping in surprise and eyes going bright with delight. She let out a hiccup of a laugh, then put a hand over her giggling mouth. Valentin put a finger to his lips to shush her.

"You can't speak to anyone about this," he told her. "You know what happens if she decides she made a mistake."

Betsy sobered, though just slightly. "I ain't gonna say nothing to nobody," she said.

The detective made a shooing gesture, and she scurried away to the back of the house. He sat down on the steps to put on his shoes, then slipped out the door into the cloudy afternoon.

He started back up Rendon to catch the Esplanade Line streetcar back to town. Then he realized that there was nothing in Storyville that needed his attention. He had nowhere in particular to go and nothing to do for now.

So he turned and walked to Dumaine, then turned west toward Bayou St. John, thinking about the case. He now knew Benedict had been murdered to silence him about what had transpired in the 1890s. It was likely that Nelson did the killing of Benedict and Charles Kane. It fit. Snatching Kane, knocking him cold, and dumping him in the river was a slick ploy. He could have easily gone down as a drunken man drowning.

The puzzle remained of why Benedict had been murdered on Rampart Street, of all places. Why there, where gentlemen of class rarely strayed? And when there were so many easier possibilities? It had to be intentional.

He stopped on the other side of the bayou. It was a long hike to Lake Pontchartrain from Esplanade, at least five miles. The rain had let up, though, and he had nothing but time and much to consider: what had just happened in the fine house on St. Philip Street; what would be waiting when he got back to Storyville; how the story would wind its way to a conclusion and who would still be standing when it did.

No one was stirring when Betsy got back from making market. She hurried into the kitchen to start preparing lunch. As she went about her chores, she heard someone pacing about upstairs.

Anne Marie had avoided her after Mr. St. Cyr had left in the afternoon and then through the rest of the evening. When Betsy came knocking with dinner on a tray, she called out that she wasn't hungry. The maid left the tray with a note that she was taking the evening out. So not a word had been spoken about what had happened in the bedroom.

In the hours since Anne Marie had awoken, she felt by turns despondent and delirious. She had been *ruined* and her body trembled with a giddy joy beyond anything she had imagined. The memories, flashing images, swirled around her: his face, his body, his mouth and hands. Though she guessed that the other women he'd taken had been more enjoyable.

It was a shock to realize that she hadn't lost her innocence in a proper seduction, but in the fashion of a common slattern. Like some ignorant peasant girl, she had let him undress and mount her without a word of protest. She hadn't made him court her for a single second and hadn't resisted another second longer. Along the way, she had risked what they called a "trick baby" and who-knew-what diseases. All that was missing was the money.

So she couldn't be incensed with him for sneaking away

without performing whatever gentlemanly duties were part of deflowering. She was actually relieved that he had slipped off and she hadn't had to face him right away.

The mattress was a mess, and as soon as she got up, she turned it over to hide the evidence of her sin. Not that Betsy would be fooled. She cringed, imagining the gleam in those black eyes. Of course, she would know.

She had heard stories of girls from good families who had been taken before marriage and ended up for the worse. Most often, the father would cast the girl out onto the street as too wanton for a decent family. A mother would be shamed to her grave. Proper neighbor ladies would trade whispers over the humiliation. There was also the option of suicide. It was all ten times worse when there was a colored man involved. The poor girl would never outlive her dishonor. If he didn't escape, the man would be castrated and murdered, and whoever made him pay for his wanton pleasure would be hailed as a hero.

Anne Marie had long ago judged such dramatics to be completely insane. Even more so, now that she had satisfied her own dark desire. She had done it, she liked it, and she wasn't about to throw her life away over it. She stopped for a few idle seconds to let the crude word for the act she'd performed cross her mind, then quivered with chagrin and put a giddy hand over her eyes, even though she was alone in the room.

A moment later, she sighed, thinking about the way he had taken her, hard and tender at the same time. He obviously knew his way around a woman's body. This came as no surprise.

For a moment the sky got darker. Now she heaved a long breath of regret, remembering how she had confessed to him, though she couldn't recall exactly what she'd said and how much she had just been thinking.

She wondered if she would ever see him again and what would happen when she did. He might well have decided what he'd done was too dangerous and already packed his bags and left the city. If that happened, she would be aggrieved. Worse than that, the case would be finished, and no one would ever know why her father had died on that lonely street.

She thought about it some more. No, he wouldn't stop and he wouldn't run away. He would see it through to the end. There had been something in his bearing, a tension, as if he was going to pounce on something. Something other than her. She sensed that it was accelerating toward a conclusion, and there was nothing she could do about it, even if she wanted to. She had surrendered, putting herself in his hands.

He walked the better part of a mile on the gravel road that ran along the lake until he came upon a line of modest houses, hoisted on pilings. Some were little more than run-down shacks, and a few were nothing but walls and roofs that leaked badly, the windows long broken, the rafters home to nesting birds.

A little farther on, he saw a familiar facade. The house was tidy, the clapboards painted solid white, the trim a deep maroon. The sun, broken by clouds, dappled a gallery that was filled with plants, down on the floorboards, up on the railings, and hanging from the rafters. There were also some strange constructions dangling here and there, voodoo sculptures of African design that were intended to ward off evil.

Valentin was a decent sneak when it came to it, but he'd never caught Miss Eulalie Echo unaware. Somehow, she always seemed to know he was coming before he got close, and he had barely placed a foot on the bottom gallery step when a melodious voice called out, "Who's that at my door?"

Eulalie Echo stepped onto the gallery and looked down at him with her dazzling smile.

She was a "good" voodoo queen who happened to be Jelly Roll Morton's godmother. She was a handsome woman, tall, angular, with smooth copper brown skin. Her eyes were black and piercing with a genial light. Her graying hair was tied back in a braid under a colorful *tignon,* and she wore a blue Mother Hubbard of washed-out cotton. Her feet were bare.

Though Valentin hadn't seen her in almost two years, she had barely aged; indeed, she looked almost exactly the same as she did the day he had met her, some seven years back. As she smiled down at him with her dancing eyes and white teeth, he considered that maybe there was something to this voodoo business after all.

"Come on up, Mr. Valentin," she said. Her voice sounded like a musical instrument, a slow tenor. "Whatchu doin' here? You in trouble again?" The question was delivered with sly reproof; she was clearly delighted with the company.

As was her custom with visitors, she invited him to her kitchen table, a massive affair of rough oak. He sat down, tired and hot from the long walk. Miss Echo poured two cups of black coffee from the enameled pot on the stove, then took a bottle of her homemade whiskey down from a shelf and poured a shot in each cup. Though it was only the middle of the day, it didn't occur to him to refuse. Not to mention that it would help settle his nerves a bit.

Her smile dipped a bit and she eyed him, her brown brow stitching, as if she was hearing an off sound. She sipped her coffee ruminatively and waited.

"Have you heard from Ferdinand?" Valentin asked her, using Morton's given name so as not to offend family sensibilities.

"All I know is he's travelin' up North, playin' in cabarets," she said. "He wrote his *maman* a letter, bragging about how he was doin' so fine."

Valentin smiled at the image of Mr. Jelly Roll, decked out in his finest to entertain the hoi polloi of all those big cities, especially the women.

They chatted for a few minutes more. His host asked after Justine, and he told her that she was in a Basin Street house and seemed to be getting along well enough. Miss Echo didn't comment, though he could see the concern in her eyes.

They came upon a quiet moment, and she said, "You were away for a long time, Valentin."

"I was, yes, ma'am."

He settled back to describe his wandering north and west, through the cities to tiny towns, making his way without plan or direction. He had been the next thing to a tramp for much of the time. She would assume that he had survived by stealing when there was no work around, which of course he had.

"How long did you stay away?"

"About fifteen months."

"That's a long time, all right."

They talked about Storyville a bit more, and she marveled at how Tom Anderson managed to keep order in that crazy place.

Once they had exhausted that subject, she gave him a look that went right through him and said, "You been playin' the rascal with some woman. But not Justine..."

He felt his face getting red. "No, not Justine."

Miss Echo's smile faded away. "And you been to a funeral lately, ain't you?"

He said, "Yes, ma'am, I have. For a friend of mine." He looked away. "And it's my fault he died."

"Ah-ha." The voodoo woman sat back. "So you got yourself mixed up in somethin'. And that's really why you come all the way out here. Ain't that right?" Though her voice was kind, there was steel behind it. He knew there was no escaping those gimlet eyes, so he took another sip of his whiskey-laced coffee and told her the story.

He began with Anderson bringing him in to fix the open-and-shut case of a white man shot down on Rampart Street.

"And right away, it got out of hand. The victim's daughter wasn't about to put up with a sham. Then another man was murdered, the first fellow's partner. Then my friend got caught up in it. He got in the way and somebody shot him dead." He pushed down the catch in his throat. "It was my fault. I should have known he was in danger."

Miss Echo eyed him. "When was the funeral? Last evening?"

"You ought to be the detective," he said.

"Ain't that hard to see. You still got it all on you. What's the rest of it?"

"There were two men came after me, but I got away from them," he went on. "Two nights later they were shot down in the alley off Marais Street."

"My, oh my. So there's...five people dead?"

"So far."

"And you know who's doing them crimes."

"I'm not sure who pulled the trigger, but I know who's behind it." He paused for effect. "It's Henry Harris."

He saw the look on her face and noted with grim satisfaction that for once he had surprised her.

"Well, good lord, son!" she said. "Henry Harris? The rich man Henry Harris? What's he got to do with it?"

Valentin said, "Everything."

Miss Echo stared, then wagged a long finger at him. "You mess in the wrong people's business, and you see what happens." She took another fast sip of her coffee. "You can't walk away from it?"

"Not now."

"Because that's what I'd tell you to do."

"That's what everybody's telling me to do."

"They're trying to save you from somethin'."

"Well, it's too late. Too far along."

She turned her regal head to gaze out the window, watching the shorebirds swoop and glide over the gray water. "I know you don't believe in it at all, but I believe in this here voodoo with all my heart," she said presently. "I'm telling you, though, there ain't a thing I can do with something like this, one way or another. Henry Harris, Valentin? Lord, you must have lost your mind!"

"My friend was murdered," he said. "He's responsible. And that's only the beginning."

Miss Echo heard the hard edge on his voice and sighed. "I hope you don't end up in a pine box, that's all." She watched him, smiling like the godmother she was. "You do take some hard roads, Valentin."

The detective didn't know what to say to that. He drank off the last of his coffee and said, "I better get back to the city."

The voodoo woman rose with him, and they went out onto the gallery. The sun was casting a glow the color of seashell over the lake's pale green waters. She was watching him closely, treating him to a look that was piercing, as if she could see his thoughts. She took his hand in hers and held it tight. "Is there anything else I can do for you?"

"I'd appreciate your good thoughts," Valentin told her.

She laughed. "I bet you would!" She regarded him with a bemused smile. "My good thoughts are that you find yourself a woman who'll look out for you. If it ain't gonna be Justine, then another one. That's what I wish for you."

When he got to the bottom of the steps, she called to him.

"One more thing," she said. "I don't know what you've got to do, but whatever it is, don't do it alone." She gave him a stern look. "You hear what I said? Don't do it alone. 'Cause if you do, I believe you'll fail, for sure. And maybe end up dead, too."

He stood still there for a moment, then waved a farewell and headed off down the gravel road. Miss Echo stood watching him until he was out of sight.

Justine was surprised when the maid came to tell her that the detective St. Cyr was waiting on the gallery outside the kitchen door. She threw on a shift and hurried down the stairs and through the rooms, grabbing a shawl off the stand in the foyer on her way. With her bare feet, her hair in two braids, and not a splotch of rouge or mascara, she looked much like the bayou girl she had been for the first sixteen years of her life.

She found him standing at the railing, looking out over Miss Antonia's freshly turned garden and the rows of young tomato, okra, leek, and onion plants.

"Valentin?"

She came up beside him and saw that his gray eyes were dreamy. A memory came and went. She peered closer, saw a certain animal serenity. She knew him well enough to recognize the signs. He'd been with a woman.

She was letting that thought settle when he said, "Miss Echo sends her regards."

"When did you see her?"

"A little while ago. I paid her a visit at the lake." He studied the garden for a few moments. "I'm sorry if I disturbed you," he said.

She gave him a wry look. "It's all right. I don't have company." She pulled the shawl tighter around her. "Mr. George has come to the door at least once a day for the past week," she said. "And now he just stopped. On the weekend, too. Did you have anything to do with that?"

"I believe he's decided to leave town," he told her. "He's afraid of what Henry Harris might do to him."

She gave him a long look. "What about what he'll do to you," she said. "He already tried once."

"I'm not waiting to find out," he said.

She was startled and a little dismayed. "Are you leaving?"

"No, I'm not leaving," he said, with a short smile. "I'm going to go see him."

She frowned. "This doesn't make sense. What are you going to do? It's Henry Harris."

Gazing out over the garden, he came up with a smile that brought another shock of memory. It was like she was seeing a person she had known a long time ago.

He repeated what he had told Eulalie Echo. "He murdered my friend."

She gave him a dubious look. "Well, I hope he doesn't do the same to you," she said.

They were waiting for him in front of Mangetta's. Nelson was lounging in the passenger seat of the Buick, and Louis Stoneman was leaning against the facade of the saloon, next to the front door.

The driver saw him and said something. Nelson unfolded his tall frame and got down from the seat.

"Gentlemen," Valentin said. "You waiting to buy me a drink?"

"Get in the automobile," Nelson said, his eyes as cold as ever.

Valentin thought about it for a moment. He took a look around to see if there were any witnesses to him stepping up into the seat, but the few souls who were on the banquettes were occupied. Storyville couldn't keep its nose out of his business until he needed someone watching and then everyone's attention was elsewhere.

He shrugged and climbed up to settle on the tufted leather seat. Stoneman got behind the wheel while Nelson stepped around front to crank the flywheel. The Buick started on the first try, settling into a placid idle. Nelson pulled himself into the passenger seat, and he and Stoneman donned driving goggles. Stoneman pushed the accelerator handle, and the automobile jerked away from the curb. Had Valentin glanced back, he would have seen Frank Mangetta just coming out the door of the saloon to stare after them.

They turned onto Canal Street and then cut west on St.

Charles. It was Saturday, traffic was light, and they made good time, cruising at twenty miles per hour by Valentin's reckoning. Neither Nelson nor Stoneman paid any attention to him as they sped along, and soon they were crossing Monticello Avenue onto River Road. Another ten minutes and they turned down an unmarked dirt and gravel road toward the river. A dusty half mile on, they came to the gate of a property surrounded by a whitewashed board fence that disappeared into the distance in both directions.

A black Ford roadster was parked next to the gate. Two men hunkered in the front seats, both dressed in black suits and derbies, both with long mustaches like cowboys wore. When they got close enough, Valentin noticed that both also sported the kind of flat stares that came from careers spent doing certain kinds of violence. He knew their type. The driver was thin, with a weasel's small eyes and pointed nose. The passenger was squat, with a head like a block and his mouth hanging open in a dumbfounded expression that looked permanent. He could see either one of them killing Cole, Smiley, ... or Joe Kimball.

He thought about that as the heavier fellow propped the shotgun he was holding in his lap and got down to open the gate. When they passed inside and he closed it behind them, his expression didn't change at all and Nelson didn't even look at him.

They were now on a shell drive that cut through the flat landscape. The property appeared to span many dozens of acres and was dotted with old oaks, black walnuts, and weeping willows. They were miles from anywhere, and Valentin realized what Justine had said was not just an idle warning; Harris might have already given an order to have him shot. They could bury his body and it would never be found.

Who? A Creole detective? No, no one like that's been out this way.

It was too late to do anything about it now; he was already trapped there. He felt the weight of his Iver Johnson nestling in his pocket. He could still put up a fight. Though if it came to that and he then escaped, he'd never get anywhere near Harris again. And yet, he felt no particular danger as they drove on. Stoneman was intent on his driving and Nelson looked bored with the errand.

When the house appeared from behind a stand of willows, Valentin was so astounded by its size and beauty that he forgot about whatever threat might linger about. It was as large as a museum, in Greek Revival design, whitewashed brick with four solid columns in front. The detective guessed that it probably contained twelve rooms. The windows were tall and opened outward to allow breezes to pass through, with black-painted shutters that could be closed when storms came along. The upper and lower galleries with their wrought-iron railings spread across the front and around both sides of the house. The driveway circled around a fountain at the door, and it was there that the Buick crunched to a stop.

The three men got down and stretched. Nelson glanced at Valentin, said, "Wait here," and climbed the steps to the broad gallery, where a Negro butler opened the door to allow him inside.

Stoneman went into his pocket for a packet of Straight Cuts and wordlessly offered the pack to the detective. When he produced a box of lucifers and struck one, Valentin regarded him over the flame, and Stoneman studied the detective blankly in return. Valentin decided that at least this man was not his executioner.

The wide front door opened, and Nelson beckoned to him with a jerk of his head. The detective dropped the cigarette onto the shells and ground it under his heel. He exchanged another glance with Stoneman, then stepped onto the gallery.

Just inside the door, Nelson held out his hand, palm up, and

Valentin produced his revolver. The stiletto and sap stayed where they were.

"You know what happens if you make the wrong move in here?" Nelson said. Valentin nodded. Nelson looked him up and down one more time, then waved for him to follow.

He'd only heard about such places, and the house was grander than any he'd ever visited, more like a palace. The foyer alone was the size of the largest Basin Street parlor, with a floor of polished marble, solid oak trim, and cut glass in doorways that opened in three directions. A cold silence pervaded the space, and in that way it reminded him of a hushed church sanctuary. That, or a mausoleum.

Nelson guided him through the door that was straight ahead, and they passed through an elegantly appointed dining room that included a table with seating for twelve and a massive chandelier overhead.

From there, they stepped through an archway and into a great room that took up a good part of the middle of the house, so large and open that the upper floor was supported by pillars rather than walls. A setting of French furniture was arranged about a Persian carpet that would have overflowed Valentin's entire Marais Street room. There were café chairs along the walls, lamp tables in the corners, plants in clay pots, art hanging on every surface. The walls were painted a pale blush of pink and trimmed in off-white. Valentin looked up to see that the ceiling was domed and someone had painted florid cherubs and cottony clouds there. In each corner was a table that held an electric lamp. On the far side of the room was the kitchen door, and Valentin saw a Negro cook standing over a massive iron stove, stirring pots.

William Little was seated on the couch in suit and tie, a journal open on his lap and a pen in his hand. He stared at the detective with a completely frigid expression, the same empty look he had given him in the back of the Grenouille dining room.

It took Valentin a moment to notice the man who stood motionless at the wide window that looked out over the west expanse of the property. He was almost faded into the background, like a model in a mural of a gentleman of means taking his leisure. That, or a statue.

The detective had seen only photographs of Henry Harris and so had expected a larger man, tall and thick like Tom Anderson, carrying the weight of power as a physical attribute. He was surprised and quietly pleased to see that Henry Harris was a diminutive gentleman, silver-haired, once delicate, now somewhat portly. His pale face featured petulant eyes, knitted white brows, a mouth crooked into a permanent frown. Shoulders that were stooped and a thin nose that hooked out of his narrow face gave him the look of a brooding vulture. He was wearing suit trousers, a pearl-white shirt with black suspenders, and a black tie. Ruby cuff links gleamed at his wrists. Valentin guessed him to be wearing at least a month's pay in haberdashery, but it hung on him. He didn't look much like that man who had created a small empire of wealth on the banks of the Mississippi. He had encountered rich and powerful men before and it never failed to surprise him how ordinary they could be.

Harris held a drink in his hand. He didn't turn around when Valentin and his escort stepped into the room. As they drew closer, Valentin could see out the window to the lawn beyond, where a Negro stableboy was helping two children ride Shetland ponies in the shade of the willow trees. Framed in the window, it looked like an old painting.

Harris let the detective stand there for most of a minute, not uttering a word as he watched the children. Then he did turn, and the flaccid statue came to life by degrees. An energy seemed to creep into his face, his light green eyes went hard, and his body straightened from its stoop into a posture that radiated a harsh vitality, summoned from some mysterious reservoir. Harris looked his visitor up and down, from his dusty shoes to his loose hair, and Valentin felt like he could have cut the contempt that the man sent his way with a knife.

"As a rule, I don't allow people of your type in my home unless they're waiting on me," Harris said, the words carrying a clipped and brittle edge. "You're not. So you have a very limited amount of time. What do you want here?"

Valentin found his voice. "I've been conducting an investigation into the murder of John Benedict," he said. He was aware of how oddly thin his own voice sounded. Harris stared at him without expression. "This is where it led me."

Harris's gaze shifted and fixed on somewhere over Valentin's shoulder. "And what does Mr. Tom Anderson have to do with your..." He smiled slightly. "...*investigation*?"

"I'm working on behalf of the Benedict family," Valentin said.

"That's not what I asked you." He returned his attention to the scene in the side yard. "You're being paid by that empty-headed fool of a daughter. What's her name?"

Valentin didn't answer. The silence lingered until Harris looked at him again. Then Valentin said, "Anne Marie. Her name's Anne Marie. She hired me to find out what happened to her father."

"Did you?"

"Yes, I believe so."

The hard green eyes rested on him for a few moments. It was a gaze that was meant to command and Valentin had to do some work deflecting it. The stare he gave back was just short of insolent.

"You still haven't said why you're wasting my time here," Henry Harris said. "The last I heard, John Benedict was dead and buried."

"So is Charles Kane," the detective said. "And a fellow named Joe Kimball."

Valentin detected a certain light in Harris's stare.

"I know about Three V, Mr. Harris."

"Do you, indeed? Know what? It was one company of the many that I owned."

"Both of your former partners are dead. One was shot to death and the other one was abducted and drowned in the river. In the space of a week."

"That's unfortunate, isn't it?" Now Harris sounded judicious.

"I have the letter you wrote to Benedict and Kane."

"Oh? You have a *letter*." Harris hiked his eyebrows, mocking him. "Do you think you're a smart fellow because you found a twenty-year-old piece of paper? What were you planning to do with this *letter*?"

"Turn it over to the authorities. And give it to the newspapers."

"What authorities? The police?" Harris's thin lips stretched in an indulgent grin, as if he was listening to a childish boast. "Who cares anymore? Who cares that people who didn't belong here in the first place went away?"

"Someone cared enough to murder five men over it."

There was no concealing the accusation in his tone, and Valentin wished instantly that he hadn't given that away. Harris's cold eyes narrowed for an angry moment, and Valentin sensed Nelson tensing behind him. The moment passed and now the white man's stare glittered with a certain cruel pleasure.

"I know about you," he said deliberately. "You're that *Creole detective*. You're half nigger and half dago. So is that what they call a Creole these days?" He saw the look on Valentin's face, glanced at Little and Nelson, and snickered. "Good lord, he looks like he wants to kill me right now." He brought his gaze back to the detective. "But I don't think you could. Even if Mr. Nelson there handed you his pistol. Because you're not a murderer. And that doesn't make you a very good dago, does it?"

He waited for a response, got none, and drew himself up. "You know I have scum try to cadge money from me every day of the week. If that's what you came for, I guess we can spare a dollar or two. If not, you really have wasted your time. And mine."

The sinking feeling in his gut told Valentin he had made a terrible mistake. Blinded by his intent, he had raced to this corrupt and venal man's doorstep with no hand to play. As if Harris would simply surrender, fall on his knees to beg forgiveness, and immediately begin a campaign of retribution to those he had so abused.

And Harris wasn't about to have him shot, either. He didn't consider him a threat at all, just another miscreant staging a foolhardy attempt at blackmail. Now it was over.

"Mr. Nelson?" Harris said. Nelson came to attention. "Please escort this *detective* out of the house and carry him to the train station and send him on his way back to Storyville." He turned away, dismissing him, and settled his placid gaze on the children and the pony.

Valentin turned to follow Nelson out of the room. Outside, Nelson told him to wait, then went back into the house. He wondered if maybe they were deciding to do away with him after all, just for the sport of it.

Stoneman was leaning against the side of the Buick, smoking another one of his Straight Cuts. He offered the pack again. Valentin shook his head.

"Your business finished here?" Stoneman inquired.

Valentin nodded wistfully. "Seems so."

Stoneman said, "You didn't get what you came for, did you?"

Valentin thought about throwing out some bluster, then realized it would be pointless. "I didn't, no," he said.

Stoneman nodded and blew a plume of smoke. Valentin regarded him carefully, reading his face and posture, relaxed and tense all at once. It was familiar.

"You've been away somewhere, Mr. Stoneman?" he asked momentarily.

"I was, yes, sir."

"In prison?"

"Angola."

"What was your crime?"

"I killed a man," Stoneman said matter-of-factly. "Stuck a knife in his heart. I did three years." His face tightened. "He came at me. He shouldn't have done that. They called it self-defense, but they said I didn't have to kill him." He sighed quietly. "It sure felt like I had to at the time."

"I'm going to guess it was over a woman."

"It was."

"Was she worth it?"

"No, sir, she was not." Stoneman sighed. "Sometimes I think it would have been better if I'd stuck it in her heart. Except that I would have had a hard time finding it."

They both smiled over the quip. Valentin gazed at the big house in its magnificent and implacable glory. It looked like it could stand forever. He shook his head and sighed over the thrashing he had just taken. Eulalie Echo had been right, and so had Justine and Frank.

Stoneman said, "What's wrong, Mr. St. Cyr?"

"He's going to get away with something terrible," Valentin said. "And I can't touch him." Another glum moment passed and he said, "I never should have done this."

Stoneman was quiet, as if there was something going on behind his eyes. His voice dropped and he said, "Yes, sir, that probably was a mistake, all right. Rather than show up here, maybe you should have just waited for him to come outside."

Valentin emerged from his funk to give Stoneman a curious look. "Come outside where?"

"He goes to town every Sunday night," Stoneman said in a low voice. "He's got a woman he visits there."

Valentin pondered for a few seconds. It felt like there was light filling his head. "A woman."

"Yes, sir."

"On Ursulines, by chance?"

"He has a fine new Essex cabriolet," Stoneman said. "We take that automobile. Usually leave right around seven o'clock."

It was all Valentin could do to keep from pounding the fender of the Buick at his own stupidity. Sylvia Cardin told him she hadn't seen John Benedict in over a month. She was finished with him. Delouche said he'd had nothing to do with her. And yet there were no signs she was leaving out of her rooms on Ursulines. She wasn't going anywhere. Because someone else was paying the fare.

He stopped to consider the possibility that Benedict's killing was nothing but a spat over a woman. It had happened before. Mr. Stoneman said that he himself had spent three years in Angola for that very reason.

Valentin now regarded Stoneman carefully, wondering if it could be some kind of a trap. "Why are you telling me this?" he said.

Stoneman's eyes lightened at the detective's wariness. Then his jaw clenched. "Because I don't owe that rich man a fucking thing, that's why. He ain't nothing to me."

Valentin heard the bitter tone and understood. Something had happened to this fellow. He looked closer. Lurking just below Stoneman's skin was foreign blood, maybe Cherokee, or something more distant. Apparently, Mr. Nelson didn't check on his help all that well.

"This here's just a job I took," Stoneman was saying. "I don't really know Nelson, nor any of them others, either."

"You wouldn't know if they did some killings down in New Orleans."

"No, sir. It wouldn't surprise me, though. Nelson's mean and them others are too stupid to think on their own. So, yeah, they could do it, all right."

He stopped then, his face changing as his gaze lingered on

the flowering fruit trees that lined the drive. "It's something to take someone's life away, ain't it?" he said.

"It is," Valentin agreed, realizing to his surprise that he and this stranger had somehow ventured into private territory. Stoneman seemed as taciturn a man as he was; and yet they were tapping a vein that ran very deep.

"That poor fellow's in the ground," Stoneman went on. "And here I stand. You know how that feels?"

Valentin nodded, thinking that maybe they both carried a mark that only certain people could discern, something drawn in blood. He didn't want to go any further down that path.

He was relieved, then, when Nelson came out the front door of the house. "Hey," he called, a warning note in his voice. "Take him to the station and leave him." He went into his pocket, pulled out Valentin's pistol, and tossed it in the air. "Give it back to him when you get there. Not before."

Stoneman snatched the pistol deftly from the air with one hand and tossed what was left of his cigarette away with the other.

They rode off the property and to the train station at Jefferson without exchanging another word. As soon as they were off Harris's property, Stoneman handed over the revolver. When they pulled up to the terminal, he offered his hand.

"Pleasure talking to you, Mr. St. Cyr," he said. "Maybe we'll meet up in New Orleans one day. Maybe one day soon. Who knows?"

Valentin hopped down. Stoneman turned the Buick around and drove off.

By the time he got back to New Orleans and walked over to Marais Street, the lamps were on, and Frank was in a rush working an early evening crowd that had the saloon buzzing.

Valentin had wanted to tell him about his visit to Nine Mile Point, and maybe the rest of it, but the bar was too busy. The saloon keeper saw him and stopped, looking relieved; then he treated him to a narrow-eyed glance.

"What's wrong?" he said, raising his voice over the noise. "Where you been all day?"

"I can tell you later," Valentin said. He looked around the merry crowd, getting a jump on Saturday night's revelry and all the loud and happy jass music that would go with it. He gave Frank a wave and edged away.

"You leaving?" Frank said. "Stay and have a drink."

"There's one more place I need to go."

"Now?"

"Yeah. I'll see you later."

The saloon keeper watched with a pronounced frown as the detective walked out the door. Then he went back to pouring drinks.

It was dark and cool when he arrived at the very spot in front of Longshoreman's Hall where he had stood three years before and watched Buddy come down the street. The look of giddy surprise on his face. *What are you doin' here?* Not knowing what was about to happen, which was the beginning of the end. In the final hours of the jass case, he had laid the trap on Rampart Street and unraveled the puzzle that had taunted him for weeks. Finally, from where he stood, he could see the place a block down where John Benedict had fallen.

He had stood there with Officer McKinney in the full light of day, when the saloons and the dance halls were all closed down, their facades looking faded and forlorn and impossibly shoddy.

The wind and rain made a mess of the street. The sanitation crews didn't get there very often. In the morning after, it would look like the circus had just left town.

It was a different place at night. Once the sun went down and the lights came on, the crowds would come, in a trickle, then a rush. First it was the regulars, stumbling out of their drunken beds. Then they came from all over the city, even from the American side. Once the music got going, it ran wild, and the fever of drinking and dancing and noisy jass lasted until just before first light. Then the dancers and the jass players, the rounders and the whores all went home, or to wherever they went when the darkness faded into daylight.

Standing there, Valentin could see that it wasn't that way anymore. It was a Saturday, and yet the crowds along the street were thin. He could hear a couple jass bands warming up, but it was only a faint echo of what was there before. All the really fine players had taken a lesson from Bolden's sad tale and had given up their evil ways, cleaned up their music, and crossed Canal Street, where the money was good.

Valentin knew that there would always be players around who couldn't mend their ways, playing that raw, fast, looping jass that had made such a rage just a few years back. They'd stay until the end, until no one was listening anymore.

It might not be long. The bright lights that had once festooned the buildings seemed muted. Indeed, a few of the former hot spots—the Little Twist and the Congo Dance Hall—were closed up for good. Another year or two, and there'd be nothing left at all.

Benedict had been lured here, then shot down, and left for the night's scavengers. Such a strange crime could only be contrived, for a reason he still didn't see.

He looked around some more. All he saw were citizens ambling around, white, various shades of Creole brown, deep black, Italian, some in between. The muted strains of real jass echoed from inside the walls of the saloons.

He thought about that. Now and forever, Rampart Street would be remembered as the place where jass was born. Instead of fading away the way some had hoped, the music was in fact catching on from New York to Los Angeles. But this was the place. This was where it began. This was where Bolden and the others broke down the wall. This was where all the crowds arrived on Saturday nights to hear a crazy man play his crazy music. This was the place where they all rubbed shoulders under electric stars and the wash of loud brass. Some of them, taken by the spirit, even danced together, and that was a scandal all its own.

It came to him in that moment. He had looked in Henry Harris's pale eyes and seen a panorama of bleak disgust that drove so much of his being. Now he understood why it had to be there.

He started walking, and in a few minutes passed the place where Benedict had fallen. Another few minutes and he turned the corner at Second Street, leaving whatever was left of the bright lights of Rampart Street behind.

He stopped for dinner at a workmen's café on Decatur Street that stayed open late, then wandered through Jackson Square, taking in the sights.

When he crossed over Basin Street, he looked up at the window of the corner room of Antonia Gonzales's mansion and saw that it was dark. Sporting girls didn't often douse the lights in their rooms; they preferred to keep an eye on their customers. Justine had done it for him, of course, but that was different. He wondered where she'd gone on a Saturday night.

Mangetta's was bubbling with noise, the swelling crowd almost spilling out onto the banquette. Valentin had already enjoyed the saloon and the music the night before, and that was enough. He now edged along the alleyway, keeping an eye on back and front. Though after his performance that afternoon, he guessed that no one would be harassing him.

He let himself in and went up the stairs. After he undressed, he opened his window and sat on the sill, listening to the laughter and music from the floor below as he gazed out on the back streets of Storyville.

He wondered if Henry Harris had any idea that the story wasn't over yet. The seeds had been sown by John Benedict as he tried to reclaim some semblance of honor in his daughter's eyes. Harris thought having his men do away with Benedict and Kane, the other third of the cabal, had finished that old business, and a Creole detective in the employ of one victim's daughter was a mere nuisance. What he wouldn't count on was a betrayal by the likes of Louis Stoneman, a blank-faced underling he would barely recognize.

Valentin shifted his position. Though there was a chink in the wall, he knew it didn't mean he could destroy someone as powerful as Harris. Everyone else had been right about that while he, in his clumsy arrogance, had been wrong. He could still hurt the man, though. That would have to be enough.

With that thought, he let go of it. The final act would arrive soon enough. He switched his thoughts to something more pleasant, conjuring an image of Anne Marie Benedict, lying back on her bed and reaching for him with longing in her eyes. As if to suit his reverie, the music that floated up from the saloon was a gutbucket blues, languid and laden with a sultry heat.

THIRTEEN

A hard storm rose up on the Gulf and came through in the middle of the night. It was early in the year for such violence, but in what seemed a sudden instant, the sky was cracked into pieces like a broken bowl, with claws of lightning turning every corner of the city an electric white for the time it took a startled heart to beat. The rain came down with a driving gray weight and cast at such an angle that those unfortunate few who were on the streets swore it was horizontal.

At its height, it shook windows and rattled nerves from Chalmette to Carrollton. Small children ran to their parents' beds, while under other roofs, the waking led to a frolic under the covers as the wild rain drummed the windowpanes. For twenty minutes, no more, New Orleans was under an artillery barrage and then, just as suddenly, the storm cowed and died, leaving a few lonely rumbles of thunder and a flash of cloudy light here and there.

On St. Philip Street, Anne Marie Benedict heard her mother moan at the first mutter of thunder, and went down the hall to calm her. As she was stepping back into the hallway, she heard a noise at the front door and came to the top of the stairs just as Betsy, all soaked and looking silly, tumbled into the foyer.

The maid whispered an apology. Anne Marie thought about asking her to come into her room, so that they could talk about what had happened. Instead, she wished her a good-night and went back to her bed.

To the west, where the river buckled at Nine Mile Point, the noise and light felt like an earthquake, and the security men who ran to one of the sheds for shelter were not surprised to see Henry Harris standing at his bedroom window in a nightshirt, blasted in deathly white light as he glared out at the storm.

As always, he was alone in the room. His wife slept elsewhere. He forced himself to stay at the window, remembering the time long ago when he had been on a boat on the river and a tremendous storm rose up. Such a feeling of terror had engulfed him as he bent under a power so much greater than his own, that it rendered him null. Now, whenever there was such a gale, he would stand in the face of its furious display. And he never shed the bottomless fear.

On Marais Street, Valentin St. Cyr came awake and sat up to watch the spectacle outside the window. In the brunt of such a tempest, his efforts also seemed so puny and useless. But for some reason, he took comfort in it.

Indeed, for the long minutes that it raged, the citizens of New Orleans were helpless, no matter what their station or color. No one could escape it.

Once the storm passed, Valentin sat up for some hours, thinking about how he was going to put an end to the case.

Sunday dawned dry, the sky such a pale and wispy blue that it seemed the night's storm had been a collective dream. Only some telltale puddles and the water that stood between the cobbles remained.

Valentin did not rise until the church bells tolled eleven. He got dressed and visited the bathroom down the hall, then went down the stairs and out the storage room door and into the saloon, where he found Frank perusing the Sunday *Picayune* and sipping coffee. He nodded to the table in the center of the floor and went off to the kitchen. Valentin took the newspaper off the bar and read it as he waited. When Frank appeared with two plates in his hands, they settled down to breakfast. They didn't discuss Henry Harris, or Anne Marie Benedict, or in fact anything of substance, and they enjoyed their breakfast in peace. Though Valentin caught Frank sneaking occasional glances over the top of a page.

It was early afternoon and Anne Marie was soaking in her bath when Betsy came knocking. For once, the maid didn't barge in, but announced from the other side of the door that Mr. St. Cyr had called and he was on his way. He'd be there in an hour or so, she said.

Anne Marie said, "You may come in," and Betsy opened the door and leaned there, waiting. "Did he say what he wants?"

"He didn't, no. About his investigation, I guess."

Anne Marie nodded blankly. There was a poised and silent moment, and then her shoulders sagged and she put a distraught hand over her eyes.

"I did a terrible thing!" she said. She sounded like she was on the verge of weeping again.

"What terrible thing?"

"With Mr. . . . with *Valentin*," she said. "You know what I'm talking about. It wasn't supposed to be like that."

Betsy knelt down next to the tub, took hold of Anne Marie's wrist, and pulled the hand away from her face. Anne Marie couldn't meet her gaze. "You didn't do nothin' wrong," the maid said. "It's about as natural as water."

Anne Marie let out a long, shaky sigh. "You think he's coming here to make amends?"

"You mean do right by you?" Betsy grinned. "Ask for your hand? No, ma'am, not that one. He ain't gonna do anything of the kind. You don't have to worry 'bout that at all." She found the idea comical and Anne Marie blushed and rolled her eyes.

"My god, what was I thinking?" she cried to the walls. She looked at Betsy, scandalized. "The man's *colored*!"

Betsy said, "Well, at least he looks white," and the two of them broke into laughter.

After a moment, Anne Marie settled herself. "I'll be out in a few minutes," she said. Betsy stood up and went into the hall, closing the door and leaving Anne Marie with her thoughts of Mr. Valentin St. Cyr.

They finished breakfast and Frank was cleaning up when Valentin asked him to sit down for a few minutes. The saloon keeper agreed reluctantly, as if he sensed what was coming and didn't really want to hear it.

Valentin took him through the prior forty-eight hours, omitting only his interlude with Anne Marie. Frank was livid when he heard about the visit to Nine Mile Point. He threw up his hands and his face went red.

"Everybody said don't go there and you went anyway? *Managgia idiota!* What the hell was to stop him from shooting you in the damn head?"

"I know, I know," the detective said.

"So now what?" Frank said, calming himself.

"That's what I really wanted to talk to you about."

He told Frank of the plan he had been formulating. The saloon keeper listened, shaking his head from side to side. When he finished, he waited for a reaction. Frank was too distressed, though, and sat in brooding silence. Valentin asked to use the phone.

He called around and finally located Tom Anderson at Gipsy Shafer's. The King of Storyville told him to come by sooner rather than later.

When Valentin got to Miss Shafer's mansion, Anderson met

him in the kitchen, where he was enjoying a midday breakfast. A pretty Creole girl stood by the stove and didn't say a thing. Valentin explained the parts that Anderson needed to know. Then he sketched the rest of it.

After listening to what the detective had in mind to do, Anderson sighed with a familiar resignation. "There's no other way?" he asked.

"There's no other *chance*," Valentin said. "What else am I going to do?"

"You could just let it be," Anderson said. They both knew that wouldn't happen now. "I'm sorry I got you into this."

"I'm not," Valentin said. He stood up to leave and the King of Storyville offered his hand. There was nothing else to say.

When he came to the door and their eyes met, Betsy was careful not to give anything away. She let him in and told him Miss Anne Marie was waiting in the sitting room.

"Good afternoon," Anne Marie said as he walked in. He could hear how hard she was working to keep her voice steady as she gestured him to the chair opposite. "Please have a seat."

For her part, it was as if it had been some other man who had come to her in her bedroom the day before. Not this fellow, the private detective, sitting at polite attention. She couldn't quite keep the blush out of her cheeks and was grateful that he was taking pains to ignore it. Or maybe it just didn't matter to him. Maybe, she thought, he seduced virgins from good families all the time. It wouldn't really surprise—

"I want to tell you where the investigation has led me," he said. "Because it's almost over. I think it's going to end tonight."

"Tonight?"

"That's right," he said, then paused for a moment. "Henry Harris was behind it. He arranged for your father to be killed on Rampart Street. Mr. Kane's murder, too. And the others lead back to him."

"Because of what my father was planning to expose, what those men did?"

"That's the part I know for sure. There are some other questions. I'll have the answers when it's finished."

"Can you tell me what you're going to do?"

"It's better if you don't know. I'll explain when it's over."

She was watching him speculatively. "Are you sure what you're planning will work?"

"No."

"Are you risking your life?" she asked him.

"They already missed their chances at me," he said wryly. "They've let down now. I don't think they'll see me coming."

"You don't think?" She frowned and looked away from him.

"Anyway, by tonight, it will be finished," he said. "If it doesn't come out the way I hope, there will be nothing more I can do. He'll get away with it. I wanted you to know that."

"Then I guess I better hope it comes out right, too," she said, a little sharply. He was too cool and distant for her taste. Especially after what had transpired on her bed. He was acting like it hadn't happened at all.

He got to his feet. "Well, then..."

She stood up, too, deciding she'd be damned if she was going to let him just go on his merry way, maybe to get himself killed.

"Wait a moment," she said, and held his eyes for the first time since he'd walked in. "I want you to know that I'm not a schoolgirl. I understand what happened yesterday. It's done. I couldn't change it, even if I wanted to."

"Do you?" he said, and she realized that his poise was not quite so stolid. He was looking abashed, like he thought she was ignoring what was between them.

"No, Valentin, I don't." They were both quiet for a few seconds. Then she said, "I won't make anything difficult for you. I can't. And you can't do that to me, either. Do you understand?"

"I do," Valentin said.

"All right, then," she said. There was a tiny waver in her voice. "I'll be waiting to hear from you."

He surprised her then, stepping close and kissing her not on the lips and not on the cheek, but somewhere in between, with a tenderness that made her heart thump. After he walked out, the brush of his kiss and the look in his eyes lingered with her.

Valentin caught a streetcar back to Storyville and spent part of the ride musing on what Anne Marie had said. Much to his relief, she remained a levelheaded young lady, even about something as momentous as surrendering her innocence. Not that it was any too soon, in his opinion. In any case, he didn't want to imagine the kind of grief she could have brought down on his head.

He turned his thoughts to the rest of his day. His plan was to spend the afternoon in his room, lying low, doing nothing to alert his prey. Later, he'd go to the grocery and make himself something to eat. Once the sun went down, he'd use the shadows to carry out his plot.

He walked through the District from the north, arriving on Marais Street a little after three o'clock. He let himself in through the back and climbed the steps. When he got to the hallway, he glanced at Angelo's door and saw a light underneath it. The *signore* was on the premises this afternoon. He was usually gone on Sundays.

Valentin locked his door and crossed to open the windows for some air. He poked around in his closet for a worn-out volume of stories and poems by Edgar Allan Poe, then stretched on his bed to read. It was something he hadn't done in a long time, and it gave him some peace before whatever commotion might come later.

Halfway through "Gordon Pym," he dozed off. It was a light, dreamless sleep, and he almost woke two or three times, imagining he heard noises and voices from downstairs. He knew that couldn't be, though. It was Sunday, and everyone was gone.

There was a sharp knock on his door that brought him awake with a start.

"Hey, Tino, *paisano mio.*" It was Frank. "Come on out of there."

Valentin sat up, blinking, and swung his legs off the bed. "What are you doing here?" he called.

"Come downstairs," the saloon keeper said.

"What for?"

Frank was moving away. "Just come on downstairs," he repeated.

When he stepped into the archway, Valentin was startled to see Reynard Vernel leaning against the bar with his foot on the rail. Then he saw Beansoup, Justine, and Betsy seated around one of the tables. Frank was behind the bar, in the process of opening a bottle of wine. It was such a bizarre tableau that he came to a stop and stared at them.

"What are you all doing here?" he said.

"Having a glass of wine," the saloon keeper said breezily.

"Is that right?" Valentin looked from face to face, and it began to dawn on him what was going on. "So everyone just happened to show up?"

"No, we were invited," Justine said.

"Invited by who?" The detective said, and looked directly at Frank.

"Anyway, they're all here," Frank said.

Valentin leaned on the bar and turned to Reynard Vernel. "And are you recording the proceedings for posterity?"

Vernel said, "I thought I might."

The detective nodded and fixed his attention on Beansoup.

"I'm going to guess you're the one who did the running to get them all here." The kid shrugged.

Valentin glanced at Betsy, who was keeping her face pleasantly blank. "Miss James," he said.

"Mr. St. Cyr," she replied.

Justine was watching the maid with some curiosity, as if she wanted to ask her something. Instead, she said, very deliberately, "But since we came, we thought we might keep you from getting yourself killed."

"Do what?"

"You've been doing some fucking stupid things," the saloon keeper said.

Valentin frowned at him. "You couldn't just talk to me? You had to call a meeting?"

"You don't listen to me," Frank said. He gestured to the others. "I thought maybe if they heard. They're your friends. They happen to care if you live or die. So..."

"So?"

"We want to hear what you've got on Mr. Henry Harris. And what you're going to do with it."

"It might be better if you don't know." Frank gave him a severe look, and he felt the expectant eyes of the others on him. He didn't want to do this now. And yet they had come there on a Sunday afternoon...

"All right, then," he said, relenting. "This all started—"

"Hold on," Frank interrupted. "We're waiting for one more."

"Who?" Valentin said, but the saloon keeper had already gone out through the archway.

In the silence that ensued, Justine watched him with such a knowing look that he wondered if Anne Marie had left a mark on him. So he was glad to hear the shuffling of feet from the grocery side. He turned his head in time to see Frank reappear in the archway with Signore Angelo on his heels.

He was so startled by this that he spilled some of his wine. The others gazed with interest at the stranger in their midst. Angelo was dressed like a peasant, in gray trousers and a white shirt, open at the neck. His eyes were round and quietly mournful. Clearing his throat, he said, *"Scusa,"* and took the chair at the table that was against the wall and closest to the archway.

"This is Angelo," Frank explained to everyone. He looked at Valentin. *"Un cugino."*

Valentin pulled his eyes off Angelo to gaze at Frank in wonder. "He's your *cousin?*"

Frank laughed shortly. "No, *paisan,* he's yours. Kind of distant, but..." He wagged a hand in the air. *"Famiglia,* eh?"

The detective was confounded. "Well, I'll be damned."

Shyly, Angelo dropped his gaze from the scrutiny as Frank fetched him his glass of wine.

"He knows about what happened on the docks," the saloon keeper explained. "He wants to hear what you have to say."

Valentin looked at Angelo. *"Parla inglese?"* he asked. Angelo shrugged, his black eyes animal calm.

"I'll translate what he don't understand," Frank said.

It took Valentin a few moments to regain his place.

"Well, then," he began. "This all started out as a favor for Tom Anderson, who was doing a favor for someone else. Mr. Benedict had been found murdered on Rampart Street. A simple case. Nothing to it. But the victim's daughter..." He felt his face warming. "...she said she wanted to know if there was more to it. And it looked like there was, because within a week a man named Charles Kane was dead. He was connected to Benedict, and to Henry Harris."

He sipped his wine. "What she didn't tell me at the time, was that she had found a twenty-year-old letter from Harris to these two victims, creating a company called Three V, and stating its purpose."

Vernel said, "What does Three V stand—"

"Wait a minute," the detective said, holding up a hand. "The company's purpose was to run the Italians off the docks. Pure and simple. The Orange Wars hadn't done it. The murder of Chief Hennessy hadn't done it. Harris wanted them gone for good. And so he created this company with Benedict and Kane. Three V."

Angelo shifted in his chair, his eyes fixed on the detective.

"They did it," Valentin continued. "They starved them out. And then they took over." He paused. "When the daughter found the letter and realized what her father had done, she shamed him into promising to fix it somehow. That's when he made his mistake. He talked to Kane, and Kane told Henry Harris, or one of his people. Benedict was killed. And Kane was next."

"Why him?" Justine asked.

"He knew too much. And he was a drunk and a loudmouth. They couldn't trust him to stay quiet." He put his empty glass on the bar and Frank moved to refill it. "It was still white people's business, and all I wanted to do was be done with it. Then Joe Kimball was murdered, because he found something I needed. And that's when everything changed. That's when I decided to go after Henry Harris. Because he was responsible."

"Just to cover up what they did twenty years ago?" Frank asked.

"I wondered about that, too," Valentin said. "There had to be something else to it. And there was." He looked over at Frank. "Can I see your chalkboard?"

Frank gave him a puzzled glance, then bent down behind the bar and reappeared with the chalkboard he used to post special meals and the name of the band slated for the evening. He handed it to Valentin, along with a thick piece of chalk.

The detective stood the board on a table and drew <u>V V V</u> on it. "This was engraved into rings that the partners wore," he explained.

"Three V's," Beansoup recited. "Like the company."

"That was their little joke," Valentin said. "Though it wasn't very funny." He stopped for a moment. "The last thing Joe Kimball did was tell me I was looking at it all wrong."

He turned the board so that it was now vertical, then wet a finger and rubbed the chalk between the letters away. "It's not V, V, V, at all," he said. The letters on the board now read:

K

K

K

"K, K, K," Justine said.

"The Ku Klux Klan," Vernel said.

"By the time Harris and the others became proud members of that group, it wasn't just Negroes they were after," Valentin said. "They'd added Italians, Greeks, Turks, and anyone else who wasn't white to their list."

Justine's brow furrowed. "So they did it because they hated Italians?"

"Well, it must have driven Harris mad to see those families prospering right under his nose," Valentin said. "He believed all the money they were making should rightfully have been in American hands. His American hands."

He stopped for a minute to let Frank make the rounds with the wine bottle.

"Harris built his name in politics on his hatred for Negroes and Italians and all the rest," he went on. "He wanted to use that in a campaign for the United States Senate. So why would he care if Benedict exposed it. Enough to have him murdered, I mean. Running a bunch of dirty dagos off the docks wouldn't hurt him all that much. Some people would call him a hero. But a lot wouldn't, so maybe it was the second nail in Benedict's coffin. Still not enough to wreck his plans, though. I thought there had to be one more. And there was."

"What was it?" Betsy asked, speaking up for the first time.

"A woman."

"What woman?" Justine said.

"Mr. Benedict had a mistress. An octoroon named Sylvia Cardin. When I spoke to her, she said she hadn't seen him in over a month, that she had ended their affair. And yet there she was, still living in those fine rooms."

"So someone else was paying for it," Justine said.

"Henry Harris?" Vernel said.

Valentin said, "He had stolen her away. He was dallying with a woman of color. I believe Benedict decided that if he couldn't get at him any other way, he'd expose him over that." He shook his head. "It was a terrible mistake. Harris could have withstood being accused of raiding businesses. And his membership in the Ku Klux Klan. That was old news. But he couldn't abide having it exposed that he had been having at a colored woman, too. After all his talk, it would ruin his chances for office. So he got rid of Benedict and Kane. Joe Kimball found the Klan connection and he might have found out about Miss Cardin before I did. So he had to go. Then I got too close and they sent those two bandits after me. They should have just shot me down and left it at that, like they did with Joe. But they wanted to play a game. Which they failed, thanks to Frank. They were both killed before they made a worse mess."

He rubbed his forehead thoughtfully. "So," he said, "I had all this, but there was nothing I could do with it." He shifted uncomfortably. "Then *I* made a mistake. I got a message to Harris that I wanted to see him. He sent a car for me, and I went to his home at Nine Mile Point."

Frank shook his head and said, "Why the hell did you go out there alone?"

Valentin evaded the question and the saloon keeper's stare. "I should have known. He's a hateful little man who made himself into an emperor. And I really had nothing to put up against him.

I couldn't touch him, and he knew it. So he just sent me on my way. But then..." He paused for effect.

"Then what?" Frank and Justine said at once.

"Then someone whispered something in my ear. Something I can use to get at him. And I will."

He stopped, and his blank expression told them he wasn't going to say any more on that subject. They were all quiet for a few moments, digesting what he'd related.

"I still don't understand how he ended up on Rampart Street," Justine asked presently.

"That bothered me all along, too," Valentin said. "Why not Canal or Marais or any other street in New Orleans? Why not on Esplanade Ridge while he was taking the air one night? I finally figured it out last night."

He drank off some wine, reminding himself to go easy before he got drunk and stupid and said too much.

"There were actually two reasons," he said. "One was to make it look like he went there for some crib girl and got caught in a robbery that went bad. Harris was betting that him dying out there would make such a scandal that the family would want it buried immediately. It was perfect. No witnesses, but plenty of suspects."

"What was the other reason?" Beansoup asked.

"That was personal," Valentin said. "He wanted to rub Benedict's nose in it. To Harris, Rampart Street is four blocks of hell. Race mixing, nigger music, drunks and hopheads, all of it. So he was saying, 'This is what you want to stand up for? This is what you get!' It was a special message."

"But they still had to get him to go there," Justine said.

Valentin said, "Harris must have let him know that if he wanted to settle it, he needed to be at a certain corner on Rampart Street at a certain hour. That was the only way. And just to rub his nose in it just a little bit more, he made him wear that ring."

The others exchanged glances, their faces belying doubt.

"The quadroon could have got him to go down there," Justine said. "He'd do it for her."

Valentin gave her an appreciative nod. "That could be. She's a bitter woman, and she wants to keep what she has. Benedict was about to wreck it." He paused. "Maybe she had no idea it was going to end in murder."

The silence that followed lasted almost half a minute. Then Reynard Vernel, no doubt thinking of all the journalistic possibilities, said, "Fascinating."

Frank shook his head. "Yeah, but what are you going to do with it?"

"I'm going to use it," Valentin said. "Tonight."

"*Che?*" The saloon keeper stared at him. "What's that mean?"

"I'm going to corner him. And finish it. Tonight."

There was another heavy pause, and then Frank said, "I'm going with you."

"I am, too," Beansoup said quickly.

"And I am, too," Vernel said.

Before Valentin could protest, Angelo cleared his throat. They all looked at him. "*Io, anche,*" he said softly. "Me, too."

Frank nodded with satisfaction, as if it was all settled. Then he looked around and said, "Who wants more wine?"

They had all been so enthralled with Valentin's story that no one had noticed the dark clouds rising. It had started to rain in thin silver slivers as Beansoup grabbed an umbrella from the corner to walk Betsy to Canal Street to get a streetcar, while Vernel grabbed another to escort Justine back to Basin Street. Both would return directly.

Valentin stood in the recess of the doorway until he spotted a couple street Arabs rounding the corner at Iberville. He whistled and they came running. He gave the two kids each a quarter and sent them off to the Vieux Carré with a message for Papá Bellocq.

In the meantime, Frank had gone into the grocery and had come out with his arms full of bread, cheese, and meat, and made up a platter. The three men sat down at one of the tables and began a quiet meal. When first Vernel and then Beansoup came back, they joined in the feast. Frank asked, and Valentin explained in more detail what he planned to do. The others listened in silence. They all had one more drink, then headed out as the last light of day was dying.

They took their time strolling through the quiet shower to Basin Street, then crossed over into the back end of the Quarter. It was quiet on this Sunday night, with few pedestrians on the streets. The men didn't talk at all.

Valentin spent the walk thinking about how much had happened in such a short span of time. Two weeks before, he had been minding his business, doing a poor job at work, hiding in his room, and aimlessly walking these same streets, sometimes all night. He had been thrown from that quiet life into the middle of a case that he could solve, but couldn't fix with any sort of satisfaction. He wasn't dealing with Storyville miscreants anymore. He had encountered someone with so much power and wealth that he didn't have to answer to anyone for anything. Or so Henry Harris had come to believe. Maybe it was true and maybe not.

Valentin thought that he had a chance to knock him off his tracks and shake his world. With a little luck, there would be no Senator Harris going to Washington, D.C. The detective realized that it was likely all he could do, without committing a murder of his own.

When they reached Bourbon Street at St. Philip, Valentin murmured for them to wait, and he cut down the alley. He knocked on the narrow door, inciting a clamor of grunts, curses, and metallic clanks from inside.

"It's Valentin, Papá," he said. "It's time to go."

Papá Bellocq threw the door open and lurched out carrying

a box camera, which he shoved into the detective's hands. The door slammed behind them, and they trudged back out onto the street.

The six of them made their way through the Quarter. The rain was a blessing; no one saw them as they drew up on their destination.

When they turned the corner from Bourbon onto Ursulines, Valentin saw that they had almost arrived too late; Harris had decided to make this Sunday's visit an early one. The Essex was parked in front of Sylvia's building. Nelson was sitting sideways in the passenger seat, under the cover of the canvas top, his legs dangling onto the running board. He looked dazed with boredom. Stoneman was standing under the balcony, next to the downstairs door, smoking one of his Straight Cuts. There was nothing except the steady rain to absorb either man's attention.

Valentin waved his companions back around the corner and under the colonnade of a restaurant that was closed for the night, then ducked along the banquette on the north side of the street, opposite Sylvia Cardin's rooms. He stopped under a balcony and before a door that was fronted by plants, with ivy vines crawling down the wrought iron. Even if Nelson turned all the way around, he'd be hard-pressed to pick out the human shadow from vegetation that was shrouded in darkness and veiled by the rain.

Valentin remained still for another minute, until he heard a small commotion on the corner of Royal Street, two men arguing with a woman's voice chiming in. As they were yelling back and forth, a hack clattered up Bourbon. With this racket as cover, he stalked across the street and came up on the driver's side of the Essex. In a swift motion, he drew his Iver Johnson, opened the door, and jumped into the driver's seat. Nelson began to turn, only to find the barrel of the pistol planted in the back of his skull. He froze. Stoneman straightened, staring but remaining still. Valentin glanced over to see something in those cool eyes that he couldn't quite read.

"I'm going to give you and your friend a chance to walk away," Valentin told Nelson.

"Or what?" Nelson muttered.

The detective pulled back the hammer on the revolver. "I know what you did, Nelson. You murdered Benedict and Kane, and you sent those men after my friend. And me."

Nelson looked over at Stoneman with some urgency, only to find his partner gazing off somewhere, as if this business had nothing to do with him. "What the hell do you think you're doing?" He coughed out a cold laugh. "You going to shoot Henry Harris?"

"It's none of your affair anymore," Valentin said. "You just lost your job."

"Is that right?"

He turned his head a half inch. Valentin pressed the pistol harder into his skull.

"Just so you know, it's not just me out here," he said.

"Well?" Nelson said after a few seconds. "Now what?"

"Now you can both leave. Start walking. Keep going, and don't look back. Because if you turn around, I'll kill you."

He realized then that if Nelson decided to be a hero, he'd have to put a bullet in his brain, right there in the street. And that would be the end of it. His finger tensed on the trigger and for the briefest instant the thought crossed his mind that he might have forgotten to load the damn thing.

He didn't need it. Nelson, taking his time to show he couldn't be pushed, did move, leaning away from the revolver and stepping onto the banquette. He strolled away languidly, refusing to be hurried by the weapon now pointed at his back.

Valentin waved the barrel of the revolver and Stoneman winked and then walked off in the other direction, disappearing around the corner at Dauphine Street. Valentin lowered the weapon and turned around again to watch Nelson crossing Chartres Street. He wouldn't be coming back.

The detective whistled and Beansoup stuck his head out from around the building on the corner. The kid, Reynard Vernel, and Papá Bellocq, carrying his Bantam Special, started across the street. A second later, Frank and Angelo appeared and proceeded along the opposite banquette.

The rain had rendered this subterfuge unnecessary. If Harris happened to open the curtains and look out the window, he'd see nothing of concern. The plan had been set, though, and once Bellocq and his two companions made their creaking way along the banquette, the six of them huddled under Miss Cardin's balcony.

The detective whispered the instructions once more to make sure everyone understood. He asked Papá Bellocq to check his camera. The Frenchman muttered irritably, something about being as ready as any of them. The other men smiled briefly. Then Valentin nodded; it was time to move.

He tried the street door and found it unlocked, a good sign. He pushed it open, stepped inside, and waited, listening. There was no sound from above. He used the time to consider his plan one more time. He hoped to find Harris in some compromising position with Sylvia Cardin. Frolicking in her bed would be best, though anything intimate would do. Papá Bellocq would make a photograph; that, and the eyewitness account of Vernel the news scribbler, would be their evidence.

Though once he had it in hand, he had no idea what he would do with it. He hadn't figured that part yet. It would be enough to hold something so powerful. It would be his own version of one of Miss Echo's voodoo charms.

He knew that what he was about to do might be a foolish ploy. It could easily fail. Bellocq's camera might malfunction. Sylvia might lock herself in her bathroom and refuse to come out. On the way over from Marais Street, he had considered another half-dozen things that could go wrong.

It was too late to reconsider. He couldn't walk away now. Henry Harris was unguarded and vulnerable, and he wouldn't get another chance like this.

Hearing no more sound, he went up the narrow stairwell and stood on the landing. Beansoup slipped inside the street door, holding Bellocq's Bantam Special.

It was so quiet inside that Valentin wondered if he had been tricked, if Harris had taken Sylvia off somewhere and Nelson was a few blocks away, convulsed with laughter at the Creole detective coming up empty-handed. He was thinking about that when he heard something on the other side of the door. It was a sigh or the shuffling of a foot or the swish of fabric, he couldn't be sure. Only that someone had moved.

He waited another half minute without hearing another thing, then waved to Beansoup. Cat quiet, the kid ascended the stairwell, placed the camera on the landing, then went back down. As soon as he slipped out the door, Frank, Angelo, and Bellocq shuffled inside.

Valentin laid his hand on the doorknob and turned. It was unlocked, and again he marveled at the arrogance of the man, to think himself so secure.

The detective gave another signal. Without hesitation, Frank and Angelo took Papá Bellocq under his elbows and hoisted him up the stairs. The Frenchman was small and light, and they made the climb without incident, though Bellocq looked positively incensed at the handling.

The two Italians dropped him on the landing. Valentin handed him his camera and Bellocq deftly filled his flash powder and stood ready. The detective laid a hand on the doorknob once more, turned and pushed.

Henry Harris was standing in the middle of the floor. After a moment of surprise at the intrusion, he glared, and the same armor-plated rich man Valentin had encountered at Nine Mile Point reappeared. It was not what the detective expected, and it gave him pause. Harris didn't look guilty at all. His next thought was that Sylvia Cardin was not in sight. He felt his stomach begin to sink.

Bellocq, Frank, and Angelo moved inside as he took a quick survey of the room. Everything was in order, and yet there was something not quite right about it. The place felt empty.

"Where is she?" he asked.

Instead of answering, Harris strolled over to the window and looked out on the street. "What happened to my men?" he demanded.

"They left," Valentin said. "Where's Sylvia, Mr. Harris?"

"Sylvia?" Harris said. "Is that what you came for?" He chuckled lightly. "Oh, I put her out. She went away this afternoon. And she won't be back." He waved a vague hand. "I'm just cleaning up a little. So you're too late." He looked over and saw Bellocq standing against the wall. "You even brought a camera." He seemed to notice Frank and Angelo for the first time. "More dagos," he murmured, with some disgust. "Well, you can all just leave. There's nothing to see here. Nothing you want." He folded his arms across his chest.

The detective understood. Harris had sensed that he was a threat after all, and went about erasing Sylvia Cardin from the equation. Maybe he paid her off and then put her on a train, or maybe he had Mr. Nelson shoot her dead and dump her body. Whatever the case, he had come to her rooms to make sure any trace of him was removed. So that the case really would be closed.

Valentin looked at that cold and self-righteous visage and realized that he had lost. Harris had anticipated his move and had beaten him.

The detective knew he could beat the details of the murders out of him, but it didn't matter. There wouldn't be anything he could use. Of course, he could shoot the man. Except everyone in the room understood that it wasn't his way.

Harris drew himself up impatiently. "If you would all leave, I want to lock the doors." He looked from face to face, as if he had no doubt they would comply.

Frank, who had remained silent since they walked in, spoke up. "Tino?" he said. "Get them two downstairs to help the Frenchman out of here." Valentin stared at him, not quite understanding. "Go on," Frank said, his voice flat and calm.

The detective looked at Angelo, saw an ancient emptiness in his eyes, and knew in that moment what was happening. "Frank..."

"Do what I say," Frank said.

"What's this now?" Henry Harris inquired fussily.

In that sudden moment, Valentin paused to give Harris a pitying look, and it seemed to dawn on the white man that he might actually be in peril. His eyes flicked and he licked his lips.

The detective went to the landing to call down to Beansoup and Vernel. They came up the stairwell and went about assisting Papá Bellocq, who was now only too glad to get out of that place. The four men in the room waited in silence for the other three to make their way down the stairs and out the door. Harris tried glaring with bluster from one man to the next, but his face paled by degrees from the stony looks he encountered.

"Now, see here," he said, with a hint of a whimper rising in his voice. "See here..." The flat gazes of the three men were unnerving him.

Valentin stepped to the front window and pushed the curtains apart in time to see Beansoup, Bellocq, and Vernel disappear around the corner at Bourbon Street. He turned around and looked at Frank.

"Now you go somewhere," Frank said. "Somewhere people know you."

Valentin studied the two Sicilians for a few seconds more, then walked out without a word. He did not look at Harris again.

He stopped when he got to the corner of Royal Street. The windows of Sylvia's rooms had gone dark. He headed west, on his way to circle around to Basin Street, and after a half block, he heard what sounded like the muffled report of a pistol. Though it might have been an engine backfiring. New Orleans was full of automobiles these days.

A quarter hour later, he was on Basin Street, passing the white walls of St. Louis Cemetery. He could just make out the roofs of the tallest vaults, geometric shapes cast in the silver light of the moon.

He walked along the street, away from the dark and somber block and into the light. He passed Willie Barrera's, then the firehouse, which was closed up and dark, save for a light in one upstairs window. The mansion run by that infamous witch of a madam French Emma Johnson was closed up as well. He walked by Antonia Gonzales's, Gipsy Shafer's, Mahogany Hall, and the rest of the line, finding every other door open for business.

When he got to Anderson's Café, he went around the corner and into the alley, slipping in through the private door on the north side, the one that important men used to veil their entrances and departures. He went inside and joined the crowd. Sunday was always a quiet night for gambling, more so when the weather was bad, and the tables were less than half full. Valentin found a place at the bar to lean an elbow and raised a hand for a drink.

At one point Tom Anderson made an appearance. He stopped to shake the detective's hand, then moved on to his other guests, those well-heeled gentlemen with their wallets full of ready cash. Valentin knew without asking that Anderson would swear that he'd been there all night.

The Creole detective cast his eye over the crowd, checking for any rascals who might be showing too quick an eye in perusing the back pockets of the other customers. He saw a couple rounders he knew, half of them flush, half down on their luck, always something to watch for. He didn't realize that he was doing it until one of the bartenders stopped to refill his drink and asked when he had come back to work.

FOURTEEN

Night bleeds into morning in a quiet way, even in back-of-town New Orleans. There's little moving in the hour before dawn, and it's as quiet as it ever gets.

An early rising workman, walking down Rampart Street to catch the first streetcar of the day, saw what appeared to be a bundle of old clothes that had been left in the doorway of one of the saloons that had gone out of business. The workman, a citizen who labored for little pay, stepped closer to check for something he might use. That's when he saw the dead-white hand sticking out from the sleeve of a nicely tailored suit coat. He yelled in fright, a sound that echoed down the street. Then he hurried to the call box on the next corner.

Within an hour the body of Henry Harris, business magnate and former state senator, had been swept from the street. It was fortunate that Lieutenant J. Picot, a cooperative soul, supervised the investigation of the crime scene. The lieutenant recognized the victim instantly, noticed the neat bullet wound, and knew what to do. Shoving aside the frantic thoughts that raced through his brain, he put a cordon around the corpse and sent a message to the chief of police himself. Henry Harris's body was collected within the hour and diverted from its proper destination at the city morgue to be delivered instead at a funeral home far out on St. Charles Avenue. There a certificate of death was issued, signed, and sealed, with the cause of death listed as a heart seizure, not unexpected in a man of the deceased's age. The fine Essex automobile that was found parked in a nearby alley was towed away to the Harris estate at Nine Mile Point.

That same afternoon, a freighter bearing the three-colored flag of Italy steamed south toward the mouth of the Mississippi. A lone passenger stood at the stern and watched the city fade into haze.

An hour later, the passenger, a thick-bodied Sicilian, received a note from the captain, informing him that the ship had passed the twelve-mile limit and was now sailing in safe waters.

News of Henry Harris's sudden passing was noted in the newspaper, along with an article penned by Robert Dodge that traced the deceased's career from humble beginnings to fantastic wealth, and included mention of his lifelong service to the city. It was acknowledged that a promising political career would never be realized. Various local dignitaries expressed condolences, though the quotes seemed rather tepid. A separate announcement stated that, in accordance with the family's wishes, the memorial service and funeral would be private affairs.

In an article on the business pages it was reported that William Little would assume the reins of Henry Harris, Ltd., for the time being.

The coverage was muted for such a prominent man, as directed by the publisher of the paper. Within another day, it was off the front pages entirely. No one spoke for the record about the coincidence of three former business associates dying in such a short period of time, with two of them ending up on Rampart Street.

———

Tom Anderson surprised everyone by walking into Mangetta's Grocery unannounced late on Tuesday morning. He left his driver outside with his yellow Marmon roadster.

Frank Mangetta greeted him with pleasure, and escorted him into the saloon, where he set a table, produced a cup of strong coffee, and, to the King of Storyville's delight, broke out a dusty old bottle of brandy. Then he went to fetch Valentin from his room.

The detective ambled in, looking sleepy. While Frank got busy making a light breakfast for his guest and his boarder, Valentin drew a cup of coffee and joined Anderson at the table. The two men regarded each other in pensive silence for a few moments. It was an old game, and somehow comforting.

"Well, then," Anderson said. "It's finished."

"I'd say so," Valentin said.

Frank came out of the kitchen carrying a large frying pan in which a frittata was still steaming. He served Anderson and Valentin right from the pan, and then put the remainder on the third plate for himself.

"Smells wonderful," Anderson said.

Frank shrugged modestly as he took a seat. "A little Asiago, some black pepper... it's nothing."

The King of Storyville put a fork to his eggs. He looked at Valentin expectantly.

"I can't say what happened to Mr. Harris," he said.

"Because you don't know or because you don't want to tell me?"

"You really don't need to hear."

Frank uttered something about how good the bread tasted this morning. Valentin stopped to take a sip of his coffee.

Anderson sighed over his eggs. "I never saw any of it."

"No reason you would," Valentin said. "No reason you would want to."

The King of Storyville mused for a few seconds more. Then he smiled at Frank. "This is a fine meal," he commented. "You could teach my cooks a thing or two."

Frank bent his head and said, *"Grazie, signore."*

Valentin was not summoned to the Benedict home in the wake of the investigation. An envelope came his way, passed from Betsy's hand to Beansoup's, and then to his. The note inside thanked him for his service. It was signed *Anne Marie Benedict* in a florid hand. He found five ten-dollar gold pieces in the envelope and wondered with an absent smile which service had earned him the additional payment.

By the end of the week, Tom Anderson had invited him to work a few nights a week, and he had received messages from Miss Lulu White and Countess Willie Piazza, asking if he might be available to resume some security duties at their mansions. He sent messages back, asking for appointments on the following Monday to discuss their situations. Except for this, his life returned to its routine.

Then one afternoon Frank greeted him with the word that Justine had been by earlier in the day, looking for him. She asked the saloon keeper to tell him that she'd come back, maybe tomorrow.

Acknowledgments

A FEW WORDS OF THANKS.

To my editor Jen Charat, a good shepherd, and copy editor Erin DeWitt, who is diligence in spades.

To Sara Branch and Marissa Riccio in San Diego, Jodie Hockensmith and Jenna Johnson in New York, and all the others at Harcourt who perform so well to my benefit.

To my corner: Kim Goldstein, Laura Langlie, and Allison Davis.

And closer to home, to my favorite muses: Anna Copello, Jennifer French Echols, Barbara Saunders, and Rebecca Wallace.